Emily's Song

by

Christine Marciniak

Emily's Song

Cover Art by *Tina Lynn Stout*

The Wild Rose Press, Inc.
PO Box 708
Adams Basin, NY 14410-0708
Visit us at www.thewildrosepress.com

Publishing History
First American Rose Edition, 2018
Print ISBN 978-1-5092-2021-2
Digital ISBN 978-1-5092-2022-9

Published in the United States of America

He looked really familiar, but she didn't remember seeing him at the wedding. She knew she'd seen that face, and she knew that if there were enough light to see the color of his eyes, they would be gray.

She knew who he was.

"You're Samuel Marshall."

"Yes," he said, as if that should be obvious to anyone.

"And this is your house."

And he died in the Civil War.

And she hadn't been able to find any light switches.

That was impossible. She had to be dreaming. Or still drunk. Or something.

No. This was a dream. That was the only logical conclusion.

Ha, did that mean that Samuel Marshall was the man of her dreams? Figures it would be someone dead for a hundred and sixty years.

Praise for Christine Marciniak

"From the moment Emily falls into the pond, I could not put this book down. Packed full with suspense, danger, and romance, *EMILY'S SONG* stayed with me long after I finished the last page."

~*award-winning author P. J. Hoover*

Dedication

To Tricia,
because she never stopped
believing in this story,
or me

Chapter One

Emily

Happily-ever-afters don't happen at someone else's wedding. Emily Parks knew this and had no expectations. Well, not many. If she could meet someone who would sweep her off her feet, that would be great. In the meantime, she was maid-of-honor and determined to enjoy herself.

If only the music wasn't quite so loud. The bass vibrated through her bones as she danced with one of the groomsmen. The loud music was the only fault she could find, though. Dayna and Johnson really couldn't have picked a more beautiful place for their reception. The nineteenth-century mansion-turned-inn had been restored to its full pre-Civil War glory. The ballroom had polished wood floors and crystal chandeliers and ornate French doors leading out to the veranda and gardens. Other than the blaring music, it was like stepping back in time. Upstairs, where the bridal party had rooms for the night, there were even canopy beds. Could life get better?

One song segued into another, and she gave a wave to her dancing partner and headed back to her table, where her drink awaited. She took a sip.

"Bet you can't wait 'til it's your turn," Dayna's mother said, practically having to shout the words to be heard.

Emily forced a smile and nodded. She drained her glass, then pointed toward the bar to indicate she was going to get another drink.

Even over by the bar it was hard to hear herself think. She waited for the tuxedo-clad bartender to mix a highball for the groom's grandfather.

"Whiskey sour," she said when he turned to her.

The bartender refilled her glass, and she stuck a dollar in the tip jar.

"You're next, eh?" the groom's grandfather said and moved on, not waiting for a response.

Emily took her glass and emptied it in a couple of swallows.

She put it back on the bar.

"Again, please."

"Another already?" the bartender asked.

"I've invented a drinking game," she told him. "Anytime someone tells me I'm next, or any variation thereof, such as, when are you going to get a boyfriend and settle down, I drain my glass."

The bartender mixed her drink and gave her a wink.

"You in need of a boyfriend, sweetie?"

She rolled her eyes and took a huge swallow. It burned her throat and made her eyes water. Or maybe that was the annoyance at it being rubbed in her face, yet again, that she didn't have a significant other.

"I'll let you know."

Out on the dance floor, Dayna and Johnson moved together like they were made for each other. Maybe they were. From the moment they started dating in high school, they had eyes for no one else. They even had a couple name: DayJon. Dayna always joked that it sounded like a good name for their first son. Every time Emily was in a relationship, she'd realize that although she was having fun, it wasn't at all like what Dayna and Johnson had. She wanted what they had. She'd never even had a couple name.

She sipped her drink. Slugging back that last glass might not have been the best idea. The edges of her vision were starting to get a little wobbly. The room was too loud and too hot and too everything.

The lobby brought some relief. She sat down on an ornate blue velvet sofa. Her feet ached. That was the problem with wearing new shoes to a wedding. Not that she had much choice. These were the ones Dayna had picked out. They'd been dyed to match the pale yellow gowns. Yellow was totally not her color, but since most of the bridesmaids were Dayna's cousins, they had the darker skin that offset the yellow beautifully. Emily more or less faded away. It didn't matter though. No one was looking at her anyway; it was Dayna's day.

Huge portraits lined the wall. A nice touch that made the historic inn seem even more like a home. The one directly opposite her was of a handsome young man with wavy dark hair, neatly-trimmed mustache, and piercing gray eyes.

"You like that painting?"

The owner of the inn, an older, professionally-dressed woman stood next to her.

"I do." She couldn't take her gaze from it. Especially the eyes, they simply gripped her. "Do you know who it is?"

"Samuel Marshall." She touched the frame lightly, almost caressing it like one might a loved one. "This used to be his house. He died in the Civil War."

"He was cute." Too bad he died in the war. Of course, the war was over one hundred and fifty years ago, he'd be dead by now either way.

"He was a poet."

Emily studied the painting with renewed interest. Old-time poets always seemed so romantic. Modern poets were a little too into navel-gazing for her tastes.

"Did he write anything I might have heard of?" She'd read plenty of poems, but his name wasn't familiar.

"I have a copy of his most famous one here." She opened a drawer in a side table, pulled out a postcard with a multi-stanzaed poem printed on the front and handed it to Emily.

"It's called Emily's Song?" she asked, bemused. "I'm Emily."

The woman lowered her glasses and studied her for a moment. "You are, aren't you. Then this was written for you." She gently patted her shoulder and moved on.

She settled back to read the poem. If she had not been drinking quite so many whiskey sours, she might have gotten more out of it, but as it was she found it charming and sweet.

Emily's Song

A sprite from the land of Faerie
Bewitching me with a glance
She touched my hand and stole my heart
Our meeting: more than happenstance

Bewitching me with a glance
Her laughter was like bells in the wind

Our meeting: more than happenstance
I knew I had to have her; if only for a while.

Her laughter was like bells in the wind
As we danced the Zingirella for the ball
I knew I had to have her; if only for a while
For when I was with her time stood still

As we danced the Zingirella for the ball
The waterfalls played the only music we needed
For when I was with her time stood still
My sprite would be my bride

The waterfalls played the only music we needed
She touched my hand and stole my heart
My sprite would be my bride
Emily you have my love forever.

Sweet and depressing. Even in poems other people were falling in love and getting married.

Dayna and one of her cousins came through the ballroom door in a burst of laughter.

"Emily! What are you doing out here?" Dayna asked. "This is my wedding you should be having a good time!"

"I'm having a great time," she insisted, shoving the poem back in the drawer. "I just needed to rest my feet, and my ears."

Dayna dropped onto the sofa next to her. "I'm sorry Brian brought a date. I figured the best man and maid-of-honor would keep each other company. But when he asked Johnson if he could bring someone, we couldn't exactly say no."

"Oh please." She waved the apology away. "I really didn't expect to have things be so easy that I'd fall in love with Johnson's co-worker anyway. And I'm having fun. But what about you, are you having fun? Is it everything you dreamed it would be?"

"Everything and more!" She looked up at her cousin, waiting patiently. "Alexis, you can go back in. Emily will help me with my dress."

"I'm on potty duty?"

"Yes, because I know you'll do anything for me."

"Are you going to expect me to be in the delivery room when you and Johnson have your first child?"

"You can cut the cord."

Dayna stood and grabbed Emily by the hand, pulling her to her feet. "Come, help your dearest and oldest friend go to the bathroom without destroying her dress."

In the special bridal bathroom, with its gilt mirrors and cushioned seats and lots of room around the toilet for people who need assistance with voluminous dresses, she held the dress out of the way while Dayna struggled with her pantyhose.

"How did those ladies ever go to the bathroom in a hoop skirt, that's what I'd like to know," she said. "And in an outhouse yet? There are some things that make me very glad I live in the twenty-first century."

"Internet," Emily said, looking discreetly away.

"And phones. Can you imagine not having phones? Not even landlines. How absolutely primitive."

Dayna finished going to the bathroom, and between the two of them, they got her clothes all situated again. Dayna inspected herself in the mirror. "Of course, in the age of hoop skirts, I don't suppose my ancestors were wearing fancy clothes."

Emily wished she didn't look so washed out and pale next to Dayna.

"Mine were struggling in the potato famine."

"Yeah." Dayna applied lipstick. "Totally the same."

"I know it's not." Nothing compared to what the slaves went through.

Dayna pushed her lipstick back into her clutch and patted her on the arm. "It's okay, sweetie, not everyone can have a backstory as tragic as mine. You make do with what you have."

She laughed and picked her glass up from the marble counter. "I suppose no matter how you slice it, neither of us would be too happy in the nineteenth century."

"You got that right," Dayna said. "They had nice houses, though."

Johnson stood in front of the painting of Samuel Marshall, tapping one foot, while pushing up the sleeves of his tuxedo jacket and shirt to check his watch.

"Couldn't live without her?" Emily gave him a light punch to the arm.

He flashed her his irrepressible grin. "You know it." With one arm, he pulled Dayna close. "We need to find someone for you, Em. Sorry it didn't work out with Brian."

She drained the rest of the whiskey sour.

Dayna stared at her, one eyebrow raised.

"Drinking game." She held her empty glass high. "Every time someone suggests I should get married or comments on my single state, I drain the glass."

"Find a safer game." Johnson took the glass from her.

"Which means you think people are going to keep saying stuff."

"Of course they are," Dayna said, snuggling close to Johnson. "It's a wedding. Matchmaking is on people's minds."

"And you are gorgeous and apparently determined to stay ridiculously single," Johnson said putting his other arm around Emily's shoulders, engulfing her.

"I haven't found the right guy. You and Dayna are so lucky." Tears of frustration pricked at her eyes. She blinked to banish them. A wedding was no time for tears.

"We are," Dayna agreed. "That doesn't mean you won't be as lucky."

"Come, dance with me, Emily," Johnson said. "Let all the other guys see what they've been missing."

"Thanks, but no. You dance with Dayna. I'm going to step outside and get some fresh air." She disengaged from Johnson's comforting arm. All those whiskey sours had been a particularly bad idea. She went through the ballroom and out the open French doors to the veranda where people milled about, engaged in quiet conversation.

The full moon was startlingly bright and huge, bathing the entire area with its glow. It was almost magical. She wandered away from the building, enjoying the cool air on her face. Moonlight reflected off a fish pond, creating an unworldly effect. The moon seemed to fill the pond. Bubble-blowing fish stopped it from being completely mirror-like.

Her reflection, warped by the ripples, mesmerized

her as she sat on the low wall surrounding the pond. Is this how we see other people, she wondered, hampered by ripples and darkness and magic?

She should definitely not have had so much to drink. The drinking game had been a bad idea.

She trailed her fingers in the water, and the moonlight caught the ring on her right hand and made it glow. The ring, gold and silver intertwined, was given to her by her parents on her twenty-first birthday. Her mother, who dabbled in new-age stuff, told her that gold represented the sun and silver represented the moon, and between them she had the power of the world at her fingertips. Good in theory.

Her dad simply told her the ring was beautiful, just like she was.

She brushed the ring against her lips.

Good old Dad. He was the only person who never got on her case about still being single. Even with all the planning for Dayna's wedding, he never said anything. He was probably glad no one was asking him to open his wallet quite yet, but still, she appreciated his restraint.

A mist rose around her, and the chill in the air raised goosebumps on her arms. She should go back inside, rejoin the party. She didn't want Dayna to think she wasn't having a good time at her wedding. She was having a good time. The music was great, if maybe a little loud. The food had been top notch. The setting was unbearably romantic. And it was the wedding of two of her best friends in the whole world. It would be even better if there was someone to gaze lovingly into her eyes and whisper sweet nothings to her in the moonlight.

Fine, she'd admit it. She was lonely.

It wasn't the fault of the wedding though.

She shivered and wished she'd brought a wrap out with her.

The mist grew, emanating from the pond. It was all-encompassing, enveloping her, obliterating the light of the moon.

The fog filled her eyes so she could see nothing, her ears, so she could hear nothing, her mouth, silencing her. It filled her soul. She wanted to get up to go back inside now, but the fog held her pinned in place.

The world around her disappeared, the only thing solid was the ledge she sat on. Then the ledge crumbled from under her, and she tumbled into the fish pond.

The water engulfed her, waking her out of her stupor and shocking her system into stone cold soberness. She floundered to the surface to find that the fog had disappeared.

Perhaps she had dreamed it all. Or not, dreamed, exactly, but it had been a result of one too many whiskey sours.

Emily, her dress a sodden mess, her carefully styled hair soaked, climbed out of the pond. That was an interesting turn of events. She laughed as she tried to wring out her dress. Dayna and Johnson would say only she could manage to fall in a fish pond at their wedding. And look at that, they'd be right.

Luckily, the rooms were right upstairs. She'd change into the dress she'd worn for the rehearsal dinner last night and then rejoin the wedding party. Maybe take a quick shower to get the fish pond gunk out of her hair. The moon once again illuminated the yard. The music from the party had changed tone. It was quieter, more classical, less rock. A little something to make the grandparents happy.

She didn't want to run into anyone in her bedraggled and sopping state, so she headed to a back entrance. Her room was right near the top of the stairs. The upstairs hall was dim. Perhaps they turned down the lights at night to give the place more ambiance. The candle sconces on the wall did give a charming cozy glow to everything. She found her room and went in.

She reached for the light switch but couldn't find it. Enough light came through the window that she could see the canopy bed in the center of the room, but she couldn't see much else. She shut the door and turned to the bathroom door. But that wasn't where she thought it should be either. Was this the right room? She stepped back into the hallway and checked. First door by the stairs, definitely her room.

Maybe that dip in the pond hadn't sobered her up as much as she thought it had. Nothing seemed to be right. What she needed was to lie down and rest for a few minutes, then when her head cleared she'd figure out where everything was. She stripped out of her wet things and climbed, naked, between the sheets on the bed.

A few minutes to clear her head. That's all she needed.

Chapter Two

Sam—1861

The quartet played a waltz.

Sam Marshall looked across the room to where Dinah gazed at him expectantly. He had promised her this dance, and it would not do to disappoint her.

Next to him, sipping from the silver flask he always carried, his friend George Phelps didn't seem to notice the music had started again.

"Maryland has to stay neutral. It's her only chance." George wiped his hand across his mouth.

"No one is going to be able to stay neutral." Sam didn't want to think of war tonight. "No state and no person. Everyone is going to have to pick a side." He took a step toward where Dinah stood, too much the lady to come collect him, but the expression on her face told him her patience was not unlimited.

"I see you've picked yours." George nodded toward Dinah.

"Sometimes people make decisions, and sometimes decisions simply happen."

George grinned. "She's a good girl. She'll make you a fine wife."

"So everyone tells me."

With a nod to his friend, Sam made his way to Dinah, past the couples who already filled the dance floor, dodging hoop skirts as he went.

"I was afraid I would be left without a partner." She tapped his arm with her folded fan. "That would never do."

"It would not. I completely agree." He made a courteous bow, took her gloved hand, and led her to the dance floor where they joined in the waltz.

She was very pleasing to look at, with her blonde curls, her creamy skin, and mesmerizing blue eyes. She looked lovely in whatever she wore. Right now, she had on a blue ball gown with wide hoops, that made her waist appear impossibly thin. Her dress was low cut, showing the white curve of her breasts. He could write a poem about those breasts.

She was also a good conversationalist. She was not one of those girls who only spoke of hair ribbons and dresses. No, she was very nice to talk to.

She could dance as well.

Sam had also been assured she could manage a house quite capably.

She would give him handsome children.

It was a good match.

Certainly it was.

Except he didn't love her.

His mother assured him love would come in time. He supposed that was true. And it would have been enough had he not known what true love was. He had loved Anna. He'd known her since they were children and loved her from the time they were sixteen, until she died of fever the summer before they were to wed.

It had been five years now, and his mother, father, sister, friends, and pretty much everyone he knew were insisting he had to move on, to get married, to settle down. So, he would.

Dinah wasn't Anna, but she was delightful on many levels. She'd make a suitable wife.

"You're not thinking about war again, are you?" Dinah asked as they circled the dance floor.

"Of course not," he answered. "I'm thinking about what a beautiful bride you will make." A little lie at times like these was completely acceptable.

Her whole face lit up as she smiled. "Does that mean we officially announce our engagement today?"

Sam couldn't think of a person in the room who did not know an arrangement had been reached between the two of them, but yes, that was the purpose of the party, to announce their engagement.

"We do." He squeezed her hand gently in his. Yes, she would make a fine wife.

The song ended, and Dinah's dance card indicated she was to dance with her brother next. He had promised the next dance to his younger sister. He found Elizabeth surrounded, as usual, by preening men.

"I believe this is my dance." He held his hand out to her.

She moved to the dance floor with him, and the band began playing a polka. "I'm sure Joseph is going to propose to me," Elizabeth said, bubbling with enthusiasm. "Perhaps even tonight. We can have a double wedding."

Joseph had not been one of the half dozen men fawning over her. He may be her favorite, but Sam hadn't seen any reason to believe the feelings were returned.

"You made the right choice in Dinah," Elizabeth said, paying no mind to his silence. "I'm so glad she's going to be my sister." The girls had been best of friends since they were tiny.

"I aim to please." He was pleasing everyone but himself.

For each dance of each set, he found himself a sought-after partner. Dinah, of course, would have liked him to herself, but since his family was hosting the ball, he needed to make sure all the ladies present had a dance partner if they desired one, and sometimes that would be him.

Honestly, Dinah didn't suffer much, she had a partner for every dance.

At the end of one set, the musicians once again played a grand march. Sam sought out his intended, and they followed the line of people heading into the supper room. The servants carried around platters of cold meats and breads and cheeses. He procured a glass of punch for Dinah and a glass of wine for himself.

His father, as host of the party and owner of the house, though he had given over all responsibilities of running the plantation to Sam, clanked a knife on the edge of a glass to attract everyone's attention. The room fell silent, and he beckoned to his son. Sam tucked Dinah's hand into the crook of his arm and led her to where his father stood. Already sixty, Mr. Marshall was still a powerfully built man with a full head of hair, that had turned mostly gray. His bright green vest lent a dash of color to his otherwise dark suit.

The past couple of weeks, when he'd been sitting with the assembly in Frederick trying to figure out what the state of Maryland should do in this unprecedented struggle, had been hard on him. Now he looked happy though. Happy and relaxed. And maybe a little bit drunk.

"Family and friends and all gathered here. It gives me great pleasure to announce that my son, Samuel Marshall has promised to take Miss Dinah Johnson as his bride!"

The assembled group clapped politely, and friends soon surrounded Sam and Dinah offering hearty congratulations. He let himself be led, by George and the others, out to the veranda where it was cooler and one could breathe easier, without the overwhelming scent of perfume and sweat that permeated the ballroom.

"Caleb Howe volunteered for the Union army today." George took a swig from his ever present flask.

"Daniel Hanson volunteered for the Confederacy." James Miller lit a cigar, not giving away his thoughts on that turn of events.

"What are you going to do?" George clapped Sam's shoulder.

"Me?" Why did he have to do anything? He wasn't interested in war. He didn't particularly care if Maryland was part of the United States or part of the Confederate states. That was something for the assembly, his father included, to decide. But he wasn't a naïve boy either. He would have to pick a side.

There was no winning in this situation.

"I'm going to get married." He still held his wine glass, and he raised it as if in a toast and took a sip.

The other men laughed. "You think that gets you out of anything?"

"I know it doesn't." He drained the wine in his glass.

"You own slaves." George waved James' cigar

smoke away from his face. "We all do. We side with the Union we lose everything."

Slavery was not illegal in Maryland like it was in the states to the north. Bonne Terra, like every other big plantation in the area, used slaves to work the fields and to serve in the home. People from up north where there were mainly small, family farms didn't understand the economics of the situation. It wasn't as simple as saying 'make all the slaves free.' Maybe if Maryland joined with the Union there would be a way to see that the slaves were free and their farms didn't collapse into ruin around them.

It was not an easy decision.

But one he would be expected to make soon. Not now though. This was a party, a party to celebrate his upcoming wedding. Why ruin it with talk of politics?

"I don't know what I'm going to do." He grabbed George's flask and took a swig before returning it to him. "Tonight, I'm going to do nothing except enjoy the ball."

James slapped him on the shoulder and laughed. "That's the way of it, Sam. You enjoy that pretty girl you got in there. You're a lucky man."

For a moment he envisioned Anna with her dark hair and shining eyes. He didn't feel particularly lucky.

The quartet started warming up for the next set.

"You better retrieve Miss Johnson from the supper room." George tucked his flask into an inside pocket of his dinner jacket. "You wouldn't want her to think you abandoned her the moment your engagement was announced."

"Right, that can wait until you enlist with one of the armies." James took a deep puff of his cigar and exhaled slowly.

That was not a prospect he looked forward to, but it did sit, rather ominously, on the horizon.

He allowed himself to simply have a good time for the rest of the night.

After the next set of dances, Dinah complained of being hot, so he escorted her out to the veranda.

"What a lovely full moon." She gazed up at it, an enchanting smile lighting up her heart-shaped face.

"Yes." He wrapped his arm protectively around her shoulder. "But its loveliness does not compare to you."

She giggled. "Sam, you darling. Such a poet! I'm so glad you finally agreed we should be married. I promise to make you very happy."

His heart softened to her even more. She wasn't Anna, she never could be Anna, but then no one could. She wanted to make him happy, and he would promise her the same. In time he might even love her.

The final dance set of the night began. He and Dinah had both promised all but the last dance to others. By the time he led her to the dance floor, many of the invited guests had left, since it was well after midnight.

"I feel positively decadent, staying out this late," Dinah said as they circled the floor to the farewell waltz.

"Your mother and father look like they wish to have already left." He nodded his head toward the older couple, top hat and shawl already in place, waiting by the door.

Dinah laughed. Her laugh reminded him, pleasantly, of the waterfall on the plantation. "Mother and father are too happy to have me settled. They won't care about a late night."

His own parents would feel much the same way when they were able to announce Elizabeth's betrothal.

The dance ended. The musicians, all negroes who most often worked as footmen, put away their instruments. Sam found Dinah's cloak and wrapped it around her shoulders.

Goodbyes were said, and the last of their guests climbed in their carriages and rode away.

"Up to bed with you, Elizabeth. It is way past your bedtime." Their mother pulled a shawl tighter around her own shoulders, her eyes dark with exhaustion.

"I'm nineteen, Mother, much too old to have a bedtime." She yawned, ruining the effectiveness of her protest.

"I'll escort the ladies upstairs," his father said, already taking his wife's arm in his own. "Meet me in the study, and we'll have a drink before retiring."

Despite the fact that he'd be more than happy to head to bed himself, he went into the study. He lit the candles in the sconces on the wall and the lamp on the desk. His desk now. He had a hard time getting used to all of this being his. It was especially difficult when his parents were here, instead of at their house in Frederick.

He went to the decanter on the sideboard and poured a splash of whiskey for himself and one for his father. Then he gazed out the window at the full moon until he heard his father's footfall behind him.

"There's something about a full moon that is almost mystical," his father said.

"Makes you believe in all those old fairy tales." He walked to the sideboard and handed his father one of the glasses of whiskey. They settled into the wingback chairs. "How are things in Frederick?"

His father waved the question away. "Plenty of arguing, no real solutions. But that's not what I wanted to talk to you about."

He knew what was coming. "I suppose you want to tell me again how glad you are that I am finally settling down and getting married."

His father took a sip of whiskey and smiled. "While all that is true, no, that wasn't my main concern right now either."

Sam rubbed his stubble-sprouted chin. "So, you think there will be war, then?" It was the only topic left.

"War has been declared by both sides." His father leaned back in the chair and closed his eyes for a moment before continuing. "No one is going to back down. Yes, there will be war."

"Maryland will stay Union?" He wasn't sure how much this was a question or simply wanting confirmation of what he already suspected.

"That is the way things are going."

"And you want to know what I am going to do?" He wished he had an answer for him.

"I do."

Sam took another sip of his whiskey. He'd like to drain the whole glass. He looked around the study, the hub of the plantation, his legacy. He could go to war and support the south, against his own state, in the hopes of everything returning to normal when he was done. He could go to war and support the Union, and if that side won, what would be left of the plantation when he was done? How would he run it? For certainly he wouldn't be using slaves. And then there was the aspect that he'd rather not own people. The more he thought about it, the more repulsed he was by the idea, but he hadn't figured out any viable alternative. There was one more thing to consider. If he went off to war, there was no guarantee he'd be coming back, and he now had to be concerned with Dinah and her future as well.

"I don't know," he said finally. "I really don't."

"If things progress as I expect they will. Eventually you'll be expected to join up."

He didn't doubt it.

"You might be able to send someone in your place. Tobias, for instance."

His shoulders tensed. He wasn't a coward, but he didn't relish the idea of going to war. He wouldn't mind finding a way to avoid going, but to send someone in his place, a slave who had no choice, no, that he couldn't do. He had another sip of the whiskey. It burned going down, but it was a good burn.

"I couldn't."

"You could," his father said. "It would be perfectly legal and perfectly acceptable."

"Not to me," he answered, a little harsher than he'd intended.

His father drained his glass.

"You don't have to worry about running this place. I'll manage it while you are gone, if it comes to that."

"And Dinah?"

His father grinned. "I'm afraid I won't be able to manage her." He got serious. "We'll look after her as well. That is, if you decide to get married before you join up. You may want to wait."

"Do you think things will happen that quickly?"

"Things are already happening quickly, son."

21

"This isn't the future I pictured myself preparing for." Sam stared out the window at the mystical full moon. "By now Anna and I should have had a couple of children. I should be worrying about ways to improve Bonne Terra, not going to war to defend it."

"Life often doesn't turn out the way we expect, but things have a way of working out."

"What should I do?" He was a grown man. He shouldn't have to ask his father for advice, but his thoughts were a swirl of contradictions. He was lucky enough to still have his father around. There was no harm in taking advantage of whatever wisdom the old man had to offer.

"You can't remain neutral." His father ran his finger around the rim of his now empty glass.

"I know that." His voice came out like more of a growl than he'd intended.

"Maryland is going to side with the Union," his father continued. "If you side with the confederacy, and the Union wins, you lose everything. There is little hope you'd be pardoned; you'd be considered a traitor. You would lose Bonne Terra."

That did not even bear thinking about.

"If you side with the Union and the Confederacy manages to break away, you will not be a traitor, you will still be in your own home state, having fought on her side. I don't see how you could do otherwise."

All his thoughts, swirling as they may have been, had led him to that same conclusion.

"You don't have to decide anything tonight." His father put the whiskey glass on the tray. "Get some sleep. Think about it more tomorrow. Your mother is expecting me upstairs. I'll see you in the morning.

Good night, son."

"Good night."

The door clicked quietly behind his father, and Sam was left, once again, alone with his thoughts.

He poured himself another couple of fingers of whiskey and drained it in one swallow. He lit a small candle to light his way to his room and extinguished the others. As his father said, there was time enough in the morning to ponder these deep thoughts. For now, he needed sleep.

From the ballroom, he could hear the slaves cleaning up. It would be a late night for them, and they would be up early seeing to the running of the plantation. He would be up early as well. There were things to do tomorrow, and he had to be awake to do them.

The candle's flickering light made strange shadows on the walls. He was used to them, but between the extra whiskey he had consumed and the late hour, the shadows seemed otherworldly.

He opened the door to his room. He wanted nothing more than to slip into his bed and drift off to sleep. He lit the lamp on the dresser with the candle he carried. Then he shrugged out of his jacket and kicked off his dancing shoes. He removed his stock from around his neck and placed it on the dresser.

As he slid his braces off his shoulders, he pulled back the covers on the bed and found himself staring at a sleeping naked woman.

He took in the roundness of her breasts, the slope of her hip. He reached out a hand to see if she were real, intending to touch her shoulder. His hand, of its own accord, touched the creamy breast instead.

The woman's eyes flew open, and she screamed.

Chapter Three

Emily

Emily screamed and pulled the sheet close around her.

There was a man in her room. Staring at her. He'd been looking at her naked. He'd touched her. Oh. My. God. She was about to be raped. She opened her mouth to scream again, but the man, his eyes wide, mouth agape, looked as astonished as she was. Maybe he wasn't about to rape her.

"What are you doing in here?" Her heart beat a rapid staccato. He looked familiar. He must be one of Johnson's friends. She was sure she'd seen that lean face, that wavy hair, that mustache somewhere before.

"You're in my bed." The inflection was almost that of a question, but not quite.

"I'm not," she insisted and then looked around. Now that there was some light, she could see that this was most definitely not the room she had checked into earlier. The furniture was dark and heavy as opposed to white and delicate. The canopy was not some Laura Ashley print but a brown and gold paisley. "Oh crap. I'm sorry. I thought this was my room."

"Who are you?"

"Emily Parks. Maid of Honor."

His features smoothed out, and a hint of a smile

25

came to his eyes.

"Ah, you're friends with Dinah."

"Dayna," she corrected, but she didn't think he was listening. "I'm really sorry I'm in the wrong room. Really sorry. You see, I fell into the fish pond and I came up here to change, but I'd been drinking and I guess I got the wrong room, so I thought if I rested for a minute or two…and I took off my clothes because they were wet. If you'll be so kind as to hand me my dress and perhaps turn your back for a minute, I'll get out of here and into my own room."

"I didn't know anyone was staying here tonight."

It was common knowledge the bridal party was staying. Besides, if this were his room, then obviously he'd been planning on staying here tonight as well.

"Like I said, if you give me my dress, I'll go find my own room."

He picked up the dress.

"It's wet."

"Yes, I told you, I fell in the fish pond."

He looked really familiar, but she didn't remember seeing him at the wedding. She knew she'd seen that face, and she knew that if there were enough light to see the color of his eyes, they would be gray.

She knew who he was.

"You're Samuel Marshall."

"Yes," he said, as if that should be obvious to anyone.

"And this is your house."

And he died in the Civil War.

And she hadn't been able to find any light switches.

That was impossible. She had to be dreaming. Or

still drunk. Or something.

No. This was a dream. That was the only logical conclusion.

Ha, did that mean that Samuel Marshall was the man of her dreams? Figures it would be someone dead for a hundred and sixty years. She pulled the covers back over her head and closed her eyes. When she woke up for real, everything would be back to normal. She heard the creak and sigh of a door opening. Her mystery dream man was leaving. Maybe, since it was a dream, she should have invited him into her bed. No harm in having a little fun in a dream after all.

"Do you need anything, sir?" A soft male voice said.

"Yes. One of the party guests has fallen asleep in my room. Make sure the green room is ready and then have Beck come up here with a wrapper or shift for her and get her situated in that room."

This didn't seem quite like how a dream would go, but then again, who could tell with dreams.

Emily lowered the blanket and peered about. A dark-skinned man in a loose fitting white shirt and brown pants stood in the open doorway.

"Yes, sir." He closed the door and left.

"Beck will be here momentarily to take care of you," Samuel Marshall, dream man, said, and then left.

A very strange dream.

She was somewhere in that state between sleep and not-quite-asleep when the door opened again. Soft footsteps approached the bed. She opened her eyes to see Dayna standing there holding a candle.

"Dayna! What are you doing here? You should be with Johnson! It's your wedding night!"

The woman holding the candle tilted her head. "Sorry, miss?"

Her voice was not Dayna's. As Emily's eyes adjusted, she realized the face wasn't Dayna's either, though maybe it had been a minute ago. This was a dream after all. Anything could happen in a dream.

"I thought..." It didn't really matter what she had thought. "Are you Beck?" She felt like Ebenezer Scrooge asking the first ghost if he was the spirit foretold to him.

"Yes, miss." Her voice was soft and melodic. "Mister Marshall say you need a shift and to be settled in the green room."

"My room wasn't green." Her protest was ignored.

"I have a shift here for you." Beck held out a white cotton night gown.

Emily snaked a hand out from under the blanket and took it. She waited for Beck to turn her back or leave the room or something, so she could slip it on, but she didn't seem so inclined. So, she employed the getting-dressed-under-the-covers trick she had learned as a seventh-grader at sleep-away camp. Then, since it seemed, dream or not, she would have to switch rooms, she threw back the covers and got out of bed.

Beck, holding the candle, led the way out of the bedroom and down the hall to another room. This one was smaller, but a lit candle sat on a side table and the blankets had been turned down in anticipation of her arrival.

"I'll bring you fresh clothes in the morning, miss." Beck stifled a yawn.

"Thank you." She climbed under the covers. In the morning, all she had to do was find her own room and her luggage and no one would have to bring her anything, but she was too tired to argue the point right now.

Beck blew out the candle and left. This was a strange dream, but she'd had stranger, like the time she dreamt that she and all her friends were puppets. That had been way stranger than this. Especially when Johnson sang "It's Not Easy Being Green."

****

Emily's head hurt. The sun coming through the windows hurt her eyes before she even opened them. She needed a glass of water and some aspirin and then maybe a huge cup of coffee. Yes. Coffee. A cinnamon latte. Certainly, they'd have those at breakfast in a nice inn like this.

She opened her eyes, and squinting to adjust to the morning brightness, looked around. The furniture was white with gold trim. The canopy and curtains were light green. The wallpaper was pale green with giant pink flowers on it. This was not the room she had checked into yesterday.

That room had yellow walls and oak furniture. The canopy on the bed had been pink and yellow. There had been an easy chair in the room and an armoire that hid a TV. None of that was in this room. There was a stand with an old-fashioned basin and water pitcher. There was a dressing table with a mirror. There was a wooden rocking chair. It was tastefully decorated, but it wasn't the room she remembered. A quick glance around confirmed that her garment bag and overnight bag were not here.

Then, as if parts of a dream coming to her, she remembered falling into the fish pond and getting undressed and dropping into bed. She wasn't undressed now, though. She looked at herself to see the unfamiliar cotton nightgown. Where had this come from?

Waking to a man looking at her, touching her. A woman who looked like Dayna, but wasn't, leading her to this room, giving her this nightgown. She shook her head and then immediately regretted it. What exactly had happened last night?

She'd had too much to drink. She knew that for sure.

Had she really fallen in the fish pond? Doesn't seem like the kind of memory she'd make up, so it probably happened. The man though, that was probably a dream.

First step was to find her room and her clothes. Then she'd go down to the dining room and have a kick-ass cup of coffee, and tomorrow she'd be back at work with quite a story to tell about her weekend.

The rooms weren't numbered, they were named, and she had been in the Mary Todd Lincoln Room. There had been plaques on each door. It should only take a minute to find the right room. She opened the door and peeked into the hallway. If she could do this without being seen, all the better.

She checked the door to see what room she'd spent the night in, but there was no plaque. Maybe it wasn't one of the regularly rented out rooms. There were half a dozen doors up and down the hallway. None of them had plaques. She'd definitely remembered a sign. It was white with gold trim and the words Mary Todd Lincoln had been engraved in it and painted gold so they stood out.

Someone was coming up the back staircase. Emily

ducked back into the room, but the footsteps came right to her door. There was a soft knock. With her heart beating loud enough she was sure whoever was on the other side could hear it, she cautiously opened the door. The woman from last night stood there, holding an immense armful of fabric.

"Your dress from last night was near ruined in the water, miss." She edged past Emily into the room. "I borrowed this one from Miss Elizabeth. I think you are close to the same size."

"Oh." Whatever kind of dress she held must be some bridesmaid dress extraordinaire. There had to be yards and yards of fabric in her arms. "Thank you, but that's not necessary. I just need to find my bags. They should be in the room I checked into. The Mary Todd Lincoln room."

The woman tilted her head and furrowed her brow. "You was in a room with the President's wife?"

Emily got the distinct feeling that she and this woman were speaking different languages, or at least having different conversations.

"No. That was the name of the room. All the rooms are named, right?" But were they? She had looked at all the doors, and none of them had name plaques. What was going on here? She reached out and grabbed hold of the nearest thing to steady herself. It was the old-fashioned water pitcher and basin. It moved slightly when she grabbed it, and water sloshed around inside. Water? She glanced in. Yes, water. She scanned the room quickly. There was no door that would lead to an ensuite bathroom. There were no light switches on the wall. The woman in front of her, still holding the yards of fabric, wore a floor length dress, and her hair was under a kerchief.

"Who are you?" she asked, not able to keep herself from staring.

"Beck. I'm Miss Elizabeth's lady's maid."

"Her lady's maid." It was like something out of a book. Who had lady's maids anymore? "And who is Miss Elizabeth?"

"Why, the daughter of the house of course, Mr. Marshall's sister."

"Samuel Marshall?" Her voice sounded faraway in her ears.

"Yes, miss. Do you mind if I put this down?"

"No, not at all. Go right ahead." She moved aside so the voluminous dress could be placed on the bed. She shivered and wrapped her arms around herself. Something wasn't right here. Maybe she was still dreaming.

"There was a party in the ballroom last night, right?" Best to get the essentials worked out.

"Yes, miss," the woman answered. "You was a guest, right? A friend of Miss Johnson?"

"Who?" Emily started at hearing Johnson's name. Where were Dayna and Johnson? Where was the rest of the bridal party?

"Miss Dinah Johnson."

Dinah. That's what the man had said last night too. Dayna and Johnson. Dinah Johnson. Close. That must be what they meant. At least that much made sense.

"Yes, I'm her friend. Do you know where she is?"

"She went home last night, miss."

That, however, didn't make sense.

There had to be some mistake. She was sure that Dayna and Johnson wouldn't have already left. She walked to the window so she could see if Johnson's Mustang was still in the lot. She pulled back the curtain and gasped, gripping the ledge as her knees buckled. Instead of the parking lot with cars parked neatly in lined spaces, a grass yard with a gravel drive led to what looked like a barn or stables. In the distance, instead of the neighborhood that surrounded the small acreage of the inn, were fields. Lots of fields. All with green plants growing in them. And black men and women tending them.

The sunlight glinted off the ring on her right hand. She glanced down at it, and her heart skipped a beat. Instead of gold and silver intertwined, it was only gold. The silver part of the ring was missing. It was impossible for it to be missing, the two sections were twisted together, one part could not simply leave, yet it had.

She stared at the pastoral scene in front of her again, and she tried to get both her breathing and heartbeat under control. There were no light switches or door plaques in the inn. A black woman had brought her a huge dress to put on.

What exactly had happened when she fell into that fish pond?

"Are you ready to get dressed yet, miss?"

Emily turned and stared at the dark-skinned woman. Was she a slave? Could she ask her that without sounding like a complete idiot?

"So, have you worked here long?" she asked, trying to sound casual, and failing miserably.

The woman's eyebrows shot up. "My whole life miss, my whole life."

"You ever want to do something else?"

"Like work in the fields instead of tend to Miss Elizabeth?" She laughed, a soft musical laugh, very much like Dayna's. "No, miss, I don't want that."

"Could you do something else if you wanted to?" This was as close as she could get to asking if this woman was a slave. All the signs seem to point that somehow she wasn't in her own time anymore but had landed back at the plantation before the start of the Civil War. It wasn't possible, but sometimes the impossible happened, didn't it?

"I better be getting you dressed, miss," Beck answered.

That pretty much answered her question.

What had happened? Had she actually fallen back in time? Right now, she had two choices, curl up in a ball and cry or go with it until she could figure out what to do and how to get back home. Crying might be cathartic, but it wouldn't get her home. She took a deep breath and squared her shoulders.

"Right," she said to Beck. "Let's get me dressed. What's first?"

Beck handed her a pair of long cotton drawers. She took them and started to put them on, but stopped when she noticed the seam was open.

"These are ripped." She handed them back to Beck.

"No, miss. That's for to make it easier to use the outhouse."

Oh. She supposed that was the sort of thing she should pretend she knew. "Right. Of course." She pulled the drawers on under her nightgown.

Next Beck held out a contraption of cloth and ribbon that Emily immediately recognized as a corset. Oh. God no. Women had progressed way past being trussed up like this. She was not going to let her innards be squeezed for the sake of some artificially thin waist. Beck held it out expectantly.

Maybe it wouldn't be so bad. Besides, what a story to tell Dayna when she finally got home.

She allowed Beck to strap her into the corset. With each tug on the strings her breath was squeezed out of her.

"It's too tight!"

"Another inch or you won't fit in Miss Elizabeth's dress." Beck tugged some more.

Spots floated in front of her eyes, and she was sure she was about to pass out, but then Beck stopped tugging and she took a tentative breath. She could still breathe, and it probably did wonderful things for her posture. It seemed unlikely a person could slouch wearing one of these. And it did more for her bust line than the latest push-up wonder bra.

The next item Beck produced was an actual, honest-to-goodness set of hoops. Emily watched in fascination as they were fastened around her waist. Getting dressed was quite the ordeal, not the kind of thing you could roll out of bed and accomplish in only a couple of minutes.

Finally Beck slipped the yards of fabric over her head. The brown and red dress belled out over the hoops and cinched in at the waist. She felt rather elegant.

"Sit down, miss, and I'll do your hair for you."

Emily submitted to her hair being brushed and tugged into an unfamiliar style. She studied the result in the mirror. She could be an extra in *Gone With the Wind*.

"They'll be expecting you at breakfast."
No going back now. It was show time.

Chapter Four

Sam

Flowers. Roses particularly, but other flowers as well. And talcum. Sam wasn't sure what other scents lingered on his sheets from that woman who'd been asleep there, but he found them intoxicating and he didn't want to get out of bed, even though the sun shone through the opening where the drapes hadn't closed completely last night.

He forced his feet over the side and stretched. Mornings came way too early for his liking, especially after a ball. He splashed water from the ewer onto his face, shocking himself into alertness. Who was the mysterious woman, and why had she been in his bed?

Taking hold of the strop, he gave his razor a few swipes to sharpen it, then mixed some water with his soap to create a good lather. Adjusting his shaving mirror, he brushed the lather on his face.

If she had fallen in the pond, why had she not gotten help from someone? Yet none of the servants had mentioned such a mishap.

He cleaned the stubble from his chin and cheeks, leaving his mustache intact, then splashed more water on his face and used the linen towel on the stand to dry off.

A friend of Dinah's, but not one he remembered

ever meeting before.

He had no objections to meeting her again.

Dinah, however, could never know her friend ended up in his bed. That was not a scandal he wanted to deal with.

He put on a pair of freshly pressed trousers and secured them with his braces. There was a lot of farm business he wanted to go over with his father today before he and his mother returned to Frederick. He tied his stock and rubbed some pomade in his hair to tame it.

The door to his room opened, and Tobias stood there with the coffee tray.

"Thought you might need a little pick me up this morning, sir."

"You know me too well." He gratefully took the proffered cup of steaming brew.

"I'm supposed to help you dress and shave, sir." Tobias frowned at Sam's half-dressed state.

"I've been dressing myself since I was a boy, Tobias. And who says I want you near my throat with a razor?" He teased. They'd grown up together, he may be the master and Tobias the servant, but they behaved more like brothers at times.

"Jonah always helped your father."

Sam took a swallow of his coffee. "I feel we've had this conversation before." Of course they'd had this conversation before, it had become a regular part of the morning routine. "I am not my father. But if you want to be useful, you can bring me my tan jacket."

Tobias did as directed, and Sam slid his arms into the sleeves.

"Did our visitor get settled in the green room last

night?"

"Yes, sir. And Beck is making sure she has something to wear this morning."

"Good, good." Sam adjusted his sleeve cuffs under the jacket. "Have a carriage ready to take her home after breakfast. Perhaps we should send a messenger to let her people know she is here and safe."

"Yes, sir. I'll send young Lucas."

Sam didn't care who he sent as long as the action was taken.

"Fine. See that Moses has two horses ready after breakfast. I want to take a ride around the grounds with my father before he leaves this morning."

"Yes, sir. Anything else, sir?"

"No, that will be all for now."

Tobias left, taking the coffee tray with him.

Sam gave his hair one more smoothing pat and headed to breakfast. He heard rustling noises as he passed the green room. Presumably Beck was getting their visitor ready for the day, which meant that Elizabeth was already dressed, or wished to sleep in. He'd wager she wished to sleep in. He'd have to speak to his parents about her. She was too old for any formal schooling and spent her days either sleeping or visiting with friends. His parents had left her here with him to learn the tasks involved in managing a house so she'd be ready when she was married and had her own house to run. The problem was that not only was she not interested in taking charge, the house slaves had been doing the job so long, that none of them needed any direction. The house purred smoothly along with no input from Elizabeth.

His parents were already downstairs. He could hear

their voices rise and fall in conversation, as he approached. The dining room table was set for five, which meant that word had spread to the kitchen staff about the unexpected guest.

"Good morning, Mother." He stopped by her chair and gave her a kiss on the cheek. "Father." He nodded to his father.

"We were pondering who the fifth place is for, Samuel," his mother said. "Did George spend the night?"

"No." He sat down next to the extra place. He'd gotten in the habit of sitting at the head of the table with his father gone, but he certainly wasn't going to argue his father's right to that spot. "A friend of Dinah's apparently had a bit too much of the punch and fell asleep upstairs."

"Oh dear." His mother's hand fluttered to her mouth. "That is unfortunate."

Sam made no comment. Fortunate, unfortunate, either way, the image of her lying in his bed was probably not going to leave him any time soon.

"We'll be getting an early start this morning." His father peered at him over the top of his spectacles and spread jam on a slice of bread.

"We'll wait until Elizabeth is up, of course," his mother added, tapping on the shell of her soft-boiled egg with her spoon.

"Then you might not be getting such an early start." Sam signaled to the serving girl to fill his coffee cup, which she did.

"What do you mean?" his father asked and his mother put down her spoon and leaned forward, waiting for him to go on.

"She's taken to spending a good portion of the morning in bed." He watched for their reactions from over top of his coffee cup.

"What does she do with her time?" His mother leaned even closer.

"Not much, as far as I can tell, but," he added, to be fair, and because he still had to share a house with Elizabeth for the time being, "I'm often out of the house most of the day, perhaps she is busy with things I am not aware of. You had better ask her."

A movement in the doorway caught his eye, and there stood the woman from last night. She wore one of Elizabeth's day dresses, a brown and red affair. It looked much better on her than it ever had on Elizabeth. He and his father both stood.

"Welcome," he said, even though, perhaps, given seniority, it should have been his father who spoke. "Please, join us at table, Miss…" For the life of him, he couldn't remember what name she had given him last night.

"Parks," the woman said. "Emily Parks."

She started to sit in the chair that had been pulled out for her, but the front of her skirt bounced up when she sat on her hoop wrong. He stifled the instinct to laugh when her face turned a deep shade of red.

"Oh, Elizabeth sometimes forgets to lift her hoop when she sits, too, dear," his mother said, so smoothly that no one would think she was giving instruction at all. But, he had never seen his sister have trouble navigate her clothing, at least not since she was out of short skirts.

"Would you like some coffee?" his father asked, casually covering any lingering embarrassment as Miss

Parks took her seat.

"God, yes," she blurted out. This time, Sam didn't even bother hiding his smile. "I mean, yes, please, that would be delightful."

"Hannah," his mother called to the serving girl. "Please pour Miss Parks some coffee."

Soon Miss Parks had coffee and an egg and bread and ham on the plate in front of her.

"Did you sleep well?" He immediately regretted the question. He didn't need anyone finding out where she had fallen asleep.

"Yes, thank you." She held her coffee cup as if it were a lifeline.

His father came to the conversational rescue.

"I understand you enjoyed our hospitality so much last night, you stayed."

"I fell in the fish pond."

His parents stared, both frozen in mid action. His father's bite of ham hung precariously on the immobile fork, his mother's coffee cup tipped at a dangerous angle.

There had been a reason why Sam had left out that little piece of information, but apparently this woman had very little sense of decorum or self-preservation, which actually made her quite interesting.

"My goodness, however did that happen?" His mother's voice was unnaturally high as she set down her cup and leaned toward their guest, eyes wide.

Miss Parks glanced around the table, and her grip tightened on her coffee cup until her knuckles whitened. Perhaps she realized she was revealing too much, hopefully she wouldn't also reveal how he had encountered her the first time.

"I'm not really sure." Her voice quavered slightly. "I was admiring the moon, and next thing I knew I was in the water. It's possible I had a little more to drink than I should."

"It was a hot night," Sam said, wanting to help her out in some way, although the night hadn't been unusually warm. "I'm sure you didn't realize how much you were drinking."

"That must be it," she agreed and happily sipped her coffee.

"Parks," his father muttered to himself. "I don't recognize the name. Do we know your people?"

She froze, and fear danced through her eyes as she darted her glance once more back and forth across the table, but then she took a breath and her face relaxed.

"I don't think so. We're pretty new to the area."

"We'll have someone ride out to your house this morning, and as soon as you are ready, a carriage will bring you home," his father said.

Once again, he noticed that she looked unsure. She took a sip of her coffee before answering. "Yeah, that's really nice, but I'm okay." She continued to hold the cup, he got the feeling she was trying to hide behind it. "If no one comes for me, I'll walk home. That is, if you don't mind if I stay around a little while."

"Not at all," he was quick to answer, though there was something about her response that didn't ring true. He certainly wasn't going to call her out as a liar in front of his parents.

With a rustle of skirts and an over-exaggerated sigh, Elizabeth entered the dining room. Her blonde hair was in perfect sausage curls, her dress a bit too frilly for breakfast.

"This is ridiculously early."

"If we delayed breakfast any longer," Mother said, "it would be dinner."

Elizabeth tossed her curls and daintily sat down.

"Can I go to Frederick with you? There is absolutely no social life around here anymore. It's dreadfully dull." She looked up, big doe eyes ready to wrap Father around her little finger when she noticed the visitor, and her tone changed abruptly. "Who are you?"

Sam was appalled at his sister's lack of decorum, but at the same time, found it interesting that Elizabeth did not know this woman who claimed to be Dinah's friend.

"Friend of Dinah." Miss Parks answered without batting an eye. She'd been prepared for this, he realized. "You're Elizabeth, right? Dinah has told me so much about you. She says you are the best friend anyone could ever have, so sweet and caring."

Who was this vixen who had landed in their house? He would bet any amount of money that she had no idea who Dinah was. How had she ended up in his bed last night?

Elizabeth, always easy prey to flattery, settled her napkin in her lap, while she smiled at the newcomer. "I don't remember meeting you, but then there were so many people at the ball last night."

"I didn't feel great early on," Miss Parks explained, "so I went to lie down. Imagine my surprise when I woke up and it was morning."

"Is that my dress?"

Sam could almost see the wheels turning in Miss Parks' head before she answered.

"I couldn't exactly wear my ball gown to breakfast, Beck loaned me one of yours. I hope you don't mind. It's a lovely dress, though I'm sure it looks much nicer on you." She took another sip of her coffee.

He glanced at his parents. They seemed as fascinated with this performance as he was. With a small shake of his head, his father turned his attention back to Sam. "Do you want to go over any accounts before I leave?"

"I want to ride the estate with you." What he wanted was confirmation that he was doing things right. He shouldn't need it. He was a grown man after all, in charge of running a large plantation. His father trusted him to do it. Why couldn't he trust himself?

"I'd like that."

"So, can I go to Frederick with you?" Elizabeth asked again, while signaling to the serving girl to pour her coffee.

His parents exchanged a glance across the table, and in that way that long-married people had, managed to have a whole conversation without saying a word.

"If Sam can manage here on his own." His mother looked at him instead of his sister.

"I'll manage." Honestly, life would be easier without having to worry about Elizabeth.

"Fine." His mother let out a small sigh. "You may come. Have Hannah pack for you."

"Why not Beck?" Elizabeth demanded, pausing as she reached for her coffee.

"Hannah will go with us."

"But Beck's my girl!" Elizabeth's protest sounded very much like whining to Sam's ears.

The look his mother gave her was enough to

squelch any more complaints. "If you are not here to see to the running of the house, then Sally needs Beck. Hannah can be spared."

Elizabeth's mouth puckered into a pout, but she didn't protest any further. Instead she turned her attention back to Miss Parks.

"I'm sorry, I didn't catch your name."

"Emily Parks."

"We'll get acquainted while Hannah packs my things."

Miss Parks' smile looked genuine and relaxed. "Sounds lovely."

What was that woman's game? He supposed it didn't matter too much. She'd be gone by midday and his parents and Elizabeth would also be on their way. He could settle into running the estate and figuring out what to do about the war. He almost wished everyone wasn't leaving. He'd prefer the distraction of a full house than all kinds of quiet to stew in his own thoughts. Despite all the things on his mind, he kept looking at and wondering about this Miss Parks. Perhaps it was his rather unorthodox introduction to her that made her loom so large in his mind. But partly it was that her story didn't add up, he knew his father realized it, too. There was also something refreshing about her, something different, but he couldn't quite pinpoint what that was.

Breakfast ended, and Sam and his father bowed politely to the ladies and headed out to their horses. Sam placed his foot in the stirrup and mounted his stallion, Echo. He gave the sorrel beast a pat on the neck. He was a good horse, maybe later he'd take him for a good long run. They could both use it.

His father mounted his horse as nimbly as if he were twenty years younger. He took the reins from Moses and squinted into the sun, surveying his land.

"Any problems with the field hands?" his father asked, as they rode toward the fields.

"Nothing out of the ordinary." Quite frankly, it was not surprising that enslaved workers weren't always thrilled with their lot in life, nor were they as motivated as one might like.

"You're keeping them in line?" His father glanced at him, waiting for an answer.

"I'm letting Wilkins deal with it." He had never felt comfortable disciplining the field hands. Daniel Wilkins had been the overseer for almost ten years now. He knew his job, and Sam let him do it.

"You may have to take a more direct hand in the matter." His father clucked to his horse who had decided that some clover by the path would make a tasty treat.

"Why is that?" Sam ducked his head as Echo walked under a blossom-laden tree.

"Things are changing, Samuel. I don't have to tell you that."

"I know." His response was perhaps a bit testier than strictly necessary. "But Wilkins knows what he's doing. You always trusted him."

"It's not a matter of trust," his father said and then, running his hand through his hair, changed his answer. "Maybe it is. Wilkins is good at his job, it's true, but I don't trust him, not like I trust you. I left you to run this farm. You have to manage Wilkins like you manage everyone else."

"I don't see why I can't let people who know what

they are doing simply do their jobs." Frankly he found the minutia of running the farm tedious.

"Because they will take advantage of you," his father answered. "Wilkins especially. He'll keep the slaves in line, but incapacitate some of them so you lose the man hours. That's not a good pay off. You need to keep him in line. Punishing is fine, as long as the bucks can still work."

Sam rather wished he were like Elizabeth and could cajole people into doing his will. Then he would convince his father to leave the politics in Frederick to others and come back here and manage the farm. Sam could then devote himself to poetry.

They rode the path between the fields of sprouting tobacco.

"Looks like a good crop." His father nodded approvingly toward the fledgling plants.

Sam gripped his reins tighter. How would his father feel about the changes he had made? "I put in several acres of potatoes."

"Why?"

Sam relaxed as he realized his father wasn't angry, merely curious.

"I know my history, Father. If this disagreement between the north and south isn't resolved quickly—"

"And it most likely won't be." His father was always the realist.

"Right. If that's the case than we could be in for a protracted war. In which case there are likely to be shortages. Tobacco's a cash crop, but you can't eat it." He knew his history, but at the same time, he couldn't imagine any life but the idyllic farm life he saw before him.

"Sound thinking," his father said. The morning sun had turned warm, it was going to be a hot day. "And what about this young woman who stayed too long at the ball. What do you know about her?"

"Not a thing," he answered honestly. "I don't remember seeing her at the dance."

"She's not telling the truth." His father swatted at a fly beleaguering his head.

He'd come to that same conclusion himself.

"Perhaps not all of it." He thought perhaps she had been misused by some male guest at the ball, and naturally she'd make up a story to cover that. "I'll get to the bottom of it."

"Don't forget you announced your engagement to Miss Johnson last night."

He had been looking across the field but jerked his head toward his father. "What do you mean by that?"

"I mean, I saw the way you looked at Miss Parks at breakfast. Do not do anything to jeopardize your alliance with the Johnsons."

"Of course not, Father," he said. "You have nothing to worry about."

Miss Parks, whoever she was, however intriguing she might be, would be gone by this afternoon. She posed no threat to Dinah. None at all.

Chapter Five

Emily

Emily followed Elizabeth to the parlor after breakfast. She'd seen parlors like it before, when touring historic homes. This was even more amazing than being in a museum, because everything was real and functional, unlike the wax fruit they'd put on tables, or the checkerboard that would be left set up with a half-finished game to make it look like a room was lived in. Here there were a couple of books stacked on an end table next to a gas lamp. There was a writing desk with a pile of correspondence on it and a jar for ink. There was a basket of embroidery on the floor by the rocking chair. The fireplace clearly was used regularly, she could smell the lingering wood smoke from it, even though it was not in use now, on a warm morning. There was even a blue parakeet in a wrought-iron cage preening himself.

"How long have you known Dinah?"

She really wished she'd never said she knew Dinah. It was hard enough to pretend she was from this time, even for a couple of hours, without adding that to the mix. She needed to find a way to get back to the fishpond and fast. If these people didn't already know she was lying through her teeth, they'd figure it out pretty quickly, and their hospitality would come to an abrupt end.

"Oh, it's hard to say," she answered with a dismissive wave of her hand. "Dinah's one of those people who once you meet them you feel you've known them forever."

Elizabeth seemed to consider this answer and apparently didn't find it lacking, for she smiled. "How true. We can wait in here until your people come for you."

That would be a long wait.

Her one hope was that the elder Marshalls and their daughter would leave before long, and then she could wander, unobserved over to the pond and dive in. Would it work? Would it take her home? If she knew for certain it would, she could enjoy her little sojourn in the past, but as it was, she couldn't concentrate on anything but wanting to go home.

For now, though, she needed to play the role she'd assigned herself, so she didn't get hauled off to jail for breaking and entering before she had the chance to get back to the pond.

"Come, sit with me." Elizabeth sat on the horsehair sofa and patted the seat next to her expectantly. Sitting itself was slightly problematic. Mrs. Marshall, the epitome of old-fashioned grace, had not mocked her inability to work her clothing at all at breakfast but had instead given her the hint she needed to succeed. She repeated that process now, lifting the back of the hoop slightly before settling into the sofa.

"Since you were ill, I suppose you missed the engagement announcement." Elizabeth picked up a piece of embroidery from the basket and set to work on it.

"Um, yes, I suppose I did." She wished she knew how to embroider so she could have something to do with her hands. "Who got engaged?"

Elizabeth looked up from her embroidery and frowned.

"Why Sam and Dinah of course. You would know that, being her friend."

"Oh, right. Of course." So the handsome Mr. Marshall, the man of her dreams, such as they were, was not even available for her. Why else would she be dumped back more than a hundred and fifty years in the past, if not to find the one man for her? Great. She'd found him, and he belonged to someone else. "I knew about that. I thought you meant that someone else got engaged. Yourself for example."

Elizabeth busied herself with her embroidery again.

"No, not me. Not yet." She glanced at Emily, from under lowered eyelashes. "Did Dinah say anything about Joseph maybe going to make his intentions known soon?"

She sounded so young and hopeful, Emily felt a tug at her heartstrings. "She didn't say anything. But you know she's been rather preoccupied." That was a safe answer. Anyone announcing an engagement or planning a wedding was bound to be preoccupied, as she had every reason to know.

Would Dayna and Johnson even know she was missing, or would they have left for their early flight, reasonably thinking that she was still comfortably asleep in her room? She needed to think about something else. Anything else.

"Tell me about Joseph." Any girl in a state of infatuation loved talking about her guy. If that wasn't considered a universal truth, it ought to be.

Elizabeth's face lit up. She had a dimple on one side of her face. It was quite endearing, actually.

"Mr. Fitzsimmons." She gave a contended sigh. "I only call him Joseph because we've known each other since we were children. It's hard to remember to be proper sometimes."

If she had to be proper, she wouldn't even know the rules.

"So, he's your beau?" The word sounded old fashioned on her tongue, but saying anything else in this setting would have seemed ridiculous.

"Oh yes, I'm sure he'll be proposing to me any day now. Honestly," she lowered her voice. "I thought he'd ask me last night, or at least ask Father for my hand. But, I suppose with Sam's announcement, the timing wasn't right. And then, there's the war. I'm sure he'll enlist, but will he want to get married before he leaves, or wait until he comes back?"

Emily stopped paying attention after the word war. *War*.

"He died in the Civil War." The inn owner had told her. That handsome, young, dynamic man who had smiled at her at breakfast, and, her cheeks flushed, who had discovered her last night, though she still held out hope that she had dreamt part of that. He was so alive now. But he would die in the war. And the war was starting. Now.

"He's going to go off to war?" She struggled to keep her voice even.

"Of course," Elizabeth answered, as if it were the most natural thing in the world. "He hasn't enlisted yet, but as soon as he figures out which side to join, I'm sure he will."

"Which side?" She echoed faintly. She knew her history, at least to a point. Maryland had been a Union State during the Civil War. She was fairly certain she was still in Maryland. Other things from history lectures over the years came back to her. The people of Maryland were very divided, many young men crossed the border to Virginia to fight for the Confederacy.

What side would Samuel Marshall be fighting for when he died?

It didn't matter, of course. He'd be just as dead and she'd be far away and back home.

"I don't pretend to understand it all," Elizabeth said as she stabbed her needle into the linen. "All the menfolk can think about anymore is war. Frankly, I'm getting tired of it. I hope it's over quickly so things can get back to normal."

Four years. That's how long the war would last. Four long and bloody years. Things would never be normal again. Not the way that Elizabeth meant. She didn't say anything though. What could she say that wouldn't make her appear like some sort of lunatic?

"Why are you going to Frederick with your parents?" She turned the conversation from talk of war. "If Jo…Mr. Fitzsimmons is here, why go there?"

Elizabeth tossed her curls casually behind her shoulder. "The parties here are boring. All the men are leaving."

"Do you think there will be more men in Frederick?" What she didn't ask was if she was so sure of Joseph, why be so concerned about the lack of men?

"One can always hope."

Mrs. Marshall glided into the parlor. "I hope you

are making our guest welcome, Elizabeth."

"Yes, Mother." Elizabeth kept her eyes on her embroidery. Emily took that bit of body language to mean that she didn't want to discuss men in front of her mother. She didn't blame her in the least.

Mrs. Marshall, with her gray-streaked hair in a tidy bun, turned to Emily. "Beck tells me the dress you wore last night is quite damaged. I suppose you can send this one to Elizabeth in Frederick once you get home."

"Oh, let her keep it," Elizabeth said with a casual flip of her hand. "It's last year's style, and those colors never looked right on me anyway."

Mrs. Marshall's lips tightened to a thin line. Emily suspected she had a better sense of possible economic hardships to come than her daughter did. She'd happily promise to send the dress back, but that might prove impossible, so she simply thanked Elizabeth for her generosity.

"Should we send someone with a message that you are here?" Mrs. Marshall folded her hands in front of her, waiting for an answer.

Oh, if only they could. Emily forced a smile. "I'm sure someone will be here within an hour. There's no need to trouble yourself. Unless, of course you want me gone before then?" She really hoped they didn't. It would be so much easier to get to the fish pond if she could stay nearby until she had a chance to jump back in. And when she emerged from the water, she'd be back in her own time and have no need to bother these fine people anymore. That had to be what would happen. It was the only thing that made sense. Making sense, being relative in this case.

"You can stay as long as you need. Perhaps we

should delay our departure until someone comes for you." From the way Mrs. Marshall hesitated before suggesting it, Emily could tell that was not what she wanted to do.

"That's not necessary. Really. I don't want to inconvenience you anymore than I already have."

Mrs. Marshall's face relaxed. "Elizabeth, you should go make sure that Hannah is packing what you need."

Elizabeth put aside her embroidery and headed up the stairs. Mrs. Marshall took the seat her daughter had vacated and faced Emily. She folded her hands primly in her lap, and Emily got the uncomfortable sensation she was about to be interrogated.

"You were at the ball as a guest of Miss Johnson's?"

The only way forward here was to be consistent with the story she'd already told. Besides, by the time they could check it, she'd be long gone.

"Yes, ma'am." She never called any one ma'am, but something about the clothes and the setting made it seem appropriate. "I hope you don't mind that she invited me." Maybe it was better to go on the offensive here. "She wanted me to meet Sam, since she'd be marrying him, and we are such good friends."

"Odd that we never met you before." There was a distinct hardness to Mrs. Marshall's voice.

Emily affected her most innocent look, eyes wide, smile unforced. "It is, isn't it? Funny how that happens. How two people can know a third but yet never meet?"

"Yes." Mrs. Marshall looked momentarily flustered, fidgeting with her fingers and blinking rapidly. "Yes, that's quite true. I am sorry you weren't feeling well yesterday. You are much better this morning, I presume."

"Oh, yes. Thank you. The delicious breakfast certainly helped. I appreciate your hospitality."

Mrs. Marshall wasn't ready to give up quite yet. "Perhaps we should send word to the Johnsons that you are here."

"Really, it's not necessary." Because they wouldn't care in the least, not having the slightest idea who she was. "You've done more than enough already. I don't want to be underfoot. In fact, why don't I go sit on the porch and wait for my ride? That will leave you free to get ready to go without having to worry about me."

Mrs. Marshall put up a small protest, but ultimately that plan seemed to work for everyone and Emily rather enjoyed sitting on the rocking chair on the porch, listening to the quiet that existed a hundred and fifty years ago. There were no car tires kicking up gravel, no motors, no radios blasting, no airplanes overhead.

There were also no modern bathrooms, and she had lasted as long as she could. She needed to find an outhouse, or whatever passed for it. Beck, brought her a glass of lemonade, but she couldn't consider even taking a sip until she had relieved herself.

"Excuse me, is there an outhouse or something I can use?"

"Out back by the kitchen," Beck answered, barely making eye contact.

"Would you mind much showing me where that is?"

"Yes, miss, follow me," she said, and tried to hide a sigh.

Emily followed her through the house, past the

paintings in the hall. How long had those portraits hung in those same spots? Beck led her out back to a small whitewashed building a short distance from the main house. She had been expecting something from *Little House in the Prairie* with a half moon in the door and corn cobs for wiping purposes, a situation she was not looking forward to. She held her breath as she opened the door, anticipating a smell much like a port-a-potty at a concert, but while she could detect the lime used to sanitize, the odor wasn't that overpowering. The small room was whitewashed inside as well, and there was a window near the ceiling in the back to let in light. A lantern on a shelf would provide light at night. There was even a small open-topped box with what, thank the good lord, looked like toilet paper.

She tried to hitch the dress up, but if the front went up, the back went down. She decided it was more important to have the back up, and suddenly she was very grateful for the bloomers with the split. She'd never have been able to get panties down without help. As she sat and relieved herself, she wished Dayna were here, not only to help her, after all, fair was fair, but in order to witness this incredible world. Then again, maybe it wouldn't be so incredible for her. She wouldn't be treated as a visiting guest, but as a slave.

Finally, she finished what she had to do and got her clothing situated once more. Either this got easier with practice, or people waited until they were fairly bursting before bothering to go. Luckily, she wouldn't need to find out. She looked for a spot to wash her hands, and not seeing one decided her next stop, before going back to the porch to drink her lemonade was back to the bedroom she'd spent the night in. She could use the wash basin there.

She found the room with no problem. She hadn't been wrong when she'd gone to the first room at the top of the back stairs last night. That had been the room she'd been assigned. She was tempted to open the door and look at it again, see if it offered any clues to her present situation, but she heard voices coming up the stairs and decided not to risk it, not yet.

She ducked back into her own room, at least if found there she'd have to come up with no excuses.

"I'd feel better about things if Miss Parks was safely on her way home before we left," Mrs. Marshall's voice drifted down the hall.

"Sam can deal with it." Mr. Marshall sounded like a man who had bigger things to worry about. "We need to be on our way. Waiting for Elizabeth to be ready has already delayed us longer than I would have liked."

A door closed. and she figured they must have gone into their own bedroom. She went back downstairs and out to the porch to drink her lemonade.

Really it was a fascinating thing, being here. She'd always loved historical homes and places where people dressed up to try to recreate a lost time. But this was real. At living history museums, she could never quite get past the fact that everyone was acting a part, and it made the past seem very distant. Here, people were basically the same, except clothes and technology were different. She glanced out at the fields. And slaves. That was different as well.

How had she gotten here? She sipped her lemonade, and the sunlight glanced off the gold of her ring. What had happened to the silver? How did a metal just dissolve? What had happened in that fish pond?

How did it work? Perhaps it was like the wardrobe that led to Narnia. The fish pond was a portal to another world and time. She had to go back into the fish pond, like going back through the wardrobe, and she'd be home in her own time. Perhaps the silver had been the price of admission so to speak. Maybe the gold would disappear on the way home. She'd have a hard time explaining to her father what happened to the ring he gave her, but it would be harder to have them wonder what happened to her if she didn't get back home, and soon.

The quiet was refreshing, but as she closed her eyes and breathed in fresh air, unpolluted by cars and asphalt, she realized it wasn't exactly silent. The birds sang loudly; she barely noticed them at home. In the distance people called to each other, presumably the slaves at work. Thumping and clanking came from the stables. Perhaps someone tossing hay, cleaning up the dirty, putting in new. The clanking could be someone getting the carriage ready. The fresh air wasn't particularly fresh either. With a deep breath she caught smells from the stable of horse and hay and manure. Bread baking and ham roasting provided a more pleasant aroma.

She opened her eyes again as the family joined her on the porch.

"Your people have not come yet?" Mrs. Marshall adjusted her be-feathered bonnet.

"Not yet." She put down her glass of lemonade and stood to see them off. "I'm sure they'll be here soon."

"If you need anything before they get here, be sure to ask Beck." Mr. Marshall pulled kid leather gloves over his hands.

"I'll do that," Emily assured him. "And thank you so much for your hospitality."

Elizabeth was the only one to look her straight in the eye and smile. "It was delightful to meet you. Hopefully at the next ball you won't feel ill."

The odds of Emily ever seeing them again were very slim, but since she had told them she was friends with Sam's fiancée, it wasn't unreasonable for them to assume. She returned the smile. "Hopefully."

Sam helped his mother and sister into the carriage, shook hands with his father, and stood back as the carriage rode off down the drive. He came back onto the porch and sat beside her.

"Do you suppose you'll be here for lunch?"

"I don't think so, no." It might be interesting to stay here and get to know him a little more, but it was more important to get back to her own time.

"I could show you around the plantation." He tugged at his own gloves as if they were constricting his fingers.

Tempting, but better to have him go about his business so she could dive into the fish pond. She really didn't need, or want, an audience for that.

"Thank you, but no. Don't mind me. I don't mean to interrupt your routine."

"It's really no trouble."

Sam looked at her with his soft gray eyes, and she really wanted to say yes.

There was something so gentlemanly about him, something grander than she was used to, that she wouldn't at all mind spending time with him. But he was engaged to be married to someone else and going to die in the Civil War. There was no reason to encourage pointless fantasies.

The decision was taken out of her hands when a young man on horseback rode into the yard. He dismounted in a fluid motion and was up the stairs to the porch in a few bounds.

"Sam, I need to talk…" He stopped, noticing Emily on the porch. His round baby-face turned red, right to his protruding ears. "Oh, sorry. Didn't know you had a guest."

"This is Miss Parks, a friend of Dinah's. She fell ill at the ball and spent the night." He cleared his throat and turned toward her, and gave her such a warm smile that her insides melted a little. "Miss Parks, this is Mr. George Phelps, a neighbor and friend."

"Nice to meet you, George." She held out her hand to shake his.

His face got even redder. He took her hand, delicately, as if not sure quite what to do with it. "The pleasure is mine, Miss Parks."

At his formality, she wondered if perhaps she shouldn't have used his first name. The etiquette of this time was a minefield she did not want to have to navigate.

George glanced around, his eyes lingering on the door, while he fidgeted with his hat.

Emily didn't need it spelled out for her.

"It's all right if you two need to speak in private. I'll walk down to those gardens over there."

"No." Sam reached out a hand but stopped short of touching her arm "It's fine, you don't have to…"

"I really do need to talk to you, Sam." George sounded terribly apologetic. "And it would be easier in private."

She had no right to make things difficult for the two men. She shouldn't even be here at all. She smiled graciously. "Please, don't mind me. I'll be fine."

She stepped off the porch, the wide skirt cumbersome around her. She walked away from the house, letting the two men have whatever private conversation they might need. She glanced back and saw they had stepped inside. Perfect. She could go to the fish pond and get home. Sam would come back out and figure her ride had arrived. They might question why she had not said good bye, but she doubted they'd worry about it too much.

She followed the path to the pond. It was not nearly as stylized as it would be in the future. There was no stone wall surrounding it, allowing for sitting and dreaming. Instead it was simply a pond, the size of a small swimming pool. The sky and nearby trees were reflected in it, giving it a very picturesque quality. On closer look the water wasn't particularly clear, and there were long strands of algae or some other native-pond growth obscuring the water. How deep was the pond? She had no idea. She supposed it didn't matter, except, she didn't want the dress to pull her down and drown her. Could she drown in a fish pond? If it was over her head and the dress kept her from surfacing again, sure she could.

She felt the row of buttons that went down her back. There was no way she could get herself out of this dress without help. She was not going to let a dress drown her. She was a strong swimmer. Plus, the pond couldn't be that deep. And it had a muddy edge, a bank, it wasn't like it was a cliff she was going to suddenly drop off. She took off the white leather shoes she'd been given. She couldn't make herself wear such nice shoes into the water. The mud squelched between her toes, and she had to steel herself to continue. The hem of the dress started to soak up the water and got heavy. She was ruining this dress, just as surely as she had ruined the bridesmaid dress. Not that it mattered, she certainly wasn't going to wear either one again.

Suddenly the muddy bottom dipped away, and she was over her head in water. The weight of the dress pulling her down, down. The water filled her ears and her eyes, and she could see nothing in the murkiness. Concentrate. Get head above water. This was what she needed. She needed to go under water so she could go home. She was under water now. Next step, get out.

There had to be a bottom. When she hit it, she could kick off and get her face above water again. She hit and let herself sink far enough that she could bend her knees. Then she kicked off with all her might and pushed her arms through the water to get back to the surface. She could see the light of the sun above her. She was almost there. Her lungs burned. Her vision was starting to go dark. She needed to get to the surface.

And when she did she'd be home and have quite a story to tell.

The surface of the water was only inches from her face.

Her face broke through. She gulped in the air before her dress started to drag her down again. Hands grabbed for her and pulled her out, and she looked into Sam's gray eyes.

She hadn't gotten home.

Chapter Six

Sam

Sam pulled a dripping Miss Parks from the water. It was one thing for her to fall in the fish pond if she had too much to drink, but to fall into it stone cold sober in broad daylight. That was another matter entirely.

"You seem to have an unnatural affinity for this fish pond, Miss Parks." He tried to keep his voice light, but he wasn't sure he properly masked his concern.

"You could have drowned." George took her other arm to help her out of the pond.

Miss Parks, her hair dripping and hanging in rivulets around her face, her dress wet, muddy and hanging limply so that every rib in the hoop showed, looked from one to the other and burst into tears.

Sam looked over her head and caught George's eye. This was not the kind of situation either of them was prepared for. Going off to war they could handle. Crying women who threw themselves into ponds? That was beyond them.

"We'll get you up to the house," he assured her, speaking softly to the crying woman by his side like he would to a colt that needed gentling. "Beck will take care of you. Don't worry. You'll be fine."

A small boy, one of the kitchen maid's sons,

watched him, fingers in his mouth.

"You there," Sam snapped. "Go find Beck and have her come here at once."

The boy nodded and scampered off, bare feet kicking up dirt as he ran.

They had nearly gotten Miss Parks to the house when Beck appeared. She took one look at their sodden burden and seemed to sum up the situation. She was quick; he had to give her that.

"I will take care of her. Leave it to me," she said with calm assurance. They gratefully left Miss Parks to Beck's tender mercies.

He led George to his study and poured them both some whiskey.

"Who is this mysterious woman?" George settled into one of the wing chairs.

What he wouldn't give for an answer to that question. "I don't know. She showed up here last night. In my bed, if you must know."

George's raised eyebrows were enough to keep him telling the story.

"After falling in the pond—"

"She fell in the pond last night, too?"

Sam held up a hand. He hadn't even gotten to the good part yet.

"Apparently had too much to drink. Fell in the pond. Went to my room, stripped naked, and climbed into my bed."

"Naked? In your bed?" George's blue eyes opened wide. "Why can't I have your kind of luck? What did you do?"

"Called for Beck and had her given something to wear and moved to a different bed."

"This is the difference between you and me." George grinned, showing bottom teeth that overlapped slightly. "I would have figured she was fine right where she was."

"I had just announced my engagement," he reminded him. "Besides, I'm a gentleman. I wouldn't take advantage of a woman like that."

George sipped his whiskey before answering. "Being a gentleman is overrated."

He sat in the other chair. "Isn't it, though?"

"So, who is she? Where did she come from?"

"She says she was at the ball. That she's a friend of Dinah's."

"You don't believe her?" George tipped up his glass and took another sip.

He shrugged. Her story made sense. She could have been at the ball. There were people there he didn't know, and although, as host, he'd tried to speak to everyone, if she had left early, he may have missed her. But if she were such a close friend of Dinah's, it surprised him that he'd never heard her name mentioned. It was time to get to the bottom of this.

"I don't know if I believe her." He walked to the desk and pulled out a piece of paper and his pen.

"Dear Dinah," he began. He supposed since they were engaged he did not have to begin his correspondence with 'Miss Johnson' anymore. He dipped his pen in the ink again while deciding how to word what he wanted to say. "Do you know a young woman by the name of Emily Parks? She had a slight mishap and was forced to stay overnight here after the ball, and we are awaiting the arrival of her people to pick her up. She says she is a friend of yours, but I do not recall you mentioning her." He looked at what he had written, crumpled the paper, and started again.

"Dear Miss Johnson," maybe it was better to stay formal. "Your friend, Miss Emily Parks is here. Would you care to come visit?" Everything else was too difficult to explain in a note and too apt to be misconstrued.

He signed the note, blotted it, folded it, and sealed it, then rang for Tobias. "Have Lucas deliver this to Miss Johnson, at once."

"Yes, sir," Tobias said, taking the note from him.

"What are you up to?" George asked from the comfort of his wing chair, one leg casually crossed over the other.

"I suppose if we want to find out if our Miss Parks really knows Dinah, we ask Dinah."

"You think maybe she's a little crazy?"

"She fell in the fish pond twice in two days." Sam stood and looked out the window toward the pond. Why would that woman go straight for the pond again, after having fallen in it only yesterday? Most people would stay clear of it, for fear of repeating the unpleasant experience. Yet, she had not. Why?

"Remember those stories Moses used to tell?" George set his empty glass on the table beside him.

Moses, the man in charge of the stables, had been an old man even when Sam was young. He told stories that weaved magic around the listener.

"Which ones?"

"The ones about the spirit in the pond."

He remembered those. Moses had a whole host of stories dealing with spirits that lived in the pond and fed on the fish there. Most of them had to do with monsters rising out of the water to devour little boys who got too close.

"I think those were designed to keep us from swimming there." After listening to those stories, they never had been tempted. They'd swam in the creek and in other places but never in the fish pond. They knew better than to take chances with monsters.

"Yes, but why?" George joined him by the window. "He wasn't afraid of us drowning. We knew how to swim. Why keep us out of that particular pond?"

"What are you getting at? Do you think Miss Parks is the monster from the pond?"

"Or bewitched by it."

A shiver went down Sam's back. Could it be? Could there really be evil monsters or spirits or demons there? Had one bewitched Miss Parks and beguiled her to enter the water? It almost made sense. Except it didn't, because those stories weren't true, they were fairy stories.

He picked up George's glass and brought it to the sideboard. He was tempted to pour them each some more, but it was barely noon, and if Dinah were to come, he would want to have a level head. Actually, he needed that simply for figuring out the story behind this strange guest.

"I don't think our pond is bewitching anyone." He tried to sound firm and certain but wasn't sure he succeeded.

"You must admit it's intriguing." George picked up a paperweight from the desk and turned it over in his hands.

"I'm sure there's a less fantastic explanation Perhaps she's incredibly clumsy." He sat back in the wing chair. "So, you're going to sign with Yuengling?"

This was what George had come to discuss with him this morning. Events were spinning quickly out of control. This was no time to sit back and spend a lot of time evaluating options. It was time to make a decision.

"He's putting together a company for the area." George continued their conversation from where the rescue of the mysterious Miss Parks had interrupted it

It made sense to sign up with the company of a local man he knew and trusted.

"Union," Sam said, mostly to himself. He knew that was the side he needed to join, but yet he hesitated to commit himself.

"Of course." George cracked his knuckles. "You know there's really no other option. Consider this. If we fight for the Confederates and they win, great, we made the right choice. If they lose? We're traitors. If we fight for the Union and they win, great, we made the right choice. If they lose, then the Confederate States are their own country, and we go home and lick our wounds. The only real negative outcome there is fighting with the Confederates."

"Very logical." Sam rose and walked back to the window. He appreciated that George was able to approach this so logically, but it didn't feel logical to him. It felt visceral. Emotional. It didn't seem as simple as a pro and con chart.

"So, are you in?"

Sam stared out the window at the fields of growing tobacco tended by slaves. His father said not to worry about the farm, that he'd take care of it, but it still felt wrong to simply walk away from his responsibilities here. But didn't he also have responsibilities to his country?

His great-grandfather, for whom he was named, had proudly fought in the Revolutionary War. His grandfather had fought in the War of 1812. How could he not help his country now? Of course he had to go. And if he was going to go to war, he might as well go with George. They did everything else together.

"Yes." He turned back from the window to face his friend. "I'll go."

George nodded, as if he knew that would be the ultimate outcome. "He'll be in town in the next couple of days, recruiting."

He thought he'd feel a sense of relief, now that the decision had been made. Instead there was a hollowness in the pit of his stomach. Is this how all men felt when they knew they were going off to war?

The door to the study opened, and Tobias stuck his dark head in. "Will Mr. Phelps be staying for dinner?"

Sam glanced at George, but he knew the answer without asking. George never turned down a meal.

"I'll stay."

"And your lady guest? Will she be dining?"

"You'll have to check with Beck. If she is hungry she is more than welcome to dine with us. Have a place set for Miss Johnson as well," he added before Tobias shut the door.

"You think Dinah will come?"

"I can almost guarantee it." Yet, at the same time he almost dreaded it.

His prediction proved to be well founded. They heard the carriage drive up before they were called to table.

Sam stepped off the porch to give Dinah a hand

and help her out of the carriage. Her face was flushed, and her curls were a bit windblown. She looked lovely.

"What's this about entertaining female guests while I'm not here?"

She sounded annoyed, but in a mostly joking kind of way. He took her arm and walked with her up to the porch, where she and George greeted each other.

"So, you know Miss Parks?" Sam asked.

"Never heard of her," she answered. "She says she's a friend of mine?"

"That's what she told me."

Dinah toyed with her closed fan, tapping it against her hand. "What is she doing here?"

He told her what he could.

"I don't recognize the name," Dinah said, wrinkling her brow. "But perhaps I know her with a different name. I'd like to meet her."

"Naturally. I'll find out if she's coming down to dinner. I assume you're staying."

"Of course." Dinah adjusted her skirt which had caught on the banister. "Where's Elizabeth?"

"She went to Frederick with Mother and Father." Sam leaned against the porch railing.

"Frederick!" Dinah spoke as if it were the ends of the earth. "When did she decide to do that? Why didn't she tell me?"

"She apparently decided this morning. That's all I know."

Dinah stamped her foot in the daintiest way possible and effected a pout.

"Don't complain to me." Sam was sympathetic, though he did find her pouting amusing. "I had nothing to do with her decision."

"You could have convinced her to stay," Dinah pointed out. Sam supposed that was true, but he hadn't particularly desired that she stay. Her sleeping to all hours and mooning over Fitzsimmons when she was awake were getting a little hard to take.

"She'll come back when her parents do." George toyed with his hat.

Dinah turned her attention to him. "When is that?"

"When Sam and I go off to war, Mr. Marshall will come back to run Bonne Terra."

George may be his oldest friend, and as close to him as a brother, but right now, Sam wanted to hold his head underwater and keep it there. This was not the way to inform Dinah that her betrothed was going off to war.

She spun around, her eyes gleaming in her fury. "You enlisted and didn't tell me?"

Sam held up his hands in surrender. "I didn't enlist yet. George only now convinced me to go with him to join Yuengling's company."

The pout was back.

"You should discuss these things with me. I'm to be your wife, after all."

"I suppose I should." It hadn't even occurred to him that Dinah would want a say in the matter.

"We'll have to have the wedding before you go. Then I can move in here as mistress of Bonne Terra."

Sam's eyebrows shot up. He was fairly certain that if his father moved back to run the plantation, his mother would quite rightly expect to be mistress of the house, but those details could be sorted out later.

"I don't know when we'd need to leave," Sam said. "I'm not sure I want to rush into anything."

"It's hardly rushing, Samuel." Dinah tapped him on the arm flirtatiously with her fan. "We are engaged, after all. No one would think it odd if we got married before you left. In fact, they would think it mighty odd if we did not."

"There will be so much to do." Agreeing to marry Dinah was one thing, actually doing it, in the next couple of weeks, he wasn't sure he was ready for that.

"It wouldn't be fair to you to not be able to give you a proper party." If he knew anything about Dinah, it was that she enjoyed a good party.

"Oh, we can make a party on short notice." She brightened as if all the objections had been swept away. "That isn't a problem. My mother can work magic in that regard."

"It's hardly fair to marry you and then immediately leave."

"Is it any more fair to leave me, promised in marriage, but not actually with benefit of marriage when you go off?" She quirked one eyebrow at him.

Tobias came onto the porch. "Dinner is served, sir."

He breathed a sigh of relief. He'd have to sort things out with Dinah, figure out if they were to get married before he left or wait until he came back. These were things they could only discuss once he had a bit more information himself, and it was a discussion they could have without the presence of George Phelps.

He tucked Dinah's arm into his and led her into the dining room. When they got there, Miss Parks stood by the table, in a brown and gold dress, looking most uncomfortable.

"Who are you?"

Dinah clutched at his arm, and he patted her hand reflexively while glancing between her with her eyes narrowed in accusation, to Miss Parks, pale and uncertain.

Who was their mystery guest?

Chapter Seven

Emily

Emily had been stripped and scrubbed and dressed again, all while completely numb, inside and out. She was still here. Still trapped in the 1800s. She didn't get home. What would Dayna and Johnson do when they couldn't find her? What about her parents? They were going to panic. And who was going to pay the rent on her apartment? She'd be evicted. And she had to get to work tomorrow. She'd worked too hard to get her CPA and a job with one of the biggest accounting firms in town to lose her job because she'd fallen into the past and couldn't call to explain.

Ha! Like any explanation was possible. She could picture the call to Toni, her boss. "Hi, Toni, I can't come to work today, I'm in eighteen sixty-one." Yeah, that would work. At least tax season had ended, maybe they'd forgive her if she only missed a day or two. But how on earth was she going to get home?

"Mr. Marshall is expecting you downstairs for dinner." Beck finished her ministrations. "That is, if you feel well enough."

Dinner. Could she even think of eating at a time like this? But if she had to stick around a little longer, she would need her strength. Forgoing meals was not the way to do that. True she was probably in a state of shock, if her freezing, shaking hands were any indication, but she wasn't actually physically ill.

"Thank you, yes. I feel fine." Fine might be a bit of a stretch.

"Mr. Phelps is here, too," Beck continued.

That made sense, since he helped pull her out of the pond.

"And your friend came by. I imagine she'll be dining as well."

"My friend?"

"Miss Johnson."

Suddenly she didn't feel particularly hungry. It was one thing to say she was friends with this person she'd never met when she was only going to be around for a little while. But now she didn't know how to get home and Miss Johnson would know she didn't know her.

"Are you going down, miss?"

She could say she felt ill and put off the inevitable. The thing about the inevitable though, it always gets there eventually. She might as well deal with it now.

Oh, how she wished Dayna were here. Dayna would help her come up with some solution; she was quick on her feet like that. Emily looked at the maid who had tended to her and dressed her. She looked so much like Dayna it was scary. Maybe she could help her. It was tempting to ask her, but when she opened her mouth to speak she remembered this woman was a slave, she had her own troubles.

She was on her own.

"Yes, I'm going down." She took a deep breath and stuck her chin out. She might be going down, but she'd go down fighting.

She dragged her feet on the way to the dining

room, which seemed much closer than it had at breakfast. She'd have to admit she lied. That would be fairly obvious to everyone. But what explanation could she give?

How about the truth? She'd been at her best friend's wedding in the twenty-first century, fallen into the fish pond and ended up in the nineteenth century. Sure. Everyone would believe that.

She'd have to come up with another lie.

Maybe she could faint. Weren't nineteenth-century women known for having vapors and passing out whenever it was convenient? If they were always trussed up in corsets like this, she could believe that would happen regularly.

No one else was in the dining room when she got there, but she could hear them approaching. She clutched the carved back of the dining room chair. She wished she were anywhere but here, but this was the reality she had to deal with right now. Reality. That was a laugh. Maybe it was all a dream. Let it be a dream. If she willed herself to wake up, maybe she would. She could sometimes do that during bad dreams.

Wake up. Wake up. Please, wake up.

Nothing changed.

Samuel Marshall entered the dining room with a petite girl with blonde curls and dimples. She was probably one of the prettiest girls Emily had ever seen, making her feel large and dumpy in comparison. So, this was Dinah Johnson, fiancée to the handsome Sam Marshall. They certainly made an attractive couple.

"Who are you?" Dinah's eyes narrowed menacingly, her tone somewhere between accusatory and confused.

"Emily Parks." At least that part she could say without lying.

"Why did you tell Mr. Marshall you are my friend? I don't know you."

Dinah knew how to get right to the point.

"I'm sorry," she said. "I thought it would be an easier explanation. And I didn't plan to be here for very long." All very true.

"An easier explanation than what?" Dinah demanded.

Okay, now the lies were going to have to start, because no one would believe the truth. Then again, what did she have to lose by telling them the truth? It was the truth after all, and it was always better to tell the truth. Right?

She swallowed hard and blinked back tears. How had she gotten herself into this mess? She was never playing a drinking game again. "Do you think I might have a glass of water?"

Samuel nodded to a young black girl standing in the doorway, and she rushed off. George Phelps hurried to Emily's side and pulled her chair out for her.

"Please, sit down, Miss Parks," he said.

Soon she was seated and had a cold glass of well water in front of her. She took a sip and looked around at the expectant faces. They didn't trust her. Why should they? She showed up out of nowhere and lied to them. What were they expecting her to tell them now? Certainly not what she was about to say.

She opened her mouth to speak, but a serving girl came in with a platter of ham and put some on each plate. Next, they were dished up potatoes and applesauce. Finally, when their plates were full, she spoke.

"I'm sorry I lied. The thing is, I don't know how I got here. You see, I—"

She couldn't do it. She couldn't tell them she was from the future. They'd think she was crazy. And what did they do to crazy people in the nineteenth century? They locked them up in asylums that were positively primitive. No. She couldn't take that chance, not with people she didn't know.

"No, that's not entirely true. I was at a party in the ballroom." That part was at least true.

"Who did you come with?" Sam asked, his voice surprisingly gentle.

She supposed saying the bridal party would raise even more questions. They were going to know everyone at the ball. She couldn't make someone up.

"I came by myself." Also true, to a point, since she hadn't brought a guest to the wedding.

Dinah covered her mouth with her dainty hand. "Alone? No escort? No invitation?"

Apparently, that wasn't something a person would do in this time and place. Though showing up at a private party without an invitation or as the guest of someone else pretty much wasn't done in any time. Emily would certainly never do it and would look quite askance at someone who did. In that, she was in full agreement with Dinah.

It shouldn't matter. She would go home and never see these people again, but she didn't want them to think badly of her. She wanted to justify her appearance here, even though it really wasn't justifiable, even to her.

"I'm new to the area," she said, casually cutting her

meat and pretending this was the most logical explanation in the world. And maybe it was, at that, since the only other explanation she could come up with was that the fishpond was some sort of a time portal, which wasn't a very logical explanation. "And I don't know anyone that well. I heard about the ball. People were talking about it downtown, so I decided to come. I thought no one would mind an extra person, and I thought maybe I could meet some people, make some friends. I've been lonely."

She watched Dinah to see if her story would get her sympathy or more censure.

Dinah however kept tight control of her face. It would take a lot to win her over, if she even needed to, which really she didn't.

"Why didn't you and your mother go visiting in the neighborhood?" Dinah leaned forward, watching her intently.

"My mother is not with me any longer." It was true enough as far as it went. Her mother was in a different time and place and soon would start to panic about the whereabouts of her only daughter.

"I'm so sorry," Sam said with genuine emotion. Emily shifted her gaze to him. It probably wasn't Dinah she needed sympathy from, but Sam. After all, she needed his continued hospitality until she could figure out how to get home.

"So," George, seated beside her, sounded amused. "You simply invited yourself to the ball?"

She looked at him. His bottom teeth were crowded, and he could use a haircut, but he had a round, open face that made him seem like the kind of person you really wanted for a friend.

"I know it was wrong." This was not the time to go on the defensive. "And I'm really sorry."

"Where do you live?" Sam voice was still sympathetic. "We'll drive you home after we eat."

Oh. She hadn't thought this through to its logical conclusion, had she?

"Really, there's no need. Someone should be coming for me very soon."

"You expected them before this, perhaps they do not know where to come for you." He gestured with his knife, until Dinah put her hand on his arm, and he put it down on his plate. "It is no trouble to take you home."

No trouble for him maybe, but what were they going to do when there was no home for them to drop her off at. Why couldn't she simply faint on demand? It would be so much easier.

"We have a house in town," she said finally. That seemed safe enough. There were houses in town and presumably these people couldn't know everyone who lived in them.

"We'll drive you home after we eat." Sam picked up his knife again, ready to eat, now that this was settled. "It's a nice day for a ride."

Maybe it wouldn't be so bad. Once dropped off, she could walk back to the plantation and try the fish pond again. She would just have to stay out of sight.

"Thank you." She hoped she sounded appropriately thankful instead of terrified.

"I'm sorry I didn't meet you at the ball last night," George said, pausing in cutting his meat. "I'm always looking for a new dance partner."

"That's because you step on toes, and the girls all want to preserve their feet," Dinah answered with the teasing ease of long friendship.

"I'm not a very good dancer." She wasn't bad at dancing in the twenty-first century, but if put to the test with real ballroom dancing, she'd fail for certain.

"Then you would be perfect for me. Next time there's a ball, you'll be sure to be an official guest, because you'll go with me. How does that sound?"

George grinned, and she grinned back. It was impossible not to like George. But inside she sighed. A guy finally showed interest, and it's in the wrong century. Figured.

"Lovely, thank you." Who knows, if she couldn't find a way home, perhaps she'd be around for the next ball. God forbid.

She pushed her food around on her plate. What had she done wrong when she went back to the fishpond? Maybe it was more than just the fishpond. The silver from her ring was missing. Maybe she needed more silver to make it work. She glanced at the fork in her hand. Silver. Why not be a thief on top of everything else? It's not like they'd be able to do anything about it if she got back home, and if she didn't, she, and presumably the fork, would still be here.

"Miss Parks?" Dinah's voice came to her as if through a fog. Of course, fog. Did the mist last night have anything to do with what happened? Did it have to be night? How could she reconstruct the exact situation?

"Miss Parks?"

This time the voice penetrated enough that Emily looked up to see the other three staring at her.

"I'm sorry," she said, bringing her attention back to the table. "You were saying?"

Dinah's smiled seemed forced, and Emily sympathized. If she were put in Dinah's position, she'd probably react the same way. "Would you like my mother and me to introduce you around the neighborhood?"

"Oh!" Emily was taken off guard by the offer. "That would be very kind of you." She hoped she wouldn't be around long enough to take her up on it.

When she finished her meal, she tucked her fork in her sleeve. Hopefully this bit of silver would be her ticket home.

Chapter Eight

Sam

As old Moses brought the barouche around to the front of the house, Sam watched Miss Parks. She stood a little apart from them, arms hugging her middle, staring out at the old fish pond. He couldn't figure her out. She seemed uncomfortable and awkward here among them, but apparently had enough self-assurance to come to their ball without an invitation or an escort. Perhaps there was something wrong with her. When he was little, there was a family in town who had a feeble-minded daughter. He didn't know what ever happened to her; he hadn't seen her in years.

"I wonder what her story really is." Dinah came up beside him and put her hand proprietorially on his arm.

"I imagine in time we'll find out." Sam reached out and touched her hand. He was tempted to remove it, but let it stay. "Since she's clearly moved to the area."

"Oh, I think the less time we spend with her, the better off we'll all be."

Perhaps she was right. Things were unsettled enough without adding a strange mysterious woman to the mix.

"George seems smitten with her though." Sam watched his best friend walk back and forth behind Miss Parks, clearly trying to get up the courage to speak with her.

"George is smitten with anything in skirts who looks at him twice," Dinah answered dismissively.

That characterization had a certain ring of truth to it, but he didn't like to see his best friend disparaged. He watched George assist Miss Parks as she climbed awkwardly into the barouche. She didn't do anything with grace. It was like she had never worn a long skirt before or climbed into a carriage. Sam helped Dinah in. Now she was a woman who moved with grace and dignity, no movement out of place, he was a lucky man, having her for his own and he knew that. Anna had been graceful as well. He shut his eyes briefly. There was no benefit in thinking about Anna. Not now.

He and George climbed into the barouche, Sam taking the front-facing seat next to Dinah, and George, naturally positioning himself next to Miss Parks. Tobias climbed into the driver's seat.

"Where to, sir?"

Sam looked expectantly at Miss Parks, hoping she would give some guidance as to where they should bring her. But she said nothing, just continued to stare in the direction of the fish pond.

Perhaps she was a mermaid and had landed here from some fantasy land, which was why she had appeared to him with no clothes on, because obviously mermaids would not wear clothing, and that was why everything else seemed so strange to her. Sam almost laughed at the ridiculousness of that thought but stopped himself in time. He wouldn't want to have to explain himself.

"Into town, Tobias," Sam instructed. "We'll be dropping Miss Parks off at her residence."

"Very good, sir," Tobias answered with a tip of his hat. He clucked to the horses, and they were off.

"Are you in the center of town or the outskirts?" Sam asked Miss Parks.

"Oh, quite near the center, I'm sure," she answered, with nothing like assurance in her answer. "You can drop me off in the center of town, and I'll find my way from there."

"I think we ought to see you right to your door." He was not going to simply leave this obviously vulnerable woman in the center of town with no protector.

"Really, I'll be quite all right. Please. You have done so much for me already, when I am a stranger who really did impose on your hospitality."

Next to him Dinah muttered under her breath. "It's true."

"But if we don't bring you to your door, how will I ever find you again?" George asked, making pathetic puppy dog eyes at her.

"A girl likes to keep some mysteries, you know," she answered with a touch of flirtatiousness.

Some? Everything about her was a mystery. But intriguing. Oh so intriguing.

The wagon bumped along out of their property and down the road toward town. The air had that fresh scent of moisture and pine in it that made one want to take deep breaths and perhaps race a horse through the fields. Yes. It would be a lovely day for a long hard ride, but when he got home from town there were myriad plantation details he needed to take care of. Without his father here to see to things, he seldom got time for himself anymore. He supposed once he had signed up and shipped out with the army he'd have even less time to himself.

All the more reason to enjoy this leisurely ride into town, if for nothing else, because he didn't know when he'd get a chance to do it again.

They passed the Jenkins' cottage, the homestead that Sam always thought of as the first building in town. Soon they were rolling down the main street, with the grist mill and its giant water wheel opening the way for the feed store and the bank, the school, the church, the dry goods store, and the bakery. There were side streets off the main street leading to dozens of houses.

"Which street?" Tobias asked from the front.

Sam looked at Miss Parks, but she stared out at the town wide eyed as if she'd never seen the likes of it before.

"Oh, anywhere is fine," she insisted.

Sam sighed in frustration and tapped the fingers of his right hand on his leg. He needed to make sure she was safely home. She had shown up in his bed, somehow making herself his responsibility. But how was he supposed to do that if she didn't tell him where she lived?

Dinah tugged at his hand, and he looked down at her. She gave him what he supposed was a look designed to relay information, but although he'd seen his parents communicate with a look, he and Dinah did not have that kind of a kinship yet. He shrugged, to let her know he did not know what she was trying to convey and she sighed.

"I need to stop at the milliners. Can we go there?"

"Of course." Such a trivial thing. Couldn't that have waited? "Tobias stop by the milliners, please."

"Yes, sir." Tobias pulled the carriage to the side of the road in front of the hat maker's shop. Sam jumped down and reached up to take Dinah's hand to help her down. She stepped daintily to the wooden walkway in front of the shop.

"Miss Parks obviously does not wish for us to know where she lives," Dinah said in a half-whisper, her gloved hand resting on his arm. "Allow her that. I don't know why she was at the ball, but you are not responsible for her past this point. She said she lived in town, and you brought her here. Your job is done."

He turned to see George helping Miss Parks out of the carriage. He hated to admit it, but Dinah was right.

"I thank you so much for your hospitality." Miss Parks held out a hand as if to shake his. "It's been a pleasure."

George took hold of her hand before Sam could even react. He kissed it in a gallant gesture "The pleasure was all mine."

Sam glared at his friend. It had been his hospitality, not George's.

"I hope we shall have the pleasure of seeing you again, Miss Parks." Sam took her hand and kissed it, as gallantly, if not more so, than George.

"I'm sure you don't mean that." Her eyes sparkled, and her voice held a hint of a laugh. "Not after I fell in your fishpond twice."

Next to him, Sam could feel Dinah stiffen. He hadn't told her that part.

Dinah took Miss Parks' hand in her own. "It's been lovely. Be sure to keep in touch." Her words were kind, but her voice didn't hold much warmth. She let go of Miss Parks' hand and turned to Sam. "Darling, please help me find the right hat."

"I think you can handle that on your own." Is this what having an announced engagement meant? Having to worry about hats? He did not care for this turn of events. "You know I'm hopeless when it comes to fashion."

"Oh, do go with her." Miss Parks was obviously as keen to be rid of him as Dinah was to be rid of her. "Make your fiancée happy."

He went, leaving Miss Parks to George's tender mercies.

Once in the frilly confines of Miss Maple's Milliners, he turned to Dinah. "What was that about? You hardly need me to help you pick out a hat."

She smiled up at him in her beguiling way. "Darling, that woman was bewitching you. I needed to get you away from her before you completely succumbed to her charms."

He studied her crystal blue eyes. Was she jealous? Of a strange girl? Who had appeared naked in his bed? If she knew that part she'd certainly feel justified in any jealousy.

"You have nothing to fear." He glanced around the shop filled with feathers and ribbons and shuddered. "But please don't make me help you pick out a hat."

Dinah laughed, and the joy in it warmed his heart.

"No, of course not." Her finger grazed his cheek with a feather-light touch. "You are hopeless at fashion."

So he was left cooling his heels while Dinah discussed the benefit of lace over feathers and whether both would work on a hat, and he wished he were anywhere but here. He could leave. He was not being held by force. But yet, perhaps Dinah was right, and he was being bewitched by Miss Parks. He certainly felt drawn to know more about her. But he had an obligation to Dinah. He had promised to marry her, and that meant forsaking all others. The very fact that he wanted to leave the shop and see where Miss Parks was headed was enough reason to stay within.

Finally, Dinah was satisfied with the hat she ordered and she tucked her hand into the crook of his arm and they left the shop. George leaned against the carriage, cleaning his nails with his knife. Sam wanted to ask where Miss Parks had gone, to go there himself and make sure she was safe, but he refrained.

Dinah seemed inclined to make the afternoon into a prolonged leisure outing, but Sam kept picturing the ledgers on his desk that needed to be updated and instructed Tobias to take them home.

"I really should get more familiar with the house staff and the running of the home," Dinah said as they alighted from the carriage in front of the house. "After all, it will be my responsibility as soon as we are married. And now without Elizabeth here to supervise, you really do need someone in that position."

Sam had agreed to marry her. Why did he have such a hard time picturing her running his house? More specifically, why did he find it repugnant to think of her managing *this* house? It was his mother's house and would stay so as long as his mother wished it. But this was his future wife, he had to be diplomatic.

"I have too much work to do. You would undoubtedly be a distraction." He watched the tiny pout on her face grow and he hastened to add, "A most welcome distraction, to be sure, but a distraction none the less."

He called for her coach and saw her safely off to home.

"Throwing away perfectly good women." George gave a disapproving shake of his head.

"You know I'm not throwing her away, simply allowing myself room to work."

"I suppose I must go as well." George shifted his riding gloves from one hand to the other.

He probably should. George was apt to be a bigger distraction than Dinah. Instead he clapped one hand on his shoulder. "Come inside for a whiskey before you go."

"Don't mind if I do," he said without hesitation.

Sam let himself relax once he reached the inner sanctum of the study. This room allowed him to feel like he had some control over his world. He splashed some whiskey in a glass for George and some for himself. Then he settled himself into the leather cushioned desk chair.

"So, did Miss Parks get off safely?" He tried to keep his voice nonchalant. He shouldn't care. It shouldn't matter to him, but yet it did.

"Far as I can tell." George shrugged. "She more or less slipped away when I wasn't looking. She's quite the mysterious lady, isn't she?"

Sam's face flushed as he remembered finding her in his bed. "Quite."

"Think we'll see her again?"

Was it wrong to want to? Sam shook his head. "I doubt it."

An urgent knock at the door was followed immediately by the door opening a crack. Tobias stood there, looking panicked. "Mister Sam. You got to come. He's going to beat Beck. You got to stop him!"

Sam jumped up. "Who? Why? What's going on?"

"It's Wilkins. He done say she stole a fork. He's going to punish her. Please don't let him."

Sam's shoulder slumped.

"If she stole, she has to be punished." He hated himself for giving in to the inevitable.

"But she didn't steal it. She's not been whipped before. It's likely to kill her. Please, sir, you can make him stop."

He could stop Wilkins, but was it wise? Did he want to undermine the man's authority to get on with his job. Slaves got whipped. It was unfortunate, but it happened. If he stopped him from whipping one, would they expect him to step in and stop him from whipping the next? It would lead to anarchy.

"Please, sir." There was such anguish in his voice that Sam suddenly understood what he'd never notice before. Tobias was in love with Beck.

"I'll see what I can do." He headed to the door, leaving the comforting sanctuary of his office with more than a touch of regret.

Chapter Nine

Emily

The quiet of the countryside was no match for the noise in Emily's head as she trudged down the dirt path that passed for a road. No cars rushed by, their tires whirring along on the pavement, the bass line of some teenager's favorite music making the very air vibrate. There were no airplanes or helicopters. There were no electronic buzzes or beeps to signal the world at large was trying to communicate.

The world at large.

How long before they reported her missing? How long before someone noticed? Dayna and Johnson probably left for their honeymoon before they realized she wasn't there. No one else in the wedding party would have any particular reason to look for her. If they didn't see her, they'd figure she'd left already. The inn would know she hadn't checked out, but they would charge for an extra day and think nothing of it. At least not at first. She usually called her parents on the weekend, but with Dayna's wedding, they wouldn't be surprised not to hear from her.

It wouldn't be until Monday morning, when she didn't show up for work, that anyone would really start to question where she was. And even then, no one would be too concerned. People miss work without search parties being made up.

On one hand it was good no one was panicking about her being missing yet. On the other hand, how sad was her life that there was no one to panic.

At least she didn't have to worry about the people she'd left behind. Not yet. And if she could get back home before tomorrow morning, no one would ever be any the wiser. She'd just have to pay for an extra night at the inn. It would take a chunk out of her monthly budget, but if that was the worst that happened, it wasn't too bad.

The wind rustled through the pale green baby leaves of the trees. Birds called back and forth to one another, announcing dinner plans or giving warning. It was like the original Twitter. She smiled at her own joke and tried to take a deep breath, but the corset she was wrapped into made that difficult. No wonder women didn't compete in the Olympics back then— now—it was hard to even get tenses right in her head today—they'd never be able to move properly in this getup. Were there even modern Olympics yet? Instinctively she reached for her phone to check.

No phone. No nothing.

How did people find out answers when a question occurred to them? It had to be very frustrating. It *was* very frustrating.

Her foot caught in an uneven rut in the ground. Pain radiated up her leg, and she stumbled, catching on to a nearby tree. The last thing she needed was a twisted ankle. At least she was pretty sure it was no more serious than that. She leaned against the tree and tried to reach her foot. No luck. There was too much skirt between her hands and her feet. She stretched her ankle a bit until it started to feel better and continued on her way, limping slightly.

A lot about this situation was fascinating. She had been thrust backward in time through a fishpond. She should try to learn all she could and maybe come up with new insights into history. After all, nothing was really as cut and dried as it appeared in books. She almost wouldn't mind hanging around and dancing at a ball with George and Sam. Maybe if she figured out the way the time travel worked she could go back and forth, but first she had to know she could get home. She wasn't going to be able to rest easy until she did. She took a deep shuddering breath. What if it didn't work? She pulled the fork out of the pocket she'd sequestered it in. What if simply having the silver wasn't enough to get her home?

She trudged along, with each step taking a little less interest in the scenery and quiet. Her feet hurt. She was hot. She wanted to be home. She missed home. How had something as ridiculous as this happened to her? Where was the darn house? Had she taken a wrong turn somewhere? There'd been a fork in the road awhile back, but this was definitely the road more traveled. Maybe that had been the wrong decision. Up ahead she saw a fence, and beyond that, the house.

She breathed a sigh of relief. Thank goodness. Now she had to stay out of sight until nighttime and then try the pond again. Night time and silver and pond. What other variables could there be?

The aroma of baking bread wafted through the air to her. She wished there was a way to get something to eat while she waited, but she didn't want to be seen, and she certainly wasn't going to sneak around and steal food. She wasn't that desperate. Yet.

She stopped and scanned the area. No one in sight. That was good. If she couldn't see anyone, they couldn't see her, wasn't that how that worked? Even so, someone could be looking out a window. Better to keep to the shadows as much as possible. She saw no path through the woods, only rough underbrush. She couldn't muck through that in this skirt. She'd probably even hesitate if she had on jeans and sneakers.

Her best course of action was to stay close to the edge of the woods until she came to a path or other opening in the underbrush, and then she would be better concealed. As she progressed, she could see around the corner of the house, where a crowd had gathered. It looked like mainly blacks. Slaves.

She shivered as that thought sank in. Slaves. People actually owned other people. Right here. Right now. This was a part of history she didn't want to have to experience. Dayna was black. If she or Johnson had fallen through the fishpond (though such a thing would never happen to Dayna, she would not allow it) they could have ended up as slaves. The thought made her want to be ill.

But, yet, she knew this was true. She knew slaves had existed and that people were slaves. Seeing it, didn't actually make it any more true. Except it did. To her. She didn't want to see it. She wanted to go home. She glanced up at the sky as if that could give her some clue as to the time of day. The sun was clearly nowhere near setting yet. It was going to be a very long afternoon.

There was an undercurrent of agitation in the crowd. Some stood, shoulders hunched as if anticipating a blow that would be impossible to avoid. Others tensed as if ready to jump into a fray.

"I didn't take it!" A woman's voice said, half in plea, half in anguish. "I didn't steal no fork. I swear I didn't take it!"

The ground seemed to fall out from under Emily's feet. She steadied herself against a tree. A fork. Someone was in trouble for stealing a fork. The one she had taken. It had to be. How could she not have realized it would be missed and that someone would have to be held accountable?

Then she heard a scream. A loud, pain filled shriek.

Her own shoulders winced in sympathy. Someone was being whipped for taking the fork. And Emily was the one who had it. She couldn't let someone else suffer for her actions. No longer caring if anyone saw her, in fact, wanting to be seen, she ran toward the crowd.

"I took it!" she screamed. "I have the fork. Don't hit her. Please don't whip her!"

But she heard another scream. She wanted to stop to catch her breath, but she couldn't. She pushed through the crowd, until she could see Beck, her dress pulled off her shoulders, exposing her back. A man she didn't recognize, whip in hand, was poised to strike again.

"Stop!" Emily screeched. "Stop! I did it! Not her!" She rushed forward, despite hands reaching out trying to stop her. She threw herself at Beck, covering Beck's back with herself as the whip came down.

An animal-like cry escaped from her as the impact made its way to her brain.

She'd never felt anything like that before. Her skin burned and ached and her muscles screamed in protest.

Her vision went black and white and then started to fade away entirely.

Around her people were shouting, but she didn't process what they were saying. She braced for another blow which never came.

Strong arms enfolded her, and she was cradled like a baby. She could smell cinnamon and tobacco and whiskey and rested her head on his chest. "I'm sorry," she said. "I took the fork. I'm sorry."

"Don't worry about it." Sam's voice was soft and gentle in her ear.

"I didn't mean anything by it," she said. "I didn't want Beck to get in trouble."

"Hush. It's all right."

She rested her head on his shoulder and believed him.

Soon she was back in the green room, and Beck was there, helping her out of her dress so she could tend to her back. Already the pain from the lash was fading, between the corset and the slip and the dress, the whip hadn't broken the skin. What hurt the most was the indignity of it all.

"I'll put some salve on your back," Beck said, her voice tight and thin.

"Wait!" Emily turned around to face Beck who had hastily pulled her own dress back up over her shoulders. "I should be helping you, not the other way around. You got hit more than once and without anything to soften the blow. Let me look at your back."

"No, miss." Beck took a step back, looking horrified. "I can't be letting you do that. You have to let me tend to you."

"I do not." She grabbed at her own dress, which

Beck had laid on the bed and struggled to get back into it. As she floundered amid yards of cotton, she finally sighed. "You can help me get this back on, though."

Beck did, without a word, and then Emily turned to her. "Let me see your back."

Beck's eyes were hard and her mouth set in a thin line.

"Why'd you steal the fork?"

"Please let me put the salve on your back. I know it has to hurt."

"What do you know about it?" Beck spat the words out and turned her back in defiance.

Emily could still feel the outlines of the lash on her back. "I think I know a little about it." Suddenly she remembered telling Dayna that her ancestors had endured the Irish famine, as if that had in some ways equaled a life of slavery. Her one lash was not the same as knowing what Beck was going through, but she did know it had to hurt. "Just a little. Please let me help. I'll tell you why I stole the fork if you let me help."

At that Beck capitulated and, still with reluctance, pulled her dress down over her shoulders, exposing her back. There had only been two strikes, but each had left a deep welt across her otherwise smooth back, breaking the skin in a place or two.

"Sit." She opened the jar of salve and braced herself against some strong medicinal scent, but the medicine had a pleasant peppermint smell. "This might sting," she warned, "but I'll be as gentle as I can."

Beck's back muscles tensed as Emily gently worked the salve along the lines of the whip marks. While she worked she tried to think of what to tell Beck about the fork. The truth was the obvious thing, but could she trust her to keep a secret? Did it matter? And her own rash actions had caused Beck pain, the very least she could do was tell her why it had all happened.

"I needed the fork to get home," she said as she finished rubbing in the salve.

"You needed the money?" Beck turned to look at her over her shoulder. "Surely Mister Sam would have given you money if you'd asked. He likes you. I know he does."

"Not the money." She sighed and walked over to the basin and pitcher to rinse her hands off. Once they were relatively clean and dry she turned back to Beck, who had readjusted her dress, and sat, expectantly, waiting for her to continue. She had to tell her. But somehow saying the words out loud made it both too real and too ludicrous.

She sat on the bed and twisted her fingers together, playing with the gold and silver ring that was now just gold.

"I'm from the future."

Beck's eyes narrowed, and her mouth formed a thin line above her hardened jaw. "You don't have to tell me if you don't want to, but don't treat me as if I'm dumb because I'm a slave." She stood up and headed for the door. "Thank you for helping with my back." The was no warmth in her tone.

"Please. Wait!" Emily jumped off the bed and following her. "I don't think you're dumb. And I am telling you the truth. Please listen to me. I need someone to listen to me!"

And that was it really, she realized with a sinking feeling. She wasn't telling her because of any goodness of her heart, but because, selfishly, she needed someone to know. But was it fair to burden Beck with her secret?

Beck turned to face her, and her features which had been hard and angry changed again to something bordering on compassion, her eyes showing a bit of warmth once again. "You can tell me."

Emily started quickly, not even moving from the middle of the room, wanting to get the story out before either one of them changed their minds. "I was at my friend's wedding at a historic inn and there was a fishpond and I'd had too much to drink and I sat by the pond and then I fell in and when I got out of the water, I went back into the inn but nothing was the same only I didn't realize that until later. And I'm not really sure what happened, but I think I fell over a hundred and fifty years into the past when I fell into the fishpond. And I have a ring. It used to be silver and gold, but the silver is gone. So I think I need to give an offering of silver to the pond to have it bring me back home. And I'm sure you don't believe me, but it's true, and that's why I took the fork. And I never would have done it if I thought someone would get in trouble. Will you forgive me?" She ended in a rush.

"So, it's true," Beck said, more to herself than anything else, a faraway dreamy look coming into her eyes.

"You know something!" Emily grabbed her by the hand. "Tell me what you know!"

Chapter Ten

Sam

Sam stood at the tall window in the study, hands behind his back, staring out across the fields, where the field hands were tending to the tobacco crop. How long before he had to leave? What would happen to the plantation while he was gone? What would war be like? Would he bring honor to himself, or would he disgrace himself? What if he was really a coward? He'd certainly rather write poetry than fire a gun at someone. Who was this woman Emily Parks, and what was her story? Would he ever know? Why had he agreed to marry Dinah? The impending marriage felt like a noose around his neck. He wished he were still back at University. Life was so much simpler then, not that he had thought so at the time.

George came up behind him and held out a glass of whiskey. Sam took it eagerly.

"You're a million miles away," George said. "What are you thinking about?"

Sam shook his head. "Everything and nothing," he answered turning away from the window to face his friend.

"That girl, Emily, sure has spunk." George laid a hand on his heart. "I think I'm in love with her."

"Love?" Sam almost choked on the word. "You?"

She was *his* mystery girl. He'd found her in his bed. He could still picture those lovely breasts. So soft, so inviting. But he was engaged to Dinah. He didn't know why he was, but he was. Emily could not be his. He wanted Emily. Which made no sense. He was going away. She was presumably going home, wherever that was. He couldn't have Emily.

"She's pretty, and like I said, she has spunk. What's not to like?"

There was plenty to like, that wasn't the question.

"There's something very mysterious about her." Sam took a welcome sip of whiskey.

"Isn't that part of the allure? Something to discover," George answered, eyes bright with excitement. "Take Dinah for instance. She's all out in the open, nothing to hide, nothing new to discover. What you see is what you get. That's fine for you, but I like a little mystery. I want to find out who this Emily is."

So do I, Sam thought. Oh, so do I.

He leaned against the desk and sipped the whiskey. "What do you think her story is?"

George shrugged. "I have no idea. She shows up out of nowhere, seems to have nowhere she belongs, keeps trying to throw herself in the pond, and takes a lash across the back trying to stop a whipping."

"Because she stole a fork." Sam shook his head. "It doesn't make sense. None of it."

"My grandmother would probably say she was of the fairy folk and throw some holy water at her for good measure."

A shiver went up his back.

"You don't think she could be, do you?" He had

never believed in fairy stories, at least not once he was in long pants, but it would be an explanation for Emily's presence here.

"No, I don't." George clapped him on the shoulder. "And neither do you. There's obviously a simple answer to all of it. We just don't know what it is yet. But I aim to find out."

"How are you going to do that?"

"I'm going to ask her." He grinned at his own brilliance. "I'm going to invite her for a drive and ask her. Can you think of a better way?"

Sam couldn't, and he wished he'd thought of it first.

"If she wouldn't tell us before, what makes you think you can get her to tell you now?"

"I can be very persuasive if I need to be." George brushed his fingernails along the lapel of his coat. "And a bottle of wine won't hurt, don't you think?"

"You're not to get her drunk and take advantage of her!" Sam said sharply.

"Hey! I'm a gentleman through and through." George held up his hands in protest.

Sam knew that. He would never question George's integrity with any girl, not even Elizabeth, so why did he feel so fiercely protective of Emily? It was because she had shown up in his bed. He felt a certain possessiveness over her. But surely no harm would come to her if she were to go on a drive with George. So why did he resist they idea so much? He didn't want Emily to go riding with George. He wanted her to go riding with him.

He was jealous.

He had no right to be jealous. He was going to

marry Dinah, and he had no claim whatsoever on Miss Emily Parks. Whoever she might be. And however intriguing she might be.

"So, should I ask her for a ride this afternoon, do you think?" George was suddenly his normal uncertain self.

He shook his head. "No. I'm sure she's been traumatized by being whipped. Give her time to recover."

"What are you going to do about Wilkins?"

He turned back to the window. The slaves worked tirelessly, all under the supervision of Wilkins. He made things run here in a way that Sam was sure he could not if he had to do it himself. And he couldn't do it himself. He was leaving for war. He couldn't leave it all up to his father, he was old. His shoulders slumped. "I don't know."

"You can't have overseers whipping white women." George put his glass down on the sideboard and opened the bottle of whiskey. "It just isn't done."

"I know." Sam held his glass out to George. He could do with a refill. "But he didn't do it intentionally. She got in his way."

"Still. I think you have to do something about him."

George was right. Wilkins worked for him, and that lapse was inexcusable. Something would have to be done.

He rang the bell he kept on his desk and presently a small black child appeared at the door, out of breath from running to answer the summons.

"Yes, suh?" He took a deep ragged breath. "What do you need, suh?"

"I need you to find Tobias and send him to me at once." He thought briefly of simply having the child fetch Wilkins, but that would never do. Wilkins would not respect an order given to him in that way. He would respond to a summons sent through Tobias.

The child scurried off, and George put his glass down on the sideboard.

"What are you going to do?"

"Take the lash to Wilkin's back." Sam drained his glass. He really wanted this day to be over. "Fair is fair, after all."

George nodded, but said, "He's not going to like it."

"I don't suspect he will, but as you said, I can't let this go unanswered."

"He'll take it out on your slaves."

"He wouldn't dare. Not as long as I'm here." Sam hoped he wielded that much authority with Wilkins. He was his father's hire; he might not think that Sam had any power over him.

"That's just it," George pointed out. "You won't be here much longer."

Damn. He kept forgetting.

"Regardless, the punishment seems fair."

Tobias came to the doorway. "You sent for me, sir?"

"Please let Mr. Wilkins know I wish to see him."

"Here, sir?"

No. That wouldn't do. The transgression had been public. The punishment should be as well.

"By the barn." Sam put his empty glass down. He would not refill it as much as he might like to. "I will be there momentarily."

"Yes, sir."

Sam took his jacket from the coat rack and slipped it on.

"Coming?"

George still stood by the sideboard, making no move to put on his own jacket.

"Perhaps you shouldn't do this publicly."

Maybe he shouldn't, but what choice did he really have?

"All whippings are public. Isn't that the point?"

"I always thought the pain was the point." George reached for his jacket.

"That and to discourage others from misbehaving." Sam held the door open, ready to be done with this.

"You have no other overseer."

He made a noise that was almost like a snort. He hated when George was right about things, but he still didn't see any other way to proceed. "I'm not whipping him in the study. Behind the barn will do quite well. And I won't invite everyone to watch. It will be private enough, most of the darkies are busy working."

"Have you thought this through?" George asked as he followed him from the study.

"You're the one who said I had to do something!" He said through clenched teeth and ran a hand over his face. "Do you have a better idea?"

"No, I don't. Especially since you can't fire him." George clapped a hand on Sam's shoulder. "Though you whip him he might quit."

"Only one lash." He lengthened his stride. He wanted this over with. Maybe this wasn't the right solution. But Wilkins had hit a white woman. Something had to be done. He squared his shoulders.

He would do what he had to. They reached the area behind the barn where Wilkins usually whipped recalcitrant slaves. Wilkins had not arrived yet. Sam wasn't sure how far Tobias would have to go to track him down. He went into the stables and took his riding crop from the wall.

"You want me to saddle up Echo?" Old Moses paused in raking out a stall to ask.

"No, thank you. I'm not going anywhere at the moment." He didn't explain what he needed the riding crop for. He owed no one explanations.

Back out across the packed dirt yard to where George waited. He felt the heft of the crop in his hand and tried to imagine what it would be like to feel its lash across his back. His muscles tensed in anticipation of a blow he knew was not going to come.

"I've never hit a man before," he said to George.

"What are you talking about? You've pummeled me black and blue on more than one occasion."

He raised his eyebrows in surprise. "You gave as good as you got, but that's not what I mean. I mean, deliberately, with a whip."

"Never?" George's eyes widened and his voice came out an octave above where it normally was.

"Have you?" Sam narrowed his eyes and studied his friend. He didn't think George had, but what if everyone else did this on a normal basis, and he was here with knots in his stomach at the idea. What kind of a man did that make him?

George hesitated before answering. "No." After a thoughtful pause he continued. "I wonder if I'll make a very good soldier?"

He had wondered the same thing. He couldn't sleep

nights wondering that. "I imagine we'll be able to do what we have to when the time comes."

"I hope so." George scuffed his toes in the dirt like an insecure child.

Wilkins rounded the corner of the barn then, trailed by Tobias. His face was stormy, and he snatched his cloth cap off his head in an angry motion when he saw Sam.

"What's this about then that you send your *boy* to fetch me like I'm some pup. Your father treated me with respect."

Tobias, behind Wilkins, bristled at the words, but said nothing.

Sam stood tall, shoulders squared, feet apart to give him balance. With careful carelessness he let the riding crop brush against his leg in a rhythmic motion.

Wilkins' eyes went from the crop to Sam's face. "What's this all about then?" He didn't lose any of his belligerence.

"You whipped a white woman." He kept his voice firm and even, although he felt like any moment he was going to get called on the carpet for confronting his father's overseer.

"The interfering wench got in my way. Someone stands in front of a moving whip deserves what they get."

Sam swallowed a burst of anger, but at the same time part of him acknowledged that Wilkins was right. "I can't let it go unsanctioned."

"Sure you can." Wilkins faced Sam with his legs wide and his arms crossed. He was clearly not backing down. "You and I both know that I only hit her because she ran under my arm. No one could have avoided doing what I did."

Sam let his glance drift to George who gave a half-shrug.

Perhaps a stiff talking to was enough of a sanction.

"You planning on whipping me?" Wilkins eyes narrowed, and there was an ugly twist to his mouth.

When he had imagined this scene, he had figured that Wilkins would ask that question with fear and trepidation not scorn.

"You can't whip me." There was nothing false about his bravado.

Sam tapped the riding crop against his pant leg. Part of him agreed with Wilkins and part of him, a part that grew by the minute, wanted to beat the crap out of him.

"I could fire you."

"And who would you get to run your farm? Everyone's going off to war."

He took a step toward Wilkins. "You laid hands on a white woman. A guest of this house. You must answer for it."

Wilkins held up both hands, but not in a way that could ever be considered conciliatory. "She got in the way of me doing my job, and you want to punish me. I believe you are thinking with your pants, young man and not your head."

He didn't think. He lunged toward Wilkins, whip in hand. He brought the lash down, missing his head only by the fact that Wilkins managed to duck out of the way. The lash landed hard on Wilkins' shoulder. Sam felt the reverberations in his own arm.

Wilkins' eyes flashed fire, and he bared his teeth as he lunged toward Sam.

George and Tobias quickly stepped between the two men, separating them.

"You'll pay for this!" Wilkins snarled, looking over George's shoulder toward Sam. "You'll pay for this Marshall." He shook off George and stalked away.

Sam didn't like the uneasy feeling that settled over him.

"That did not go at all as I had planned." He cleared his throat and frowned.

"I think it went rather well, considering." George slapped him on the back

Sam looked at him, eyebrows raised. "Well?"

"He didn't kill you."

"Not yet," Tobias muttered from the stable doorway.

Sam glared at his servant, who had the sense to look at the ground.

Not yet, indeed.

Maybe going off to war wasn't going to be such a bad thing after all.

Chapter Eleven

Emily

Emily watched from around the corner of the stable as Wilkins stalked off. Sam had defended her honor. Is that what you would call it? For a moment it gave her a warm fuzzy feeling inside. No one had ever fought on her behalf before. But then she recalled what he had said "you hit a white woman." It didn't matter who she was, just that she was white. And Beck had been hit more times and with less provocation. He wasn't punishing the overseer for that. It was because she was white. The warm fuzzy feeling faded.

She ducked into the stable, inhaling the scent of clean hay and horse and let her eyes adjust to the dimness within. An old man with a stooped back and cotton-white hair over his dark face was pitching hay into the stalls.

"Moses?" she called out softly, not wanting to startle the man, and not even sure he was the man she wanted.

The man's back straightened somewhat and he almost dropped the pitchfork, but by the time he had turned to face her, no surprise was evident on his face.

"Yes, miss? How can ole' Moses help you?"

"I need information." She met his eyes, but he looked away.

He leaned the pitch fork against the wall. "I reckon I don't have much, miss. But you're welcome to what I've got."

"What can you tell me about the fishpond?"

If he was surprised by her question, he didn't show it. Maybe when you are a slave you get very good at hiding your emotions. Or, maybe, he wasn't surprised by her question.

He rubbed his chin. "There's catfish in there, and sometimes trout. It gets fed by a creek and sometimes there's enough fish in there to catch your dinner, but usually it's just for looks. In fact, there's some snapping turtles that make their home there. Best to stay away from it. If you wish to go fishing, I know of a much likelier fishing hole over yonder."

"I don't want to go fishing." Maybe he didn't know. Maybe Beck had been lying when she said that Moses knew all about the legend of the fishpond and people who mysteriously disappeared or appeared. She had been sure he would be able to tell her the secret to having the pond bring her back to her own time.

"What you want to know then?" Moses didn't meet her eyes.

She looked around to be sure they were alone, but no one was there to hear. Even the horses were out in the paddock getting fresh air and exercise.

"Is there a legend? Beck said there was a legend, and that you knew it."

For a second Emily saw understanding and recognition flash through the watery eyes of the old man, and then his face resumed its placid expression.

"No," he said. "There's no legend."

Had Beck lied to her? It was possible, but she

didn't think that was the case. And she'd seen the look in his eyes when she mentioned the legend. He knew something about it, but didn't want to tell her.

Emily leaned close to him. "Nothing about the pond being magical?"

He drew back from her, blinking rapidly, and shook his head. "No. There's nothing."

Was he afraid? Of her? Of the legend? She stared him down, and he looked away

"Please," she begged as tears pricked her eye and an unwanted lump formed in her throat.

He picked up his pitchfork without making eye contact.

"I've got work to do, miss, if you'll excuse me." He went back to his work.

Emily watched him for a moment. She wanted to grab him to make him look at her, to make him tell what he knew, but she couldn't do that. The man already suffered enough indignity, being a slave. He didn't need her forcing him to tell her when he didn't want to. But he knew about the legend, Emily was sure of it.

And she needed to find out what that was.

She left the stables, stepping out into the late afternoon sun, and walked to the fish pond. What was it about this body of water? Was it some sort of a weird portal? How could something like that even happen. It couldn't. Not in any reality she was aware of. Yet, here she was, clearly back in the 1860s when the other day she'd been in the twenty-first century.

The pond didn't look magical. It wasn't even particularly picturesque. It was bigger now than it had been when it was in the yard of the inn. In the future, there would be a stone wall around it, containing it, controlling it, making it into a feature of the landscaping as opposed to a naturally occurring body of water.

She had fallen into that water in the twenty-first century and emerged in the nineteenth. That much seemed clear. Unless this was some sort of hallucination. But no, she could still feel where the whip had hit her back. This was real. So, why, when she had gone back into the water had she not come out at her own time again? Was it because she didn't have the silver? Was there more involved? It had been night. There had been a full moon. And fog. Which of these things mattered?

Moses had to know, otherwise Beck wouldn't have bothered saying something. She had to find a way to convince him to tell her.

"Miss Parks?"

She jumped, startled, and turned to see Sam a few yards behind her.

"Not planning on jumping in again, are you?" His tone was somewhere between joking and real concern.

She stepped away from the water's edge. "No. No." Not yet, anyway. "I was just admiring the pond."

"How is your back? Did the salve help? I cannot express strongly enough how sorry I am that happened to you." He took a couple of steps toward her and reached out as if to touch her.

"I'm fine." Automatically she flexed her shoulder, assessing how much it still hurt. It was a dull ache now and would probably not bother her at all by tomorrow. "It was my own fault really. If you step in front of a moving whip, I suppose you have to expect to get hit."

"I've punished Wilkins." Sam cleared his throat and tugged at his jacket sleeve.

She was about to say that she knew, but she probably wasn't supposed to know that.

"Have you?" she asked. "I'm sorry I caused you distress."

He took another step toward her. Only a few feet separated them now.

"No, please, it is I who owe you the apology, not the other way around."

This could go on all night, the two of them apologizing to each other. Emily grinned and held out her hand. "I forgive you if you forgive me. Fair?"

He grasped her hand, his gray eyes shining as he smiled at her. Instead of shaking it, as she expected, he brought it to his lips. Shivers ran up and down her arm. She'd never known a kiss on the hand could be so sensuous. How sad that it had gone out of fashion.

"Forgiven." He did not let go of her hand, but tucked it into the crook of his elbow. "Would you like to see the rose garden?"

It was surprisingly pleasant to have her arm linked with his. It made her feel protected and cared for. She would go anywhere with him right now to keep that feeling alive.

"That sounds lovely."

"The roses aren't in bloom yet," he apologized as he led her across the lawn.

"That's all right," she assured him. "I'm sure it's lovely anyway."

They walked in silence for a moment, and then he cleared his throat and said, "Is it too forward to ask why you have come back? Was it simply to return the fork you accidentally took away with you?"

She loved that he ascribed the simplest and most innocent intentions to her actions.

"Oh, yes, I meant to return the fork. Such a ridiculous oversight on my part. And I will never forgive myself that Beck took punishment on my behalf for that." And she wouldn't either. She had never realized before how her actions could have such negative consequences on others. She would be much more careful going forward.

He patted her hand reassuringly. "These things happen."

"They shouldn't." She wasn't normally one to stir up trouble, but she didn't plan to be around long and some things had to be said. "I can't believe she was whipped when no one had any proof of wrong doing. Isn't there some sort of trial system or anything for when a slave gets in trouble?"

"Generally it's left up to the overseer."

The way he emphasized generally made her wonder if he thought that wasn't such a good plan. She stole a glance at him. He stared out over the fields, as the late afternoon sun cast a golden glow over the landscape, but she didn't think he really saw any of it. What was on his mind? She almost wished she'd have the time to get to know and understand him better.

"I see." She tried to keep her tone noncommittal, though a bit of animosity may have crept in.

"It's the way it's always been done." He adopted a slight defensive, yet also apologetic tone.

"Sometimes what's always been done, isn't the right thing."

How much should she try to get involved to fix

things here? Should she try to free the slaves? Should she convince Sam to free them? The Civil War was starting, they'd all be free soon anyway, maybe there was really nothing she could do to make a difference.

They came to a garden enclosed by a white picket fence with a gate in an arching arbor. Sam unlatched it and led her inside. The rose bushes were green with new growth and covered in tiny buds. It wouldn't be long before they erupted in bloom.

"It must be spectacular when the roses bloom."

"It is." He stopped by one sprawling bush to examine the nascent buds before they continued down the crushed shell path. He cleared his throat. "Miss Parks, should I be offering you a ride back into town?"

The way he worded the question alerted her to the fact that he probably didn't believe her story and didn't think she had a place to stay in town. Should she admit everything? No. Not yet. First, she needed to find out things from Moses; of course in order to do that, she needed to stay here. She needed to think of an excuse, and she needed it fast.

She tried to match his formal tone. "I'm afraid, Mr. Marshall, that the friend with whom I thought I was staying has left town. If I could impose on your hospitality for a few days, it would be greatly appreciated."

"Of course, it is my pleasure."

He answered so quickly and guilelessly that it brought that thickening back to her throat. She was very lucky that it was Sam she had landed on when she'd fallen back in time.

"Thank you." She wanted to say more, but the lump in her throat wouldn't let her. They walked in silence, and she caught the heady perfume of lilac. The roses might not be in bloom yet, but that wasn't the only flower in this garden, and the purple lilac bushes were resplendent.

Sam pointed to some bright yellow tulips growing by the path. "My favorites. They are so cheerful looking."

"I think daisies are the most cheerful," she answered, stopping to study the flowers more closely. "But tulips make me think of Holland and windmills and canals, all peaceful things."

"Are daisies your favorite then?"

She cocked her head. Were they? "I think I have different favorites for different sorts of things. Daffodils and crocuses because they mean spring is coming, roses because they are delightfully romantic, mums because they make me think of cozy nights by the fire and pumpkin spice coffee…" She remembered where, and when, she was and amended. "I mean pumpkin pie and coffee."

"A very diplomatic answer." He squeezed her hand gently and she tingled at the touch. "You have not offended any of the flowers."

"Thank goodness." She was able to laugh with him. The overwhelming emotions from before had dissipated a bit. Maybe he knew something about the legend of the pond. Maybe she wouldn't have to bother old Moses.

"Once," she started as their footsteps crunched on the crushed shells, "when I was a little girl, someone told me a fairy story about a magic pond." They walked by a lilac bush, and the scent of the flowers was nearly intoxicating.

"Is this the story where you kiss a toad, and he turns into a prince?"

"Oh, no! But that is a good story too. Though it never did prompt me to kiss any frogs."

Sam chuckled. "My sister kissed one once. Turned out it was a regular frog, not an enchanted prince." He led her to a wrought iron bench tucked underneath an arbor with rose bushes climbing up both sides. She was careful to adjust her hoops before she sat.

"I hope this wasn't recently," she said.

He laughed louder.

"Oh, no. She was about four at the time."

"A four-year-old wouldn't know what to do with a prince anyway. She was better off with the frog."

"Undoubtedly." He rested his hands chastely in his lap, though she found herself wishing he would touch her more, put his arm around her or his hand on her knee. Those things weren't appropriate though, not now, and probably not even in her own time, since he was engaged to be married. "So, tell me, what was magic about the pond in your story?"

"It took people places," she said before she could stop herself.

"What kind of places?" he asked quietly.

"Places different than where they started out." She never should have said anything. It was stupid and foolish. She should have simply...done what? Found another fork and risk having someone else whipped for her? Forced Moses to tell her things he obviously didn't want to? What options did she have here anyway?

"Is that why you jumped in the pond?" Sam's voice was barely above a whisper. "So you could go someplace else?"

121

"No!" She jumped up and away from him. That explanation made her sound absolutely insane. "She caught her breath and tried to regain her composure, what was left of it anyway. She breathed in and out slowly once, twice. Stay calm, don't behave like a lunatic. "No," she repeated more quietly. "That was…that was an accident. Forget I said anything. It's not important. Really it's not." She turned from him, hugging her arms around her waist, made impossibly thin with the corset. She was giving herself away. She didn't want to do that. Did she? She wished she knew what was right. Tell him the truth or not? She had told Beck, why did she not feel she could tell Sam?

Maybe because Beck had no power. She could do nothing to her. But Sam had power. Lots of it. What could he do to someone who showed up and claimed to be from the future and had arrived via a magic fish pond? If it were her in his position, she'd be calling the closest psychiatric ward. She didn't need him doing that! She'd read about mental hospitals of the nineteenth century, and she had absolutely no desire to end up there. They practically kept people in cages, for crying out loud. If she wasn't crazy going in, she certainly would be in short order.

She felt a tentative hand on her shoulder, as gentle as a butterfly. "Can I help?"

"No," she said and then shook her head and turned to face him. "I mean, yes. You can let me stay here until I get myself sorted. Just a day or two, I promise. Really, that's all I need."

"There's nothing else I can do? No people I can contact?"

If only it were that simple.

"No," she said with a sigh. Suddenly her limbs felt heavy, and the weight of the world seemed to descend on her chest. Tears welled up inside her. All she wanted to do was curl up and have a good cry.

"I need," she started, her voice catching. She took a steadying breath. "I need a drink."

"That I can do." He took her hand again, tucking it back into the crook of his elbow and she allowed herself to be led back to the house, out of the garden and its enchanting scents of lilac and fresh earth. They passed the stables with it's much more pungent odors of horse and manure and fresh hay. As they approached the back of the house, they passed an outbuilding with smoke rising from the chimney. Mouth watering aromas of fresh baked bread and roasting meat filled the air. That would be the kitchen.

He led her into the house by a back door. In the dining room, a young black girl set the table. The portraits on the wall stared down at her, the same as yesterday. How had it only been yesterday that she'd been at Dayna's wedding? Hadn't she lived a lifetime since then?

Soon they were in a book lined study. He brought her straight to a sumptuous red leather wing chair. She sat, letting the coziness of the room, the luxuriousness of the chair envelop her. She watched as he went to the sideboard and sorted through various bottles before opening one and pouring the amber colored drink into a ball-shaped glass.

He handed it to her. "This should help."

She took it gratefully and sipped.

It didn't solve all her problems, but it certainly helped.

Chapter Twelve

Sam

Sam removed the empty brandy glass from Miss Parks' inert hand and covered her sleeping form with a crocheted blanket. Teardrops lingered on her long eyelashes. He wished he could do more to help her, but until she gave him some clue as to what was going on, he couldn't do much.

He sat back down at the chestnut desk and buried his head in his hands. When had he lost control of his life? He was engaged to be married to a woman he did not love, he was going to sign up for a war he didn't want to fight, and he was supposed to be running a plantation he felt unqualified to run. And now this mysterious woman had dropped into his life. He picked his head back up and sighed. He had work to do.

The large ledger lay open in front of him, but the numbers had stopped making sense long ago. Things were purchased, but never seemed to appear in any other ledger; they were never used. What happened to them? The books simply didn't add up, and he didn't know why.

He took a piece of blank paper out from the desk and dipped his pen in ink. He glanced at Miss Parks, peacefully sleeping in the wing chair. Where had she come from? Why was she here?

A sprite from out the land of Faerie
Bewitching me with a glance

He scribbled on the page. Was she really from the land of the faeries? That was certainly an attractive explanation. Had she bewitched him? Dinah certainly thought so. But bewitched? No, intrigued was a better term.

In the chair, the woman shifted, and the afghan fell to the ground. She opened her eyes, and he shoved the paper into the desk drawer. He watched as she looked around, confused, taking in her surroundings.

"You've had a long day." He kept his voice soft so as not to startle her. She reminded him of a wild animal about to bolt. "You drifted off after drinking the brandy."

Her face flushed, and Sam's heart melted a little more toward her.

"Did I? I'm so sorry. What a horrible way to repay your hospitality."

"Not at all," Sam said.

He glanced down at the open ledger and sighed. If he could solve one of his problems, either the uncooperative numbers or the origins of Miss Parks, he'd consider it a good day, week even.

Across the room, she craned her neck to see what he was looking at. "Accounting problems?"

"Of a sort," he answered. "I can't make the numbers add up."

"May I take a look at it?"

He should say "no." The running of the farm was none of her affair. She was a stranger, a woman, a complete unknown, but yet, he was so tired of looking at it himself that he stood and offered his seat to her.

"If you'd like."

She sat down in his desk chair, adjusting her skirts the best she could. Instead of looking slightly bewildered, or intentionally flirtatious, she looked intent and serious. She turned the pages back to get a larger feel for the numbers.

"This here is what you've purchased from outside sources? And this is items used, correct?" She pointed at two columns.

"Yes. So you can see here." He pointed to one number. "This is how much flour was purchased last month, and this is how much was used."

"You used a lot less than purchased."

"So it would seem." That was the crux of his problem.

She looked up at him sharply. "There's no physical excess?"

"Not that I'm aware of. And it's not the only item either."

"I see that," she said. She turned more pages, running her fingers up and down the columns. "Who does the purchasing?"

"I do." He moved the lamp closer so she wouldn't have to strain her eyes.

"And what do you base your numbers on? How do you know how much to get?"

She was so business-like and sure of herself. This was an entirely different Miss Parks than he'd been dealing with the rest of the day. Who was this woman?

"Depends on the source. Some things, it's Sally in the kitchen. Some things it's Wilkins."

He could see her shoulders tense at the name.

"I don't like that man."

"Understandable." His voice caught on the word, and he cleared his throat.

She continued poring over the ledgers. "The income comes from the tobacco you've sold?"

"Mainly, yes." He perched on the edge of the desk and walked her through the way the plantation was run and how the numbers were supposed to match up.

"Someone's stealing from you." She looked up at him with her clear brown eyes.

That was the solution that had presented itself to him as well, but he hadn't wanted to see it.

"I think it's Wilkins." She said the name as if even speaking it left a bad taste in her mouth.

He thought so, too. The problem was that he didn't have enough proof, and even with it, he still couldn't fire the man. He needed an overseer, and everyone else was going to war. He ran his hand over his face. He should have gone over this with his father this morning. Why hadn't he? Because he'd been too proud to admit he was having trouble.

"You need to do an inventory." She tapped her finger on the page. "You need to find out how much of everything you actually have in stock, if anything, and then only order what's been used. Don't rely on Wilkins. Sally may simply be telling you what Wilkins wants you to hear. I wouldn't come down too hard on her."

"Oh!" He hadn't expected advice. For that matter he hadn't expected her to grasp the situation so quickly, when he'd been struggling against the obvious to figure it out himself. "No, I would never blame Sally."

"You don't want to blame Wilkins, either." He was surprised how quickly she was able to sum up his feelings.

"He's quite good at his job, and he's been here ten years. I find it hard to believe he would steal from me."

Her shoulders twitched, and he remembered the lash that Wilkins laid across her back. She of course would have absolutely no reason to trust him.

"You obviously know him better than I do." She sat back in the chair and rubbed her hands over her eyes. "But the numbers are showing something out of whack, and if you want to find out why, I think he's the place to start."

The door opened, and Tobias came in. His wide eyes took in Miss Parks sitting at the desk.

"Supper is ready, sir."

"Thank you, Tobias. We'll be right in." How did it look to his servant, to see this stranger studying the books, sitting at his father's desk? His desk, he reminded himself, and he had the right to let anyone sit there he wanted.

Sam held out a hand to his guest. "May I escort you into dinner, Miss Parks."

"Thank you, Mr. Marshall." She tucked her hand into the crook of his arm as if they'd been doing this their whole life.

It was just the two of them at dinner, and he found himself discussing the various aspects of running a plantation. He'd tried to discuss this with Dinah once, and she'd simply laughed and said she trusted him implicitly to take care of that. She maintained she had no head for numbers or organizational details. Miss Parks on the other hand knew the questions to ask and didn't simper and giggle but was able to discuss things reasonably.

After dinner they sat in the parlor and had another glass of brandy and talked about the coming war and the political implications of it. There was no discussion of hats or fashion or even when the next ball would be. It was more like talking to George than to a woman.

When he saw her hide a yawn, he realized she'd had quite an eventful day and perhaps was ready for sleep.

"Should I ring for Beck to get you ready for bed?" He was reluctant for the evening to come to an end.

"Oh." She looked liked she was about to protest, but then nodded. "Yes, please. I'm sorry. I'm very tired. It's been a long day."

"No need to apologize."

He escorted her upstairs and turned her over to the ministrations of Beck before heading back down to the study.

Back at his desk he closed the ledger. Miss Parks was right. Someone was stealing from him and he needed to investigate but the ledgers wouldn't give him any more answers tonight. He took his started poem out of the desk and stared at it. All that talking this evening and he still didn't know where she came from, or how the pond figured in.

The pond.

That seemed to be important.

But why?

He let his mind drift to a long ago day under the cottonwood trees, listening to Moses tell stories.

"You believe in fairies?" Moses had asked, directing the question straight at him. He was eight or nine, definitely too old to believe in fairies, and he balked at being asked the question.

"Course not," he'd said, his young voice squeaking, trying to make himself tall as he sat on a cut log.

Moses had fixed him with a long hard stare, and he started to squirm under the scrutiny.

"Fairies aren't real!" he'd finally defended himself.

"Aren't they?" Moses cleaned a saddle while he spoke. His hands were never idle.

"Only fools believe in fairies." He knew he was on solid ground here.

"If you don't believe I guess you won't want to be hearing my story then."

He squirmed. Despite himself, he was curious. Should he hear a fairy story, or was that only for babies? But Moses didn't tell baby stories, and he did want to know why he'd been talking about fairies, of all things.

"You don't have a story about fairies." He stuck out his lower lip and balled his fists.

"Don't I?" Moses was maddeningly nonchalant about it.

He needed to know the story.

"Tell me then!" He jumped up from the log and stared down at Moses who calmly continued working the damp sponge in small circles on the saddle.

"Sit down." Moses never got excited about anything. Sam didn't know how he always kept so calm. He sat down and waited for the story to begin.

"It was a long time ago." Moses' deep voice had a soothing sonorous quality to it.

He snorted. "All fairy stories always say they were a long time ago. That's so no one can ever check to see if they were true."

Moses looked at him for a long moment and then continued. "A long time ago, when I was a lad, about your age."

Oh. That was different. A long time ago, but when Moses was little. This story could be true then. He leaned forward, giving all his attention to the old groom.

"One day the fairies brought DayJon and took away Elsbeth."

"Wait!" He put up one hand, feeling the right as the master's son to interrupt. "Who is Elsbeth?"

"You don't know Elsbeth?" Moses glanced up from the saddle and studied the boy as if he couldn't believe that was true.

"How could I? If this story took place when you were a little boy, why then my father wasn't even born yet."

"That's right; he wasn't." Moses concentrated once more on the saddle, this time running a dry cloth over it. "Elsbeth would have been his aunt. Your grandfather's sister."

Aunt Elsbeth? He'd never heard about her. Clearly this story was as made up as any other fairy story.

"And who was DayJon?"

"You gonna let me tell the story, boy? Or are you going to keep interrupting?" Moses gave him a stern look, but then went back to concentrating on the saddle, putting linseed oil on a cloth and rubbing it into the leather.

"You can tell it," he said, but he wasn't at all convinced it was real.

"Elsbeth, she was this real pretty lady. Everyone said she was the most beautiful girl this side of the

Mississippi. I didn't know where the Mississippi was, but I knew she was pretty. She was engaged to be married, and the wedding was days away. All the slaves in the kitchen were working extra hard to make party foods, and I wasn't allowed even to touch one pastry."

That Sam could sympathize with. Why was it whenever they made things that looked especially good he was never allowed a taste?

"Then one day they couldn't find her."

"Did she run off and get married in private?" he asked, feeling very grown up to have thought of that solution. Someone in the neighborhood had done that a year ago, and for weeks it was all the grown ups could talk about.

"She left her fiancé here, so that seems unlikely."

He frowned. "Did they ever find her?"

"They looked and looked everywhere they could think of but never found a trace of her, except for one shoe by the pond."

"A shoe?" He rolled his eyes. "Can't you even be original Moses? That's Cinderella. Everyone knows that story."

"And tell me that story," Moses said.

He didn't often get to be the story teller. He cleared his throat and began. "A long time ago in a land far away. That's how all good stories start," he explained. "There was a girl who lived with her mean stepmother and stepsisters because both of her own parents were dead. You ever notice how so many stories are about children whose parents are dead?"

"Maybe it's because children with parents to watch out for them don't get into the kind of trouble that makes for good stories," Moses said, working the oil into the saddle.

That made a certain amount of sense. "Anyway, there was going to be a ball so the prince could pick a wife, and all the girls in the kingdom were supposed to go, but the stepmother wouldn't let Cinderella go because she wanted her own daughters to get the prince, even though they were ugly. So she made Cinderella stay home and do lots of work while everyone else went. But then her fairy godmother magicked up a dress and stuff so she could go. Then the prince fell in love with her, but she had to leave at midnight because the spell would wear off. So she ran away, but one shoe stayed behind. And that was lucky, because that old prince tried that shoe on every girl in the kingdom until he found Cinderella." He left out the boring part about them getting married and living happily ever after.

Moses shook his head. "Then it's not the same. In Cinderella they found her because of that shoe. They never did find Elsbeth."

"Never?" That made it a mystery. He and George were always looking for mysteries to solve.

"That's what I said." Moses shifted in his seat and stretched his back

"But how do you know the fairies took her?" If it was a mystery there had to be clues.

"Fairies never take something without leaving something in its place."

"Really?" He hadn't heard that before, but it sounded reasonable. "What did they leave?"

"They left DayJon."

"What's a DayJon?" Maybe this was a clue.

Moses got a faraway look in his eyes. "If Elsbeth was the most beautiful lady this side of the Mississippi, then DayJon was the most handsome man."

"The fairies left a man?" He wasn't sure he liked the way this story was turning out. Couldn't they have left a horse or something interesting like that?

"Not just any man. He was taller than most and muscular and intelligent."

Sam snorted. "Sounds like you were in love with him, Moses!"

Moses raised his eyebrows at the boy. "Everyone was in one way or another."

"How is this a fairy story?" he demanded. "You're telling me that one person showed up and another one disappeared. I'm not a baby. I know there can be lots of reasons for that."

"Okay, then I'll tell you what DayJon told us. He told us he was from the future, and that there would be a war between the northern states and the southern and when it was over the slaves would be free. He told us that sometime a black man would be President of the United States."

He laughed so hard at that he nearly fell off his log. "That ain't never gonna happen! A slave as president! No way!" He slapped his knee as he laughed some more.

"He said men would walk on the moon and drive in carriages with no horses. He said there would be buildings hundreds of stories tall, and people would as easy as you like get on a contraption that could take them to Europe in a couple of hours."

"Sounds like he was the one telling fairy stories, Moses." He was disappointed. He'd heard much better stories from Moses.

"Could be." Moses stood up to put away the

linseed oil and the saddle. "Just the same, be careful of fairies boy; you never know what they might do."

He stood up, brushing dirt and dried bark from his breeches. "I don't believe in fairies, Moses."

"Maybe you should."

He had walked away that day and hadn't thought more about it until now. What was it Emily had said? Some sort of story about a magical fish pond? And this mysterious man had predicted the current unrest? How was that possible? Walking on the moon? Going to Europe in a few hours. Those things were all ridiculous embellishments on the story, but now he wondered. What did Moses know? What had he been trying to tell him, and how was it connected with Emily?

It was too late to go and speak to Moses, that would have to wait until morning.

One thing he could check now, though. He stood from his chair, stretching his tired muscles and studied the book shelves behind him. It didn't take more than a minute to locate the family Bible. He pulled it out and laid it gently on the desk. Opening it to the front where births and deaths were recorded, he scanned the page for the name Elsbeth. His heart skipped a beat when he found it, there, beneath his grandfather: Elsbeth Marshall with a birth date inked in and information on her sacraments, even her wedding date was penned in, obviously by someone figuring there was no harm in putting it in a few days early, and then scratched out. After that no more information. No children, no death date, no mention at all of what might have happened to her.

Then he remembered the portrait in the hall of a beautiful young girl. All he knew about it was that it was his grandfather's sister. He'd always figured she'd died young and had never questioned it.

Could she have been spirited away by fairies?

He rubbed his hand over his face again. He was too tired. Obviously there were no fairies. He'd known that as a boy, and he knew that now. But what happened to Elsbeth? Who was DayJon and where had he come from and where did he go? How could he have known about the war that was starting now? Where had Emily come from. and why was she so attracted to the fishpond?

Somehow the thought that the fairies had brought Emily to him was rather nice.

He needed sleep. He'd figure this out in the morning.

Chapter Thirteen

Emily

Cinnamon buns.

Emily smelled them before she even opened her eyes.

The soft pillowcase under her cheek, warm sunlight coming in through the window and cinnamon buns with a trace of nutmeg, like Dayna's mother always makes. She stretched, luxuriating in a morning spent sleeping in. She knew exactly where she was: the Gordon's house after a sleep over. A sense of peace and security washed over her. She'd had a bad dream, something about being lost in time, but the details were already getting lost in the haze of new morning.

She opened her eyes and saw Dayna holding a tea tray.

Except it wasn't. It was a woman about the same size and coloring, but wearing a long dress, her hair wrapped in a scarf.

There was a canopy over the bed, and the windows were on the wrong side of the room.

She was not at the Gordon's.

And then it all came back to her. It wasn't a bad dream. It was reality.

A bad reality.

She closed her eyes tight, in the hope that when she

opened them things would have changed and she would be in Dayna's room and they would be in high school again and everything would be right with the world.

"Miss Emily?" Beck said. "I've got tea and buns. Miss Elizabeth always likes something to eat before she puts on her corset."

Emily sighed. This was her reality now. At least until she knew how to fix it. As tempting as it was to burrow under the covers and cry, that wasn't going to accomplish anything.

She sat up, leaning against the tall headboard. She took the proffered cup of tea and sniffed it. There was a touch of lemon in the tea.

"Thank you."

Beck put the tray down on the dressing table and pushed open the drapes so the room was bathed in sunlight. She came back to the bedside and looked around furtively as if she might be seen doing something wrong. "Did you talk to Moses?" she whispered. "Did you get answers?"

Emily took a sip of the tea before answering. It was warm and soothing, and she kind of wished her real life included people who would bring her breakfast in bed. Then she remembered that Beck was a slave, and the thought of being waited on wasn't nearly so appealing.

"He wouldn't tell me anything." It was so discouraging that the one person who might be able to tell her something refused to help.

Beck frowned, twin lines forming between her eyes.

"He wouldn't tell you the spell?"

She sat up straighter. "A spell? Like magic? You never said anything about a spell."

If it were as easy as a magic spell, then her problems were solved. Her hands started to shake; she was so close to finding the answers. She put the cup down, so she wouldn't spill the tea.

"So, I have to get him to tell me the spell, that's it?"

"I don't know if that's it." Beck shook out the dress Emily wore the day before. "I mean, we all have it memorized, but it never seems to work. So we figured he was making stories up, but you're here." She turned suddenly and stared at her, eyes wide. "Wait. You don't know the spell? How'd you get here?"

"I'd like to know that too." She picked her tea cup back up; she needed the restorative warmth. Naturally it wasn't going to be as easy as saying a few words. But how had she gotten here? She'd said no spell. At least she didn't think she had. Had she muttered something in her drunken state? She couldn't be sure. No more drinking games ever. That much at least was clear. She scrunched up her forehead in thought. "But you said you have it memorized, why do I need to ask Moses?"

"In case there's something else," Beck said reasonably. "Or in case I have the words wrong."

"What are they?"

Beck closed her eyes in concentration. "It goes like this: *Lorska la loon romp leet le tong Fair John Ah March ee sur lee face der lumier ah un otre mo mant*"

Her confusion grew as she listened to the nonsense words. "That doesn't make any sense. It's not even English."

"Who said magic spells have to be English?" Beck laid out the knit stockings that Emily would soon put on.

"What's it mean?"

"How should I know?"

Emily sighed. Why couldn't this be easier?

"Are there slaves in your time?" Beck asked, not meeting her eyes while getting the rest of the clothes ready for the day.

"No." It was true as far as it went, though she supposed, technically slavery still existed in some parts of the world.

"I want to be free."

"You only have to wait a little." She tried to be reassuring. "By the time this war is over, all the slaves will be free."

Beck didn't look like she entirely believed her. "You want to wait 'til this war is over before you go home?"

When you put it that way. "No."

"So, I help you find out how it works, and you take me with you."

She had another sip of her tea. Why not? Beck could adapt quite easily to the twenty-first century. She could even room with her, since Dayna had moved out.

"You have a deal." Tension eased out of her. It was always good to have a friend, partner, and ally.

Beck visibly relaxed. "Eat the bun. My mother makes the very best cinnamon buns I've ever tasted."

"Your mother made this?" She took the fragrant, warm bun from the plate.

"Sally. The cook. She's my mother."

"If you come to the future with me, you'll never see your mother again." She needed to be sure Beck understood what she was asking.

"And either one of us could get sold away and

we'll never see each other again anyway. If I'm not going to see her, she'd at least like to know I'm free."

Emily tried to imagine a life where she would know for a certain that her mother was still alive, but inaccessible to her forever. Of course, if she couldn't get back home that was exactly the kind of life she was destined to live. She swallowed over the lump in her throat and took a bite of the bun.

It was divine. It was heavenly. It tasted like home. More specifically it tasted like Dayna's home. It was almost exactly like the cinnamon buns Mrs. Gordon made and that she had promised to teach both Dayna and Emily to make. She said it was an old family secret recipe, and she was breaking with tradition by showing Emily, but she considered her another daughter so she would risk it.

"Risk what?" Emily had asked.

"The wrath of my slave ancestors," Mrs. Gordon had said with a laugh. "It's a very special recipe because it came from my great-great grandmother Rebecca. She was an escaped slave. Isn't that fascinating? I wish I could have met her, but at least I get to eat her cinnamon buns."

Emily hadn't quite known what to say to that. She didn't feel comfortable talking about slavery, much less joking about it.

But if Dayna had slave ancestors, did that mean Beck had descendants somewhere in the future? If she took Beck home with her, what would happen to them? Would a whole line of people cease to exist? But maybe that was what was supposed to happen and she never would have had children in the past but only in the far future.

But what if she were Dayna's slave ancestor? What if the old family recipe came from Sally and if Emily brought Beck into the future with her Dayna wouldn't exist anymore? What if she saved Beck at the expense of Dayna? But cinnamon buns were cinnamon buns, how many ways to make them could there possibly be? Lots of people probably had the same recipe and called it a secret.

Was it so unlikely that Beck and Sally were Dayna's ancestors? And if they were, and she helped Beck get to the future, then she was dooming Dayna. But if she left Beck here was she dooming her? Was there a right answer to this?

"You ready to get in your corset?" Beck stood over her, holding the obnoxious contraption. She didn't think she'd ever really be ready for that, but for the time being it was what she had to do.

Beck helped her into all the same clothes as yesterday, and then with gentle hands fixed her hair so she looked like a proper nineteenth-century woman. Too bad she couldn't get a photo of herself looking like this. It was even better than those Old Time Photo places at the boardwalk. As long as it was temporary. She didn't even want to entertain the notion that it might not be.

"You're expected at breakfast." Beck stood back and examined her critically.

"Breakfast? But I just ate." She held one hand to her trussed up middle.

"A cup of tea and a bun. That's not breakfast."

"It's about what I usually eat."

"More than I do," Beck responded with a wry laugh. "But I ain't white. You go down and have breakfast with Mister Sam."

"I need to go home soon." She stared at the door that would take her out of the sanctuary of this room where she could be herself, and back into a world she wasn't equipped to deal with. And Sam. She wasn't sure she was equipped to deal with him either.

"Why's that?"

"Because otherwise I think I'll fall in love with Sam, and since he's engaged to be married to someone else, that could be a problem."

"Engagements get broken." Beck was very philosophical about it. "But it doesn't matter. You'll get home, and you'll take me with you."

She couldn't bring Beck to the future, that was clear. Not if she didn't want to destroy lives of untold, unknown people. But she could help her escape. She could do that. Besides, how could she spend any time in a slave-owning state, no matter how she got here, and not try to help someone escape? If she didn't then she'd have no moral superiority over all the people who lived in these times and did nothing. She'd always wanted to think herself better than that. Now was the time to prove it.

In the dining room, Sam stood when she came in and smiled as she lowered herself with a modicum of grace into her chair.

"I was wondering." He adjusted his linen napkin and didn't meet her eye as he spoke. "If you would be interested in going for a ride around the plantation this morning. I can have Sally pack us a picnic lunch."

"I'd like that very much." A warm glow spread through her, a ride and picnic with Sam sounded lovely. Besides, the only other thing she had on her agenda was figuring out how the magic spell worked, and Moses didn't want to tell her anything.

"Thank you for your help yesterday on the books."

His gray eyes met hers, and she felt a flutter in her stomach that had nothing to do with tight corsets. She could not fall in love with him. He was engaged. Though, as Beck had said, engagements get broken.

"You're welcome." She ignored the flush of her cheeks and concentrated on her breakfast, taking a few birdlike bites. "It's the least I could do after you've housed and fed me."

"So, rather a quid pro quo?"

She looked up and saw the grin that spread across his face.

"Or a friend helping a friend," she responded with a grin of her own.

She couldn't eat much breakfast because her corset constricted her stomach, but she did enjoy a nice cup of coffee. It wasn't her usual latte, but it would do.

After they ate, she stood on the porch and watched Moses get the carriage ready. It was a different one than yesterday. This one only carried two people. It had two large wheels and a cushioned seat between them. There was a canopy, but it was down and a black woman was placing a picnic hamper behind the seat in the limited cargo space. The whole thing was painted a shiny black with gold accents. It was the equivalent to a modern day sports car.

"You'll be wanting this." Beck held out a pink parasol.

"Really?"

Beck pushed the parasol into her hand. "Mister Sam likes the top down, but the sun gets hot. I've heard

Miss Elizabeth complain about it often enough. Best to take this and be prepared."

"Thank you." Now she really felt like a nineteenth-century lady.

Sam came to the steps of the porch and held out a hand for her. "Shall we?"

His smile was perfectly heart-melting. Why oh why did he not only have to be from the wrong century, but engaged to someone else? Was this the universe's way of telling her that she was never going to be able to find true love?

He helped her into the carriage and waited for her to get her skirts situated before climbing in himself. She caught a whiff of sweat and body odor emanating from herself. The dress hadn't been washed. She hadn't bathed. She had no deodorant. To put it bluntly, she smelled. Good thing she wasn't trying to win him over after all.

He settled in beside her. The sheer masculinity of him was rather overwhelming. Except maybe for Johnson, she couldn't think of any guys she knew who really exuded such manliness. It was almost intoxicating. He didn't smell like soap and aftershave or expensive cologne like so many of the people she knew, instead he smelled of sweat and tobacco smoke and leather, and there was a hint of cinnamon too. Or perhaps she still smelled the cinnamon from the breakfast bun.

"Are you ready?" he asked, and with a nod from her, he flicked the reins, and the horse took off at a leisurely walk.

"Is there anything you'd particularly care to see?"

"Can I see where the slaves live?"

His muscles tensed. "Why?"

Oh. Maybe that hadn't been the most judicious request. He was trying to show her the pretty places, and she wanted to see the dark underside. There was nowhere to go but forward on this. "I'm curious," she said and tried to think of a reasonable explanation as to why she would be. "I know some abolitionists, back home, and they always go on about the horrible conditions slaves live in. Yours seem healthy though." She wouldn't go as far as to say they seemed happy.

"The slaves here are well cared for," he said, defensively, giving the reins another flick. "They have adequate housing and food."

"And an overseer who beats them without evidence of wrongdoing."

She felt the slump of his shoulders, but she didn't look at him. She knew she'd gone too far. She was dependent on his hospitality until she could get back home, and to jeopardize that by pissing him off was probably a really bad idea.

"I'm sorry." She tried to sound properly contrite.

"I don't live under a rock." There was no anger in his voice. "I know that in many places the owning of slaves is considered morally objectionable."

One eyebrow shot up, and she studied him. "Don't you think it is?"

He didn't answer at first, and she watched his hands work the reins, the large hands that didn't have to do a tremendous amount of hard labor because that was done by slaves.

"I do, actually." He stared ahead as he spoke.

"Then why do you own slaves?" She couldn't keep incredulity out of her voice. She would never own slaves. Couldn't imagine the possibility.

"First of all, I don't, with the possible exception of Tobias. My father owns them all."

"But not Tobias?"

"Tobias and I grew up together. He's been my friend and valet for as long as I can remember. I believe my father officially turned him over to me when I turned twenty-one, but I didn't care too much about the details at the time. I'd need to check."

"So can't you at least free Tobias?"

"No," he said with such finality that she stared at him, startled.

"The manumission laws make it very difficult, if not impossible to free slaves. But it might interest you to know that my father never purchased a slave. Everyone here was born here."

She didn't think it made it any better, but maybe on some level it did. She remembered Beck telling her about the constant fear of being sold away from her mother. "Did you ever sell one?"

"My father has once or twice. It's a business," he added as if that were an explanation. Maybe to him it was.

A row of cottages, all newly whitewashed came into view. There was a kitchen garden at the end of the row and wooden benches outside some of the doors. "The slave cottages." He waved a hand in their direction "They could do worse."

"They could also do better." She was unable to let it go.

"Undoubtedly, but I do the best I can for them." His shoulders slumped momentarily as he stared out at the compact cabins. With a deep breath, he straightened up and grasped the reins more firmly. "Can I show you something more interesting now?"

She supposed she'd been enough of a nudge for right now, and she was in an intimate carriage with a handsome man, this might never happen again, she should take advantage of it.

"Yes, please." She flashed him a smile.

The grin he gave her back showed he didn't hold any ill will against her.

It was time to allow herself to enjoy the day.

Chapter Fourteen

Sam

One thing was certain about this mysterious Miss Parks: she was not shy about voicing her opinions. And although, it might appear they were on different sides of the subject, she apparently being a fierce abolitionist, and he, the owner of a plantation that used slaves, he really didn't disagree with her.

Unfortunately, as he told her, it was not a simple matter to free slaves. The abolitionists would have you believe that all you need do would be to wave a magic wand and say "be free" and that would be the end of it. But the state demanded payment, insurance against the possibility of the freed black becoming a burden on society. Quite frankly he couldn't afford to free his slaves.

He had been going to show her the fields next, with their green sprouts of tobacco and the workers industriously watering and weeding, but he thought perhaps that would bring up more conversation about slavery, and that was the last thing he wanted to discuss with a beautiful woman.

Instead he drove her to the apple orchards. The trees with their pastel buds were particularly picturesque this time of year.

"It's beautiful!" She lifted her face as apple

blossoms floated around them like snowflakes. Her open smile warmed his heart. This is what she looks like when she is happy. He wanted to keep that smile on her face all the time.

He shifted the reins in his hand, letting his shoulders relax.

"When I was a boy, I used to love climbing the apple trees. Especially at harvest time, so I could get the freshest and best apples, but also in the spring, when it felt like being in the midst of a warm snow shower."

"My parents have an apple tree." She kept her gaze on the fluttering petals, and a dreamy quality came into her voice. "I used to like to climb up in it, until one day I discovered I shared my branch with ants. I decided the bugs could have the tree. I'd read my book someplace more civilized."

He laughed, and she gave him a grin, while a rosy blush formed on her cheeks. He envisioned the young Miss Parks indignant that a bug would share her space. He could picture it all too well, because he remembered the squeals and screams from Elizabeth whenever anything creepy or crawly got near her. Of course, as her older brother, he'd often made sure to point out any creepy crawly thing just to enjoy her reaction.

"Do you have any brothers?" It was amazing how little he knew about her.

She nodded, still mesmerized by the falling blossoms. "One. Patrick."

"Older or younger?"

"Younger. He's…" She broke off from whatever she was going to say as if momentarily confused, but then continued. "He's away at school."

So, she had parents, though he did remember her

saying her mother was gone, and a brother, and apparently a happy childhood that included time for climbing trees and reading. Why was there no one she wanted him to contact on her behalf? Had she run away? What had interrupted that idyllic life?

"You must miss him." He clucked to the horse who had started to wander to munch on a patch of clover.

She nodded, but didn't answer. When he looked closer he saw a tear glimmering on her eyelid. Something wasn't adding up here.

"Hopefully this war will be long over before he has to worry about leaving school and enlisting." He took a shot at what might be bothering her.

Her eyes widened. They were almost honey colored. "The war!" she said as if she had forgotten about it, though it seemed impossible anyone would have. It's all anyone could talk about these days.

"I'm sure it will be over by Christmas." He tried to sound reassuring and certain, although personally he had his doubts that this would be a quick rout.

"Ha!" she said, but there was no humor in her voice. "It will be long and bloody and thousands upon thousands will die."

She said it with such certainty that his blood froze within him.

"Perhaps it won't be as bad as all that." He hoped. He prayed.

She looked at him then, a pitying look. Then a small smile came across her face, making her beautiful. "I'm sorry, I'm not a very good picnic companion, am I?"

"I never should have brought up war. It's not a pleasant picnic topic." He was quite foolish to be out

151

with a beautiful woman and talking of war.

The lovely open smile had vanished. She didn't seem to notice the falling apple petals anymore. She faced forward, hands primly folded in her lap.

"Show me something beautiful."

"More beautiful than this?" He waved his arm to encompass the orchard, but already he knew of the exact place to take her and he clucked to the horse and turned his head toward the woods. The horse followed the track toward the creek. If she wanted someplace beautiful he'd show her the waterfall. The coolness of the glade enveloped them. It had rained a few days ago, and still the earth here held that damp, loamy scent. He inhaled deeply. He would miss this when he went off to war.

A squirrel scampered in front of them, but the horse barely noticed. He could hear the crash of the water as it fell from one level to another in the creek. The trees thinned, and he reined in the horse in the clearing by the creek. A little later in the season it would be awash in wildflowers, and already there were violets and daffodils and tulips adding a bit of color to the green of the meadow. The creek ran cool and clear, jumping playfully over stones, and at the edge of the clearing was the waterfall, bringing the water down ten feet from the creek above.

"Do you like it?" He couldn't say why he so desperately wanted her approval, but he nearly held his breath until he saw the smile once again transform her face.

"It's wonderful!" She clapped her hands together in delight. "Is this where we will have our picnic?"

"I can't think of a better place." He looped the

reins around a tree and helped her down from the carriage. She was not particularly graceful. Not for the first time he got the impression she was not used to the clothes she wore or even getting in and out of carriages. Perhaps she was from some poor family living in the backwoods somewhere and was trying to improve her situation. That would explain any number of things, including why she was so hesitant to tell him where she was from.

She hurried to the creek edge while he got the basket from the carriage. What on earth had Sally packed in this thing? Was she expecting him to feed a battalion as opposed to one lone girl? He spread a white and red checkered quilt on the ground by the water and went to stand beside Miss Parks.

"Beautiful enough for you?" He clasped his hands behind his back, to keep himself from reaching out and touching her.

"It's perfect. Like something the fairies have conjured up for our pleasure. Surely a place like this can't be real."

She didn't speak like someone from the backwoods somewhere, she spoke like an educated, wealthy woman, but a shiver went up his spine at the mention of fairies. Certainly it was a coincidence she would say that. She didn't really believe in fairies, did she? Could fairies really have brought her?

"Didn't know fairies were known for their beautiful scenery." He tried to keep the right amount of humor in his voice, while behind his back he twisted his fingers together.

"Oh, I don't suppose they are." She turning to him, her eyes filled with light. "But sometimes it's easy to forget that such beautiful places exist. Thank you."

He wasn't sure what she was thanking him for. Taking her to a beautiful picnic spot? That was hardly a chore on his part.

"Are you hungry, shall we eat?"

"Is it lunchtime already?" She glanced at her wrist quickly as if by instinct and then put her arms behind her back.

He shielded his eyes and peered through the trees to gauge the position of the sun. It was close enough to noon to warrant opening that picnic basket. "Aren't you hungry?"

"Famished," she admitted with refreshing candor. He could never imagine Dinah being so honest about hunger. "This corset makes it hard for me to eat, it squeezes me so."

He'd been regretting thinking about Dinah, and now with the image the word corset brought to mind, his cheeks flushed. "Don't you normally wear a corset?" He tried to make his voice casual, as if discussing women's undergarments wasn't the most inappropriate thing he could do under the circumstances.

She couldn't hide the wide-eyed look of fear that flitted across her face, but almost as soon as it appeared, she grinned, blushing, making him wonder if he had imagined it after all.

"I. Well. I guess Beck must tie it tighter than I'm used to." She turned from him, staring out at the water, hiding whatever her expression might give away.

He couldn't exactly offer to loosen it for her, though he certainly wouldn't mind.

"You'll have to speak to Beck, perhaps she can tie

them looser from now on."

"Not as long as I'm wearing Elizabeth's borrowed dresses. It's the only way I'll fit into them." Her tone was matter of fact, but he wondered if she was blushing as deeply as he was.

He should have known better than to mention corsets and such. There was a reason they were called unmentionables. She did fill out Elizabeth's dresses better than his sister ever had. And he had to force himself to look away from her bosom and concentrate on something else. It was true, though, that she had no dresses of her own. Should he offer to buy her some? He had the means. But if she were only going to be here for a few days, perhaps it wasn't worth the effort. On the other hand, if she had run away from someplace and was starting over, then she might not be at all adverse to the idea of being properly dressed. He'd mention that later, now might not be the best time. Instead he opened the picnic hamper.

A bottle of chilled wine sat right on top. Perfect. A little wine would relax them both.

He extracted the cork and sniffed. A lovely Chardonnay. He poured it and brought a glass over to Miss Parks.

"Wine!" She had managed to compose herself and smiled at him as she took the proffered glass. "This is very luxurious, a picnic with wine in the middle of the week."

"It is, rather," he agreed. Not the wine so much, he often had that with lunch, but the picnic. It made his problems seem very far away. "I don't often do this myself. Perhaps I should more often."

"What do you normally do?" She took a sip of her

wine and looking over her glass at him with those big brown eyes.

"A lot of figuring numbers. It's the most boring part about being in charge." How many beautiful afternoons had he spent in the study, poring over the ledgers when he'd rather be sitting by the waterfall composing poetry?

"You must do something for fun now and then," she said, and he could have sworn that her tone was almost flirtatious.

"I go riding. That's fun. Oh, and the occasional ball." He grinned and imagined her in a sweeping ball gown with low décolletage. He had to stop thinking about her breasts. "Perhaps you'll be at the next ball in the neighborhood," he said with more than a little hope.

"I doubt it." There was regret in her voice, but he couldn't imagine why she wouldn't be there. He'd invite her himself if he had to, though being engaged to Dinah that might prove problematic. He'd have Dinah invite her. That would work.

She took another sip of her wine. "Besides, I don't think I know any of the dances."

"I find that hard to believe." Every girl he knew had at least enough in the way of dance lessons to get successfully through a ball. But perhaps it was another clue that she was not who she said she was.

"I can teach you." He took her wine glass from her. "I would not want you to be at a disadvantage when you find yourself surrounded by beaus at a ball."

Her cheeks turned a delightful shade of pink. "Oh, I hardly imagine that would happen."

"I'll teach you anyway." He set the glasses carefully on the blanket.

"We'll start with a waltz." He put one hand lightly on her waist and took hold of her hand. She was not wearing gloves, and the warm smoothness of her hands made his heart beat faster. He took a breath to steady himself. He was just showing her dance steps. That was all. He had to remember that.

"Watch my feet and do what I do. It's quite simple, really. Remember it's a one-two-three count." He counted one-two-three as he took her through the steps. At first he thought she was catching on, and then she tripped over her own feet between two-and-three. He steadied her, feeling the blood rush through his body as he held her a bit closer.

"You can do this. Anyone can waltz." At least he assumed anyone could. Even children of ten could waltz.

"I may prove the exception to that rule." There was a tone of defeat in her voice.

"Feel the beat of the music," he whispered in her ear. "One, two, three…one, two, three" he counted in a sing song.

It didn't take long before she got into the rhythm of the dance. They glided around the glade, and he was convinced that there really was music playing, even though they were alone.

"Are all the dances waltzes?" she asked, as they moved as one through the grass.

"Oh no." He almost lost count as he danced. "That would be very boring."

Her face darkened at that, and the light went out of her eyes. "Oh."

"I will teach you the others," he said quickly; he didn't like seeing her so disappointed. "One of my favorites is the Zingirella."

"The what?" She stopped dancing and looked at him in incomprehension.

"You've never heard of it?" Clearly she hadn't. He reluctantly let go of her so he could demonstrate. It was hard without a partner, but he pretended he held someone in his arms while a Zingirella played. "Slide the left foot forward, so, then bring the right foot up behind. Then bounce on the right foot, and bring the left foot behind—being sure to not touch the floor. Then bounce again on the right foot and bring the left foot in front. And then slide the—"

"Stop!" She laughed and held up her hand. "That's beautiful and all, but I tripped over my own feet when I tried to waltz. I'll never be able to do that!"

"With a little practice," he assured her, but she shook her head. "I know, how about a Polka?"

"Roll out the barrel, we'll have a barrel of fun," she sang. It sounded like a polka tune, but he wasn't familiar with that particular one.

"What song is that?"

"Beer Barrel Polka," she answered, but then squinted in uncertainty and bit her lip. "That's a polka, right?"

"Of course." He gave her what he hoped was a reassuring smile. Why was she suddenly so unsure of herself? "I've never heard that one before. It's catchy."

"All polkas are catchy," she said, once more composed. "But I don't know how to dance to them."

"Then I will teach you." He took her hands in his. "It's a little hop, then step, step, like such." He led her in a dance around the meadow until they were both gasping for breath. And then he pulled her close. He could feel her heart beating close to his, and she smelled of roses. Without even thinking about it, his lips met hers. Her soft lips separated to welcome his touch. Every nerve tingled as if he were alive for the first time in years.

She kissed him back, and the world fell away. There was nothing but the two of them in the spring air. He held her tight. Their heartbeats synchronized as if they were one person. Nothing else existed and he wanted to keep feeling like this forever.

It took a minute too long for him to come to his senses; he stepped back in horror. What had he done? "I'm sorry! So very sorry. That was unacceptable. I never should have done that. I…please accept my apology."

She looked at him in a way that was hard to read. She gently touched her lips. "You don't have to apologize."

"It was wrong of me." But how could something that wrong have felt that right?

"Dancing does make one forget oneself, doesn't it?" She gave him a sweet and very forgiving smile.

Yes, that was a perfect excuse. It was the dancing that made him do it.

"It does." He cleared his throat and glanced toward the picnic basket Sally had packed. "Are you hungry? We should eat."

"Yes, that sounds like a good idea."

Sam tucked her hand into the crook of his elbow and led her back to the blanket. Emily sank to a sitting position, letting her hoops and voluminous skirts pool around her. He handed her wine glass back to her.

She took a sip. "Thank you, for dancing with me."

Christine Marciniak

They were apparently not going to discuss the kiss. They'd pretend it never happened. Perhaps that was for the best. But he knew he'd never forget it. It was selfish of him, but he hoped she wouldn't either.

"My pleasure. I only hope someone has a ball before I have to leave."

"Leave?" She looked up at him, confused. "Where are you going?"

"I'll be signing up for the army. I don't know how much time I'll have before the company musters out."

"Oh." She didn't sound enthusiastic about it.

"I need to do my duty." He wasn't enthusiastic about going either, but there was no point in dwelling on that.

"Oh! Of course."

He put some of Sally's fried chicken on a plate and handed it to her. They ate with the rushing of the waterfalls their musical accompaniment. It was peaceful and refreshing. He wished he could do it every day. They didn't talk much while they ate, but he was sure to keep her wine glass full. One way or another, he would find out her story.

By the time the bottle was empty, all his inhibitions had fled. He leaned in close to her, and although he was tempted to kiss her again, he merely whispered, "Who are you really, Emily Parks and where did you come from and what are you doing here?"

She looked at him with wide open eyes. "I really am Emily Parks, I came from the future, and I don't know what I'm doing here."

The future?

He sat back and stared at her. Clearly, he had let her drink too much wine. He'd wanted an honest answer from her and what he got was something out of a novel.

She recoiled from him almost as soon as she'd spoken, her hand going to her mouth as if to try to recall the words.

He watched various emotions flit across her face from upset and confused to resignation until finally her features settled into a look of defiance.

"You're serious?"

"I am," she said. "I was at a wedding in the twenty-first century and I went to sit by the fish pond and a fog came and next thing I knew the wall crumbled away and I fell in the water and when I got out, apparently I had slipped back in time. I don't know how it happened. I'm not sure how to get back. I thought silver would make the difference. I'm not sure."

The future. It wasn't possible. But all the questions he had about her mysterious appearance and strange behavior were answered by that impossibility.

Tears rolled down her face. His heart nearly broke for her. If what she said was true, then she must be so scared and lonely. If it wasn't true, the truth must be bizarre indeed. Either way, this was clearly a girl in need of his protection and help. He fished his handkerchief out of his pocket and handed it to her. She accepted it gratefully and wiped her face.

"You don't believe me." She sniffled.

Did he believe her? It was impossible, but yet, why on earth would she lie about something like that?

"It is hard to believe." He didn't want her to think he didn't believe her, but did he? Could he believe something that was clearly impossible simply because he had come alive when he kissed her?

"Agreed." She took a deep breath and squared her shoulder, getting herself under some semblance of control. "If it hadn't happened to me, I wouldn't believe it."

"Can you tell me something about the future?" He wasn't sure if he'd be able to tell if she were telling the truth or not by what she said, but he had to admit he was curious.

"We have cars. They are like carriages but don't need horses to run."

That seemed plausible. He knew there were people working on technology for such a thing.

"And airplanes." She pointed up to the sky. "We can go places in planes…um, like big ships…that fly through the air at hundreds of miles an hour."

"Really?" He knew his skepticism showed.

"And we've sent rocket ships to the moon," she continued, with each statement getting more outlandish. "And a black man was president of the United States."

He laughed. Now she was clearly pulling his leg, but he glanced at her and she was watching him, one eyebrow quirked, not even a trace of a smile.

She was serious. He remembered that Moses's mysterious man had made those same predictions.

"And this war that's starting?" he asked, even as he got a funny feeling deep inside when he said it. Did he want to know? Would it make a difference? Maybe it would. If he knew which side won, he could choose which side to support. Forewarned is forearmed after all.

"You want me to tell you?" she asked, and a shiver ran down his back as he realized that she thought she could.

Did he want to know?

"Yes." He pushed away his doubts. If she knew, he wanted to know.

"The south loses. Slaves are freed. The war lasts four years. Many many people are killed. More than any other war."

No. That wasn't what he wanted to hear. His stomach suddenly felt unsettled. Was it the wine? Or the information?

"They say it's going to be a short war." His voice sounded weak and uncertain.

"They're wrong."

He studied her eyes. She didn't have that wild crazy look he'd seen in people who clearly had lost touch with reality. There was honesty and intelligence behind her eyes, not insanity.

He wanted to believe it would be a short war. He wanted to think that he and his friends could march off with the army, fire a few shots at the other side, have them put their hands up in surrender and say, never mind, we didn't mean to cause a bother, we'll all go home now. That's how he wanted it to work. He wasn't sure he liked confirmation of his worst fears.

"How can I help you?" Better to focus on what he could do for her; the coming war was largely out of his control.

"I want to go home," she said, and the longing in her eyes was unbearable. "But I can't figure out how to make it work. I think Moses knows something, but he won't tell me."

The stories Moses used to tell him. Did they have some basis in reality? Were they not just strange tales to keep him from playing in the fish pond? And what about the story of DayJon? Who was that mysterious person? Had he come from another time like Moses said? Had his aunt gone to one?

"I can get Moses to tell me what he knows." He wished they hadn't drunk all the wine; he could use some more. "Why did you think you needed silver?"

She held out her right hand and showed him a ring. It was a twisty piece of gold, very beautiful and delicate. "When I got this ring, it had gold and silver intertwined. When I came out of the pond the silver was gone. I thought maybe the pond needed silver as a sacrifice or something to make it work. I didn't get a chance to test the theory, though."

"Do you want to test it now?" he asked. "I can get you silver."

The hopeful look in her eyes was heartbreaking. "Can you? Can I? It's not that I don't appreciate your hospitality and everything, but, oh, I do want to go home."

"Yes, of course. Let's get you home," he said and began packing up the remnants of the picnic. It was good to finally have answers. To have a way to help her and to get her home. Not that he minded having her around. She was attractive and friendly and funny, and he enjoyed spending time with her. But he couldn't keep her around for those reasons; first of all, it was wrong. Second, Dinah would never stand for it. Perhaps he should have thought of Dinah first.

He helped her back into the carriage. She fumbled with the skirts, but after a minute or two managed to get herself situated.

"Tell me," he asked as he settled beside her and picked up the reins. "What do you wear in your time?

You seem unused to these clothes."

"Oh." Her cheeks flushed becomingly. "Generally jeans. You know, trousers. But if I'm going out somewhere I'll wear a dress, but it only comes past my knee, and doesn't have all this other stuff like hoops and corsets."

Trousers, on women? He could feel his own face getting hot at the thought. And short skirts with no hoops and corsets? He wouldn't mind getting a chance to see this world she came from.

They rode in silence for a moment. He frankly wasn't sure what to say to her. She was some exotic creature that shouldn't even be here. What could he possibly say that she would want to hear? Unless she was as curious about his time as she was about his.

"Is there, um, anything you'd like to know about now? Anything you'd like to see or do?" His voice cracked on "do" which it hadn't done to him since he was fourteen. He cleared his throat. "Or do" he repeated solemnly.

"I wouldn't mind seeing a ball," she admitted, with a touch of longing in her voice. "But I'd much rather go home. You don't mind, do you?"

"Not at all." He pointed the horse back toward the house. They left the fairy glade by the waterfall.

"Perhaps." He cleared his throat. "You should go into the water in your shift. Less chance of accidental drowning if you are not over encumbered. And…" He hated to bring this part up, but it had to be said. "If you get to where you are going, it might be hard to explain to Elizabeth what happened to her dress."

Next to him Miss Parks laughed. She had a lovely laugh, free and unfettered, unlike so much of the tittering that girls he normally saw did.

"Yes, that might be hard to explain...on both ends." A moment where the only sounds were the clop of the horse's hooves, the jingle of the harness and the rumble of the wheels over the hard ground. "Thank you for being so understanding. I know it sounds unbelievable, and if it weren't happening to me, I wouldn't believe it. But thank you. You don't know how much it means to have you believe me."

Transferring both leads to one hand, he reached over and took hold of her hand. "It is hard to believe it is true, but I will do everything I can to help you."

And if holding a bit of silver did not send her back to where she said she came from, he'd have to figure out what to do with her. It would certainly be easier if her story were true and she went home. He drove the buggy straight to the pond. There was no one around, which certainly worked to their advantage. He helped her out of the carriage, and they stood awkwardly looking at the dark water of the pond.

"Do you want me to help you out of the dress or would you rather I call Beck?" He wasn't sure what answer he wanted her to give. On the one hand, he had no objections to undressing her. On the other hand, there were the proprieties to consider. Did rules of etiquette apply in a situation like this?

She started a bit at hearing Beck's name and turned pale. "Better not call her. If you don't mind messing with the buttons and ties and what not, I don't mind."

Was she remembering being naked in his bed? How could she not be? But he wasn't going to get her naked now. She'd still have her shift on. She'd still be covered. It was all perfectly innocent. Part of him wished it wasn't.

His fingers felt fat and awkward as he worked the tiny buttons on the back of the dress. He'd always thought that when he got around to undressing a woman it would be a prelude to bedding her, not to sending her away.

The dress fell away from her shoulders. "Perhaps you can help me lift it over my head?"

He tried to control his breathing as his fingers touched bare skin on her arms and shoulders as she emerged from under the dress. He pulled his hands back quickly, so as not to be tempted to touch her like he had that first night when she appeared in his bed. No. He had to remember Dinah. He had to remember not to take advantage of Miss Park's unfortunate situation.

She didn't appear to notice his distress as she unbuttoned the hoops from her corset. Once they had fallen to the ground she turned her back toward him. "Would you mind untying the corset?"

Mind untying the corset? It was every man's fantasy, untying the corset and getting to what was underneath. He had to remind himself this was not a prelude to anything. His body was reacting as if something else might happen. He took a steadying breath and fumble-fingered loosened the laces on the corset for her.

She stood in her shift before him, her arms crossed protectively in front of her. She looked so scared and vulnerable. He wanted to take her into his arms and protect her and kiss her again. He couldn't do that, though.

"You said you had silver?" Her voice quavered. Perhaps she was uncertain about this endeavor as well.

Was it the prospect of going back into the pond, even if it meant bringing her home, or was she afraid she was about to be exposed as a fraud?

He pulled a ring from his pocket and spent a moment studying the small circle in the palm of his hand. Anna had given it to him when he went off to University. He had joked that he was supposed to give her a ring, and she had smiled coyly and told him that could come later. But in the meantime she didn't want to be forgotten. He could never forget her. Never had, never would. But he would be marrying Dinah soon, and Miss Parks needed silver, and the time had come to sever the ties with Anna. He handed the ring to Miss Parks.

She gave him a searching look. "If this works I won't be able to give it back. Is this something you can part with?"

"It is." His voice was thick and he spoke brusquely to hide his emotions. "Take it."

She took it and gave him a shy smile. "Thank you."

They stood a few feet apart, but with a world between them. How does one say goodbye under these circumstances? He rocked back and forth on the balls of his feet, remembering the kiss they'd shared and wishing it didn't feel like his heart was being wrenched out of his chest by being forced to say goodbye.

Her hair had started to come loose, and she pushed a lock back behind her ear.

"Thank you," she said again. "For everything."

He didn't even think. He pulled her to him and kissed her again. She melted in his arms, but then she found her strength and pushed herself away from him.

"I must go." She gently touched her lips.

"Don't forget me." What he should have said was 'good bye,' but those were not the words that came out of his mouth.

"I won't." She blinked quickly a couple of times, and then with a small nod toward him, she turned and walked into the dark water of the fish pond. He heard her muttering something as she walked but couldn't make it out. He watched as she got to knee level. Waist level. And then with a final wave toward him, she ducked under the water.

Ripples spread out from where she had gone under. Bubbles from her breath floated to the surface with encouraging regularity. If he stopped seeing those bubbles would it mean that she had gone to where she had meant to go, or that she had died? He stared at those bubbles.

They stopped. It took a moment to realize they weren't there anymore, that another wasn't about to surface, but they were gone. She was gone.

He stared at the water, waiting for something else to happen. Should he dive in? Was she trapped, and drowning? He should. If he couldn't find her, then she was safe in her own time, but what if she were still here and suffering. He couldn't let her suffer. He was about to kick off his shoes when the bubbles started up again in the pond, and then, she emerged.

She stared at him, wide-eyed and then those beautiful brown eyes filled with tears and her face crumpled as she began to cry.

Christine Marciniak

Chapter Fifteen

Emily

It hadn't worked.

Sam wrapped her in a blanket and held her in his arms while she sobbed.

She kept trying and trying, and it never worked. She wanted to go home. Why couldn't she get home? Did she have to click her heels together like Dorothy or something? She'd do it. Anything. But the fishpond had brought her here, and she didn't understand why it wouldn't take her back again. What did it want from her?

"It will be all right," Sam whispered in her ear. "It will. Let me get you upstairs and into dry clothes. Trust me, it will be all right."

It will be all right. The words penetrated her haze, and she nodded. She sniffled and wiped a hand across her eyes to dry them. Sam scooped up the discarded dress and hoops and then, guiding her by a light touch on her elbow, led the way back to the house.

She stumbled over rough ground, and Sam dropped the clothing in order to steady her. She would have sat down right there and started crying again, but he kept up the soothing chatter and got her moving.

It will be all right. He kept repeating it. Maybe it was true. It had to be true, otherwise how would she keep on going?

Women were coming in and out of the kitchen, and she froze. She didn't want to be seen like this, dripping wet, wrapped in a blanket. But Sam nudged her gently along. "It's all right. No one will notice a thing"

Probably a convenient fiction. Weren't people with servants always convinced they saw or knew nothing. She had read enough books to know that was never the case, but she chose to believe him so she could get inside. If she could get inside, things would be all right.

They made it over the threshold into the house, and she would have stopped there had he not once again steered her along. "We'll get you upstairs so you can change."

Under the blanket she shivered. Yes. She needed to change. They went up the back stairs, where no one but servants were likely to see them. She kept putting one foot in front of the other, trying to push all other thoughts out of her mind. It had not worked. She would never get home. What was she going to do now? How on earth could Sam say it would be all right?

When the door of her room finally shut behind them, she dropped the blanket to the floor and stood in her wet shift, uncertain what to do next.

"You should get out of the wet clothing." He dumped the dress and hoops on the bed. "Where is a dry shift?"

"How should I know!" Emily blurted out, coming back to life as anger surged through her. "This isn't my house, my things, my time! I have nothing. Nothing except a bridesmaid's dress that has apparently disappeared."

"Okay, okay." Sam put a soothing hand out but

didn't touch her. "I'll get you something dry. Don't go anywhere."

He left her standing, dripping in the middle of the room. Like she had anywhere to go.

The anger left as quickly as it had appeared, leaving her with no emotion but hopelessness once again.

She still had the ring Sam had handed her on her finger, and she twisted it around. The silver hadn't worked. The magic spell hadn't worked. There had to be another variable. Night time? Full moon? The fog? What was it? Maybe all wasn't lost. There was a way to get home. There had to be. They hadn't tried every variable. Moses still hadn't told her what he knew. She had to be patient and remain calm. Right, remain calm, while trapped in the past with the Civil War starting. Calm. Ha.

Sam came back holding a white muslin shift. "I found this in Elizabeth's room. It should work. Take off the wet one."

"We have to ask Moses what the trick is." She ignored his injunction to undress. "I need to know what we did wrong."

"Right. We will. But first you need to get out of the wet clothing." He held the shift out to her, but she didn't take it.

"It could be darkness. Maybe we have to try again when it's night. Or maybe it has to do with the full moon. When is the next full moon?" Her voice rose in pitch as she edged ever closer to panic.

"Miss Parks." Sam took a step toward her. "Emily." His voice was thick with emotion. "It will be all right. I promise. Let's get you into dry clothes." He came even closer and touched her shoulder. "You'll get sick. That won't help anything."

Somehow his touch unfroze her, and the panic retreated into the dark corners, for now. "Right. I need to take this off." She stepped behind a room dividing screen. The shift clung to her, and her skin was still damp when it was removed. "Do you think you can find me a towel?" she called out to Sam.

"Certainly." A moment later, a hand holding a towel appeared around the edge of the screen. She took it.

"Thank you." She dried herself off. There was a man in the room with her and she was naked and all that separated them was this screen. She wasn't someone to simply fall into bed with someone, and Sam was engaged, which made him off limits, but yet, part of her felt a pull to simply walk out from behind the screen and offer herself to him. But no. That was a silly and strange romantic kind of notion, probably stemming from panic and fear and the desire to take control of something, anything in her life. But she couldn't do that. It would be foolhardy on so many levels.

Yet, she was drawn to him. He was handsome and charming, and here.

"Emily?" He called from the other side of the screen. It wasn't lost on her that he had stopped calling her Miss Parks. She wasn't entirely certain what that signified. "Are you all right?"

She wrapped the towel around her sarong-style and stepped out from behind the screen. "Yes, thank you." He was close enough to touch. "I need the dry shift," she said, barely able to make her voice work. Her heart beat fast, and she wanted him to hold her. It was wrong, but it was what she wanted, and damn it, shouldn't she get something she wanted? Everything else was working against her.

She took one step closer, and so did he, and soon she was wrapped in his embrace. She put her arms around him, holding tight. His hands were on her shoulders and moving down her back and the towel was coming loose and she didn't care in the least. His mouth found hers and she was surprised that she could even breathe, that she was still standing.

His hands were warm and strong on her back, his kisses reached deep inside her, turning her to liquid. She could melt away right here. She didn't even know what was keeping her upright except for Sam's arms. She clung to him like a lifeline. He was all that was real and solid and here and nothing else mattered as long as he was touching her like this.

A small portion of her brain kept its grip on reality and was able to think straight. It sounded alarm bells in her head. This was wrong. On lots of levels. Not least of which was Dinah.

She pulled away from the kiss and put both hands against his chest and pushed away, forgetting that there was nothing holding the towel up. It fell to the ground, pooling around their feet. What was she doing? Naked with a practical stranger.

She bent and grabbed the towel, wrapping it around herself even as she ducked back behind the screen.

"I'm sorry." Her voice shook, betraying her emotions. "We shouldn't have done that. You are getting married. We shouldn't have. I'm sorry."

"I'm not." His voice was so soft that at first she

didn't know if she really heard him say that.

"You're not what?" She peeked out from behind the screen. She really needed the dry shift, so she could get dressed.

He seemed to divine this, for he handed it to her.

"I'm not sorry."

He wasn't sorry? Neither was she. But shouldn't they be? She dropped the towel and slipped the shift on over her head. Shouldn't they be concerned about Dinah? Wasn't that only right and proper? Though, she got rather a thrill out of thinking of the possibilities of not observing the proprieties. There were no dry bloomers, but she figured that didn't matter too much right now. At least she was covered again. So much for being a rebel.

"And I'm not marrying Dinah."

Her breath caught in her throat and she steadied herself against the flimsy screen. "You're not?" She came out from behind the screen. Had she misunderstood? She was certain she'd been told he was getting married. If he wasn't...well she still couldn't jump into bed with a practical stranger, but it gave them room to become less strange to each other.

"I don't think I can." Sam's gray eyes bored into her. "Not when I'm not in love with her."

Her heart soared at these words. Was he saying that he was in love with her instead? But she didn't belong here, she had to go home. And he was going to war. He was going to die in the war. There were no happy endings here.

"You can't be in love with me." She tried to keep her voice light and flippant even as that formerly sane part of her brain chanted 'He loves me! He loves me!'

"We've only just met."

The shocked look in his eyes told her more than she wanted to know.

"Oh, you're not in love with me." She suddenly felt two inches tall. Her cheeks burned and she couldn't bear to meet his eyes. "Do you think you can get me back into this corset, or should we call Beck," she rambled on, trying desperately to change the subject.

"Emily," he said, his voice cracked and he cleared his throat. "Miss Parks. I think perhaps in time I could love you. You are right that we don't know each other. But the fact that I think I could love you tells me that I do not love Dinah." He cleared his throat. "Come here, I'll tie your corset for you."

She did as she was bid, her whole brain such a mix of emotions she wasn't even sure which direction to let her thoughts run anymore.

"Why did you agree to marry Dinah if you are not in love with her?" She finally settled on a question as Sam tied her corset tight.

He sat down on the edge of the bed and twined his fingers together in his lap, staring at the ground. She stood and watched him for a minute, but he seemed to be getting his thoughts together and maybe it was better not to rush him. She settled in the rocking chair, it looked like she wasn't going to finish getting dressed any time soon.

"Have you ever been in love?" he asked, finally looking up from the ground. The pain in those gray eyes made her want to rush to him and hold him, but instead she clutched the arms of the chair and rocked gently.

"I thought I was a time or two." She didn't want to

think about Mark or James right now. Mark, her first real boyfriend in college, and James, the one she thought would give her the kind of happiness that Johnson brought to Dayna. It hadn't worked out that way. Mark had gotten drunk one night and hit her. That was all it took for her to know there was no future with him. James had cheated on her with a woman he worked with. If it weren't for the fact that Dayna and Johnson had found true love, she would think it didn't really exist.

"I was in love once." He got up and walked over to the window, staring out at his land.

His voice was so sad that Emily would have known the story didn't have a happy ending, even without the use of past tense.

"What happened?" She kept her voice soft and non-demanding. What she wanted to do was to go to him and wrap him in her arms and take away whatever pain he was in. She didn't think that was really what he wanted right now, though, so she stayed in the chair, barely rocking.

"She died." He turned from the window and she saw his eyes were bright with unshed tears. He came back across the room and sat on the bed again, placing his hands on his knees and taking a deep breath before continuing. "Five years ago. She got a fever and died. We were going to be married, and I was the happiest man in the world. And then she was gone, and the light left the world."

"Tell me about her." She pleated the shift with her fingers, trying to release nervous energy. She wasn't sure she really wanted to hear about the person who gave Sam's life light, but he needed to talk about her, and she did want to understand him more.

"She made me happy." He touched his fist to his chest. "Deep down in here. We knew each other as children, but when we were sixteen I fell in love. She was beautiful, but that wasn't why I fell in love with her. And maybe she wasn't even beautiful, objectively speaking. George told me that her teeth were crooked and she had freckles, but I never really noticed. She could make me laugh and…I can't even describe her."

"You don't have to, I get it. I'm sorry." Tears came to her own eyes. To have loved that deeply and lost, how does one get over that pain? Or maybe one doesn't, as evidenced by Sam, so clearly hurting even five years later.

He shook his head as if coming out of a trance. "I'm sorry. I shouldn't have told you that."

"Whyever not?" She affected the matter of fact tone of a school teacher. It was the only way to keep from being overwhelmed with emotion herself. "You were in love with her. You should feel free to talk about her." She watched his fingers play with the crease in his trousers, and she softened her tone. "What was her name?"

"Anna. She was Anna."

"And why were going to marry Dinah?" That was the million dollar question.

He took a deep breath and gave her a sad half-smile. "My family and friends said I needed to move on with life, and I suppose they're right. And Dinah is a lovely girl, she really is. It's not like with Anna, it never could be, but I thought perhaps that wasn't possible. That I couldn't have that kind of love again, so I agreed. Only a few days ago, mind you, I agreed to marry her. But now, I'm not sure."

"Why?" She didn't want to jump to conclusions.

"Because now I think the kind of love I had is still possible."

Oh! A flock of butterflies took flight in her belly and her heart pounded as if it were growing too big for her chest. He had the best kind of love possible and he thought he could have it again. With her. It was what she had always dreamed of and it might be happening.

Sam gazed at her in a way that made her uncomfortably aware that she was only wearing her shift and corset. Should she go and sit beside him? Should she have him loosen the corset and get naked with him? No. She still didn't really know him. And that a wonderful love was possible was not the same thing as saying he was in love with her.

And she was going home.

And he was going to die in the war.

She couldn't do this.

She stood up and she wanted to go to him, to hold him, but instead she picked the hoops up from the bed next to him. "Maybe you can help me into the dress." She tried to keep her voice even. "People may start wondering where we are."

This broke Sam out of his trance. "Yes. Happily."

She managed to get her hoops buttoned on and he helped get the dress over her head. Sun glinted off the ring he had given her. "You should take this back."

"You may need it later." His eyes stayed glued to the ring. It had to have special meaning for him, she shouldn't keep it.

"Are you sure?"

He nodded, but his lips were pressed into a straight

line.

"Was it Anna's?" She touched the ring as if it had some magic power.

"It was." His voice was tight.

She wanted to refuse it, to give it back, but yet, if he was willing for her to have it, who was she to throw that kind of a gift back at him? She looked into his eyes and smiled. "Then, thank you. I'll take good care of it."

He bowed to her and took his leave. She sank down on her bed. What had happened? Was she falling in love with him? Of course she was. Was he falling in love with her? She glanced at the ring on her finger. Possibly. She wanted true love, had dreamed about it for years. Now after all those years of wishing, her wish had finally come true.

Maybe the pond wasn't a time portal, but a wishing well?

She sat up straighter, then slumped as much as her corset would let her when she realized that it probably wouldn't matter at all. Either way, it had brought her here and didn't seem inclined to let her go home.

Chapter Sixteen

Sam

Sam paced the length of the study, hands behind his back. Was he falling in love with Emily? He could still feel her soft skin beneath his fingers. He'd longed to touch her all over. It had taken almost inhuman strength to stop himself. But was that love or lust? He'd never seen that much of Dinah; would he feel the same way about her if he had? He'd also never seen that much of Anna, and he'd known he'd loved her. How does one tell these things anyway?

And from the future? Was it true? He doubted it. Which maybe made her crazy, which wasn't really the best quality in a mate, come to think of it.

She didn't act crazy though, that was the thing. A little out of the ordinary, but that could easily be explained by being from the future.

Damn, did he actually believe her? If he believed her, did that make him crazy too?

Then there was the war. It would be long. It would be bad. He didn't want to believe her on that, but deep down, he did. And he wanted to see her naked again.

He stopped behind his desk and poured himself a few fingers of whiskey. He needed something to settle his mind. He needed to be logical about this. Moses might have answers to some of the questions, and it was time to ask him. He drained the glass and went out in search of the old groom.

He found him raking out the stables, the late afternoon sun making stripes of light in the dim barn.

"You need a horse this afternoon, Mister Sam?" He stopped raking and gave a differential tip of his head.

"No, I need to talk to you." There was no use beating about the bush. He took a deep breath, inhaling the fresh sweet scent of hay and the earthy smell of horses.

"Anything wrong, Mister Sam?" The old groom leaned on his rake and a worried look came into his eye. "Something wrong with one of the horses?"

"No, nothing like that." Sam rested his hand on the rough wood of the stable enclosure. The mare he'd taken out earlier with the chaise was stabled. With a start he realized he'd left her by the fish pond when he had escorted a dripping Miss Parks back inside. Luckily someone had been on top of things and taken care of the horse. Probably Tobias. He'd have to thank him later. He took a deep breath and turned to Moses. "I need you to tell me everything you know about the fish pond."

Moses rubbed his chin. "Well. there's catfish and some trout in there. Snapping turtles, too, like I told you when you was a boy."

Sam slapped his hand against the stall, causing Moses and the horse to start. "The legend, Moses. Tell me the legend."

"That's a fairy story to tell the children." Moses reached toward his rake, ready to go back to work.

Sam was not done with this conversation. "What about Elsbeth and DayJon? Elsbeth was real. What about DayJon?"

Moses dropped his hands to his side and sighed. "Oh, he was real enough, Mister Sam."

"And you said the faeries used the pond to take people to other places…or times."

"DayJon told us he was not from this time." Moses stared over Sam's head as if looking into the far distant past.

"Did he say how he get here?"

Moses sighed. "Mind if I sits down Mister Sam? This might take awhile."

"Fine, sit." Sam waved a hand toward an upturned barrel.

"You might want to sit as well," Moses said, settling onto the barrel. Sam nodded, bowing to the inevitable and sat on a conveniently placed bale of hay. "I was but a boy, you have to remember," Moses began. "I only know DayJon appeared around the same time Elsbeth disappeared. I saw the two of them together once and crept into a place I shouldn't have been and listened. They were repeating something over and over, magic words, it sounded like. I had a good head for remembering, so I learnt those words well. Then later, over the campfire after Elsbeth disappeared he told those words to us young uns, and said they held the key to getting free when the time was right. He said he'd explained more to the elders, and they'd tell us when they thought we were ready to know. Then…well, what happened happened, and they never did tell us." Moses cleared his throat before continuing. "I've gone to the pond and said those words, and I'm still here. If there was more to it, I don't know it. They was stories, Mister Sam, that's all. Stories. DayJon probably was a free black captured up north. It happens. And he wanted to sound more interesting. Elsbeth probably didn't want to get married. There's always a logical explanation."

Was there? Then what was the logical explanation for Emily's appearance and insistence she was from the future. Right now, he tended to believe that DayJon wasn't captured up north, but from the same time as Emily. They told the same details of this future world. But how to get back to it? That's what he needed to find out.

"Did DayJon use the magic words to leave?" He rubbed his palms on his knees, he was getting close to an answer, but he wasn't entirely certain he wanted one.

Moses shook his head. "No, sir. He was done made a slave, since he couldn't prove he was free. And he weren't used to working like a field hand. He died of a whipping."

A feeling of shame washed over him. He had never met DayJon or done anything to him, but apparently his own grandfather had taken this man who said he was from the future and decided he owned him. And then killed him.

"What are the magic words?" He knew he was being cowardly by not acknowledging the horror that Moses had exposed, but there was nothing he could do about it now anyway.

Moses closed his eyes and very carefully enunciated.

"*Lorska la loon romp leet le tong, Fair John, A March ee sur lee face der lumier, a un otre mo mant.*"

"What does that even mean?" It was a bunch of nonsense syllables. Though maybe all magic spells sounded like that to the uninitiated.

"I don't know as they mean anything, sir." Moses shifted in his seat and a horse nickered as if looking for attention.

"I won't keep you much longer," he assured him. "Do you know anything about silver?"

"No, sir." Moses's eyes opened wide at the question, and Sam suspected he'd never associated silver with the legend. Did it have anything to do with it then, or was Emily wrong about that?

"Do you know of anyone who has come or gone that way, since DayJon and Elsbeth?"

"Nothing I can swear to," Moses said and he believed him. "The young ones always want to try the spell when they hears of it. They want to be free."

The dissatisfaction in Moses's voice was obvious. And why shouldn't he be dissatisfied. He was a slave. There was no honor in that.

"I'm sorry," he heard himself saying. "I don't like slavery any more than you do, but I don't see a way to fix it."

"Then you ain't looking hard enough, boy." Moses stood up, ready to get back to work

His eyebrows shot up at the blatant disrespect. But this was an old man, a man who had known him since he was born. He would let it go.

"That girl," Moses asked suddenly as Sam stood, ready to leave. "She come from the same place as DayJon?"

His mouth dropped open, but why should he be surprised that Moses had figured it out? He knew the secrets of the fish pond after all.

"I think so, yes." He let out a weary breath. Why couldn't life be uncomplicated? "Maybe you better tell me those magic words again."

So once again the old man repeated the string of nonsense syllables.

"*Lorska la loon romp leet le tong, Fair John, A March ee sur lee face der lumier, a un otre mo man*"

Sam repeated them to himself a few times before he felt fairly certain he remembered them.

He left the stable. One thing was clear, even if nothing else was. Emily might be here for a while as they figured out the mystery, and she would need dresses and other things. And Dinah. What should he do about Dinah? It made no sense to cut her free when Emily would be gone before long. But it wasn't really because of Emily he was thinking of letting her go, at all, was it? If he had to be honest with himself, he had to admit that he was pretty sure he didn't love Dinah the way she deserved to be loved, and so many things could change during a war, he needed to free her from their commitment, so she could find someone who could give her what he couldn't. That sounded reasonable. Would Dinah see it the same way?

He rounded the corner of the house as George rode into view. He dismounted and casually handed the reins to Lucas.

"I was just in town," he said, his words rushing together in excitement. "Yuengling's going to be there tomorrow taking recruits. If we leave right after breakfast, we shouldn't have any trouble both getting in."

Sam ran his hand over his face. Why now? He did not need the extra complication of a war to deal with. Then again, it would get him out of here and every one could sort out their own problems. There was something to be said for that.

"You are still in, aren't you?" George put one hand on Sam's arm and looked into his face.

He shook him off. "Yes, I'm still in. It's perfectly normal to have qualms about going off to war. In fact, if you don't there might be something wrong with you."

George shrugged. "I've always been up for adventure."

"Lots of people are going to be killed." He echoed what Emily had told him earlier.

"Pshaw," George waved that concern away. "It's going to be over by Christmas. We'll show those rebels what's what and come home to a nice roast goose."

"You really think it's going to be that easy?" Why couldn't he have that kind of confidence. Go off, kick some rebel butt and come back home again. He'd sign up for that in a heartbeat.

"Don't you?" George tilted his head and studied his friend. "You don't think the rebels have a chance of winning, do you?"

"No." Even without Emily's take on it, he still felt this way. The south did not have the manufacturing to fuel a war. How could they win? "But I do think they are going to put up a good fight."

George preened a bit, like a rooster entering the hen house. "I'm always up for a good fight. Aren't you?"

"Yeah, yeah." He wished he felt more enthused about the whole thing. "I'll sign up with you tomorrow, but things have gotten more complicated. My father is not here to look after things, I don't trust Wilkins, and then there is Emily." He hadn't meant to actually say that last bit out loud.

"Who?" George asked, eyebrows drawn together. "Oh, you mean Miss Parks, mystery woman. Hey, do you think I'll get a chance to take that picnic with her before we leave? Is she going to dine with us today?"

"Us?" He didn't recall inviting George to dine with him. Somewhere in the back of his mind he'd been envisioning a quiet, romantic meal. But that probably wasn't the most prudent move anyway. It would be better of George were around.

"You were planning on inviting me to stay for supper, weren't you?"

"Yeah, sure." He always invited George to eat if he were around at mealtimes. Why should today be any different?

"And I'll get a chance to woo Miss Parks." George waggled his eyebrows in a way that Sam suspected he thought was seductive.

Over my dead body. He winced, with war on the horizon, that might be truer than he cared to admit.

"Wilkins give you any more trouble?" George bent to adjust his boot.

"No, it's been quiet today. Though I wasn't really around."

"No? Where were you?"

He grinned, he had no compunction at all about needling his friend. He didn't even need to waggle his eyebrows. "Picnicking with Miss Parks."

"No!" George stared at him open mouthed. "You dog!"

"Took her to the waterfall," he added with a sideways glance at George.

"Wouldn't want to be you when Dinah hears about this."

"She won't." He gave him what he hoped was a stern look, and then sighed. "But it doesn't matter. I'm going to break the engagement with Dinah."

George couldn't seem to lose that bug-eyed stare. "Because of Miss Parks?"

He shook his head. "Not directly, no. I'm not in love with Dinah. She deserves someone who is."

"You in love with Miss Parks?"

"Quite possibly," he answered and with a slap on the shoulder, brought George inside for a pre-dinner drink.

Chapter Seventeen

Emily

George was there for dinner again, which kept things from getting too intimate or awkward. Emily wasn't sure if that was a good thing or not. She was still trying to sort out what had happened this afternoon and what it meant. She couldn't be in love with Sam. They were from different worlds, and that wasn't even metaphorical, they really were from different worlds, different centuries at least, they couldn't build a life together. But yet... No. They couldn't. She would go home as soon as she could figure out how and that was that.

In the meantime maybe she could repay Sam for his hospitality by helping him figure out what was happening to his missing supplies. She didn't bring it up at dinner, unsure of how much he had shared with George. There would be plenty of time to discuss it once they were alone.

When the final dishes were cleared, Sam dabbed at his mouth with his napkin and stood. George pushed back his chair, and Emily realized they were heading to the study for an after dinner smoke. She put her napkin on the table and pushed her chair back. Was she expected to join them? Was she even allowed to join them? From what she could tell it was rather a male-bonding ritual. Besides, she didn't smoke.

Sam's eyes widened, and he looked around the table and realized that there were only the three of them. "George, perhaps we should retire to the parlor instead. No one is here to entertain Miss Parks."

"Please don't change your plans on my account." She was an uninvited guest here, she should try not to cause more trouble than necessary. "I'll simply go in the parlor and read for a while."

Her selflessness was rewarded with a grateful smile from Sam which made her heart flutter. Why did he have to have this effect on her?

"We won't be long," he assured her. "Only a quick smoke."

****

The gas lamps in the parlor gave off a cozy glow, and she studied the books on the shelves looking for something that piqued her interest, settling on *Pride and Prejudice*, an old favorite. She read the first chapter and realized that Sam and George had not emerged from the study. She suspected that like any old friends, they got caught up in talk and lost track of time.

She, however, needed to use the ladies' room. She sighed. Outhouse. She hoped she wasn't here long enough to actually get used to that.

She set the book on the end table and headed outside. When she had finished what she needed to do, she walked past the kitchen. Inside she could hear cheerful voices and the sounds of cleaning up. She should go in there and see what they knew about the missing inventory. At the very least she could find out how much of any given item they regularly used. Then she could see how their numbers matched up with what showed in the ledger.

She hesitated at the open door of the kitchen. The room inside was cast in shadow, lit only by the fire in the hearth and the fading light of the setting sun coming through the window. The aroma of the night's roasted meat and fresh bread hung in the air. Three women worked inside, their long skirts sweeping the stone floor, all three with their hair hidden by faded scarves that had once been colorful. They chatted and laughed as one swept the floor, another scoured a large pot, and the third banked the fire. Did she really have a right to intrude on them? But if she didn't ask, she wouldn't get answers. She knocked on the doorjamb. The room fell silent, and three dark faces turned toward her.

The woman who had been bent over the hearth, straightened. She was tall, lean, and wiry and seemed to be the senior of the three. Emily could see the muscles in her forearms and knew this was a woman who worked hard, all the time. "Can I help you?" Her voice was formal and clipped with no warmth in it.

"Are you Sally?" Emily asked, taking a guess and stepping into the room, which was hot and airless even though the evening was cool

"I am. Do you need something?" The words were spoken as one of whom something was always being demanded. Emily wanted nothing but answers, but was even that asking too much?

"May I ask you some questions?" She tried to keep her tone light and respectful, to let them know they could say no if they wished.

"You one of those abolitionists come to find out if we like being slaves?" the woman with the broom asked harshly.

The question took her off-guard. "I wouldn't expect anyone would like being a slave." Perhaps if she showed them she didn't consider their work beneath her it would help matters. "Can I help with the washing up?"

"We're quite able to do it ourselves," the third answered, bitterness in her voice.

"I'm sure." She took a step back. She had thought they'd be happier to talk to her, chalk up another misconception about people and the past. "Actually, I was wondering who is in charge of placing orders for flour and sugar and other things that the farm doesn't produce."

"Mister Sam places all the orders." Sally kept hold of the iron poker while she spoke, and Emily wondered if she posed that much a threat to this woman. She couldn't imagine how, but there was a lot about this time she didn't comprehend.

"How does he know how much to order?" She took another step backward, to prove she was no danger to them.

"Wilkins tells him," the woman with the broom answered. Sally gave her a squelching look, and she began sweeping more industriously.

That was about what Emily had suspected. "And how much do you need a month?"

"I don't see how that's any of your business, seeing as you are a stranger here." Sally didn't actually lift the poker in a threatening way, but Emily saw the strong muscles in her arm flex. She was not helping matters by being here.

She could tell them she was trying to help Sam catch a thief, but he hadn't really given her permission to ask questions.

"I'm sorry for intruding." She stepped out of the kitchen entirely, and then, with one hand still on the doorjamb she said, "For what it's worth. If I knew of a way to free you all, I would. But know this…by the time this war ends you'll all be free."

"From your mouth to God's ears," Sally muttered, and turned back to the fire.

She left them to their tasks, feeling rather lonely and desolate. The sun was near the horizon, and the shadows were long. Honeysuckle was sweet in the evening air, and birds chirped cheerfully in the trees. It was so lovely here, now, so peaceful. It was hard to believe that somewhere, battles were being fought, men were dying in a war that was going to go on and on and destroy so much. How could that even be possible when the world seemed so serene?

She should go back inside to the cozy parlor and her book and quietly wait for someone to want to spend time with her. She sighed, that prospect did not exactly fill her with joy either. She wanted to do something, to help Sam out in some way.

There were other outbuildings here behind the house. Sam had pointed them out to her when he took her around the plantation. Storehouse, smokehouse, spring house, overseer's house. Where might Wilkins hide ill-gotten gains? If it was indeed Wilkins behind the thefts. His house would be a likely spot, but she wasn't going to snoop around in a person's private home. She wasn't an idiot. But maybe that would be too obvious, anyway, perhaps he would utilize one of the outbuildings.

No one was around, so she decided to channel her

inner Nancy Drew and do a bit of sleuthing. The first building was the storehouse. Barrels of flour and cornmeal and sugar and beans were neatly stacked along the walls. Dwindling piles of apples and potatoes were in the corners. After all, this year's crop wasn't in, and last year's would be almost gone. This was the sign of a home well cared for, well-provisioned. What would the war do to it though? Would they starve like Scarlett O'Hara in *Gone With the Wind*? Hopefully it wouldn't come to that.

She shut the door on the storehouse and went to examine the next building. This was empty but had the definite odor of smoke lingering about it, clearly the smokehouse. The building after that Sam had called the spring house, and when she stepped inside she saw why. It housed a cool natural spring, surrounded by rocks. However, it was clear nothing was hidden in this building.

Back in the evening air, she hesitated. Obviously Wilkins hadn't hidden anything in a place that people frequented, and how was she even going to find places people didn't? It was a fool's errand.

"What do you think you are doing?" A gruff voice from behind her asked.

She turned and saw Wilkins standing behind her. A leer spread across his ugly face when he realized who she was.

"I think you better come with me." He grabbed her by the arm.

"With you?" She tried to jerk her arm free from his grasp, but he had a grip like a vise. Don't panic. That was the key to situations like this, right? "Why would I do that? No, I was just getting a bit of air. Sam is expecting me back any moment."

"Sam is it? You two getting nice and cozy with each other?" She didn't like the look in his eye and his breath smelled of onions.

"Let go of me." She jerked her arm again, but it made no difference. Should she scream for Sam? Would he hear her? The ladies in the kitchen might. Would they help her if they did? She wasn't so sure.

"No. You're a trouble maker, and I'm going to put a stop to it."

She didn't like the sound of that at all. "I'm not causing you any trouble," she insisted, trying to push down her rising panic, even as he pulled her along the path, her feet reluctantly moving to keep herself from falling. "Honest."

"You caused me to take a whipping," he snarled. "That ain't ever happened before, and it ain't ever happening again."

"Oh, if that's all. I'll be sure to ask Sam to never whip you again." She wanted to sound firm and confident, but her voice quavered as she spoke.

He laughed. It was not a cheerful sound.

"I took that whipping because of you." He tightened his grip on her arm. She'd have bruises there for certain. He dragged her toward a small house on the hill, the overseer's house.

Enough of being conciliatory. "That's because you whipped me. You big jerk."

"Jerk am I?" He snarled and tugged her arm up behind her, wrenching her shoulder painfully, and grabbed her face with his dirty fingers. "You'll pay." He whispered the words, which made them all the more frightening.

She struggled, but it only made him hold her more roughly. He moved his mouth closer and closer to hers. Her stomach clenched. He was going to kiss her. When his mouth was only an inch or so away and she could smell his dirty teeth and onion breath, he whispered, "Oh, I'm not going to kiss you yet, don't get all excited. There's plenty of time for that. But then again, why make you wait, when you so obviously want me."

Oh, hell no. She wasn't sure particularly what he had planned, but she was having none of it.

She opened her mouth to scream, but no sound at all came out before he had actually planted his mouth on hers. She squirmed, but he only held her tighter. She brought up her knee, to get him in the crotch, a move she'd seen often on TV and in movies but had never had reason to employ herself, but that proved physically impossible with all the hoops and layers of skirts.

Finally he released her mouth, and she tasted blood on her lip where he'd bit her.

"Don't try to scream again, or you'll be sorry."

She was pretty sure she'd be sorry if she didn't scream, but she had no breath with which to even whisper yet.

Wilkins let go of her face and grabbed hold of both her arms so quickly that she wasn't even aware he was going to do it until he already had both hands behind her back and was tying them with something. A bandanna or handkerchief perhaps? Whatever it was, it didn't bite as hard as rope probably would, but he tied them tight enough that she could already feel her fingers go cold.

"Let me go." She pulled her hands apart, but it only made the knot tighter. There'd been some video on

Facebook awhile back on how to get out of a situation like this. Too bad she hadn't watched it.

He propelled her forward and soon she was in his house. He pushed her down onto the floor, and she cried out. She'd be a mass of bruises tomorrow, if she lived that long. She was face down and managed to turn herself over. With her hands behind her back, it was hard to maneuver. He stood over her, his hands on his belt, leering at her. If he came closer, she would kick him. And she would scream. And spit. Anything to keep him from raping her. But then he moved his hands from his pants and gave her an evil grin.

"No, that can wait. There's plenty of time. And anticipation is half the fun, don't you agree?"

"No." She spat the word at him.

"You're like an alley cat." He didn't seem bothered by that. "I look forward to subduing you."

"You won't—" He shoved a bandanna into her mouth and tied it tight behind her head before she finished her sentence. The cloth bit into the sides of her mouth. She wouldn't be screaming now. That must mean he anticipated she would want to. That couldn't be a good sign.

She tried to kick him, but her skirts and tied hands really limited her mobility.

"None of that now." Next thing she knew he was sitting on her legs, tying her ankles together.

Tears pricked her eyes. There was no reason Sam would come looking for her, and when he did, he certainly would have no reason to look here. If she was going to get away, it would have to be on her own.

Her muscles tensed waiting for a blow she was sure would come. But instead she heard the door open and close, and she realized she'd been left alone on the floor. This was unexpected.

She lay still for a moment letting her heartbeat go back to normal and assessed her situation.

She was in a combination front room and kitchen. A fire was banked in the hearth; a pot of what smelled like stew hung over the embers. A table and chairs took up much of the center of the room. Perhaps there was a knife of some sort around, and she could manage to free herself. She struggled and wiggled until she was able to sit up. It was awkward and uncomfortable, but better than lying on the ground like an upside down turtle. She stretched and craned her neck and did see a knife on the table, but unless she could stand, she wasn't sure she could get it. And she didn't see any way of standing. Maybe she could knock it off the table and then somehow get a hold of it and then manage to free herself.

Yeah. Maybe if she were in some action movie or was the least bit nimble. She'd never even been able to touch her toes in gym class. And forget yoga positions. How had she managed to get herself in this situation anyway? Where had she gone wrong? Was it so dangerous to walk around outside by herself? Apparently it was. Okay. Think. What did he want from her?

Probably rape. Or perhaps he wanted to whip her some more in retaliation for Sam's punishing him for whipping her in the first place. Though that seemed like a no-win for him. If Sam were to find out, which she would make sure he did, then Wilkins would be in even more trouble. And in either of those situations, why had he left her here like this? That made no sense.

She noticed a canvas sheet in the corner hiding something. Was it the stolen goods? Maybe she could inch herself over there and find out, but before she'd managed to scoot herself more than a foot across the floor the door opened.

Wilkins entered, pushing ahead of him a small black girl, maybe five years old.

"Comfortable, I trust." He sneered at her, and evil seemed to glow in his beady eyes.

Since she couldn't answer with the gag in her mouth, she just glared at him.

The child trembled, and Emily wanted to reach out and hug her and assure her it would be okay. Though, honestly she wasn't sure at all, and she would rather like it if someone would offer her those reassurances. If she'd been able to, she would have beckoned the child to come sit by her and said some comforting words. She hoped that the look in her eyes would comfort the child somewhat.

"You're a compassionate woman, aren't you?" Wilkins asked Emily.

She nodded, not at all sure where this was going.

"And you wouldn't want anything to happen to young Dolly here, would you?"

She shook her head, but a sick feeling crept into her stomach.

"Marshall will pay for humiliating me." Wilkins mouth twisted up into an evil smile. "And you are going to help."

She must have moved her head even though she hadn't meant to, because his face had that awful sneer again. "Oh, yes. You will. Because if you don't help me, then this child will be punished. I may not be able to whip you with impunity, but I can do whatever I want to her."

He was serious. He was freaking serious. This man was a monster and a sadist and all kinds of bad things, and she had to sit here and listen to him because she was so damned trussed up she had no choice. He walked toward her, and she tried to back away from him, but there was nowhere for her to go. He pulled the gag from her mouth.

"Am I making myself clear?" he murmured menacingly into her ear.

She choked on her own spit before she could answer. "Yes. Untie me."

"Before I do," he said. "I want to make one thing clear. You are in my power."

She was not now nor would she ever be in anyone's power. He could hurt her, but he had no power over her.

"I can and will do anything I want to you, and if you tell Marshall one word of it then this girl gets whipped."

Emily's heart lurched. The child. No. She was powerless to stop this. No. She wasn't. She would not give in to this. There had to be a way out. She would find a way to tell Sam. She would take the child under her personal protection. Everything would be okay.

She would not let him get away with this, but for now she agreed. Arguing with him would only prolong everyone's agony. "Fine," she said. "I understand. Untie me."

"Not yet. Let's test your resolve."

She did not like the sound of that at all. He moved his face close to hers and she pulled back, repulsed by everything about him.

"That's not being very agreeable." He straightened up and slapped the little girl in the face so hard that she fell over, clasping her hand to her cheek and sobbing quietly.

"Don't do that!" Emily shouted, straining at her ties. As if anger alone could free her.

"Then don't fight me," he snarled like a rabid dog, approaching her once again.

Emily took a steadying breath. She would not fight. She would be as passive as possible so this child would not get hurt on her behalf. Wilkins kissed her, and she didn't resist. Although it was hard not to gag when he pushed his tongue between his lips. When his finger traced the curve of her breasts, she didn't let herself move an inch. How much was she going to have to endure with this poor child watching?

And then as suddenly as it had all started, it stopped. Wilkins stopped kissing her. He untied her hands and untied her feet, and even offered her a hand up to get her back to her feet.

"Very good." He looked inordinately proud of himself and she had to resist the urge to punch him in the face. "You understand the terms of our agreement. I can call on you at any time, day or night, to continue what we've started here. And I won't refrain from punishing Dolly if you don't comply." He moved his mouth close to her ear, and she tried not to wince. "Keep in mind, that if you find some way to protect Dolly, I can choose another pickaninny. There are plenty of them. Oh, and one more thing, if you think I won't know if you've spoken to Marshall about this or not, I've got spies everywhere. Any private conversation and I'm going to assume you've told and start the punishments."

His words hit her like a sucker punch to the stomach. Every out she had thought of for herself, he had an answer for. But when it came right down to it, Sam was in charge here, and he could put a stop to this, as long as he stopped it before anyone, like Dolly, got hurt.

"I won't say anything," she lied. She wanted to go directly to Sam and tell him everything, but the risk to Dolly was too great. If only the pond would finally take her home. Everyone would be safe then.

Chapter Eighteen

Sam

The mantel clock in the study chimed eight, and Sam glanced at it startled, he'd no idea so much time had passed. He placed his pipe on its mahogany stand. It had gone out while they'd talked anyway.

"We've been most neglectful of Miss Parks." How could he have left her on her own that long? He knew it was unacceptable as a host, but the afternoon had shaken him more than he cared to admit. He didn't know how to handle being alone with her again. So, shamefully, he'd left her to her own devices while he'd smoked and drank with George. There was no excuse for it, and now he had to face the music.

"And I must be on my way." George stood and stretched. "I'll come by tomorrow morning, and we'll ride into town."

"We'll take the carriage." Sam turned down the gaslight on the desk.

"Why? It's much more convenient to ride."

Sam cleared his throat, not sure what George would make of what he had to say next. "Yes, but I'm taking Miss Parks into town to have some dresses made up."

"So, she's staying, is she?" George crossed his arms and studied him, one eyebrow quirked.

"For the time being." She had nowhere else to go. It would be ungentlemanly to turn her out. "Which is another reason I can't be lax on my hospitality."

"Should I stay and chaperon?"

Sam wasn't entirely certain his friend was joking.

"Don't be ridiculous." He walked George to the front door and then headed to the parlor to see if Emily needed anything. Perhaps he should bring a glass of brandy, was the evening cool enough for that? Was it too forward of him? Considering what had happened this afternoon could anything be considered too forward?

He expected to see her sitting in the big chair by the fire, or perhaps the davenport, but the room was empty. Tobias, as always, was near at hand. "You don't happen to know where Miss Parks is, do you?"

"No, sir." Tobias shook his head as he answered. Of course he didn't, Sam realized, he'd been in the study with him and George, refilling their drinks as needed. "Can I say, though, Mister Sam, that Mr. Phelps is right. You should have a chaperon here if Miss Parks is going to stay. It's not right."

Sam frowned at him but knew he was right. It would be cause for scandal in the neighborhood if it were discovered, but he didn't particularly care, and he suspected Emily wouldn't either. His mother, on the other hand, would be livid if word got back to her.

"Especially after what happened by the pond this afternoon," Tobias continued.

Sam gave him a sharp look. "What did you see?"

"Enough," Tobias answered.

Damn. That was all he needed.

"Anyone else?"

"Not as far I as I know."

"And you'll, of course, keep your observations to yourself." It came out sounding much more like an order than a request to a friend.

Tobias bowed his head slightly. "Of course, sir."

Sam took a deep breath and let it out slowly. "Perhaps I should wire my sister to come back. That would provide sufficient chaperonage, don't you think?"

"I think that would be fine, sir," Tobias answered.

Sam rubbed his chin. "First things first. I need to find her. Can you send Beck to me? Perhaps Miss Parks has retired for the night."

It didn't seem likely, eight o'clock wasn't that late.

Beck came to him and the worried look on her face did nothing to put his mind at ease.

"Do you know where Miss Parks is?" He tried not to let panic seep into his voice, but if Emily wasn't where he'd left her, where might she be? That was the problem. She could be anywhere. She could be gone. For good. That didn't bear thinking about. "Has she retired for the evening?"

"She has not." The girl looked at her feet as she answered. "I haven't seen her either. I was hoping she was with you, sir. If you don't mind me saying so, sometimes I think she needs a bit of extra help managing things."

He looked at Beck sharply. What did the girl know? Would Emily have confided in her about her unusual situation? Quite possibly. Would Beck be one of those slaves trying to get free using the magic words? Also quite possible. He said the words over to himself again to make sure he remembered them.

"Lorska la loon romp leet le tong, Fair John, A March ee sur lee face der lumier, a un otre mo mant."

If he could only figure out what they meant then maybe everything would be clear. It certainly wasn't clear now.

For that matter, would Emily have tried again tonight? Had Beck told her the magic words? Would she have left without saying goodbye? He hated to think so, but perhaps everything that happened this afternoon was too much for her and she didn't want to see him again.

"Perhaps you should look by the pond, sir," Beck said, daring to look him in the eye.

"My thoughts exactly," he answered, not worrying about the deference that should exist between master and servant. He headed outside and managed not to break into a run until he was out of sight of the maid

But Emily wasn't by the pond. He looked into the dark water, but there was no sign that she had thrown herself in. Would there be a sign? Could she simply be gone? Gone as quickly as she had come? And if she was? Then what? He still knew he didn't love Dinah enough to marry her. But should he simply go through with it anyway, because everyone expected it? No. It wouldn't be fair to Dinah and that was the truth.

Maybe he wasn't destined to know love, real love, in any more than fleeting glimpses. It wasn't the future he wanted for himself, but he was going off to war and that wasn't the future he wanted either.

He headed toward the stable, out of habit. Even when a boy he would go to the stable to sort out his problems. If Moses couldn't solve them, just being near the horses, petting them, feeding them, often made him calmer. He repeated the magic words again, softly, under his breath, *"Lorska la loon romp leet le tong, Fair John, A March ee sur lee face der lumier, a un otre mo mant"* What meaning did they hold?

The horses were all stabled. Some were munching on hay, some sleeping. Moses, done with his work for the day, was either down by the slave cabins or asleep in the loft. Sam breathed in the earthy scent of the horses. Then he heard a sound that was different than the horses chewing or shuffling in their stalls. It was the sound of a child crying. He struck a match and lit the lantern hanging by the barn door and took it in hand, searching the hidden corners of the barn that he knew so well from his own childhood.

He found the child in an empty stall, nestled in the hay and tears running freely down her cheeks. "Hello, there," he said quietly, so as not to frighten or distress the child further. "What seems to be the problem?"

"Oh, sir, I can't be talking to you. I'll get whipped for sure." Her voice was so quiet and tremulous he wasn't sure he'd heard her right.

He squatted near the child. She was about five or six. "Dolly, is it?" he asked.

"Yes sir." She sniffled and wiped her nose on her sleeve. Sam handed her a handkerchief, and she looked at it as if it were spun gold.

"It's okay," he said, fighting the urge to smile at her hesitancy. "You can use it to wipe your nose."

"Oh, no sir." She handed it back. "It's too good."

"It's what it's for." He nodded encouragingly until she used the handkerchief in such a delicate manner that he wasn't sure it did any good at all. "Now, tell me, who is going to whip you?"

"Wilkins, sir. He's a bad man. If he knows I'm talking to you, he'll whip me for sure."

"Why?" Why on earth would the overseer have such a rule in place for such a small child? Or for anyone? This was his plantation, these were his people, he of course could talk to anyone he pleased, but why should they be afraid of repercussions?

"It's because of the lady, sir," the child said, her voice stronger and more certain now, perhaps since lightning bolts did not strike when she spoke to her master. "If she tells what happened, Wilkins will beat me for sure. He already hit me once. And if I tell, I'm sure I'll get hit."

He wanted to ask what happened, the words were on the tip of his tongue, nearly falling out of his mouth, but if the child were afraid she was going to get beat for telling him, it wasn't fair to her to ask her outright, it would only scare her more.

"Come inside with me. He stood up and held out a hand to the child. "Wilkins will not hurt you."

"He'll hurt someone else if I'm safe. That's what he told the lady."

"What lady?" He had a strong suspicion that he knew.

"I don't know her name, sir. She's new around here."

Emily. Definitely Emily.

"Come inside with me, Dolly. No one will hurt you. I'll see to that."

"But what about my little sister? Maybe she'll be hurt instead. I better stay here and not talk to you anymore."

"No one will get hurt," Sam assured her. With the

possible exception of Wilkins.

Reluctantly he got the child out of the hay and brought her into the house. There he sat her in a chair in the dining room and had Sally bring her a large glass of milk.

"What's Dolly doin' in here? She pestering you? I'm training her to be a house slave, but she's too young to do much but peel potatoes yet."

"She's not pestering me." Sam put a reassuring hand on Sally's arm. "I brought her in here so I can speak with her."

He sat down opposite the little girl. "What did the man do to the lady?"

Dolly looked left, right, up, and down, as if both hoping for an escape and to see if anyone would see her talking to the master. "He kissed her," she whispered.

Sam's back stiffened. Kissed her?

"And then he untied her and told her if she told you about it he'd whip me." She put her hand up to her face, and Sam could see the darker outline of a bruise on her cheek.

"Untied her?" Sam nearly jumped out of his chair, but he gripped the edge of the table and forced himself to remain calm. He needed to get the whole story "He had her tied up?"

"Yes, sir. Please don't tell him I told. I don't want to get whipped."

"I won't tell him you told me anything." The anger nearly burst out of him, but he had to remain calm in front of the child. He had known he couldn't trust Wilkins, but he'd left him in place anyway, and now the man had abused his guest and his slaves. He'd have none of it.

Sally hovered in the doorway, her face thunderous with anger, and Sam turned to her. "Can you find this child a place to sleep somewhere in the house for tonight, please. I do not want her going back to the cabins."

"I'll keep her safe. She will stay with me in my alcove tonight."

"Good."

"What you going to do about Wilkins?" Sally asked, her look challenging him to get it right, even as she took Dolly by the hand and started to lead her off.

"First I need to find Emily and see if she's safe. As for Wilkins, he'll be lucky if I don't kill him."

Chapter Nineteen

Emily

Emily rocked back and forth on the bench tucked away in the rose garden, hugging her arms around her and waiting for the panic and nausea to subside. When Wilkins had freed her, she'd grabbed Dolly's hand and run from the cabin. She'd gotten as far as the rose garden when the child broke free from her grasp and ran off on her own. Emily hadn't pursued her but instead found the bench and collapsed onto it. She didn't know how long she'd been sitting there, but the sun had fully set, and she was stiff and cold, and still she had no plan.

Sam had to know, but she couldn't risk telling him. Not yet, not until she knew Dolly and the other children wouldn't suffer.

What could she do, though? She obviously wasn't planning to let Wilkins abuse her in any way. What she needed to do was get the goods on him with the thefts. Then Sam would fire Wilkins and the rest of the threats wouldn't matter. First she needed proof. To get that she needed to go back into the overseer's house. And for her own safety she had to make sure Wilkins wasn't there when she did.

To do any of that she needed to leave the sanctuary of the bench. Taking a deep breath, she stood. She could do this. She had to do this. It was dark now, with only the light of the waning moon to guide her way. She stepped carefully over the stones in the path, keeping an eye on the light coming from the overseer's house. Since there was a lamp lit, she assumed he was still in there. With the only lights being live flames, she didn't imagine people left a light burning when they left the house.

Would he go out at all, or was he in for the night? Should she risk dealing with him, so she could find out what was hidden under that tarp? No. That much was clear. He would rape her, whether he got in trouble for it or not. She was pretty sure the only reason he hadn't already was that he liked keeping her in a state of fear. It was working. No. She would not allow him to control her in this way. Breathe. She had to remember to breathe.

She couldn't wait out here all night, especially if he wasn't planning to leave. She would give him ten minutes. She crept closer to the building and through the open window, she heard voices. Since he obviously wasn't listening to the TV or radio, someone was in there with him.

"That wench?" Wilkins's voice, full of derision, came clearly through the night air. "Yeah, she was here. She couldn't wait to bed me. Damn good lay she was, too. I suppose she told you I was the aggressor?"

"She hasn't told me a thing." Emily's heart skipped a beat at the sound of Sam's voice. Why was he in there with Wilkins, and who were they talking about? "I haven't seen her in several hours. As I told you I'm looking for her. But you say she was here?"

He'd come looking for her. Her shining knight to

the rescue. And what was that damn overseer telling him? Her hands clenched into fists. He said he'd slept with her. And that it was her idea? That cur! That jack ass. That… She couldn't even think of words bad enough to describe it. She needed to go in there and set the record straight.

She took two steps toward the door and stopped as the voices continued.

"She was here. Like I said. Great in bed that one. You should try her."

And then there was the sound of flesh hitting flesh and a thump and crash as someone hit the table. She didn't waste any more time but hurried into the cottage, where Wilkins was getting back to his feet.

Sam stood in a boxer's stance, ready to take him on, but she didn't like his odds. Wilkins clearly outweighed him and had a few inches on him as well. There wasn't much she could do to help. In a fight he would squash her like a bug. She could perhaps whack him on the head with a frying pan or rolling pin, but neither of those things were in evidence, and she had to act quickly.

What she could do was cause a distraction. Perhaps keep them from killing each other. She darted into the room and pulled the tarp off the things in the corner, hoping beyond hope that it really was the stolen goods and not an innocent pile of dirty clothes.

She'd been expecting perhaps a barrel of flour like she'd seen in the storehouse. What she uncovered were two crates full of wine bottles.

"What's this?" Her voice was surprisingly steady and loud considering how shaky her knees were.

Wilkins, who was about to punch Sam in the face,

stopped, nearly losing his balance.

"What the hell are you doing in here?" he snarled, at the same time Sam called out, "Emily, get out."

She ignored Sam, since she was here to help him, and concentrated on Wilkins.

"This your wine?" She hoped that if he came after her with his fists she could duck fast enough.

"That's *my* wine!" Sam's eyes narrowed and his face turned red as he glared at his overseer. "What's it doing in here?"

The two men stared at each other, the tension between them filling the room. At least they didn't seem about to kill each other yet, so that was a plus. Emily stood by the wine, the canvas cloth still in her hand, not sure what her next action should be.

"I can explain." Wilkins took a step back, most of his bluster gone.

"I'm waiting." Sam crossed his arms and tapped his foot.

"The cellar was full. I needed to store it somewhere."

"The cellar is not full." Sam didn't move, but his eyes were hard and cold.

"Though it should be," Emily said, surprised her voice sounded as steady as it did. "Based on the numbers in the ledgers. If I remember correctly, the numbers were off by about four dozen." She glanced significantly at the twenty-four bottles she'd uncovered. "Where are the rest?"

Wilkins shifted his glance quickly from Sam to Emily, his breathing labored. He gave off the impression of a trapped animal, and she knew that could be dangerous. She looked around for some sort of a weapon, should Wilkins lunge at either of them.

"Let me explain," A sheen of sweat glimmered on his forehead. He licked his lips and his eyes darted around the room. "It's not what it looks like."

"It looks like you're stealing from me." Sam took a step toward Wilkins

"Yeah. It looks like that. But that's not the case. I don't know how those bottles got there. In fact," with renewed vigor he stood straighter and pointed to Emily. "She did it. I didn't even know they were there. But she did. She put them there. She came in here earlier, seduced me, and then found a good spot to store her ill gotten gains, all in the hopes of pinning blame on me."

"What?" She could hardly believe what she was hearing. "None of that's true."

"Hush," Sam hissed and Emily glared at him. Was he not going to let her tell her side of the story? Was he going to believe this evil man over her? But when she got a good look at Sam's face, the worry seeped from her. It was clear he didn't believe a word Wilkins said.

"I'm placing you under arrest." Sam uncrossed his arms and took another step forward.

"What?" The larger man bristled. "On what grounds? I told you I didn't put those things there. It was her. How can you believe her over me? I've worked here since you were a boy. Your father trusts me implicitly."

"I can't speak for my father. I'm arresting you for theft and for assault on Miss Parks."

"Assault? What with the whip? You already lashed me for that. You can't punish me twice for the same thing, besides it was her own fault. She walked in between me and the black wench."

"You know perfectly well what I'm talking about," Sam growled.

She stared at him. Did he know? But how could he? She hadn't said a word. She hadn't even seen him, and if she had, she wouldn't have said anything. She didn't want to risk little Dolly, or anyone else, getting hurt on her account.

Wilkins shot her an evil glare, and she forced herself not to look away. He would not intimidate her. She had Sam here, on her side; she had nothing to worry about. Except that Wilkins didn't seem to be taking the news of a possible arrest easily. With a swiftness that belied his size, he lunged for Sam, grabbing him around the neck.

She reached for the closest thing she could use as a weapon, which happened to be one of the bottles of wine, and swung it at Wilkins' head with all the force she could muster. The bottle broke, spilling wine everywhere. Wilkins dropped to the floor, letting go of Sam, who righted himself, rubbing his throat.

The neck of the bottle still clutched in her shaking hands, she looked at the unconscious Wilkins. What had she done? Had she killed a man? She never even liked to squish bugs, and she thought mouse traps were terribly mean. "He isn't dead, is he?" Her voice trembled, and her words were no more than a whisper.

Sam knelt by the wine-covered overseer and held his hand in front of the prostrate man's face. "He's still breathing as far as I can tell." He stood then and took the broken bottle from her hands. "Thank you. He caught me unawares."

Her hands, now cold as ice, wouldn't stop shaking. Her knees had the consistency of wet noodles. Her vision started to go black and white and get spotty.

"I'm going to pass out," she managed to say before everything went black.

Chapter Twenty

Sam

He scooped Emily up in his arms and hurried toward the house. He needed to get her safe and cared for and then deal with Wilkins. He wasn't dead and would eventually come to. Sam had to make sure he was in control of the situation when that happened.

Emily began to stir as he passed the kitchen. "It's all right," he murmured, his face close to her hair, breathing in the scent of her. She buried her face in his shoulder and he held her a bit tighter.

"I'm so sorry." Her words were muffled against his jacket.

"You've nothing to be sorry for." Sorry? She had saved his life. In fact, she had helped him quite a bit in addition to that. He pushed open the back door to the house and bellowed for Tobias, who appeared in seconds.

"Get Beck. Sally. Anyone who can help." He carried Emily into the front parlor and placed her on the sofa. She started to sit up, but he put a hand on her shoulder. "Rest." He kept his voice quiet, but firm, and she settled back down. It would probably be better to bring her upstairs to her room, but he needed to get back to Wilkins. He kept picturing him rousing and taking off. Sam couldn't risk him being at large.

Neither he nor Emily would ever be safe if that were the case. He needed to take him into town for the law to deal with, but that would have to be tomorrow. For tonight he had to make sure he was locked up somewhere, secure and safe.

Sally bustled into the room, stopping when she saw Emily on the couch.

"She fainted. I leave her to your care." He turned to Tobias. "Come with me." He didn't wait to see if his directives would be followed, he knew they would be. He headed out, with only a quick glance at Emily. He'd be back with her once he'd taken care of Wilkins.

In a few words he told Tobias the basics of what happened. "I need a secure place to lock him up for the night."

"Smokehouse is best. Nothing being smoked right now, and the door fits securely."

"Good. Come help me with him." He picked up his pace, afraid to leave the man alone for long.

"What are you going to do about an overseer?" Tobias asked as they approached the cabin.

"I'll figure it out." He had no idea. He had to have an overseer. He couldn't even say he could fill the role himself because he had promised George he'd go off to war with him. Damn the war. Life was complicated enough without that.

Inside the cottage, which smelled strongly of a good Bordeaux, Wilkins still lay where he'd fallen. It would be rather convenient, actually, if he really were dead, except Sam didn't think Emily could cope with having killed a man. He could finish him off right here, right now. Take that knife on the table and jab it into his heart. It would be easy. Physically easy anyway. It would also be cold-blooded murder, and he didn't think he had it in him to do that.

He knew, going off to war, that he would likely have to kill someone. He knew it intellectually, but it didn't seem real, and for now, he didn't think he could kill a person, not in cold blood, someone he knew. Did that make him weak? Which was the more valiant option, to let the law have him, or to simply protect his loved ones himself?

He took a deep breath to steady himself. He was a poet, not a fighter.

On the ground, Wilkins groaned.

"Hand me that rope." Sam pointed to a coil near the door, and Tobias reached for it. "We have to get him tied up before he comes to."

Wilkins opened his eyes as Sam tied the final knot. He tried to move and cursed.

"Hell, Marshall, what you got me trussed up for?"

"I need to make sure you don't take it in your head to run off before I bring you to the law tomorrow."

"Where the hell am I going to go with my head feeling like a boulder fell on it? What the hell hit me?" His nose twitched like a rat terrier, and he seemed to become aware he was wet to the skin. "Damn. That was good wine. A shame to waste it."

"I think it was put to rather good use, myself."

"Listen, I never harmed the girl." Wilkins remained defiant, trying to ease himself up on one elbow. "I was just scaring her. I wanted to get back at you for whipping me. I didn't hurt her. You can ask her. She left me unharmed."

According to what Dolly had told him, that was true, but there are many ways to hurt a person. You don't have to injure them physically to inflict harm. Until he could talk to Emily about it and see how she fared, he wouldn't know how much damage Wilkins had done. But his attack on Emily was not the only issue.

"What else have you stolen from me?" Sam turned a kitchen chair backward and straddled it, looking down on his overseer.

Wilkins seemed to shrink slightly. "Stolen is such a harsh word."

"Can you think of one better?"

"I was looking out for myself. You didn't even notice."

"Of course I noticed." Though sadly it had taken him way too long to figure out what was going on, and even then only with Emily's help. If she could help him run this plantation they'd be unstoppable, but sadly neither of them would be here to do that.

"Untie me, Sam." Wilkins adopted a docile expression, even so far as to giving him a wide-eyed innocent look. "I'm sorry I jumped at you before, though to be honest, you hit me first. You take the wine. We'll be square. Right?"

"I don't think so." It would be easy to let things go back to how they were. But was how they were so good? Wilkins was stealing from him, and not treating the slaves fairly either, and then there was his treatment of Emily and his threats to the slave children. That could not be ignored. Sam stood and pushed the chair aside. "You are relieved of your duties here." He needed to be sure there was no confusion.

That caught Wilkins attention. "You're firing me? You'll never find anyone to replace me. Everyone is enlisting."

"That's not your concern."

He pulled the man to his feet and motioned for Tobias to grab Wilkins' other arm.

"Where you taking me?"

"The smokehouse for the night. In the morning I'll take you in to town for the law to deal with."

He steered Wilkins to the smokehouse.

"This isn't the end." Wilkins spat the words out, dropping all pretense of reasonableness.

"It could be," Sam said in what he hoped was an ominous tone. They reached the smokehouse, and Sam shoved him inside.

"Can you at least untie me?" Wilkins wheedled, adopting a pathetic tone.

Sam glanced at the slaves standing around observing. Wilkins never had any concern for their comfort, especially if they were undergoing a punishment.

"No." Sam shut and bolted the door.

"Find some strong young bucks to guard this place, will you?" he instructed Tobias. "Oh and send Marcus to me."

He wasn't leaving the smokehouse until he knew there was a guard set on it for the night.

Inside the smokehouse Wilkins shouted and cursed and kicked at the door. Keeping his hands tied had been the right choice. If he had not, the man would tear the building apart plank by plank.

Tobias returned with several strong field hands, including Marcus. Sam sized them up. They would do.

"I need a constant guard on this place overnight," he said without elaborating further. "Marcus, come with me." He led him a few yards away so they could talk privately.

"The child, Dolly, is sleeping up in the big house with Sally tonight." This was not the main thing he needed to tell Marcus, but it occurred to him that someone might be worried about the child.

A look of relief briefly passed over the slave's face. "I'll let her mother know. She was afraid she had wandered off and gotten lost. But I don't imagine that's why you wanted to speak to me in private."

"No." Sam sighed. He was not a natural manager, like his father was. "I'm going to need you to take over as overseer, starting tomorrow."

Marcus's eyes widened and Sam hastened to add, "I will pay you what I was paying Wilkins."

"I thank you kindly, sir." The man's voice was thick with emotion. "May I ask what has happened to Wilkins?"

"Right now, he's locked up in the smokehouse. Tomorrow I'm taking him to the law."

Sam knew Marcus would not ask what Wilkins had done, and he didn't feel inclined to tell him. He did not need the story of Emily's abduction and humiliation spread throughout the slave quarters.

"Make sure he doesn't get out," Sam added and headed back up toward the house and to Emily.

Emily, who had come to his aid without being asked, who had put her own safety at risk, so she could help him. He couldn't imagine Dinah ever doing that, though he never would have expected her to. The man is supposed to take the risks, not the woman. The man is the one who should come to the rescue and protect the woman, not the other way around. But yet, knowing that she had done that for him made him feel loved in a way he hadn't since he was a small child at his mother's knee.

He and Emily, they would take care of each other. That's what really being in love was about, wasn't it? He needed to see her and tell her he could never live without her.

Chapter Twenty-One

Emily

She couldn't stop shaking. Even when Sally wrapped a crocheted afghan around her shoulders. What had she done? She could go to jail for assault, or murder if he died. She hoped he didn't die. Yet, she wouldn't be terribly sad if he did. She shivered again.

Dolly had followed Sally into the room like a little duckling and now snuggled up next to Emily. "Did the bad man hurt you again?"

"No." She wrapped her arm around the child, drawing from her warmth. "I'm afraid I hurt him this time."

The little brown eyes opened wide. "Did you whip him?" the child asked in an awed whisper.

"No, I hit him over the head with a wine bottle." It was hard to admit. She was not a violent person.

Sally raised her eyebrows at that but betrayed no other emotion.

"Is he dead?" Dolly asked as matter of factly as if she were asking if dinner were ready.

Was he? Sam had said he wasn't. But what if he died since then? Could she have killed a man? But it was in self-defense. Defense of Sam anyway, that had to count for something. She started to shake again. "I don't think so." She wished she sounded more confident.

"Too bad," the little girl murmured, snuggling closer.

Sally gave an exasperated sigh and reached for the girl. "Come out of there, you pesky child. You leave Miss Parks alone now, you hear. And we don't go wishing people dead."

"Not even bad people?" Dolly looked up with big innocent brown eyes.

"Not even bad people." Sally answered, but there seemed to be a certain lack of conviction in her tone, and Emily understood her ambivalence. Would it really be so bad if Wilkins were dead?

"Now off to bed with you."

Emily wouldn't have minded having the small warm body snuggled against her for comfort, but she knew better than to interfere. Dolly climbed off the couch and obediently headed out of the room.

"You need anything else?" Sally asked, a solicitousness in her voice that was new. She had apparently softened to her since Emily had invaded her kitchen earlier tonight. "Some brandy maybe?"

"That would be nice, thank you." Emily pulled the blanket tighter around her shoulders. Where was Sam? Should she go look for him? Would he come back to her? Had she somehow messed everything up between them?

Between them. What could possibly be between them? Except, she felt a warmth deep inside when she thought of him that she didn't remember ever feeling before. What was that? It couldn't be love? Could it?

Sally placed a glass of brandy in her hand. "I'll send Beck to you."

"I don't want to be a bother." It would be nice to have someone sit with her, but she didn't want people ordered about for her benefit.

"Mister Sam wanted to make sure you are taken care of, and that's what we're going to do." She hustled out of the room.

Beck came in and stirred up the fire, pushing the wrought iron poker into the dying embers, sending up glowing sparks of light. The fire flared up and she put some wood on it to feed it.

Emily took another sip of her brandy, which had an amazing warming effect, while Beck stood by the fire, watching.

"It probably be good if you were to head on home to your own time now, don't you think?" Beck's eye were bright and eager. "There's too much trouble for you here."

Especially if the overseer died. She should go home. She wanted to go home. She kept trying. Nothing worked.

"I can be ready whenever you are. I just need time to say goodbye to my mama."

Emily was startled out of her reverie. She'd never gotten around to telling Beck how future generations might be impacted. She opened her mouth to explain, still not sure what to say, when her gaze caught on the necklace Beck wore.

She was sure Beck hadn't been wearing it before, she would have remembered. A new set of shivers went through her, and she took a gulp of her brandy.

She remembered when she had first seen that necklace, a flat round, pink and white stone with a hole in the middle and a leather thong through it, on Dayna's neck. "That's an amazing necklace, where did you get it?" she had asked.

Dayna had fingered the stone and grinned broadly. "Don't tell my mother I have it, she'd have a cow. This belonged to her great-great-grandmother Rebecca. The story goes that she had it when she was a slave, one of her few personal possessions."

Emily stared at that same necklace now, around Beck's neck. That settled it, she absolutely couldn't let Beck go to the future. If she did, Dayna and her whole family might cease to exist. There had to be another way to help her. But first, she had to try to explain.

"Beck." Emily licked her lips tasting the brandy on them, as she tried to think of how to start. "Is that short for Rebecca?"

"Not yet," Beck answered, standing tall. "It's just a short name, but I vow, if I'm ever free I'm going to call myself Rebecca, because that is a powerful dignified name."

"It is." She took a deep breath. She did not feel up to having this conversation right now. "Sit down next to me, please." She patted the seat next to her. Beck did, but with obvious hesitation, sitting on the very edge of the sofa and poised to jump up should anyone come in.

"My best friend is the descendant of slaves." Saying the words, while sitting here with an actual slave gave it all new meaning. She'd known the truth of Dayna's history for years, but had never really internalized what that meant. "She told me a story once of her great-great-great Grandmother who escaped from slavery. Her name was Rebecca, and she used nutmeg as a secret ingredient in cinnamon buns. She also had a necklace, exactly like yours. I've seen it before, around my friend, Dayna's neck."

Beck clutched at the necklace, but her face was completely still. Finally after a very long moment she said, "You think I'm her great-great-great grandmother?"

"I think so." Her voice cracked, and she cleared her throat. "I can't be sure of course, but it does seem like it." If she was wrong was she denying Beck a chance at freedom? But what if she were right?

"I can't wait to meet her!" Beck said, delight shining in her voice.

Emily took a fortifying sip of brandy. There was no easy way to say this.

"I don't think you can." A lump formed in her throat. She didn't want to destroy Beck's dreams, but she couldn't risk Dayna. "If you go forward in time before you have any children here then she won't exist."

"Oh," Beck thought about that a second and then shrugged. "Too bad for her, I guess. When can we leave?"

"Beck!" Tears pricked Emily's eyes. "I can't take you. It's not only Dayna that won't exist but her ancestors, too, and cousins. One of her uncles is a doctor who won some prize for medical advancements. You can't take all those people out of the world."

Beck's eyes widened, and she fingered the pendant around her neck. "All those people are mine?"

"They are." Perhaps she was finally getting through to her.

"And she says I escape?" The words were barely above a whisper.

"Yes." She put the brandy snifter down and

breathed a little easier. It was a relief to be able to give some good news.

"Do you know how?"

Emily stared at her blankly. How? She had never asked. How could she not have asked? But maybe Dayna didn't know. Chances were Dayna did know though, and Emily hadn't simply thought to ask.

"I don't know, I'm sorry. But I can help you, if you have ideas. I don't know enough about everything that goes on here to come up with my own plan, but I'll gladly help you if I can." She wanted to reach out and touch Beck, to comfort or reassure, like she would if it were Dayna sitting next to her, but didn't know how the action would be received, so she clutched at the blanket instead.

"So, you're saying you won't take me to the future, but you will help me escape." Beck wrung her fingers together in her lap.

Emily watched those anguished fingers, those work rough, slender fingers. Why couldn't there be easy answers to any of this? "Yes, if you want my help."

"I'd rather go to the future." She wasn't giving up on this easily.

"But, your people!" Emily tried again to get Beck to see why it wouldn't work. "You are going to have many distinguished descendants. You can't let them down."

"Tell me about these descendants of mine." Beck leaned forward, her fingers still wound tight.

What did she know about the relatives on Dayna's mother's side. She picked up the brandy snifter and had another sip while she collected her thoughts. "Okay, I said there's a respected doctor. There are also a few college professors and a journalist. There are lawyers and accountants, and I think one of Dayna's uncles was a mayor of his town for a while."

"Mayor! A black man?" Beck snorted in derision.

"Yes!" Emily needed to make sure Beck believed her. "And they are all because of you. Because you escape and start a family and teach your children how to be brave and strong and determined like you are."

Beck gave her a sideways glance. "You're laying the flattery on a bit strong, there, Miss Emily, but I get your point."

The back door opened, and the thud of boot steps sounded on the wooden floors.

Beck jumped up, smoothing her skirt. "I best be going." She hurried from the room, getting to the door as Sam came in.

He rushed to her, sitting by her side, but not touching her. She yearned for his touch but clutched her glass to keep from reaching out to him.

"Are you all right?" His voice was harsh with emotion.

"A bit shook up." She took a sip of brandy. There was definitely a soothing restorative quality to it. "I can't believe I hit him."

"I can't either." His eyes caught hers and she felt she could get lost in them. "I'm very grateful." He swallowed and broke eye contact, as if it were too much for him. "What's that you're drinking, brandy?"

"I believe so. Sally poured it for me." She hated that her voice quavered. She wanted to appear strong and independent, not weak and needy.

He got up and poured himself a glass. He stood for a moment, staring into the fire, his back to her, and she studied the lines of his body, the slim hips and shoulders, the wavy dark hair. He was not built like a fighter. What would this war do to him? A shiver ran through her, because of course, she knew what the war would do to him. It would kill him. And a very nice lady would show people his portrait hanging in the hall and say this is "Samuel Marshall, he died in the Civil War." How could she have said it with such calmness, when the very memory of the words were ripping Emily's heart out?

After a long moment, he came back and sat beside her on the sofa, not touching, but close enough that she could feel the heat emanating from him. "Tell me what happened. Earlier. With Wilkins."

She wanted to tell him, she needed to tell him, but she couldn't bring herself to look at him as she did so.

"He surprised me. I was coming from the outhouse, and he accosted me and told me I'd pay for him being whipped. Then he grabbed me and kissed me. It was horrible." Her voice broke, and she found herself reaching out to Sam. He took her hand in his large, warm one and she continued. "He tied my hands behind my back and dragged me to his house. Then he gagged me and tied my feet. I was so scared and helpless, and I've never felt so powerless before." Sam's hand tightened on hers and she took strength from him.

"Did he violate you?" His voice cracked, betraying his concern.

Violate her? Of course. He grabbed her and tied her up and gagged her and kissed her against her will, but she was pretty sure Sam meant rape.

"No. But the threat was implicit." She took a deep breath to steady herself. "He went and got Dolly and said that he could do anything to me, and if I told you about it he would punish Dolly, then he smacked her across the face so I would know he was serious. He even told me he would hurt her if I so much as spoke to you. And he said that if I found a way to protect Dolly, he'd hurt someone else. I didn't want to be the reason someone gets whipped. I really didn't!" Tears came unbidden and she had to stop.

"No one's getting whipped." He squeezed her hand. "Dolly's a brave little girl. She told me everything that she knew about what happened. That's why I was confronting Wilkins." He took her glass from her hand and placed it, with his, on the side table. He wrapped his arms around her and whispered into her hair. "Remember, none of this is your fault. Wilkins is a vile man, and if he hurts someone it's on him, not you. But he won't hurt anyone. I give you my word."

Everything would be okay. She trusted Sam on this. It was true that she didn't know him well, but this was his time and his place and now that he knew, he would make things better.

"I was so scared, Sam," she breathed the words out in relief, her mouth against the smooth linen of his shirt. "So very scared and the worst part was that if I gave into his demands and didn't tell you, you would be hurt and I didn't want that. I didn't want you to be hurt."

"Shush, it's okay now," he murmured, smoothing her hair. "You're safe with me."

She relaxed further into his arms. She was safe. She was protected.

"What are you going to do to Wilkins?" Now that she was in his arms and could relax it was time to worry about the particulars.

"For now, he's locked in the smokehouse and there is a guard outside. Tomorrow I'll take him into town and turn him over to the sheriff." He cleared his throat and added apologetically, "You may have to explain what he did to you."

"I don't mind telling about it, if it keeps him locked up." She'd rather not have to recount the incident, but she'd tell everyone if it would keep the creep behind bars. "What about an overseer?"

"I'm giving the job to one of the bucks. Marcus can do it."

"Man." She stiffened in his arms.

"What?" He moved back from her a little so he could see her face.

"Not a 'buck'," she explained. "That's what you call a deer or some other animal. I'm assuming Marcus is not a deer."

"No, but he's a negro." It was clear by his befuddled expression that he didn't see the problem at all.

"A man," she repeated. "He's a man. Call him that."

There was a pause, and she wondered if she had offended him, but then he said. "You're right, of course. I never thought of it that way before."

"Don't you think of Tobias as a man?" It was clear that Tobias was not only his valet, but one of his best friends, almost a brother.

"I think of him as Tobias, but yes, I do think of him as a man. You make me think, Miss Emily Parks, I thank you for that."

Just the romantic words she always wanted to hear from a man. She made him think. Not that it was a bad thing, but she'd like to make someone swoon instead one of these days.

He pulled her close again and whispered into her hair. "May I kiss you?"

"Please," she answered.

His mouth found hers, and she could taste the brandy he'd sipped, and a hint of tobacco. His lips were soft and his tongue, searching. It was safe and warm and exciting and not at all frightening or imposing as it had been when Wilkins forced himself on her. She wanted to melt into Sam, to become one with him. She held him tightly and his arms were wrapped around her as if he never meant to let go. As the kiss deepened, she let her hands roam his back feeling the softness of his shirt and the strength of the muscles underneath. His hands, also started to move, caressing her softly. But then Sam stopped, he took his mouth from hers and said, "I cannot take advantage of you."

"It's not taking advantage if I don't object." She could barely catch her breath to answer him.

"Just the same." Sam took a deep breath, still holding you tight. "I think you should leave."

The words were so unexpected, so hard, that she wasn't sure she heard them properly.

She pushed away from him so she could look into his face, but the anguish she saw there didn't explain anything. "Leave? But I have nowhere to go!"

"I mean"—he wiped his hand across his face—"I want to marry you."

"What?" She glanced at her glass of brandy but she was pretty sure it didn't have hallucinogenic properties. Sam suddenly knelt in front of her, taking both her hands in his. Leave here? Marry him? Her thoughts bounced around the room, not sure where to land.

"I used to be good with words." He smiled crookedly at her, his eyes holding hers and not letting go. "Emily. I can't think of anything in the world that would make me happier than to spend the rest of my life with you, but I am going off to war, and I don't know if I'll come back…"

Her face must have given something away.

"You know something, don't you?"

She shook her head, tears blurring her vision.

"Okay then, that settles it." He took a deep, steadying breath and swallowed. "I won't come back. I can't ask you to stay here, trapped in this world, this time that is not your own, when I can't be here for you. You need to go back."

"I don't even know if I can." He wanted to marry her. Did he actually say that? Was this a proposal? Was she allowed to accept or had it already been rescinded as not being practical?

"I found something out," Sam said. "It seems there's a magic spell or something. Did you say a magic spell when you came through?"

"No, but Beck told me about it," she said, not stopping to think if she shouldn't mention Beck's involvement. "I tried saying it when I went in last time. But it didn't make a difference."

"Were these the words?" Sam closed his eyes and concentrated on the what he was about to say. "*Lorska la loon romp leet le tong, Fair John, A March ee sur lee face der lumier, a un otre mo mant.*" Yes, that sounded like what Beck had said, what she had repeated when she'd stepped into the pond, but yet it sounded slightly different when he said it.

"Say that again." Now she closed her eyes and listened carefully.

He repeated the words slowly, but that didn't help.

"Say it quickly, running the words together."

He did and she opened her eyes.

"It's French!"

"What?" He looked at her in surprise. "That's not French. It's nonsense words."

"No. Listen, and she repeated it the way she had heard it the last time he said it. "*Lorsque la lune remplit l'étang/Offrez-argent/Et marcher sur les faisceaux de lumière/à un autre moment.*"

There was something about the moon and silver and time. Even as she translated it in her head, he was several steps ahead of her. "When the moon fills the pond/Offer it silver/And walk on the beams of light/to another time." He looked at her, eyes wide. "It's not a magic spell. It's instructions!"

"When the moon fills the pond," she said. "It must mean a full moon, and the moon has to be reflected in the water. It was like that the night I came."

"And silver," he said. "You were right about that."

She breathed a sigh of relief. There was a way for her to get home. But not until the next full moon. That was almost a month away.

Sam must have been thinking along the same lines, because suddenly he grabbed her hand. "Would it be wrong to marry you and have you as my wife for the next month?" The words came out as hardly more than a whisper, but this time she knew she had heard him correctly.

"No." The answer came automatically, but she'd only known him a few days. Did she want to marry someone who she barely knew and who she would be then separated from forever after? How was that really any better than hooking up with someone you met at a bar for a one-night stand? When she got married she wanted it to be real, and to be forever. But her heart ached to be with Sam. Forever. Why couldn't they have that? Why was life so unfair? "I don't know." She choked on the words, not wanting to admit any hesitation.

Sam bent his head over her hands. "It would be wrong." The words sounded strangled, as if it pained him to admit it. "But yet, I want you so badly."

She leaned over his head and whispered in his ear. "Then come upstairs with me."

His head jerked up so quickly, she was lucky they didn't collide. "You don't mean it."

Did she? She'd never done anything like this before, but she'd never been in a situation like this before, where it really felt as if there was no time. There'd always been time before to get to know someone, to develop a relationship, but not now. At the most they had until the next full moon. Maybe less if Sam had to leave with his unit. Why waste time?

He kissed her hands. "I do want you, but it wouldn't be right."

"Forget what's right. Can't we do what we want?" She couldn't believe she was suggesting it. This wasn't her at all, but maybe that was the problem, she'd never really gone after something she wanted before.

There was a small chuckle from Sam. "So very tempting, but I have not yet broken my engagement to Dinah, and I won't come to your bed unless I am free to be there."

She wanted to say 'Forget Dinah,' but the more rational part of her brain kicked in. She was not the kind of person who slept with another girl's boyfriend or fiancé. Okay, quite frankly, she was not the kind of person to sleep with anyone. No relationship ever got to the point where that felt right. Why was this different? Was it really right or was she caught up in the moment? How could a person make sure?

"Perhaps we should finish the brandy." He let go of her hands so he could stand up, retrieve the glasses, and hand her one. He sat down next to her, so close their thighs touched.

"So, am I allowed to accept your marriage proposal?" She smiled at him over the top of her glass.

His eyes opened wider in surprise. "Would you?"

"You don't think I would offer to go to bed with someone I wouldn't marry?"

He opened his mouth to speak, but no words came out.

Emily smiled at him, feeling her heart expand with love for him. "Sam, I want to be with you more than anything."

"But we can't. I'm going to war."

"Not yet." She held onto that thought like a talisman. "Not yet."

"Soon. And if I don't come back… You know I won't, don't you?"

She couldn't lie to the man she was offering to sleep with.

"The wedding I was at, before I fell though time, was here, at this house, only it was an inn and your portrait—the one in the hall—still is there and I saw it and thought how adorable you are and the woman who runs the place said 'That's Samuel Marshal. This used to be his house. He died in the Civil War.' "

Next to her a shiver run through Sam's body. "That's that then."

"Maybe not." She wanted more than anything for it to not be true. "Perhaps the lady was wrong. I mean, maybe that's the story that got handed down, but it didn't really happen."

"There's no way to know." His voice was thick, and she hated that she'd ever let him know what she'd heard. Maybe it would have been better to let him have hope. But hope didn't have to be completely gone.

"There's no way to know if anyone going into battle is going to survive. But you might. It could happen." How many times were lists wrong or bodies not properly identified? Anything was possible. They couldn't give up hope.

Sam shook his head and there was a certain finality to the set of his jaw. "I will not have you wait here for me on the very small possibility that I might survive. I'll be able to rest easier if I know you are safely back in your own time where you belong."

The thing was she had no objection to going to her own time, she just didn't want to leave Sam, but he was leaving her soon regardless. She took a sip of her brandy. He wrapped one arm around her and she relaxed into him.

"You know." There was hope in his voice, as if he'd reached a conclusion he liked. "It might be for the best if we do get married."

"Really?" She craned her neck so she could look into his face and he smiled at her.

"If you can't get home again, which is a possibility

we have to consider, and you were married to me you'd have the protection of the plantation and my family. It would keep you safe."

As safe as anyone could be in a war zone, Emily thought. As much as she didn't want to think of the possibility of not being able to get home, he was right.

"Would you do that? Marry me to keep me safe?" She snuggled close, feeling so loved and protected it was almost scary.

"Not only that. I want to spend forever with you, and if forever is only a month, well then, we'll spend a month together."

"A month won't be nearly enough." When she thought of forever, she always thought of it lasting more than a few short weeks.

"If it's all we have, then it's plenty." There was confidence and cheer in his voice again. They would find a way to make this work. "Tomorrow I'll get things sorted with Dinah, and write to my parents, they'll want to be here of course."

"For what?" she asked and took another sip of brandy.

"The wedding of course."

"Wedding."

Now why when they talked about being married had she not considered a wedding? She rather imagined that they would go out in a forest glade, perhaps by the waterfall and take each other's hands and promise themselves to each other, after all they didn't have time to plan a wedding. But, of course if it were to be official and help her should she need it there would have to be things done properly. And of course his parents would be there. A small pang pierced her heart. Her parents wouldn't be here. Or Dayna. How could she get married and not have Dayna by her side? How could she not have her father walk her down the aisle?

"What's wrong?" He peered into her eyes, his forehead wrinkled in concern.

"My family. They can't be at the wedding. I always thought they would be with me when I got married."

He hugged her tighter. "There's really not much we can do about that, but if you'd rather not get married…" he let the words trail off.

"I want to," she insisted. "I do. I guess I have to adjust my expectations." Then she remembered that he had lost one fiancée to sickness and would soon have to go fight in a war that he didn't want. Hers were not the only expectations that needed to be adjusted.

She was taking a crazy leap here, but it didn't feel crazy at all.

Chapter Twenty-Two

Sam

Tobias brought him a cup of coffee along with the shaving things in the morning.

"No time." Sam was already pulling his pants on and adjusting the braces over his shoulders. "I've got to get Wilkins to town before anything happens." He grabbed the cup and took a few quick gulps. That would have to do him for now. "Have Moses hitch up the wagon," he instructed and headed out the door.

The sun was barely over the horizon as he stepped outside into the cool morning air. The grass was wet with dew and the air smelled fresh and full of promise. Once he got Wilkins to town he could relax and think about the other tasks he needed to accomplish today. Not that the other tasks were much more pleasant. He rather wished he hadn't promised to enlist with George, and Dinah was not going to be happy at all to have him break the engagement.

Today was really a day better spent in bed, despite the promising glow of the early morning.

The one good thing he had to look forward to was spending time with Emily. How she had managed to steal his heart in such a short time he might never know, but he did know that he hadn't felt like this about someone since Anna. That had to mean something.

He approached the smokehouse, and there was no one standing guard. His shoulders tensed, and he clenched his fists. Perhaps there was a perfectly logical explanation. Most likely the slaves had to get out to the fields. They all started their day early. That had to be it. And besides, the smokehouse was locked tight, and Wilkins was tied up. What difference could it really make if someone stood outside the door or not?

He slid back the bolt on the door and peered inside. He didn't see much before a punch to the jaw laid him flat on his back. Wilkins leaped over him and ran. Sam jumped up to chase him, but his head swam and his vision was full of spots. He closed his eyes momentarily to settle the spinning in his head. When he opened them, Wilkins was already out of sight, and Sam couldn't be sure which direction he had gone.

Damn. Damn. Damn.

Marcus and some of the other slaves came running toward him.

"Where was the guard?" Sam sputtered. "Which way did he go? Did you see?"

"Into the woods." Marcus pointed to where leaves still rustled in the wake of the fleeing man. "Want me to chase him down?"

Sam tried to make his mind work logically. Of course it would be nice to have someone else chase Wilkins down, but that wasn't likely to end well. Besides, he'd made Marcus the overseer, which meant he had a job to do this morning.

"No. Run up to the stable and tell Moses to saddle Echo. I'll stand a better chance of catching him on horseback."

Within minutes he was seated on his horse and

heading in the direction he hoped Wilkins had gone. He spurred his horse to go faster and faster, ignoring brambles and branches that smacked him in the face and arms as he careened down the path. After fifteen minutes of hard riding, he had to admit that he would have caught up with him had Wilkins actually gone this way.

He pulled his panting horse to a halt. There was little to no way to find him, wandering blindly around the woods, especially when there was no guarantee he'd even gone this way to start with. But he needed to protect Emily from him. Right now, Wilkins might be back at the house causing problems. That thought alone was enough to make him turn Echo toward home and gallop back nearly as quickly as they had left.

Moses met him by the stable.

"Did he come back here?" Sam demanded, gulping for breath.

"No sign of him, Mister Sam."

That was good. His heartbeat started to come back to normal; it became easier to breathe. Wilkins wasn't here, but he didn't know where he was, and until he did, he could not rest easy. "I'm going in to town to alert the sheriff. You get Tobias to keep an eye on Miss Parks. I don't want her left alone."

Sam turned once more, urging his indefatigable horse into town. He scanned the roadside as he rode, hoping to catch a glimpse of Wilkins, but he saw nothing before getting to town. He dismounted in front of the large brick building that served as courthouse and jail and tied Echo to the hitching post.

He took the marble steps two at a time and once inside strode quickly to Sheriff Fallow's office.

The sheriff, a friend of his father, who had spent many evening at Bonne Terra, looked up when he walked in. The older man smiled. "What can I do for you, Sam? I trust your father is well."

"My father is fine, thank you," Sam answered, eager to be done with the pleasantries and get to business. "But I have a problem." As succinctly as he could, he laid out the situation for the sheriff, not even bothering to drop into the seat that sat empty opposite the sheriff's desk.

Sheriff Fallow listened carefully, steepling his fingers as he took in the information.

"Do you have proof of his stealing?" He sat back in his chair and idly picked up a paper knife.

"I do," Sam answered. "At least I have proof that the numbers in the ledgers don't add up, but that what he was hiding under tarps in his cabin goes a long way to making up the numbers. Seems fairly conclusive."

"Perhaps," Fallow said, tapping the knife on the table. "But you don't have proof he put it there, do you? Could have been one of the slaves."

Sam said nothing. He supposed that Wilkins could say that in his defense, and what proof would Sam have that he was lying? None.

"There's more." He hadn't wanted to bring up the assault on Emily. He preferred to leave her out of this, but if he wanted Fallow to take the situation seriously, he would have to tell him everything.

Fallow's frown deepened while Sam told his story.

"Very serious allegations." Fallow still fiddled with the knife.

"They are." Sam wanted to snatch the knife from his hands, to make him understand how urgent this matter was.

"Hard to prove." Fallow used the knife to scratch the back of his neck.

Sam wanted to scream at him. What would Fallow consider proof? If he'd seen it for himself. He gripped the back of the chair in front of him and fought to keep his voice calm. "There's a witness."

"A slave child." Fallow raised one eyebrow to show what he thought of that witness. "You know full well that no judge is going to admit the evidence of either a slave or a child. Or a woman," he added softly.

Sam tapped his foot in frustration. "I need to make sure he stays away from Miss Parks."

"Certainly you can keep her safe." The sheriff finally put down the knife.

"I've agreed to enlist. I don't know how long I'll be around." Even saying the words were difficult. This would all be hard enough without the damn war.

"But this Miss Parks, certainly she won't be around here much longer, she'll be returning to her family."

"I'm going to marry her," Sam blurted out, surprised at how good it felt to share his secret.

Fallow's eyebrows jumped up. "But Miss Johnson…"

Sam dropped into the chair. "It's a long story," he said. "The thing is that I don't know if I'll be around to protect her."

"Sam," Fallow said, his tone paternal, "let me give you some advice. Send Miss Parks home. Don't marry Miss Johnson if you don't feel so inclined, but send Miss Parks home. When this war is over, which God-willing won't last long, you can sort out what you want to do. But Miss Parks needs to be with her people. They will protect her from Wilkins."

If only it were that simple.

"You may be right." It was easier to agree than to explain why he was so very wrong. "But what about Wilkins?"

"I'll keep an eye out for him. I'll bring him in if I see him, but I want you to be prepared that the charges may not stick."

Sam rubbed his hand over his face, feeling the stubble on his chin because he'd not shaved this morning. His stomach rumbled, because he'd forgone breakfast. And all for what? Nothing. Wilkins had gotten away and might never have to pay for what he'd done.

He sighed and stood. "I thank you for your time."

"Sam, I don't mean to discourage you. I'm being realistic. If we find him, we will do everything we can to make sure justice is done."

"Of course." Sam wasn't entirely certain he believed that. "Thanks. I appreciate it."

He walked back outside, unsatisfied with how the morning had gone. He untied his horse. He should go home and get cleaned up and eat something, and then he could see Dinah and explain to her that they were not meant to be. He should do that, but he was already most of the way to the Johnson place now, and really, why put off the inevitable? Perhaps the news that he was breaking their engagement would be easier for her to take if he wasn't well-groomed when he did it.

He mounted Echo and headed toward his next unpleasant task.

Even as he stood on the front porch waiting to be given entry to the house, he had no idea what to say.

Dinah was a sweet girl, really she was. She deserved someone who could truly love her. Maybe that was the best way to bring the subject up. He was shown into the parlor, and he paced the room, staring at objects and paintings he'd seen dozens of times, but not really seeing them this time, as he waited for Dinah to appear.

"Sam! What a pleasant surprise," she trilled from the doorway.

He turned to her and wanted to smile but found he couldn't. She was beautiful, that much was true, and her dress was stylish and fit perfectly, but she wasn't Emily and never could be.

"I've been so busy making plans for the wedding. Do you think our ballroom is better suited to the dance, or should we have it at Bonne Terra? Papa would be sad if he thought he could not send me off in style, but it wouldn't do to squash the guests."

Sam shook his head, momentarily voiceless.

"What's the matter?" Dinah came forward and took his hand. "Has something happened? You look positively morbid! Is it your parents, or Elizabeth?"

"They're fine." The words sounded strangled. This was going to be much more difficult than he'd imagined.

"Have you already gone and enlisted. Do they want you right away? Is that the problem?"

"Dinah," he said firmly, putting an end to her babbling. "It's not going to work. I could never make you happy."

She frowned, her brows coming together in confusion. "Don't be silly, you already make me happy."

"No." He needed to make her understand. "You

need someone who can love you like you deserve to be loved."

"And you can't?" she choked on the words.

He shook his head hating the pain he saw in her eyes. He hadn't wanted to hurt her, even though he knew that would be inevitable.

She pulled her hand back from his. "Is it still Anna holding you back, or the mystery girl, Miss Parks?"

He ran his hand through his hair. Anna. If it were still Anna it would be so much easier. She'd understand that. Everyone did. They pitied him, even as they urged him to move on. But it wasn't Anna. Finally he felt free of her. It was Emily, but how could he tell this to her? It would be better if she thought it was the ghost of his first love she couldn't compete with, instead of a woman he'd just met. He swallowed hard and looked at the ground. He couldn't meet her eye. She read the answer on his face even as he tried to keep it from her.

"The mystery girl, I see." She turned from him and studied a shepherdess statuette on the shelf

"It really has nothing to do with her," Sam said, although he didn't think he sounded at all convincing.

She spun around to face him, tears in her eyes. "Doesn't it?"

He took a deep breath. There was no going back now.

"You deserve better. You deserve someone who can love you whole heartedly."

Dinah blinked back her tears and held her chin up proudly. "You're right. I do." Her voice was firm and surprisingly in control. "Thank you, Sam, for being honest in your deficiencies in that regard. I suppose I ought to go inform my mother. You can see yourself out?"

He bowed respectfully to her and didn't try to say anything else. Everything that could be said had been, and anything else would make things more difficult.

His heart was heavy as he left the house, knowing that he had hurt her. He mounted Echo and headed toward home. He had one more unpleasant task to accomplish today. He had to enlist in the army, but that could wait until he had eaten something.

Was he a weakling or a coward since he didn't relish the idea of going off to war? George and some of the others seemed so excited at the prospect it made him wonder if there were something wrong with him. Shouldn't a man want to fight for his family and country? That is exactly why he would sign up, because ultimately it did come down to fighting for his family and country.

For Emily.

His face relaxed into a smile as he thought of her. His future wife.

Was he crazy to marry her? He barely knew her, and her story and background were almost impossible to believe, but he did believe her, and he had not felt like this about someone since Anna. He couldn't let her slip away. Though, he sighed, he supposed she would. She would go to her own time, and he would go to die in battle. That was still hard to believe. He couldn't imagine himself not existing a short time from now. But he thought she was wrong. He would survive, and he also thought she'd still be here when he got back. Some part of him refused to believe that she would actually be able to return to her own time, assuming she had come from another time at all.

Despite all evidence to the contrary, he couldn't picture anything but a happily-ever-after for them, living at Bonne Terra.

Chapter Twenty-Three

Emily

Emily sat on the porch, waiting for Sam to come back. She twisted her fingers around in her lap. If she could lose herself in a book, it would help the time go faster, but she couldn't. She couldn't think of anything except that Tobias had told her Wilkins got away and Sam went after him.

"Why didn't you go with Sam?" she had asked, picturing the bigger man pulverizing her beloved.

"He told me to stay and watch over you," Tobias answered, and she detected a bit of resentment, as if he'd rather be with Sam instead of guarding her.

Even now he sat on the porch steps, idly whittling, while constantly scanning the area for danger.

Little Dolly came out on to the porch carrying a tray nearly as big as she was. "Would you like lemonade, miss?" Emily hurried to take the pitcher and glass from the child. She placed it on a small table and poured a glass of lemonade and handed it to Dolly.

Dolly's eyes grew wide, and she took a step back. "No, miss, that's for you!"

"Have it," Emily insisted, holding the glass out to the child.

Dolly's serious face broke into a grin, and she glanced around to be sure no one was about who would chastise her and took the glass.

"Thank you, miss."

"How are you this morning?" Emily studied the little face. There did seem to be a bruise on her cheek, but it wasn't as bad as she had feared.

"Fine, miss. My face don't hurt hardly at all anymore. Is the bad man really gone?"

"He is," Emily assured her and tried not to think about the fact that they didn't know where he had gone, and they didn't know if he'd be back. There was no reason for little Dolly to worry more than she had to. "You were very brave yesterday."

"I was plum scared." Dolly clutched the lemonade glass in both hands.

Emily leaned toward the girl in the threadbare dress. "I'll tell you a secret, so was I."

The girl turned her big dark eyes, open wide with wonder, to Emily. "I didn't think white folks ever got scared."

"All the time," she assured her. "All the time. How's the lemonade?"

Dolly took a tentative sip and then her smile grew wide and she took another, longer drink. Finally, she licked her lips and smiled up at her. "It's like maybe what heaven tastes like, don't you think?"

She had never thought about what heaven tasted like, though she had described certain flavors of ice cream as heavenly from time to time, but she supposed that tart and sweet and cold and refreshing was nearly a perfect drink. Why shouldn't heaven be like that?

The distinctive sound of clip clopping hoof beats came down the street. Tobias stood, putting aside his whittling, but keeping his little knife in his hand. She rushed to the edge of the porch and strained to see down the drive, hoping this was Sam coming back, but the person who came into view was George.

"Hello." He swept his hat off in a grand gesture as he came to a stop before the house. "Go fetch your master, little one," he instructed Dolly and then turned back to Emily. "You look ravishing this morning, Miss Parks."

"Thank you." She knew he was flattering her; she couldn't possibly look ravishing. Not after what happened last night. She was operating on way too little sleep, and no make up. "And Sam isn't here." She put a restraining hand on Dolly who'd looked up at her with questioning eyes, not quite sure how to follow the directive she'd been given.

"Not here? But he knew we were going to go into town to enlist today."

"I know." She hated the fact that Sam was going to enlist, especially since she knew how it would end. "But he had some business he had to take care of first."

"He had to catch the bad man first," Dolly piped up, and Emily was unable to repress a smile. Small children were the same regardless of the century they grew up in.

"What bad man? What's been going on here?" George looked back and forth between Dolly and Emily, as if trying to decide who was likely to give him a better answer. Finally, he settled on Emily, one eyebrow quirked in query.

"Come on up and have a glass of lemonade," Emily said and turned to Dolly. "Go get a glass for Mr. Phelps, please." Dolly scampered off, and George dismounted.

"You didn't go with Sam?" George handed the reins to Tobias.

"No, sir. He told me to stay here with Miss Parks. In case." He led the horse to the stable.

"In case of what?" George directed his question to Emily. "What's going on, Miss Parks?"

Emily wasn't sure how much Sam wanted to tell George, for that matter, she wasn't sure how much she wanted George to know about what happened yesterday, but clearly she had to tell him something.

"It's Wilkins, the overseer,"

George nodded impatiently. "I know who he is." In a couple of long strides, he was beside her on the porch.

Of course he did. She was the newcomer here.

"He…" There was nothing for it but to say it. "He's been stealing from Sam, and he attacked me yesterday and Sam fired him and was going to bring him to the law this morning, but he escaped. He went to try to find him."

George looked properly horrified by this news. He took her hands in his. "My dear Miss Parks, were you injured?"

"I'm fine." She gently tried to take her hands back from him, but he had rather a firm grip and she didn't want to be rude.

"I'm so glad." He gazed into her eyes with a sincerity that was touching. "I always knew that man couldn't be trusted. Do you think I should go try to find him, to help Sam?"

She really didn't know. Had Sam caught up with Wilkins and if he did, where were they? Did he need help, or was everything under control? If George went to help him, where would he even go, where was Sam?

What she wouldn't give to simply be able to text him right now and find out what was going on.

Dolly came back with the glass and poured the lemonade. She held it out for George and he had no option but to let go of Emily's hands so he could take the glass. At the same time, the sound of hoof beats came to them on the spring breeze.

"That must be him now." Relief flooded through her that he had made it back safely. How would she ever manage when he went off to war? Of course, she wouldn't be here, she'd be back home. It all seemed impossible.

Sam came into view, whole and alive, and she couldn't stop the smile that spread across her face at the sight of him.

"In love with him, are you?" George's mouth turned up at the edges into a crooked smile, even while his eyes looked sad.

She nodded.

George sighed. "Story of my life. In my next life, I'm picking an ugly best friend."

All she could do was smile at that. In truth, she understood the feeling. People were always falling in love with her friends, especially Dayna. Not that it mattered because Dayna had been devoted to Johnson for years, but that didn't stop every guy they met from being infatuated with her.

Sam gave Emily a searching look, as if to see how she was holding up. She smiled reassuringly at him, and he grinned back, melting her heart before turning to his friend. "I had to take care of some things this morning. I hope I didn't keep you waiting long."

"I was early." George put the glass down and stuck

his hands in his pockets "Miss Parks said you had a bit of trouble with Wilkins."

Sam shot Emily a look that seemed to ask 'how much did you tell him?'

"I told him he attacked me."

Sam nodded. "He attacked her, threatened her, tried to blackmail her. Stole from me as well. I can't have that here."

"Of course not." George leaned against the porch railing. "Did you find him?

Sam shook his head. "No sign of him, but I spoke with the sheriff, and he'll keep an eye out. If he's spotted, he'll be arrested."

Emily's heart sank. She didn't want to have to worry about Wilkins appearing out of the woodwork, there was enough to worry about.

"What are you doing about an overseer?" George took his hands out of his pockets and crossed his arms.

"I put Marcus in charge," Sam said.

"I wonder what your father will think of all this."

"I plan to write to him today." He gave Emily a significant glance.

She was rather amazed that already she could interpret his looks. He'd broken it off with Dinah, and they were now free to get married. That letter would not only include information about Wilkins and Marcus, but tell his parents about his engagement to Emily. How would they react? Did they particularly like Dinah? That aspect of things hadn't occurred to her before. How many people's lives were they messing up as they worried about making themselves happy? And was it worth it? But she looked at Sam and her heart overflowed with happiness, so she tended to think it was.

"Are you ready to go?" George asked, moving away from the railing and looking like he was prepared to spring into action.

Sam broke his gaze with Emily and looked at George as if he couldn't remember why he was there.

Emily wasn't ready for him to do that, but it wasn't up to her.

"Not yet. I need to clean up and eat something and Moses has to hitch up the buggy." He took a step toward the front door.

George rolled his eyes. "Oh, I forgot you wanted to make this a regular outing."

"It will not interfere with our plans. We'll simply escort Miss Parks and Beck to Mrs. Barnes' dressmakers before we meet up with Yuengling."

Sam turned to little Dolly, "Go fetch Beck." The child darted off, and he took hold of Emily's hand. "Are you ready?"

"As soon as you are." Was he talking about getting married or buying dresses? It didn't matter; she was ready for either. "What dresses will I need?"

"I would think an everyday dress, a visiting dress and a ballgown, which would double as your wedding dress, would be sufficient for now."

"Wedding dress?" George's voice cracked on the word wedding.

Sam did not let go of Emily's hand but squeezed it a little harder as he turned to his friend. "Yes, I spoke to Dinah, and we've ended our understanding. Emily and I plan to be married before we go off to war."

George looked at them blankly as if the words didn't make any sense to him.

"But you just met her," he sputtered.

"Sometimes that's how life works," Sam said with a small shrug. "I haven't been this happy since Anna."

"If that's the case, then I'm all for it." He smiled and bowed to Emily. "Welcome to the family, so to speak."

She grinned back at him. "Thank you."

Sam went inside to freshen up and get some nourishment, and fifteen minutes later they were ready to go. Beck joined them, and Moses brought the two-passenger buggy out from the stable. Sam helped Emily and Beck into it and then handed the reins to Beck. "You've driven this before, right?"

"Yes, sir," she answered.

He mounted his own stallion, and soon their small party was on their way into town.

Emily rather wished she were riding side by side with Sam instead of Beck in the little buggy, but at the same time, the trip fascinated her. She'd been on this road going into town the other day but had been too dazed to pay much attention. In her time it was lined with subdivisions and shopping malls. Now it was fields and orchards and woods with an occasional house set far back from the road. She would almost believe she was really in a different place entirely, except that every now and then she recognized something. That house there was a big doctor's office now. The church on the corner was now an Italian restaurant, or would be, rather. Tenses were hard to keep track of.

They turned onto Main Street. A street she knew as filled with cute shops and cars parked up and down both sides of the street. Now there was a large courthouse at the end of the street, wooden sidewalks, and shops like milliners, feed and seed and dry goods. It was a far cry from modern coffee houses and drug stores.

Beck stopped the buggy in front of a shop with a painted sign proclaiming it Mrs. Barnes Dressmaker, and Sam dismounted and helped the girls down. He addressed Beck. "I trust you know what she needs and will make sure it is ordered. Have them bill everything to me."

"Yes, sir." Beck nodded in agreement.

Sam grasped Emily's hand. "We'll be down the road at the grange building. We'll meet you out by the carriage. You will be safe here. Even if Wilkins is in town, he wouldn't approach you with other people around." That was a bit reassuring anyway. Sam mounted again and he and George headed down the street to sign up for their fate and she went into the dressmaker's to be properly dressed for hers.

They were greeted by a plump little woman, her hair tucked primly under a cap which incongruously had pins sticking through the edge. It reminded Emily of her father's favorite fishing hat and the fishing flies he would stick to it until needed.

"Who have we here, Beck? Where is Miss Elizabeth?" the little seamstress asked.

"Miss Elizabeth is with her parents in Frederick," Beck answered, keeping her eyes on the ground with a deference that Emily imagined must be hard to keep up. "This is Miss Emily Parks. She's going to marry Mister Sam and needs two day dresses, a Sunday dress, and a ball gown, as soon as possible."

Emily realized Beck added a dress to the order, but Sam had said to make sure she got what she needed, and in reality, only four dresses didn't seem nearly enough to get through life, not if that was what you were supposed to wear every day.

"I thought I heard Mister Sam was marrying that Johnson girl, the one with the curls."

"Yes, ma'am, he was going to, but things changed," Beck answered. "Do you think you can make Miss Parks some dresses, right quick?"

"I'm certain I can." She crooked her finger, signaling Emily. "Come around back, and we'll get your measurements." Beck came too and helped her out of the brown dress, the petticoats, the hoops and even the corset. Emily felt almost naked standing in front of Mrs. Barnes in nothing but her chemise and bloomers.

With a deftness that belied her plumpness, Mrs. Barnes wrapped the tape measure around Emily's hips, her waist and finally her bust hmmming and muttering to herself the whole time.

"A lovely shape you have," she said, "not so starved in the middle as some of the young ladies. You're a girl who likes her food."

Her face burned. It's not like she was fat or anything, but she would agree she wasn't the skinniest twig in the bundle.

"Don't be ashamed; it's good to be healthy. But you need a new corset. One that works better with your shape." The dressmaker rooted around on the shelves behind her and pulled one out and handed it to Beck.

It didn't look any different than the first one as far as she could tell, but when Beck tied it up as tightly as she could, Emily could still breathe. She didn't feel quite as stifled.

Mrs. Barnes pulled out another hoop. "That one is

last year's model, the newer ones are easier to maneuver," she explained as Beck fastened Emily into it. The brown dress was slipped back over her head, and they moved from behind the screen.

Mrs. Barnes put fashion pictures in front of Emily. "You can have this kind of neckline, or this is another popular style. Wide sleeves are essential."

Words swirled around her. She didn't understand these fashions. She didn't know what she liked or would look good in. Her mind drifted back to bridal shopping with Dayna. They'd gone to dozens of shops. Dayna must have tried on hundreds of gowns, and in each place they were petted and made much of and Dayna looked like a queen. Her own wedding gown was apparently going to be a ball gown in rose silk with hoop skirts and lots of lace. Not exactly the kind of dress she pictured herself wearing to her wedding. But then again, this was hardly going to be the kind of wedding, or marriage, that she had ever imagined.

Decisions had to be made regarding necklines, sleeves, decorations on the skirt, type of material, color, for each of the dresses. She was overwhelmed, but Mrs. Barnes, while asking for input always answered her own questions and soon was satisfied with the four dresses she planned to make.

Finally, Mrs. Barnes assured them that the first of the dresses would be ready in less than a week. She handed Beck the package containing the discarded hoop and corset, and they went out to the carriage to wait for Sam and George to come back.

"I wish I could have fancy dresses sometimes," Beck said with a touch of wistfulness as she stowed the bundle in the wagon. "I suppose all those frills and fripperies wouldn't be too practical as I worked."

"I don't imagine they're practical for anyone, but they do make a person not stand out quite so much."

"My thoughts exactly," Beck said with an emphasis that caught her attention.

She cocked her head and gave the other woman a questioning look.

"If it should come that you do decide to help me get away, a nice, fashionable dress could certainly make things easier," Beck said, not quite meeting her eyes.

Emily smiled. It certainly would.

A shadow fell over them and she looked up, expecting to see Sam and George. Instead it was the gorgeous, petite blonde Sam had been engaged to until this morning. Emily glanced around for some means of escape. Encountering Dinah was way down low on her list of things she wanted to do today. There was nothing short of running down the street, and in these clothes, she knew she wouldn't get far.

"Man-stealing hussy," Dinah hissed at her.

She wanted to defend herself, but from Dinah's point of view she could see how it might look that way. Okay, frankly from anyone's point of view it might look that way.

"I didn't mean for it to happen." The explanation sounded weak even as the words left her mouth.

"Who are you really? Why are you here with nothing? Why have you no people? What do you want from Sam? Bonne Terra?" Dinah fired the questions at her.

"No. I want nothing. I just… I love him." It was insufficient, but what more was there to say, really?

"Ha! Why? He's a fickle dreamer who will never

amount to much."

Her back stiffened. "Then why did you want to marry him?"

"Because Bonne Terra is destined to be mine. That's why. And you will not stand in the way."

If all this girl wanted was the plantation, she didn't deserve Sam. "I'm not sure what you can do about it. Sam knows his own mind."

"He only thinks he does. And what's more, his father has some say in what happens to the plantation. I'll get my way. You can count on it."

"Good luck to you." Emily's voice was cold and hard. She'd never let that bitch win.

Chapter Twenty-Four

Sam

Sam stood quietly, hands behind his back, while his father paced back and forth across the study, haranguing him. He had been quite surprised when his father showed up at dinnertime. He'd only sent the letter yesterday explaining that he had ended his agreement with Dinah and would be marrying Miss Parks. His father had wasted no time.

"You don't know anything about her," his father repeated for perhaps the twelfth time. "You don't know her parents or her background or even where she lives."

The things he did know, he did not feel comfortable telling his father.

"I had a telegram from Dinah saying you were being taken in by a charlatan, that Miss Parks was not what she said and is simply after the estate."

"It's not true." Heat rushed to his cheeks. How dare Dinah interfere in that way? "Emily is not after Bonne Terra. That is not what interests her. Dinah is simply angry at my breaking our engagement."

"As well she might be." His father waggled a finger at him accusingly.

Sam shrugged. True, Dinah did have reason to be unhappy but he wasn't the man for her and they both knew it.

"You had a perfectly good arrangement with the Johnsons," his father continued. "Your marriage would double the size of the land you owned. It was advantageous on all sides. What does a union with this woman bring you?"

"Love." What more was there to say than that, really?

His father stopped pacing and sighed. "Sam, lust and love are not the same thing."

"I said nothing about lust." He struggled to keep his voice calm. "I do not love Dinah. I never have."

"And you love this Miss Parks?"

"I do."

His father wiped his hand over his face.

"How could you possibly? You don't know her."

"I know her well enough."

"Did you get her pregnant?"

"No!" He wondered if he could get away with pouring himself a glass of whiskey about now; he could use it.

"Because if you did, you don't have to feel obligated to marry her, a nice financial settlement will take care of everything, and you can go ahead and marry Dinah."

"You're not listening to me, Father." He took a step forward and rested his hands on the back of the red leather wing chair. "First of all, I am not a child who can be directed. I am a grown man, about to go off to war, and I know my feelings. I do not love Dinah, have never loved Dinah. You knew that. Even when I agreed to marry her, everyone knew that I didn't love her."

"Love will come." His father stopped pacing and faced him, arms crossed.

"Love is already there with Emily," Sam shouted. He took a deep breath to calm down. "I love her, Father. I haven't felt this way since Anna. I know it's real." Why did no one believe him when he said he loved Emily? True he hadn't known her long, but how long did it take to fall in love?

Now it was his father's turn to sigh. Invoking Anna's name may have been the winning move here. No one had ever been in any doubt how he felt about Anna.

"But you don't know her." He waved a hand helplessly in the air.

"I know enough." He knew she was kind and smart and beautiful. He knew that when he was with her time seemed to have no meaning.

"Where is she from?" His father leaned against his desk, arms crossed.

"I don't know." He assumed she was local, but that would only raise more questions from his father that he really couldn't answer right now.

"Who are her parents?"

"I don't know." He could answer that they were Mr. and Mrs. Parks, but that wasn't what his father wanted to know. He wanted to know what her father did. He wanted to know if they had money. He wanted to know if they would be accepted into their social circles. Sam didn't think it was worth pointing out that it didn't matter, because they would never come here, never try to infiltrate their society in any way.

"Are they rebels or union?"

Considering what she had told him, he felt fairly confident answering this question. "Union. Definitely Union."

"That's something anyway. How do you know insanity doesn't run in her family?"

"I don't." He wasn't at all certain it didn't run in his. He seemed to remember a great uncle who could best be described as odd.

"What if she is after your money?" His father caught his eye and held it as if he'd played the winning card.

"She's not." Sam didn't break eye contact. "But if she is, she can have it."

His father began pacing again. "You are not being reasonable!"

"I'm being perfectly reasonable. I am going to marry Emily Parks as soon as possible."

"That's another thing. Why the rush?" His father turned to face him once more.

"Because in three weeks I report for duty with Yuengling's outfit. I need to be married before then."

"Why? So that the plantation can go to her if you don't come back? Go to someone we don't know? Go to someone who might destroy all our work?" His father ran his hands through his hair and shook his head.

Sam understood his father's frustration, but he wished he could get him to see that there was nothing to worry about. At least not on that score.

"Alter your will father. Don't leave the plantation to me until you are sure I will survive and come back. I don't care and she doesn't care, but I do have a favor to ask you."

His father arched one graying eyebrow at that.

"As you've pointed out, she has no one near to protect her. By marrying her I am offering her not only my protection but that of the family. You will take care of her, won't you, until I come back?"

His father went to the sideboard, poured a glass of whiskey, handed it to Sam, and then poured one for himself.

"Why are you marrying her, son?" He sounded tired, and drank half his glass before speaking again. "Is it because she needs protection? Because she is a good tumble? Is she blackmailing you? What's going on? The truth."

Sam gulped back two-thirds of the glass at once, which maybe wasn't the best idea, but it kept him from screaming at his father over the ridiculous notion that he would upend his whole life because some girl was good in bed.

"I have not bedded her." He struggled to keep his voice even and calm. "She is not blackmailing me. She does need my protection, it is true, but I could offer that without benefit of marriage. I love her. And I am going to marry her. In less than three weeks."

"But you'll have no time together before you go off to war. She will be married to a cipher, a person she doesn't even know, and so will you, what good will that do either of you?"

"She will have the protection of my name and family." This was the most important point. It was true they would not have much time as husband and wife, but if she were still here, she needed to be protected. It couldn't be stressed enough.

"She would have that anyway, Sam." His father sounded more angry than exasperated at this point. "We are not monsters. If this person is important to you, you don't have to marry her to ensure that we will see to her safety when you can't be here."

"I'm going to marry her." This time it was his turn to catch his father's eye and not look away. This was not up for discussion, and he hoped his father would realize that.

His father sighed, drained his glass, and poured himself another.

"And you've enlisted." It wasn't a question, but Sam answered him anyway.

"George and I went down and signed up yesterday."

His father sipped his whiskey thoughtfully for a second. Sam thought he looked old, older than he ever remembered him looking before, his shoulders seemed stooped, his hair thinner and grayer, his face less animated.

"I'm proud of you, son." He stared at Sam as if memorizing him.

Proud. Now Sam sighed. Would he be proud of a son who signed up to near certain death? If it was in protection of country and family, then yes, and besides he'd never have a son. He wasn't going to survive this war. He didn't tell his father that, though, no point in making him even more of an old man overnight.

His father took a deep breath. "Now, tell me what happened with Wilkins? I wish you had consulted me before firing the man."

"There was no time to consult you." He gripped his mostly empty glass. Consult? Wasn't he supposed to be in charge? Wasn't that what his father was always telling him. He'd taken charge. And he'd been right to. There was no second guessing here. "He stole from us, and he attacked Miss Parks. I needed to do something immediately."

"Attacked? Raped?" His father put down his whiskey glass and looked concerned.

"According to her, no, he did not violate her." Though, what was tying her up like that other than a violation of her person. His shoulders tensed, and he took a deep breath to keep from exploding. "But he threatened to. He confronted her when she was alone and brought her to his cabin where he gagged her, tied her hand and foot, and told her he could do anything he wanted to her." He strode to the window and looked out on the last vestiges of daylight across the fields. How frightened Emily must have been. But what had she said to him, that her biggest fear was that he, Sam, would be hurt if she didn't confide in him. The man was threatening her, and her worry was for Sam. He had to marry this girl. There could be no one else for him. "To prove his point, he grabbed one of the slave children and told Emily that any resistance on her part, or any going for help, would result in severe beatings for the child. Then he manhandled her a bit, to show her who was boss and let her go. She was very shaken."

"Shaken!" His father sounded horrified at the blunt account of what had happened. "My lord, if that's true, the man deserves to be hanged."

"It's true." He turned from the window to face his father. "The child confirmed it."

"Then you were right to fire him. Though, frankly, if someone had done that to the woman I loved, they'd be looking for the body for years to come."

"That had occurred to me." He didn't want his father to think he was a coward. "It seemed better to let the law handle it."

273

"And is the law handling it?"

"They will if they can find him."

His father took another sip of his whiskey. "I'm beginning to understand your urgent concern for Miss Parks' safety." His father joined him by the window "But you don't have to marry her, son. We can look after her without you tying yourself to her forever."

He turned so that they were both looking out into the gathering darkness. "I know I don't have to, Father. I want to. I need to in the sense that I want her more than I ever imagined possible. If all I have left of real life is the next few weeks, why can't that include marrying the woman I love?"

"You think you won't survive the war?" his father asked.

"I'm being realistic. Some…many won't. Why do I think I'd be one of the lucky ones?"

His father's voice was tense when he spoke next. "When talking to your mother, you are to assume you will be one of the lucky ones. Understand?"

Sam nodded. "Understood."

They stood side by side, their matching reflections shining back at them, his father a smaller, older version of himself. When had his father become smaller than him? When had that happened? How many years of straining to be even as tall as his father, and now he had outpaced him and he'd never noticed until now.

"You're sure about Miss Parks?"

"I couldn't be any more sure."

Now it was his father's turn to nod. "Then I suppose we have a wedding to plan. Your mother and Elizabeth will be here tomorrow to take charge. Don't expect Elizabeth to be happy that you threw over her best friend," he warned.

"Dinah can still be her best friend, and now Emily will be her sister. I'm sure she'll love her as much as I do, once given the chance to get to know her."

"We shall see," was his father's ominous reply. He put his glass down and gave Sam a hearty clap on the shoulder. "Well, it's time for me to get to know my future daughter-in-law, don't you think."

He smiled with relief. "Indeed, it is."

He hoped Emily was all right. He had left her to finish dinner alone when his father had burst in upon them. The last time he had left her alone, she had fallen into Wilkins' clutches. He was fairly confident that wouldn't happen this time, but he hoped she had found a safe way to keep herself occupied.

They found her in the parlor, sitting in the rocking chair, a novel in her lap, but he didn't think she was really reading it, for she closed it and put it aside as soon as they came in. She stood to greet them, though a proper woman wouldn't stand when a man entered the room. But yet, as she hurried to his father and took his hands in hers, he could see his father was entranced by the greeting.

"Mr. Marshall, what a pleasure to see you again." Her tone was honey sweet and not at all cloying. The perfect way to greet his father. "I realize that Sam's announcement must have come as a shock to you, but I want you to know that I love Sam for himself, not anything he might have. Penniless or rich wouldn't matter to me. It is Sam I love, not Bonne Terra. Though it is a beautiful plantation," she added quickly, as if afraid she had offended him.

"What about Wilkins?" his father asked, being too

much the plantation owner, and not enough the prospective father-in-law. Sam reddened with anger that he would even bring that name up. "Would you love Sam if he could not offer you protection from him?"

She cocked her head as if the question made no sense to her.

"Of course. It's not what Sam can do for me that I love; it is who he is. Himself."

"He is going off to war." His father was very blunt about it, almost cold.

Sam saw tears pool in Emily's eyes. How he hated the thought of leaving her.

"I know," she answered with a deep sigh. "I wish he didn't have to."

"You wouldn't try to stop him?"

"Would you?" She gazed directly at his father, and Sam fought the urge to reach out to her.

"In a heartbeat if I thought it would make a difference." Sam saw moisture in the corner of his father's eyes and a lump formed in his throat.

"Same," she answered and gave his father a sad smile. "Same."

His father turned a smiling face to Sam. "Break open a bottle of champagne, my boy. We need to celebrate your engagement to this charming woman."

Sam hurried to the wine cellar to get one of the best bottles of champagne. Maybe Emily really was from the fairy folk, the way she was able to enchant his father like that. Or perhaps he was the luckiest man alive to have met the perfect woman.

Chapter Twenty-Five

Emily

Emily sighed as Beck helped her once again into the brown dress in the morning. "I wish my new dresses were ready. What will Sam's mother and sister think when I greet them wearing Elizabeth's old dress?"

"There's nothing wrong with Elizabeth's old dress," Beck said as she did up the dozens of tiny buttons in the back. "Except maybe that it has too many buttons for my taste."

It wasn't so much the dress as it was the fact it was borrowed. From them. "But I come to them with nothing. And it's so obvious. And they'll hate the fact that I'm marrying Sam."

"If you won over Mr. Marshall, you'll win over his mother and sister." Beck's tone was reassuring, but Emily wasn't convinced.

She looked at Beck through the reflection in the oval mirror. "That's not how it works. Mothers always hate the woman their son is going to marry. They feel jealous and threatened."

"I don't think so," Beck said as her nimble fingers did up the dozens of buttons. "Mrs. Marshall liked Dinah well enough, she wasn't threatened by her. And she loved Anna."

"Anna." The perfect Anna. Could she even

compete with her? "Tell me something about her. Was she as perfect as Sam seems to remember?"

"Pretty much."

That was not the reassuring response she wanted.

"They grew up together." Beck continued and motioned for Emily to sit at the dressing table so she could do her hair. "She was small and sweet and made him laugh. When she died, we despaired of him ever being happy again, and it's been close on five years. That's a long time to be sad. But you make him happy. His mother will see that, and she'll love you."

That was some relief at least. "And his sister?"

"Leave her to me." Beck ran the brush through Emily's hair. "I've got a plan," she said after a moment.

"About Elizabeth?" Emily looked at her in the mirror but Beck shook her head.

"No, to get free. You said you'd help, right?" Defiance flashed in her eyes.

"Sure." She'd really rather deal with one problem at a time, but since there was nothing she could really do about Mrs. Marshall or Elizabeth right now, she might as well hear what Beck had in mind. "What is your plan? What can I do?"

"Once Sam has gone off to war, you remember some people in Philadelphia you want to visit and take me with you. Then I'll conveniently get lost, and you'll return alone."

The family certainly wouldn't be happy with her, but she couldn't force Beck to stay enslaved just to make her own life easier. "Sounds good."

"When does he go off to war?" Beck asked as she arranged her hair in a chignon.

"A couple of weeks." The words hurt her heart as

she said them. A couple of weeks. That was all they had left, and then he would be gone.

Samuel Marshall, he died in the Civil War.

Why did she have to know that? It broke her heart. But if she were to be honest with herself, if she didn't know that, would she have agreed to marry him, effectively trapping herself in the past forever? She couldn't be sure. She'd like to say yes, she would, but would having Sam be enough to make up for everything she would be leaving behind? When she was with him, she felt more protected, more loved, happier, than she had remembered being since she was a small child. She was more concerned about his well-being than her own, if that wasn't love what was? All her thoughts were of him. Yes, she would give up everything for Sam. And that was what she was doing, because unless she knew that he was definitely dead she was not going back to her own time. She would be here waiting for him to come back, until she knew he wouldn't. He would know she was here for him.

"A couple of weeks gives me time to get things together before we leave," Beck said, putting the finishing touches on the hairstyle.

Right. They were talking about Beck's plan. She needed to concentrate.

"Do you have a place to go when you get to Philadelphia?" She turned so she could look at Beck directly, not through the mirror.

"Not specifically, but I'll figure it out, don't you worry about that. I just need you to get me out of Maryland without anyone stopping me." The determination in her eyes was proof that she'd be fine.

"I can do that." It felt like far too little.

Sam and his father were both at the table when she got downstairs for breakfast. They stood and bowed politely toward her as she entered the room. There were aspects of this time period that she could get used to, this respect was definitely one of them. Sam hurried and pulled out her chair for her.

"You slept well?" he asked.

"Quite, thank you," she said. "I'm looking forward to seeing your mother and sister today."

She was actually quite nervous about encountering them again as Sam's fiancée, but she wasn't going to admit that.

"And they are looking forward to seeing you." Mr. Marshall's words were meant to be comforting, but he didn't sound completely convinced as he said them, and she became even more nervous.

When Mrs. Marshall and Elizabeth arrived, shortly before lunch, they immediately went to the study with Sam and his father. Emily was left anxiously awaiting the outcome of their conclave. She picked up *Pride and Prejudice* again. She never seemed to get past the first chapter, and today wouldn't be any different. She couldn't concentrate.

His mother would hate her, she was sure, despite what Beck had said. Emily had been able to charm his father, but that didn't work on mothers. Would his mother convince Sam this was a horrible idea? Was it a horrible idea? Would he go back to Dinah? What would she think if she were the mother? She'd think her son had lost his mind. Maybe he had. Maybe they both had, but yet, it felt so right.

She had read the same page at least five times, when she heard the door of the study open. Soon Sam hurried into the parlor. She stood, and he took her by the hand.

"My mother is looking forward to getting to know you," he assured her, squeezing her fingers gently, as the rest of his family came into the room.

"Miss Parks," Mrs. Marshall said, sounding completely pleasant and not at all like she hated her. "When you dropped into our lives, I did not expect you would stay, but Sam is happier than I have ever seen him, and I look forward to having you in our family. Perhaps you were dropped from heaven for my boy."

"Perhaps." She smiled at her future mother-in-law. That was as good an explanation as any for how she ended up here. She stole a glance at Elizabeth, who had crossed her arms and glared at her through narrowed eyes, her lips making a thin line across her face. Perhaps her brother's happiness wasn't as important to her as having her best friend be her sister-in-law.

Mrs. Marshall glided across the floor and seated herself on the horsehair sofa. "And Sam tells me we are to plan a wedding at the same time we prepare him for war."

"I'm afraid so," Emily said. She was really turning this household upside down. How could they not hate her? "We really don't have much time, but of course an elaborate wedding is not what's important to us."

Elizabeth's eye's widened, and she nearly skipped across the room to her mother. "We should have a ball!" she said with sudden enthusiasm. "That's what we should do. Have a small wedding in the church of course, because it has to be a church wedding or it doesn't count, and then come back here and have combination wedding/farewell ball for Sam. Mother,

I'll need a new dress."

Emily managed to suppress the laugh that threatened to bubble over. Elizabeth was truly selfless in a mercenary way.

"Of course," Mrs. Marshall said, putting her hands together in delight. She seemed almost as excited about the idea of a ball as Elizabeth. "And you will of course need a dress, Miss Parks."

"Oh, Sam took me to Mrs. Barnes yesterday and we ordered some dresses." She wondered if she should sit, but Elizabeth sat in the chair she'd been occupying and decided for now she'd stand.

"Just the same, we can take you back to Mrs. Barnes. A mother knows what a girl needs for her wedding." She gave Emily a tender smile. "And your own mother, will she be able to be at the wedding?"

"My mother…my parents are not living." A lump formed in her throat as she said the words. It was true as far as it went. Right now, in this time, her parents were not alive. She of course had every hope and confidence that they were alive, healthy, and probably torn apart with worry, back in her own time.

"I am so sorry, dear." Mrs. Marshall stood and hurried to Emily, taking both of her hands in hers and looking into her eyes. "But you are our family now. We shall take care of you."

Tears came to Emily's eyes. How was it that these people should be so nice to her? Of course they were doing it because they loved Sam and he loved her. Why did this all have to end?

With Mrs. Marshall in charge, suddenly the day turned into a whirlwind of activity. They headed into town to arrange things with the priest and then back to

Mrs. Barnes so that Mrs. Marshall could approve the dresses already ordered. It turned out that one of the day dresses was pieced together, and Emily tried it on so that Mrs. Barnes could get final measurements. They ordered a dress for Elizabeth, and Mrs. Marshall agreed to pay more so that Mrs. Barnes could bring in help to get the dresses done in time. Then there was a stop at the dry goods store to get Emily a workbasket and supplies so she could begin to sew some of her trousseau. Emily had her doubts about this. If they were relying on her sewing skills for her to have underwear, she'd be going commando the rest of her life, but she went along with it to make her future mother-in-law happy.

When they got back from town, all she wanted was to go off somewhere alone with Sam. She needed to be with someone she didn't have to pretend with. She needed to have him hold her and kiss her, but as Sam took her hand to escort her out to the garden, Mr. Marshall clapped a hand on Sam's shoulder. "I think we need to go over the books."

She watched with regret as Sam was led behind the closed doors of the study.

"Shall we have tea in the parlor, girls?" Mrs. Marshall said, and without waiting for an answer headed to find a servant to bring the refreshments.

Emily followed Elizabeth into the parlor where the afternoon sun had warmed the room to slightly past cozy, and moved on to oppressive. As soon as they'd crossed the threshold, Elizabeth turned a cold face to her.

"What's your game?" Elizabeth waved a finger in her face. "Who are you? Why do you want my brother?

Where do you come from? What's your story?"

It was tempting to tell Elizabeth the truth, but she wasn't at all sure how that would be taken. Better to save that until there was more trust between the two of them.

She held up one finger. "First, I have no game." She tried to sound as sincere as possible, the only problem, she found was that when you were tried to sound sincere you often didn't. She held up a second finger as she answered the second question. "I'm Emily Parks. I have no particular family significance. I can't tell you I'm of the Oak Ridge Parks or anything like that." She'd always thought people who introduced themselves that way were pretentious, and she supposed they were, but it was a way to prove your bonafides to strangers who doubted you. Third finger up. "I want your brother because I love him like I've never loved anyone before in my life. And I know he has to go off to war, but I want him to have what happiness he can first, and to know I am waiting for him when he returns." She crossed her arms. She'd answered the questions; the ball was back in Elizabeth's court.

"Don't you think Dinah could have given him that happiness?" Elizabeth narrowed her eyes as if daring her to actually answer the question.

Emily sighed and sat down on the sofa. She wiped a sheen of sweat from her forehead and wished that Dinah were not collateral damage in all this. She had nothing against Dinah. She'd had no intention of stealing Sam away, but he insisted he wasn't in love with Dinah and Emily was not going to argue with him about that. "I'm sure Dinah could have made him happy. I'm sure she wanted to. What happened with me and Sam wasn't planned. I didn't go out to steal him away or anything. We fell in love."

"Very quickly," Elizabeth interjected her eyes narrowed disapprovingly.

"Yes," Emily agreed. "Very quickly. And if I were you I'd have my doubts too. I'd say how could they know they love each other after such a short time? I'd say, they barely know each other what are they doing making a lifelong commitment? And you know what I've said those same things to myself. But I'll tell you this, I've never been happier than with Sam, and he's the one who wanted to get married before he left. I agreed because the most important thing for me right now is to make him happy." It was hot in here. She wished Mrs. Marshall were bringing lemonade instead of tea.

"Dinah says you're a fake who is after the plantation and don't care about Sam at all." Elizabeth sat with a flourish in the chair across from her.

Damn that Dinah, why did she have to keep poisoning people against her? "That's not true. I don't want anything from Sam except Sam. That's all."

"I'm not sure I trust you," Elizabeth said, nose in the air

"I don't blame you," she answered, clearly throwing Elizabeth off guard. "I wouldn't in your position. But hopefully as you get to know me, you'll learn that all I want is the best for Sam."

"And what if he changed his mind and said he still wanted to marry Dinah instead."

The very thought stabbed at her heart a little. She hoped that wouldn't be the case. Had Sam said something to his sister that would make her think that?

But she had said what she wanted was what Sam wanted, so she had to answer honestly.

"If that was what he wanted, it would break my heart, but I would let him go. Providing of course it was before the wedding. Once I'm married I intend it to be forever." She leveled a steady gaze at Elizabeth. She was not going to be intimidated out of loving Sam. Especially not by his little sister.

"What if Father writes him out of the will for marrying you?" Elizabeth cocked her head to one side as if she'd found and played the trump card.

That had already been dealt with between Sam and his father as far as Emily knew, but she answered anyway, and hoped that Mrs. Marshall would get back soon and they could settle into forced civility.

"If that bothers Sam, he is free to not marry me."

Elizabeth studied her through narrowed eyes. "You won't try to take over the running of Bonne Terra, will you?"

"I wouldn't dream of it," she said with maybe a bit too much passion. "I wouldn't even know where to begin."

Elizabeth seemed to find this answer acceptable. "One last question," she said. "Jane Austen or Charlotte Bronte?"

"Austen all the way," Emily answered without hesitation, even though the question was so out of the blue. "I find Bronte too dark."

"But don't you sometimes think the world is a dark place?" Elizabeth tilted her head in inquiry not inquisition.

"Exactly why I like some light in my literature," she answered. It was also why she preferred comedies to documentaries. Life was dark and dangerous, entertainment should be fun.

Elizabeth looked at her through narrowed eyes. "Maybe we'll get along, after all."

"I certainly hope so," Emily answered and allowed a hint of a smile. She felt she'd passed a major test she'd never studied for.

****

It wasn't until after dinner that Emily finally got time to spend alone with Sam. Ignoring the family gathered in the parlor, he took her by the hand and led her out to the rose garden. "We will not have as much privacy now that they have come back," he said, giving a gentle pat to her hand that he had tucked into the crook of his elbow.

"I know." She repressed a sigh. It wasn't Sam's fault that others had intruded on their little cocoon. She clung to his hand, leaning against him as they walked, wishing they could be promised a happy ever after.

"Somethings bothering you." It wasn't a question so she didn't bother denying it.

"It's Dinah. She seems to think she can get you back."

"She can't." He said it with such certainty that she hated to pursue this further, but she couldn't let it go.

"But..." How could she say this and not sound like she was having doubts about marrying him? "You're from the same world, you two. She knows how to do things like run a plantation that I never could. You've known her for much longer. You don't really know me at all."

He led her through the arbor into the garden. "Are you having second thoughts?" Was there actual worry in his voice?

"About marrying you? Not at all," Emily quickly assured him. She didn't want him to think she didn't want him. "But…"

"Don't worry about Dinah. She can't stop me from marrying you." He sounded so sure about this, but Emily had seen her eyes when they were in town the other day. She was the kind of girl who would not give up easily.

"She might try."

"She already tried. She sent a telegram to my father. But as you can see, it had no effect. We will still be married," he paused slightly and squeezed her hand. "As long as you wish it."

"Oh, I do!" Emily said, her heart feeling lighter. "I almost wish the wedding could be tomorrow, or right now and then we could spend all our time together until you have to leave."

"We can still spend most of our time together," Sam said. "Two weeks is the quickest the seamstress can promise to get the dresses done, and the priest didn't want to do it before then anyway. Besides, Mother needs a bit of time to plan the ball and invite everyone."

"I feel like I should be doing more of the preparations." She had helped Dayna with so many of the wedding preparations, it was odd to not be able to even plan her own.

"No, Mother thrives on things like this. Don't interfere, and she'll be happy as a clam."

"If you insist." She relaxed against him, feeling the warmth of his body beneath his linen shirt.

"I do." He led her to a bench under a bower of

roses that were starting to bud. They sat and he put his arm around her and pulled her close. She leaned into the kiss and let herself melt into him. Two weeks. It seemed an impossibly long time to wait, but yet, it was nearly all the time they had left. She didn't want to wish those two weeks away because then they would only have one week more together.

He stopped kissing her long enough to whisper in her ear. "I want to make the most of every moment we have left."

She wanted to make every moment last forever, was that too much to ask?

Chapter Twenty-Six

Sam

All he wanted was to spend every minute with Emily. He couldn't get enough of her, it was like he'd been in a desert and now had water again and he couldn't drink it in fast enough. But every minute of every day seemed to be filled with other things that needed doing. Getting ready to go off to war was not quite as simple as packing a few shirts in a saddle bag and heading out. He and George would be lieutenants in Yuengling's company, and they needed to get coats tailored and the rest of their uniform prepared. There were meetings with Yuengling and the other officers nearly every day. There was more involved in being a soldier than he had ever considered. At least there had been no sign of Wilkins. Rumor around town was that he had enlisted. As long as it kept Wilkins away from Emily, Sam didn't care what he did.

Spring was progressing; the trees were in bud. The roses would be in full bloom soon, and he would go off to war. He should be sitting by the waterfall with Emily composing poems to her. Instead he was riding back from yet another meeting with Yuengling, George by his side.

"Your head doesn't really seem to be in this," George observed as he stopped prattling on about some new provisions they had to procure before they left.

"It's not," he admitted. He let his gaze take in the pastel green of the budding trees and the light pinks and yellows of the wildflowers that were dotting the landscape. It was too beautiful a day to think of being a soldier. To think of death. "I'm more suited to be a poet than a soldier."

"Anyone could tell you that," George agreed taking off his hat and wiping the sweat from his brow before replacing it. "But if you are going off to war, you're going to have to be a soldier, otherwise you'll be a dead poet."

If Emily was right, he'd be a dead soldier. It didn't really matter much. Either way he'd be dead. He'd rather not be. He'd rather stay with Emily.

"I am sorry," George said quietly, plucking a bud from a low hanging branch.

"For what?" He turned to look at his friend, surprised by sympathy where there often was teasing.

"That you have to leave her," George said with a shrug. "You're finally happy again, and you can't stay. I am sorry."

So it was obvious to everyone. He wasn't sure if that was a good thing or not.

"At least you'll have her to come home to," George said and waggled his eyebrows at him.

Sam nodded, acknowledging the implication and grinned politely. But that would only be if he came home. And if she didn't leave, go back to her own time before then. Would she be there when this was over? Would he? All he knew for certain was they had a couple of weeks together, and he wanted to make the most of it.

He got back to the house and found Emily standing in the ballroom, her arms crossed tight in front of her, hugging herself, her brow wrinkled in a frown.

"Has something happened? What's the matter? Are you ill?" He rushed to her side, hoping the distress was something he could fix. They had so little time together, he wanted all of it to be happy.

She started at his voice, but then saw him and a smile spread across her face, and he relaxed.

"Oh, no. Nothing like that!" She assured him, but then the distressed look crept back on to her face. "I'm worried that I'll disgrace you."

"Disgrace me? Not possible!" He took her hand in his. Even if she used their wedding ball to make an abolitionist speech, it would not disgrace him. Instead he would be proud of her courage.

"But I can't dance. Remember?" Dancing? That's what she was worried about? She looked up at him with her big brown eyes and he wanted to laugh, but she was so honestly upset that he didn't dare. "You showed me the waltz, but it's all I can do, and I can't even do that very well. I'll be here in my beautiful gown, the most handsome man on my arm, and yet still be a laughing stock."

"You won't." He pulled her close, wrapping his arms around her and looked down into that face he had grown to love. "Come, we'll go back to the waterfall and practice some more. I think the wedding and war preparations can go on without us for a few hours."

He sent Tobias for a bottle of wine from the cellar, had Moses hitch up the buggy and soon he and Emily were alone by the waterfall, where the wildflowers provided a carpet of color and the light filtered through the emerging leaves.

Emily clasped her hands in delight and let out a happy sigh. "It's as magical as the first time. I was afraid that it wouldn't be, that I only imagined it because I was falling in love."

"Perhaps it's still magical because you are still in love." He touched her hand lightly and she gave him that smile he never tired of seeing.

"Quite possible."

He helped her down from the carriage and tucked her hand protectively in the crook of his elbow and walked with her to the edge of the creek. It was wrong of him, he knew, but he wouldn't mind simply stripping off her clothes and laying her down on the moss by the creek and taking her right here and now. A week. One more week until the wedding. He could make himself wait. He would not dishonor her by taking advantage of her.

"Shall we start with the waltz, as a refresher?"

"Yes, please. That's one-two-three, one-two-three, right?" She was so eager to please it made his heart ache.

"Yes. Come here." He put one hand on her waist and with the other held her hand. She gripped his fingers tightly, as if afraid he would disappear if she let go. "Now, watch my feet," he said and he began to sing "one two three" to the tune of a waltz. She followed easily. She may say she was not a good dancer, but he thought it was not ability, but experience she lacked. Hopefully he could make up for that with a few quick lessons. And he certainly didn't mind the excuse for holding her close.

"How am I doing?"

"Wonderfully." He could feel the heat of her body through her dress. He wanted to never stop touching her. "You dance like a dream."

She laughed at that and he had to admit that perhaps it was a bit of an overstatement.

"Do you want to try a polka now?"

"I'd love to," she answered. So he guided her through the steps of the polka, and it was so beautiful dancing with only the music of the waterfall and the birds that he didn't think any orchestra could make it better. When they stopped for breath she asked, "How about that other one? The Zinga one? Your favorite. Teach it to me. I want to dance it with you at our wedding. It will be my wedding gift to you."

He grinned. "The Zingerella. Yes. I'll teach you. But first, a break. I brought wine."

"I certainly won't turn that down."

He spread a blanket on the ground by the creek and opened the wine while Emily situated herself on the blanket. She was getting better at the wide skirts and hoops, but he could tell wearing them did not come naturally to her. He handed her a glass of wine and poured one for himself.

"Tell me about your time."

She took a sip and looked thoughtful for a moment.

"Life is more fast-paced. Everyone is always in a hurry, but yet we can do things so much faster. We can text people, instead of sending letters."

"Text?" He pictured the type used in a printing press and tried to imagine how that could be a quick way to communicate. "Is it like telegraph?"

"I suppose it started with that." She frowned in concentration, trying to figure out how to explain to him. "We have phones. Devices we hold in our hands, that we use to send messages to people, and they get them instantly." She held out her hand as if holding something, but he couldn't imagine how something small that would fit in the palm of your hand would allow someone to communicate instantly.

"Fascinating." He would like to see this world of hers but couldn't really picture it.

"And with our phones we can also get information on almost anything in the world."

"Like a library at your fingertips." He stared off at the waterfall. He couldn't conceive of the things she was telling him. A telegraph you held in your hand was the closest he could get, but that didn't seem to take in the immensity of what was possible.

"Very much like that." She took another sip of her wine and chewed on her lower lip, contemplating. "And there are fifty states. And of course no slavery. We drive cars, which are like horseless buggies and have electric lights, so you don't need to light candles but can flick a switch and the room lights up."

"It's rather hard to believe." He wasn't sure how much he did believe. It could be real, or it could be wild imaginings. He didn't really care which, he loved how animated she became when she spoke of her time. A time she belonged in.

"When I go off to war." His voice broke on the word war and he cleared his throat. "I want you to use the pond to go home."

To his surprise, she shook her head. "No. I won't. I will be here waiting for you when you get back."

He blinked, stunned, a couple of times before responding. "But you said I won't come back."

"I don't know if that's true. Perhaps the woman at the inn was wrong. And besides, the war is long. Four years. Even if you don't survive the whole thing, you may live for many years yet, and get leave to come home and if you do, I'll be here."

His heart ached he wanted that so much, but it was wrong of him to ask it of her.

"No. You don't belong here. You need to go to your own time."

"I belong where you are." She reached out and touched his hand sending shivers up his arm. "And until there is no hope, I will be here, waiting for you. You can be sure of it."

He took her wine glass from her and wrapped her in his arms. How could he have gotten so lucky to have her fall into his life the way she had? Soon they were lying on the blanket, kissing and his hand strayed to her breast, enjoying the soft contours of it. She gasped softly in response, but held him tighter. He wanted her with a longing that went deep into his bones.

"You have to teach me the dance," she whispered in his ear.

He did. He had promised he would do that. Reluctantly he removed his hands and helped her up. She picked up her glass of wine and finished it in a couple of big swallows. So, maybe he wasn't the only one who wished things could have gone further right now. When she put the glass down, he took her hands in his. The Zingirella was started side by side, left hand holding left hand, right hand holding right. He walked her through the steps, and they practiced until she was able to manage enough that she would be able to keep up with him on the dance floor.

"You'll do splendidly." He held her hands in his and gazed into her eyes as the waterfall splashed merrily beside them.

"I hope so" she said earnestly. "I know it's your favorite, and I want to do it justice. Maybe you should dance it with someone else, someone who won't get all tripped up."

"No." He brought his face close to hers. "I will dance it with you. I will dance all the dances with you."

"Is that allowed?" she responded breathlessly. "From what Elizabeth has been telling me it seems as if everyone is supposed to have a dance card and lots of partners."

"You will be my wife. It will be our wedding dance. Only I will dance with you, and only you will dance with me, and I dare anyone to complain about it." He kissed her then, dance lessons be damned.

****

Stolen minutes were few and too short, but Sam knew once the wedding came he would at least have the nights with her, there was that to look forward to. She got her first day dress from Mrs. Barnes and happily modeled it for him. She looked even more beautiful now that she wore a dress made especially for her, as opposed to one of Elizabeth's cast offs. The wedding ball gown would be ready soon, but she insisted that he could not see it until the wedding day.

The day before the wedding his father called him into the study and handed him a glass of whiskey.

"Tomorrow is the big day."

"It is." He settled into one of the red leather chairs. He had thought the day would never arrive, but it was less than twenty-four hours away now.

Christine Marciniak

"I must say, I think you've made a good choice." His father sat in the chair next to him, and stretched his legs out in front of him. "The girl is a little unusual, but she's delightful. She will make you a good wife."

"I know she will." He took a sip of his whiskey. Why couldn't he be looking forward to a peaceful lifetime ahead of him with Emily by his side. "You'll take good care of her while I'm away?"

"Of course." His father put a reassuring hand on Sam's knee. "You need not worry."

Sam knew Emily said she'd stay, but what if she got lonely and the draw of her own time was too much, should he warn his father that she might leave? But she said she wouldn't. And if she wasn't here there wasn't much his father could do about it anyway. No, he'd leave things as they were.

"The wedding night." His father cleared his throat and continued, awkwardly. "You'll be gentle with her?"

"As much as possible," Sam answered honestly and drank the rest of his whiskey.

He didn't know how much it would be possible.

298

Chapter Twenty-Seven

Emily

Today was the day. Her wedding day. Emily stretched and opened her eyes, taking in the canopy and ewer and other old-fashioned touches in the room. Funny how the dance would be in the same place as Dayna's wedding. Nothing about this day was what she had envisioned her own wedding to be like. She would not wear white. That wasn't the norm now apparently. But she did have a gorgeous rose silk ballgown that would put any modern wedding gown to shame. Her parents wouldn't be here. Her heart hurt a bit at that. She knew her mother would want to see her married, and her father wanted to walk her down the aisle and dance the father-daughter dance with her. He'd had a song picked out since she was five.

She wasn't going to Hawaii on her honeymoon. She wasn't even having a honeymoon, not really. One week spent with her new husband in his parents' house before he went off to war. The Civil War. And wouldn't return. What was she doing? Why was she setting herself up to be a young widow?

Because she loved him.

She barely knew him, it was true, but yet, she felt like she knew him better than anyone in the world.

The door creaked open, and Beck entered with her

morning tea tray.

"It's the big day." Beck put the tray down and opened the drapes letting in the morning sunshine. "Are you ready?"

"Is anyone ever ready?" She pushed back the coverlet and sat up.

"Probably not." Beck poured the tea into one of the porcelain cups.

"I'm nervous." She adjusted herself against the headboard. "I know I want to be with Sam, but he's leaving for war and what if I'm making a mistake?"

"You asking my opinion?" Beck stared at her, eyes wide.

"Yeah." Was that so strange? Maybe for Beck it was. "I mean, you kind of remind me of my best friend. Who I think is your great-something granddaughter. You don't mind if I ask, do you?"

Beck handed her the cup of hot tea.

"Honestly, I do think it's all kind of fast, but yet under the circumstances you can't go slow. Does it feel right deep down in your gut?" Beck put a fist under her breasts to demonstrate what she meant. "That's what my grandmother used to always say. If it felt right it was right. Your body knows."

"It feels right." She took a sip of her tea, reassured. It definitely felt right.

"Then you have nothing to worry about." She pulled the blue day dress out of the wardrobe and got the hoops and corset ready while Emily ate her bun.

"You know what my friend Dayna's wedding day was like?" She knew of course that Beck couldn't possibly.

"How was it?"

Emily licked sugar off her fingers. "We all went to the beauty parlor to get our hair done starting way early in the morning, like eight."

"That's not so early." She held out the corset and Emily stood so the dressing could begin.

"It was early to be getting my hair done." She held out her arms as Beck settled the corset into place.

"Who is 'we all'?" Beck tugged at the ties and Emily barely winced.

"All the bridesmaids. There was me and Dayna's cousins and a couple of friends from college and high school. There were six of us all together. Only two of us were white."

Beck looked interested at that.

"No one cares if someone is black or white where you come from?"

Emily wanted to say that they didn't, but it wasn't entirely true, some people cared very much.

"Mostly people don't," she answered while Beck put the hoop in place. "Some do. I don't."

"You're going to have to watch that if you want to get along in this house, especially without Sam to run interference. Blacks and whites, they mostly stay separate." She finished attaching the hoop to the corset.

"But not you, you are around the family all the time." She ducked so Beck could slip the petticoat over her head.

"I'm not their friend. Make no mistake about that."

"You're my friend, though, right?" She certainly thought of Beck as a friend, as a confidant, and in her relation to Dayna as a connection to home. Besides Sam, of course, Beck was the only person she really felt comfortable with here.

Beck shook her head. "No. I don't think so."

Oh.

"It's nothing against you," Beck quickly pointed out. "But it doesn't do me any good to be friends with the whites. They own me. I can't be friends with them. It's unequal, you understand?"

"I do." She wished things were different. "And I'm sorry. I will help you, though. I have promised, and I keep my promises."

"Someday, when I'm free, if we meet up again. Then we can be friends." Beck held out the blue day dress.

"I'd like that." With the promise of future friendship, she let Beck dress her.

She thought of the morning of Dayna's wedding a few weeks ago. The appointment at the hair dressers, the manicures and pedicures, dropping their bags off at the inn, everyone getting dressed amid laughing and champagne drinking in the master bedroom at Dayna's parents' house. The photographer and the endless posed pictures. Finally the limousine ride to the church and the ceremony with the string quartet. It had been magical. Everything had been wonderful until she'd gotten drunk at the reception and fell in the fish pond.

And ended up here.

Life was strange.

The morning proceeded like any other morning, except for the jumpy feeling in her stomach as she thought that this afternoon she was actually going to get married, and tonight she would share a bed with Sam. She shivered a little in anticipation.

Shortly after lunch Sam took her out to the fish pond.

"Are you still sure?" He took her hand in hers and she squeezed, holding on tight. "You will be giving up so much if you stay."

She stared into the murky water. It was true, she'd be giving up modern conveniences and her family and friends. At least for the time being. If he were to die she could go home, but for now, she would give up those things for him. And if he survived—*please God let him survive*—she would have him and the rest paled in comparison to that.

"But I'll have you." She looked into those gray eyes so full of love. "I've never been so sure. And you?"

"Very sure." He pulled her close. "So very sure. In a few hours you will be Mrs. Samuel Marshall."

"That sounds wonderful." She remembered all the different boys' names she'd scribbled on notebooks in middle school, with a 'Mrs' added as if that would make her crush fall in love with her. Mrs. Brad Conroy, Mrs. Juan Estes, Mrs. Justin Smith. And now her name was changing for real. Mrs. Samuel Marshall. She liked it.

Sam took her in his arms, but as soon as his lips touched hers, his sister's voice interrupted them.

"Plenty of time for that later," Elizabeth said, a hint of laughter in her voice. "It's time to get the bride dressed. The groom should get dressed as well."

"I'll see you in church," Sam said as she reluctantly let Elizabeth pull her away.

"Come, sister," Elizabeth said, looking back over her shoulder as she led the way to the house. "May I call you sister?"

"I'd like that. I never had a sister. I only have a

brother."

"And he cannot be at your wedding? Did you try to contact him? Or"—she looked slightly horrified at the possibility of making a social faux pas—"Has he passed on, like your parents?"

Technically, she could say that her brother was not living, because like her parents, at this time he wasn't alive, but it felt too terribly tragic to say that all of her family was dead. "He's in school, but with the war traveling is so much more difficult."

"Still, it is sad that you could not have your own family here with you." But, Elizabeth was not one who could stay morose for long. "No matter, we are your family now. And I am your sister. I did always want a sister. Let's get you ready for your wedding."

Up in her room, Emily felt like a mannequin as Beck, Elizabeth, and Mrs. Marshall hovered around her and dressed her from head to toe. When they finished, they stepped back and positioned her in front of the mirror. The dress was amazing and surprisingly low cut. She tugged a little at the front, to cover a bit more of her breasts, but Elizabeth stopped her.

"It's fine the way it is."

"I feel so exposed! And I'll be in church."

"You'll wear a shawl in church," Mrs. Marshall said, producing a lovely lace shawl that she draped over her bare shoulders.

"Ooh, this is beautiful." She looked like something out of a fairy tale.

"It was my grandmother's," Mrs. Marshall said, a misty look in her eye.

"I'm honored." Emily swallowed the lump in her throat, once again reminding herself that if she couldn't be with her own family, how lucky she was to have the Marshalls.

"Now." Mrs. Marshall sat on the edge of the bed and suddenly sounded business like. "Since you don't have a mother of your own, I feel I need to tell you what you might expect on the wedding night."

Emily's face flamed. This was bound to be incredibly awkward.

"Maybe I should leave." Elizabeth inched toward the door.

"No." Her mother waved her arm, indicating she should stay. "You'll be getting married before long, stay."

"I do know about the birds and the bees and all that," Emily said quickly, lest she have to suffer through an awkward explanation of what sex was.

"Good, but understand that it might be uncomfortable at first, but you want to be sure to try to enjoy it to please your husband."

Oh, this conversation couldn't end quickly enough.

"I'll do my best," she said, trying hard not to picture herself in bed with Sam, while his mother sat right there.

"You don't have any questions?" Mrs. Marshall asked anxiously.

"No, I think I have it under control."

Mrs. Marshall looked a bit relieved at that, maybe even more relieved than she, to be able to end this conversation. Elizabeth would perhaps need a more detailed discussion later, but that wasn't her concern.

Now that she was ready, both Elizabeth and Mrs. Marshall needed to get dressed. They hurried to their own rooms to get into their finery, and she was left alone to think.

She was getting married.

Today.

To a man who she'd only known a couple of weeks.

This was insane, yet felt so right.

She wished her mother could be here. And Dayna. Maybe not here. Dayna might not fare too well if she were here. What Emily really wished was that her wedding to this incredible man could take place in her own time. She stood in front of the mirror in her amazing rose ballgown and felt beautiful and exotic, but she had always dreamed of wearing a white wedding dress. She'd wanted to go to the bridal stores and try on a dozen dresses and feel like a queen.

It didn't matter though, she was marrying Sam. She had to focus on that.

There was a knock on her door and when she opened it, Dolly stood there. "Ooh, you look like a fairy princess!" Then remembering the reason she was there she quickly added, "The carriage is ready for you, miss."

Emily thanked her and made her way downstairs. Servants helped her and Elizabeth and Mrs. Marshall into the shiny black carriage. Sam and his father had already left for the church.

The church in town was one Emily had been in before. And not just for Sunday Mass with the Marshall family. In her time, the church had been decommissioned, or whatever it was they did to a church to make it not a church anymore, and it was an Italian restaurant. She'd gone to dinner there once on a very memorable blind date.

Memorable because her date was already drunk when she met him there, and then he proceeded to accidentally spill both a glass of red wine and a plate of spaghetti in her lap. The food, what she'd tasted of it, had been good, but she hadn't been eager to go back there again. Now of course, it was entirely different.

Now the church was still a church with light provided by what seemed like hundreds of candles, and sunlight streaming in through the stained-glass windows. There was not a huge crowd: family and close friends, some of whom she had met over the past couple of weeks, more were complete strangers to her. She should know the people at her wedding, shouldn't she? She knew Sam, that was good enough.

Mr. Marshall met her at the back of the church. He had agreed to walk her down the aisle, since her own father couldn't do it. "Are you ready, daughter?"

Tears welled up in her eyes, threatening to overflow. She wished her own father could be here.

"I'm ready." She blinked back the tears and smiled up at him. He took her by the arm and guided her down the aisle.

Sam stood at the front of the church, dressed in his brand new officer's uniform. Her stomach did a funny flip when she saw it. He looked like something out of a living history museum, but this was real. He was not playing make believe. He was ready to go off and fight the Civil War.

Sam smiled at her and she smiled back and all the worries of the day disappeared.

She was marrying Sam.

The service moved quickly, in Latin, except for the exchange of vows, and she was never quite sure what was going on until Sam put a silver ring on her finger and she said "I do."

They left the church arm in arm, husband and wife and Emily could hardly believe it was possible to feel as happy as she did.

Chapter Twenty-Eight

Sam

Sam didn't remember ever being happier. He led Emily, radiant in her pink dress, to the carriage that awaited them. Someone had decorated the two-seater with streamers of flowers. That seemed like Elizabeth's handiwork. He helped his wife into the carriage and then climbed up himself.

"Well, my wife." He enjoyed the way that sounded. "Should we go home?"

"I'll go anywhere with you, husband." She beamed at him, holding tightly to his hand.

"There will be food at the house and later, dancing." He knew he didn't really have to coax her to go back to the house, and he rather liked the fact that if he wanted to turn the horse's head in some other direction entirely she would go along with him simply because they were together. This was what happiness felt like.

"Oh, food and dancing." There was laughter in her voice. "In that case, definitely let's go home."

He drove slowly, enjoying the time alone with his wife. He loved that, thinking of her as his wife. He looked forward to the ball, but he couldn't help counting the hours until he could get her out of that dress and into his bed.

"Your mother wanted to make sure I knew what to expect on my wedding night." Emily gave him a sly sideways glance.

"No!" He jerked on the reins nearly driving the horse off the road. A frantic second later he had the carriage traveling smoothly again. "I'm so sorry." How could his mother embarrass him like that? But then again, she would have that talk with Elizabeth, and since Emily had no mother here, it was rather sweet of her to take on that position. "What did she tell you?"

"That it might be uncomfortable, but I should try to make you happy."

He glanced at his wife and saw that her cheeks were a delightful shade of pink.

"I think we'll make each other happy." He found himself getting warm just thinking about it.

"I'm sure of it." She rested her hand on his knee, and the touch of her, even through the cloth, made his heart beat faster.

Too many hours, that's how many before he could have her all to himself.

He stopped in front of the house, and Tobias took the reins. Sam helped her out of the carriage. She was getting much better at doing that gracefully. Friends and relatives were already gathering on the porch, and everyone wanted to stop them and offer congratulations. He introduced her over and over, to his uncles, cousins, neighbors. Emily, looking slightly overwhelmed, greeted everyone with the same smile and repeated again and again how delighted she was to be a part of the family and how much she loved Sam.

When he noticed Anna's parents he hesitated. What could he possibly say to them? But they approached him and there was no way to avoid them.

"Emily, I'd like you to meet Mr. and Mrs. Payne, Anna's parents." He hoped she would catch the significance of that. He shouldn't have worried.

Emily took Mrs. Payne's hands in hers. "I'm delighted to meet you. Anna must have been a remarkable girl, judging by the way Sam's face lights up when he speaks of her. I know this day must have been difficult for you, thinking that it should be Anna standing here next to Sam. I can't tell you how sorry I am for your loss."

"Thank you, dear," Mrs. Payne said and Mr. Payne turned to Sam.

"You are a lucky young man. Make sure you keep this girl happy."

"No worries there, sir," Sam said, love and happiness once more threatening to bubble over inside him.

They successfully passed the gauntlet of well-wishers and made it to the parlor where his father poured champagne. It seemed everyone had a toast to make, and some people, like his father and George, made several. Emily gamely kept up, draining several glasses of champagne, but her cheeks were flushed and she clung to him tightly. Perhaps they ought to eat before she was too drunk to enjoy the rest of the evening.

Soon the doors to the dining room opened and he led Emily to the head of the table. He held out her chair for her and helped her get her voluminous skirt situated as she sat. The feast started with oyster soup and then the fish course of poached bass with walnut ketchup, followed by roast pheasant with asparagus and fresh peas and finally lamp chops with mint sauce and baby beets. Each course, naturally, had it's own wine, and there seemed to be a never ending string of toasts to which he and Emily happily raised their glasses. If this continued for too much longer he was afraid Emily wouldn't be the only one too drunk to make it through the evening.

Sam signaled to a servant and instructed him to bring both of them some water. He wanted to make it through the dance to what lay beyond. He was not going to be incapacitated on his wedding night.

"I'm going to burst if I eat another bite." Emily murmured, putting down her knife and fork and rubbing her belly. "Or the corset will."

"That would certainly provide unexpected entertainment." His gaze lingered on her bosom as he spoke to her. The dress didn't leave too much to the imagination, not that he was complaining.

As the last plates were cleared, he could hear carriages pulling up outside as the people who were invited to the ball and not the wedding dinner arrived. Soon the dancing would begin. He hoped Emily remembered the steps to the dances. He wanted them both to be able to enjoy the ball.

Emily leaned over and whispered in his ear. "It's necessary that I...um use the necessary, before we continue."

"Of course." He signaled to Beck. "Will you accompany Mrs. Marshall and assist her if she needs it."

Emily grinned. "She's on potty duty," she said mostly to herself. "Wait until I tell Dayna."

Emily was back by his side as the orchestra

warmed up, the strings and horns making a discordant sound, preliminary to filling the air with beautiful music.

"Do I need one of those little cards?" she asked, pointing to a dance card that Elizabeth was busy having filled by eligible bachelors in uniform.

"No, your dance card is already full. You will be dancing with me." He placed a hand proprietorially on her waist. He could do that now without raising eyebrows. She was his wife.

"Is that fair to you?" She looked at him through earnest eyes. "I'm not very good. I want you to enjoy yourself."

"Do you think for a minute I could enjoy myself dancing with anyone who is not you at our wedding ball?" It didn't matter if she knew all the dances, what mattered was that she be in his arms.

"I suppose the answer to that is no." She gave him a huge smile and straightened his tie.

"That's right. The answer to that is no. Now, come, it's time to line up for the grand promenade. We must lead."

She held back. "But Sam, I don't know how to do that."

"You walk. On my arm, around the ballroom, in time to the music. Trust me, you can do it."

He led his beautiful bride into the ballroom as the other couples lined up behind them. As the orchestra played a march they walked the perimeter of the room and down the middle and then around again, until everyone had entered and the band began playing a waltz. At that, Sam guided Emily to the middle of the dance floor. He put one hand on her waist and grasped her hand with his other. He looked into her eyes, that were looking up at him with such trust and love.

"Are you ready?"

"As I'll ever be," she answered and he began leading her in the dance. No, she didn't dance as some of the other girls did who had spent years perfecting the steps, but her body moved with his, responded to his, and they glided around the ballroom, the center of everyone's attention. Soon other couples felt it was proper to join in and the dance floor became crowded, but there was always room around Sam and Emily as if they were in their own little bubble. He had no objections.

He wanted to dance every dance with her, but when his father approached them between songs and requested the next dance with his new daughter, Sam could hardly refuse.

"And your mother would like to dance with you," his father told him. Sam bowed gallantly to his wife and father and went to find his mother. Of course he should dance with his mother at his wedding.

His mother looked nearly young enough to be a bride herself, Sam thought as he approached her. True there was a bit of silver showing in her hair, but her face was smooth and her figure trim and she smiled happily at him when she saw him. He bowed to her.

"May I have this dance, Mother?"

The orchestra played another waltz, and he and his mother skimmed across the floor to the music.

"Do you like Emily?" he found himself asking as they moved together in three-quarters time.

"I think she's delightful," his mother answered, giving his hand a small squeeze. "And she makes you happy, which is the main thing."

"I hate having to leave her." That dark cloud hung over his head this whole day, he would have to leave her and soon, and he would likely never see her again.

"But you'll be back," his mother said with assurance. "Probably by Christmas. We will take care of her while you are gone, and when you come back you will not need to be separated any longer."

He wished he could be as optimistic as his mother in that regard.

The song ended, and with a bow to his mother he started back toward Emily. He had not made it halfway across the ballroom when he saw George bowing to her, asking for a dance. Emily's eyes sought out his, and he gave her a nod. He could not deny a dance to his best friend.

"You do plan to dance with you sister at your wedding ball, don't you?" Elizabeth asked, suddenly at his side.

"Naturally." He bowed properly to her and took her hand as the orchestra struck up a polka.

"Do you think Joseph is going to propose to me?"

He studied his sister with her curls and elegant gown. How was it that she was no longer the little girl in pinafores, tagging after him and George, but a woman worrying about marriage?

The polka was not as easy to talk through as a waltz, but Elizabeth deserved some sort of an answer. "He leaves with George and me. He may not want to commit himself, or you, before he returns safely."

"You did," Elizabeth pointed out, apparently intent on having a conversation while they danced.

"I did." He waited until the song neared its end

before continuing. "I needed to make sure that when I am gone Emily is taken care of. Joseph has no reason to have the same concern for you; you are safe in your father's house."

"I suppose that's true." She didn't sound convinced, and he didn't want to pursue it. He was fairly certain that Joseph never intended to propose to Elizabeth. As far as he could see any romance between the two was strictly in Elizabeth's head.

"You'll find true love, Elizabeth," he said to her as the song ended. "If I could find Emily, then anything is possible."

"You really do love her, don't you?" Elizabeth sounded almost mystified.

"I do." He stole a glance at Elizabeth's dance card to see what song was next. It was a Zingirella. He was dancing that one with Emily, and nothing would stand in his way. He made his way to his wife, and although Elizabeth's Joseph looked poised to ask her for the next dance, Sam intervened.

"This dance is mine," he said in a tone that left no room for argument and took Emily by the hand.

"It's the Zingirella," he said, bending to speak into her ear. "Do you remember how to do it?"

"I do, but it's your favorite, are you sure you don't want to dance it with someone who really knows what to do?"

"No. I want to dance it with you."

The music started, and he took Emily's hands, and they began the dance. She stumbled a bit at first, the steps were tricky, but as the song continued either she had it down, or she'd found a way to fake it, because he really wouldn't have known that she didn't know what she was doing.

When the dance ended, he took her in his arms. "You have made me so happy tonight," he whispered in her ear.

She smiled up at him and winked. "And the night's not over yet."

There was so much more night to come. As much as Sam wanted to dance with her forever, he found himself wishing the ball would end, and he could take his wife upstairs and really celebrate being a husband.

Chapter Twenty-Nine

Emily

Emily didn't know what time it was when Sam led her upstairs. The last guest had not left yet, but apparently, it was fine for the bridal couple to sneak upstairs before the sun rose. Her heartbeat quickened as they approached his bedroom, his hand warm and solid around hers. Beck appeared almost out of nowhere as they got to the door.

"Does Mrs. Samuel need help getting out of the dress?" she asked, suppressing a yawn.

"Absolutely not." Sam steered Emily through the door, and then added almost tenderly, "Get some sleep, Beck."

He shut the door, and they were alone. Husband and wife. Emily shivered in anticipation.

"Are you cold?"

She had the feeling he would throw a fur over her shoulders if she should mention she had the slightest chill. But she wasn't shivering because she was cold, quite the opposite.

"I'm fine." Her fingers trembled. Was it from drink? Exhaustion? Excitement?

He lit a lamp and set it low, so there was enough light to see, but barely. Of course candle, lamp, lantern, it didn't matter much, almost all lighting in this time period was mood lighting. Nothing ever quite dispelled the shadows, and that suited her fine.

"Are you sure you don't want Beck's help with the buttons?"

He ran his fingers slowly over her bare shoulders. Goosebumps rose up and down her arms. "I am going to undress my wife, myself."

A shiver of pleasure went through her.

"You are lovely." His breath tickled her neck as his fingers moved to the dozens of small buttons that ran down her back. He fumbled with them and she didn't know if his fingers were unsure or if he was toying with her. Either way, it only made her shivers increase. She almost wished he could unzip her dress and have it fall to the floor, but as he undid button after button and her skin tingled with yearning, she realized this was definitely the more exciting option. As each button loosened, her heart beat a little faster and her breath became more ragged. His fingertips brushed her back as he worked.

Finally the buttons were undone, and he slid the dress down her arms, exposing her corset. But the dress wouldn't slide down over the hoops. Should she have undone the hoops first? How did people get graciously naked in the 1800s?

"I think the dress has to go off over my head." She turned to face him again.

"Then that's what we'll do." His voice was rough, as if he was having trouble catching his breath. He took hold of the bottom of the skirt and brought up over her head, nearly getting lost in the yards of material himself. She laughed as she untangled him from the dress, and together they placed it across a chair, out of the way.

She stood in front of him in her corset and hoops and petticoats, and crossed her arms, suddenly shy and exposed.

"Don't hide," he said, taking her hands in his, and putting them by her side. He gazed at her longingly and her breath came faster, as the muscles in her legs weakened. "A minute," he said and let go of her long enough to slip out of his shoes and uniform jacket. He placed the jacket on her dress and stood in front of her again.

Now it was her turn to fumble with buttons. Wordlessly she reached out, the linen of his cloth smooth beneath her fingertips, undoing the three that closed his shirt, while he let his fingers touch the tops of her breasts. She nearly swooned at the touch. Swooned, like a fangirl at a boy band concert. But his touch was electrifying. She wanted him to touch more of her, all of her. And now.

She grasped the hem of his shirt, intending to pull it over his head, but with a touch to her hand he stopped her and first removed his cuff links. Then he smiled and raised his hands to assist her, as she stripped him of his shirt. One shirt off, but he still wore an undershirt. It was amazing anyone ever managed to have sex with all the clothes they had to take off first. She ran her hands over the cotton of his undershirt, wanting to be touching bare skin and afraid she'd never get the chance. Her fingers felt for the buttons on his fly and trembled as she tried to make the button go through the hole.

He took her hands in his and instead of helping her, moved her hands away and whispered. "My turn." He loosened the tie of her petticoat and lifted it over her head, then he let her unfasten his pants. She fumbled in her eagerness to get him undressed, but finally his uniform slacks pooled around his ankles. She smiled shyly at him, because, while he still had on his under drawers, it was obvious he was ready for what lay ahead. Gently she stroked him and he made an odd strangled sound as he caught his breath.

With one hand behind her neck he pulled her closer, and his lips found hers. She melted against him, feeling the heat of his body against hers with only a few layers of cloth separating them.

After a long minute, she put her hand on his chest and pulled back ever so slightly. "We haven't finished undressing," she murmured, her mouth resting against his cheek.

"It was taking too long," he replied.

"But we're almost there." She let her hand wander again. "It will be worth it."

"You're right," he said and nibbled lightly on her ear. She giggled and held him tighter. "Can't get you undressed if you don't let go."

So she took a step back and held her hands out to her sides, inviting him to remove the rest of her clothing. He undid the first hook on the front of the corset, and her breasts popped free of their restraint. He gently touched each nipple through the cloth of the chemise while electric currents shot through her body and she struggled to stay standing.

"The hoop first," she said as he fumbled with the next hook on the corset. She reached for the buttons that held the hoop to the corset.

He took her hands in his. "I'll do it," he whispered in her ear.

"Quickly, please." Her whole body tingled with the desire to be naked and in bed with him.

"Quickly," he assured her as the hoop pooled around her ankles.

She didn't bother to kick it aside but reached for his undershirt and pulled it over his head and, dropped it to the floor. She ran her hands over his warm chest, letting her fingers play in the dark curly hair.

"You have the advantage on me," he said, his voice thick. He undid the next hook on the corset.

Her breath came in rapid shallow bursts. Every cell in her body cried out for his touch. When the last hook was released the corset fell to the ground with the hoop.

She took hold of the chemise, not wanting to wait a second longer to have it off, but he removed the cloth from her hands.

He pulled her chemise over her head, and his hands went right to her breasts, making her whole body strain toward him. She untied the top of his under drawers and pushed them over his hips. He stepped out of them, and untied her bloomers. They fell with the rest of her under things to the floor.

Naked except for their stockings, he scooped her up in his arms and deposited her on the bed. She wanted him to lay down beside her, to touch her body, to become one with her. Instead he sat beside her and pulled off his socks, then he untied the garters from around her thighs, his fingers inching so close to her upper thighs that she was sure he would feel the moisture and heat she was generating. Slowly, he pulled her stockings off.

She'd never imagined getting undressed could be as sensuous as this. Forget foreplay, she was ready for the main attraction and all they'd really done so far was get naked.

He ran his fingers lightly over her skin, tracing her nipples and making her arch her back and gasp as she reached for him. She needed him beside her. Her body was crying out for full skin to skin contact. She needed to know him to feel him, to give herself to him totally and fully. She was ready in a way she had never thought possible.

"Let me turn out the lamp." He shifted his weight, as if to move, his voice was hoarse with excitement.

"No," she said, reaching out and touching his thigh. "Leave it on. I want to see you. I want to see your face when we make love."

"You do?" He raised an eyebrow as he gazed at her.

"I do." She let her fingers stroke his thigh. "At least the first time."

"First time?" He let out a slightly strangled cry and touched her hand. For a second she thought he was going to make her stop, but then instead he stroked her inner thigh.

"Oh!" She gasped as erotic sensations filled her. "You weren't planning on sleeping tonight, were you?" she managed to ask.

"That wasn't on my agenda, no." He lowered his mouth to her nipple and sucked and she bit her lip to keep from crying out.

This was her husband. Husband. Lying here with her. Touching her. Making her gasp for breath. Making her want to be one with him. Her husband who would be going off to war and never coming back. They didn't have time to slowly get to know each other. She had to memorize every inch of him, the way he felt, the way he made her feel. Every second counted in a way it never had before.

They came together as husband and wife, and she wanted the moment to never end, the sensations to never stop. She cried out, not even caring that someone might hear, and Sam collapsed on the bed next to her, breathing as hard as she was.

"Are you okay?" he asked, his voice like a caress.

"Yes." Her breathing still came in ragged gasps. "I didn't ever want it to end."

"Don't worry," he said, already stroking her breast as he held her. "We'll take our time the next time."

"And the time after that." She let her hands explore his skin, relishing the heat and sheen of sweat that covered him.

"And the time after *that*."

She laughed, delighted at the prospect.

This time when he moved to turn out the light she didn't stop him. She'd never forget the ecstasy she saw on his face when they made love.

They got under the coverlet, holding tight to each other. "I didn't know it was going to be that amazing," he whispered into her hair.

"I've heard it gets better with practice," she answered, lightly running her fingers over his nipples.

"Then shall we practice?"

"Yes." Because they didn't have years to get to know each other's body. They had a week. Only a week. She tried not to focus on that as they made love again, and she tried to memorize how it felt. She would never feel this way again. Tears brimmed in her eyes but she blinked them away. This was not a time for tears.

Finally, as the sun shone through the curtains, she fell asleep, safe in the arms of the man she loved. The man she would lose.

A couple of hours later, she awoke to his hands caressing her naked skin. This was oh so much better than any alarm clock could ever be. She wriggled closer to him and enjoyed the warmth of his skin on hers. She wanted to wake every morning to his hands on her, to her senses bursting with excitement. But she knew that was impossible.

"We're getting good at this," she said when they had brought each other to completion once again. "Must be all the practice."

"You are an amazing woman," he said. "Do you think anyone would notice if we stayed here, in this bed, until it was time for me to meet my company?"

"We might get hungry," she answered. Why had he brought up his deployment? She'd been trying to forget that. She gently circled one of his nipples with her finger.

"We can have food brought up."

"In that case we can stay here all week."

But of course, they couldn't. By the time the shadows in the room lengthened as the sun made its way across the sky, she knew they had to get up and be social. After all, when Sam did deploy in a week, it wasn't only Emily he would be leaving behind, but his whole family. They deserved some time with him.

Emily slipped into her chemise and picked scattered garments up from around the room. It didn't take Sam long to be dressed in trousers and shirt. It would take her longer. He helped her into the corset. It had been so much more enjoyable when he'd helped her out of it. She fastened the hoop to it and put on a petticoat. She hung her wedding gown in the armoire and took out her new blue day dress.

"Will you help me, husband?" She didn't want the magic intimacy between them to end by having to call Beck in to get her dressed.

"Of course, my love." He helped her get it over her head and situated around her hoop, then he buttoned it for her. "They should really make these dresses with fewer buttons."

"They will." She wasn't sure when the zipper would be invented, but it was definitely an underappreciated item.

"I'm afraid I can't help you with your hair," he said as she sat at the dressing table and studied the rats nest that had once been a fancy hair style.

"That's okay. I've got it." She did the best she could without any styling products. It might not look how Beck would do it, but it did look a little less like she'd just crawled out of bed.

"We should have a photograph made of us in our wedding outfits." He took her hand as she stood from the dressing table. "There's a man in town who does that. We can go in tomorrow; would you like that? We can have two copies made, one for each of us."

"That sounds wonderful." She kept her voice light, but needing two copies reminded her that her time with Sam was limited and every time she thought of that she got a piercing pain through her heart. She understood now how people could die of heartbreak, and he hadn't even left yet. What would it be like when he did?

They went downstairs, arm in arm, to find no one

around.

"Where is everyone?" Sam asked Tobias.

"Mrs. Marshall and Elizabeth went visiting. I believe they went to the Johnsons."

Emily felt slightly uneasy at that. Dinah Johnson, the woman who Sam had been engaged to when she met him. Naturally they had not been at the wedding yesterday, but Dinah was still Elizabeth's best friend.

"Don't worry about Dinah," Sam said, giving her hand a squeeze.

"She certainly can't stop you from marrying me now. That deed is done."

"Indeed it is." He gave her a wink and turned back to Tobias "And my father?"

"Gone to town," Tobias answered. "Everyone is supposed to be back by dinner. They wanted to give you both some privacy."

It wasn't exactly a honeymoon in Hawaii, but it had been sweet of them.

"In that case, my wife." He looked at Emily and grinned, and for a second she thought he was going to suggest they head back upstairs. "Let's take a walk in the rose garden."

That was good, too.

How any times in the past few weeks had they strolled down to the garden arm in arm. But today she was with her husband. This was her garden. Not exactly hers, but they couldn't kick her out now. She belonged. It gave everything a brighter tinge, like an Instagram filter.

The roses were in bloom now, sending their delicate fragrance through the air. They sat on the bench, a bower of roses above them.

"I want to talk baby names," Sam said as she settled her skirt around her.

"Baby names?" Baby names were nowhere near the top of the list of things she thought they should talk about. But yet, she didn't really want to talk about him going off to war, she didn't want to discuss the possibility of them never seeing each other again or whether she should stay here and wait to hear of his fate, or go back to her own time where she would be safe. She would stay here of course, as long as there was a chance, but she didn't particularly want to talk about it.

"Yes." There was a very determined tone in his voice. "I know there may be no future for us, but it is also possible that you might get pregnant before I leave."

Pregnant. In all of this, how had she not had the same thought? She wasn't on the pill. They had no condoms. She hadn't had her period since she'd been back here and attributed that to the way time travel messed with her body, so she had no idea where in her cycle she really was. But pregnant. Good lord, what if she got pregnant and Sam died? She'd be a single mother in the 1860s. Or even worse, what if she went home, pregnant with Sam's child—how could she ever explain that?

"And if you do get pregnant, I thought we should discuss possible names."

"Of course," she said, still reeling from the thought. "Would you like Sam, Junior if it's a boy?" Men often had strong feelings about that. Some definitely wanted a Junior. Others just as adamantly did not. "My friend Dayna and her husband, Johnson want to name their child a combination of both of their names if it's a boy. DayJon."

"DayJon?" He'd been stroking her thumb, but now he froze.

"Yes. It's really not that odd sounding a name for my time." She gave his hand a reassuring squeeze. "I'm not sure we could combine our names. Samily? Emmuel? Samem? Nothing would be quite right." She laughed, but Sam wasn't joining in with her, instead he looked alarmed. "What's the matter?"

"Come with me." He stood and held out a hand for her. She took it hesitantly wondering what she could have said that had changed his mood so abruptly. "There's something you need to hear."

"Is everything all right?" she asked as he pulled her toward the stables.

"You tell me," he answered which wasn't an answer at all as far as she was concerned. "Just listen to what Moses has to say."

With trepidation she found herself seated on a bale of hay in the stables.

"Tell her the story, Moses." Sam stood, arms crossed, beside her.

Moses let his gaze bounce back and forth between her and Sam and she had the distinct feeling he didn't want to say anything.

"Tell her about DayJon," Sam insisted and a chill enveloped her.

"What about DayJon?" she asked, attempting to get to her feet. Sam put a restraining hand on her shoulder.

"Just listen." He gave her shoulder a squeeze, but she didn't feel reassured.

So she listened while Moses told a completely

believable story about a man named DayJon who appeared one day and said he was free, that all men were free, but was enslaved simply because of the color of his skin, and one day whipped to death because he would not, or could not conform.

"Could it be your friend's son?" Sam asked.

Emily's hands were ice cold even though the afternoon was warm.

"She doesn't even have a son yet. I mean, they only just got married." But the thing with time travel, is linear time really had no meaning. So could a yet unborn child of Dayna and Johnson have come here near on sixty years ago? Why not? But what did this mean, other than she had to warn Dayna and Johnson? And what kind of warning exactly would she give? The easiest seemed to be to tell them not to name a child DayJon, then the tragic hero of Moses' story couldn't be their child, but was that how things worked? If he had already come back in time, could changing the future change what happened in the past?

And what if she did get pregnant now? How would that affect future generations?

It was too much to take in.

"Sam." She couldn't keep her voice from shaking. "Do you suppose I could have a bit of brandy?"

Some things were easier to deal with after a drink or two.

Chapter Thirty

Sam

Sam sat Emily in one of the chairs in the study and poured brandy into a globe-shaped snifter. He placed the glass in her shaking hands, and she took a sip.

Color started to return to her cheeks, and he breathed a little easier. It had been wrong of him to bring her to Moses and make her listen to that story, but he thought she should know, but what good did it do to know something like that if there was nothing you could do about it?

"You can go home…warn her." The thing was, for her to warn her friend, she would have to leave him. Have to go back to her own time. Of course, if he really should die in battle, it's what he wanted for her, to be safe among her friends and family. But yet, he didn't want to admit to himself that he really would die in the war. He wanted to know that she was here, waiting for him. It was a selfish attitude, he admitted, but it was true.

"This is my home now, isn't it?" She gazed at him through those big brown eyes and his heart warmed. "I said I'd be here waiting for you, and I will." It was what he hoped she'd say. "Besides, I don't see what good it would do even if I did warn her. I mean, Moses remembers it happening, it can't unhappen, can it?"

Sam strode to the window and stared out at the pastel woods and fields. Could things unhappen? If Emily had come back from the future and made a life here now, didn't that change things? Life was much easier to figure out when he had been certain time moved in a straight line.

He turned back toward Emily, who studied her glass of brandy as if it were a crystal ball and would tell her the answers. "I don't know," he said. "I really don't know."

She took another sip of her drink and her face lost that haunted look. She took a deep breath and smiled at him, though the smile didn't quite reach her eyes. "No matter. There really is nothing I can do about it if it already happened, and if it is destined to happen, there's no point in my telling Dayna and giving her something to worry about. Even if I could. And in the meantime, we have a week left to enjoy being husband and wife, we shouldn't waste it."

He gave her what he hoped was a seductive wink. "You want to go back upstairs already?"

She laughed, and even her eyes twinkled. "Oh, maybe not quite yet. Soon, though. I thought we could perhaps finish our walk in the rose garden. We were going to discuss baby names, if I remember correctly."

He took her hand and helped her up, she left the half empty brandy glass on the desk and they headed back outside.

The walked arm in arm back to the rose garden and it's entrancing colors and fragrances. The warmth of her, so close, aroused him. He would have preferred if she'd agreed to go right back up to bed. Though, he supposed a bit of fresh air wouldn't do them any harm.

"You never did answer if you wanted a Sam Junior or not." She looked up at him with an elfish smile.

"Oh, I think so." He gave her a kiss, because she was his wife and he could. "I'd like to think that I'm the start of a legacy. But what if it's a girl? Emily Junior?"

"No, she'd end up being Little Emily and I'd be Big Emily and I couldn't go through the rest of my life like that." She laughed and he laughed with her. This was real, talking about baby names with his wife. The war, time travel, that was all an illusion. "I always liked the name Sarah, but I also think I'd like to name a girl after my mother. Her name is Marie."

"How about Emma Marie, after you and your mother?" He gently stroked her palm with his thumb.

"That could work. Though it is all theoretical right now." She pulled a rose blossom toward her, inhaled, and sighed happily.

"Oh, I don't know, we were awfully busy up there, you never know what might have happened." He grinned, remembering.

"Would it be good if it had, though?" Her hands going protectively toward her womb.

"Don't you think so?" He was surprised how much it hurt that she might not be as enthusiastic about the idea of children as he was.

"I'm not sure. I don't want to raise a child alone." Her voice cracked and suddenly he understood her concerns. "What if…"

"I'll come back," he said with a sudden certainty. He could not imagine not coming back to her, and that had to mean he would. "I'll come back."

She swallowed hard and he saw a tear glisten on her eyelash. "Then I'll be here, waiting." She smiled up at him. "Or perhaps, we will be here waiting, if we worked hard enough."

He didn't think he could love her more. He wrapped her in his arms. "Thank you, my love. Thank you."

The peaceful reverie was interrupted by the clopping of horse hooves echoing up from the road.

"Someone is home." He tilted his head to listen. "One horse, so it's probably Father come from town. I'm sure Mother and Elizabeth took the carriage."

He tucked Emily's hand into the crook of his elbow and led her out of the rose garden to greet his father. Only, it wasn't his father who rode up, but George.

"Sam, Sam!" George called out when he saw him. "I just saw Yuengling. He's got orders. We leave tomorrow."

Emily clutched at his arm and Sam's shoulders slumped as he deflated with dismay.

"Tomorrow?" He nearly choked on the word.

"I know, I know," George said, from atop his horse. "I told Yuengling you were newly married, but he didn't have much sympathy. His own wife is way past when they expected her baby to deliver. He hoped he could hold his babe before he left."

"I thought we'd have nearly a week more." Tomorrow? The word echoed through his brain like a death knell. How could he leave Emily tomorrow?

"Be glad the word didn't come that we had to leave before your wedding," George pointed out. He tipped his hat to Emily. "Good afternoon, Mrs. Marshall."

"What time?" Emily asked him, her voice surprisingly strong. "Tomorrow, but what time?"

"Dawn," George answered. "He wants everyone to

muster tonight so he can march out at first light. I convinced him that you could be trusted to get there by the time he leaves, and he agreed. See, he does have some sympathy for your plight after all."

One more night. That's all they would have together. It wasn't nearly enough. Not nearly enough.

"I better go," George said, with a glance toward the position of the sun. "I need to get ready. I don't have an excuse not to show up tonight. At least I get one more good meal at home. I'll see you in the morning." He rode off, leaving Sam feeling like the world had dropped away from him. One more night.

"I'm sorry." The words sounding thick to his ears. "I'm sorry, Emily. I want more time with you."

"At least we have tonight." He could hear the anguish in her voice. "We have tonight."

"It's not enough." He pulled her close to him, holding her warm body against his. They should have gotten married earlier. They should have not waited until they were married to bed. Anything so he could have had more time with her.

"Since it's all we have," she said, her voice muffled against his chest. "We'll make it enough."

His father rode up next. "I saw Yuengling. He's pulling out tomorrow."

"I know," Sam said, still holding Emily to himself. "George was here and told me. I have to meet him before dawn tomorrow."

"It's not a lot of time." His father's eyes held so much sadness Sam thought his heart would break.

"No, but I'm essentially packed. I…" He squeezed Emily a little tighter.

"As I said," his father said, his voice full of

sympathy. "It's not a lot of time." He cleared his throat. "Your mother will not be happy."

"No one's going to be happy about it," he said taking a deep breath to fortify himself. "We'll have to make do."

His father went inside giving him a little bit of privacy with Emily. "I'm going to have to spend some of this evening with my parents, you do understand?"

"Of course I do," she said, looking up to his face. "As long as you come up to my bed tonight, I can't ask much more."

"You'll have that. I promise you'll have that."

If he had his way, he'd take her up to their bed right now and not stop making love to her until he had to dress and leave in the wee hours of the morning.

"I'll be back," he murmured into her hair.

"I know," she answered, holding him tight.

Did either of them really believe it? He wasn't sure.

"The picture!" Emily said suddenly.

"What picture?" he asked, still imagining himself in bed with her.

"The photograph. Do you think there is time to get it done?" She sounded so concerned that Sam decided that it was of the utmost importance.

"Yes." He looked down into her eager face. "Should we put on our wedding clothes again?"

"Is there time? Oughtn't we to hurry?"

"We'll make time." He called to a passing slave child to find Beck to help Emily dress. They went upstairs, and he put on his uniform. When he first put on the jacket yesterday, it had felt new and special and made him feel important, but now he realized he'd be wearing it all the time. Suddenly it didn't seem quite so wonderful.

Within half an hour, he and his wife were riding into town in the buggy, dressed once again in their finery from the night before. "I'm so sorry I have to leave so soon." He must have said it a hundred times already.

"Stop apologizing." She laid a comforting hand on his knee. "We knew we wouldn't have much time; we just didn't realize how little we would have. But we'll make the most of it. One day, one week, what's important is that we are together, and you are my husband."

He squeezed her hand. It was hard to find small talk though, his departure loomed over everything, but yet neither of them wanted to discuss that more than necessary. Maybe if they had known each other longer they would have other topics to fall back on. Maybe not. War stole all conversation from everyone these days.

"Elsbeth!" he said suddenly remembering the part of the story Moses hadn't told.

"Are we still talking baby names?" Emily asked, rightly confused by his outburst.

"No." She needed to know this. It could make the difference between her getting home safely and being stuck here without him should the worst happen. "Moses didn't tell you everything. He told you about DayJon, but he didn't tell you about Elsbeth."

"She's someone else, who came here, out of time?" Her voice rose a little in excitement.

"No. She left here. She was my grandfather's sister and disappeared without a trace right before she was to be married. Her portrait hangs in the hall. Moses says when the fairies bring someone here they take someone away." He turned the buggy down the road toward town.

"Did anyone disappear when I came?" Emily asked.

"No. But of course, we know it's not the fairies."

"Oh, I don't know. Fairies make as much sense as time portal fishing pond," she said with a wry laugh. She stared at the passing trees for a moment before speaking again. "Do you think she went to the past?"

"I don't know," Sam answered truthfully. Her disappearance may have had nothing to do with time travel at all. "But I thought, before I left, I should make sure you knew. It might end up being a helpful clue at some point."

She squeezed his knee.

"Thank you, but it won't matter. I don't need clues. I'm staying here, waiting for you to come home from war."

He certainly wasn't going to contradict that sentiment.

They pulled up in front of the photographer's studio. The door was closed and shade drawn.

"We're too late!" Emily lamented.

"No." He hopped out of the buggy. "Wait here. I'll get him." He tied the reins to the hitching post and went around the back of the storefront, where he knew Mr. Edwards had his private quarters. He pounded on the door, and Mr. Edwards, in shirt sleeves, his tie untied, answered the door.

"What can I do for you, Sam?"

"I need you to make a picture for me." He tried to

keep his voice calm and professional. He wasn't sure he succeeded.

"Tomorrow morning," Mr. Edwards said. "First thing. I've got some other appointments, but I'll squeeze you in."

"No!" His heart beat faster and his palms started to sweat as panic threatened to overcome him. He wanted to be able to leave Emily with this one thing. "I pull out with Yuengling's company tomorrow, first light. I need it now. My wife. My new wife. Please."

Mrs. Edwards, a towel in her hands, came into view. "Ah, go take their pictures, Johnnie. The lad's going off to war, and the wife needs a memento. The dinner will wait."

Sam smiled thankfully at her, taking a deep breath to slow his beating heart.

Mr. Edwards sighed and put his jacket back on. "All right then, come around to the front, I'll let you in."

Sam collected Emily from the buggy and brought her into the studio. "I'll want two," Sam told him. "One for me, and one for my wife."

"Sure, sure," the photographer said as he prepared his equipment. "You'll have to sit by the window, it's the best light we'll get right now." When he had his equipment set up, he brought a chair and placed it by the window, and instructed Emily to sit on it. Sam stood behind her, and to the side, putting his hand on her shoulder. She reached over and took hold of his other hand, and as they posed, clinging to each other for dear life, the photographer did his magic and made the exposures.

"I can have these ready for you tomorrow," he said,

already putting his studio back to rights.

Sam sighed. He would not get it before he left.

"I can mail it to you, can't I?" Emily asked, clutching his hand. "I mean, you will be able to get and receive letters."

He hadn't even thought of letters. He had been so focused on not being physically near Emily that he hadn't considered they could still stay in touch.

"Yes, of course," he said, smiling at her. "You can send it to me."

He took out his wallet and counted out the money to pay the photographer, including a little extra to thank him for opening back up to take the picture.

"Godspeed to you, Sam." Mr. Edwards clasped his hand.

Sam swallowed hard. "Thank you, sir."

He helped Emily back into the wagon, and they rode back to the house, talking about the gorgeous spring afternoon, because any other topic of conversation was too painful.

Tobias met them in the drive and took over the horses. "The family has gathered to dinner," he told them. So still dressed in their wedding finery Sam led his wife into the dining room. Despite their gay apparel, it was a somber affair, especially after the lavishness of the night before.

"Be sure to wear two pairs of socks," his mother said, dabbing her mouth with her napkin. "It will help keep your feet dry and warm. Warm, dry feet are very important."

"Of course, Mother." He was hardly listening, unable to take his eyes from Emily, wanting to memorize everything about her. Any photograph wouldn't do her justice.

"You need to get the respect of your men right away," his father said, signaling for more wine. "To be sure they listen to you in battle."

"Yes, Father," Sam said. "Respect. Got it."

He barely registered what he ate, although he was aware it was certainly immeasurably better than anything he'd be eating in the near future. Why had he signed up to go to war? What foolish, romantic notion had led him to this point?

When dinner ended, he automatically followed his father to the study. His father poured them each a glass of whiskey, and they settled in the wing chairs with their pipes. How long before he'd be able to do this again? Even here, with just the two of them the conversation was stilted. There was too much to say and not enough time to say it, so they said nothing.

"We should join the women; your mother wants time with you before you go." His father put out his pipe and placed his empty glass on the sideboard.

Emily stood when he entered the parlor where the women were waiting. He immediately went to her side and took her hand. "I'll go upstairs," she said, tenderly releasing her hand from his, "and let you take leave of your family in private."

No one told her she didn't have to do that, and he watched her go, knowing she would be waiting in his bed when he got there. Talk was awkward and forced. His mother kept dabbing at her eyes. His father sat straight, his jaw tight, occasionally emitting platitudes like "we know you'll do us proud" or "you'll be home by Christmas."

Elizabeth slouched in the corner of the couch, her

lip stuck out in a pout. "It's not fair that they gave you so little warning. Joseph didn't even have time to propose."

After about an hour, his father checked his watch and said, "You should get some sleep, son; you need to leave quite early."

Sam had no intention of sleeping tonight, and he suspected his father knew that.

"You'll all still be abed when I leave," he said. "I'll say my goodbyes now."

He hugged them all, even his father, and assured them he would be back.

"In time for Christmas!" Elizabeth said with forced cheerfulness.

"Yes, definitely. And you'll all take care of Emily for me."

"Rest assured, son," his father said, a comforting hand on his shoulder. "She is our daughter now. You need not worry."

But of course he would worry anyway. How could he not?

He took leave of his parents and Elizabeth and took the steps two at a time leading to his room. The lamp on the table burned, showing him that Emily waited under the covers in his bed. He undressed quickly, putting things where he could find them a few hours from now when he had to leave.

Naked, he approached the bed and pulled back the covers. She was naked, and he remembered that night, only a few weeks ago, when he found her like this, in his bed. Then she had been a stranger. Now she was his wife. He reached out now, like he did then, to touch her creamy white breast. This time she did not scream, but smiled up at him.

"Come to bed, husband," she said to him.
And he did.

Chapter Thirty-One

Emily

They hadn't planned to sleep at all, but two nights of virtually no sleep caught up with them, and Emily dozed off in Sam's arms. She awoke to him caressing her breast. "Do you have to leave soon?" she murmured. There was no light coming through the curtains, and at some point, he had doused the lantern. She didn't know how he knew what time it might be, but he had to be with his unit by first light, which meant leaving here in the dark.

"Soon," he whispered the word, as a caress, in her ear. "But I still have a little time."

They used the time wisely, making love slowly and carefully, memorizing each other in the few moments they had left together. They lay together, sated, for several minutes, and then Sam disentangled himself from her. She sat up and watched as he got dressed by candlelight.

"Go back to sleep," he told her, touching her gently on the knee.

"No." As if there was any chance of her sleeping away the last few moments they would have together. "I'll stay with you until you leave."

He didn't argue with her. When he was dressed in his uniform, looking like he did on their wedding day, she thought her heart might crack in two.

"I need to leave," he whispered hoarsely.

"I'll go down with you." She found her chemise on the floor and slipped it on. He took a dressing gown, his, from a hook, and put it over her shoulders.

Together they walked downstairs. The house was quiet, but when they got to the front door, Tobias stood there with the reins of Sam's horse in his hands. The saddlebags were loaded, the bedroll was strapped across the back. He had sent a separate trunk with additional supplies up the night before to where the troops were camping. That would travel with the unit by wagon.

He turned to her, standing there on the porch and wrapped his arms around her. She wanted to stay like that forever, but knew they couldn't. She breathed him in, the scent of their lovemaking was still on him, as well as the wool of his jacket and that ever present smell of cinnamon.

"Why do you smell like cinnamon?" The question was completely out of place, but if she didn't ask now, she likely would never know.

He laughed and kissed the top of her head. "It's in my hair pomade. You don't mind, do you?"

So that explained that. "Mind? No, I like it, and cinnamon will always make me think of you."

"Will you need a reminder to think of me?"

"No." She pressed her cheek into the wool of his coat. "No. I won't need anything to remind me of you."

"I'll be back." His strong arms held her tight.

Famous last words.

"I know." She was not ready to let him go yet.

"I love you," he whispered the words fervently into her ear.

"I love you." She could barely keep back her tears. There was nothing else she could say.

His mouth found hers then, and he kissed her long and hard. Her knees grew weak, and she wanted to bed him again right now but knew that wasn't possible.

Behind them Tobias cleared his throat. "It's getting late, sir."

The kiss ended, as she had always known it would have to.

"I will be back." Even as he separated himself from her, he still clutched her hand.

"And I'll be here." She let go of his hand, finally, and brought her fingers to her mouth to try to hide her sadness from him.

With that he mounted his horse and rode off to war.

She stood, his dressing gown wrapped around her, watching until even the sound of the hoof beats faded into the distance. He was gone. Really and truly gone.

"Mrs. Samuel?" Tobias spoke the words softly, standing only a few feet away. "Can I get you anything?"

"Oh, no, thank you." She stared off into the space where Sam had been.

"If you don't mind my saying so, ma'am, you should be back in bed."

"I should, you're right. Thank you." Like one in a dream, or perhaps a nightmare, she trudged up the stairs and back to the room. Sam's room. It felt cold and empty and lonely without him. She climbed under the covers, which still held the scent of him, and let the tears flow. She didn't even try to hold them back, for what was the use. She'd found her true love and lost him. She could still feel his touch on her body, it wasn't possible that she would never see him again, but yet, she couldn't forget the words of the woman at the inn "he died in the Civil War."

She woke to the smell of cinnamon and for a brief, wonderful moment, thought that Sam was back, but it was Beck, laying a tea tray on the dresser. "I wasn't sure if you were awake yet, but I thought a cup of tea would do you good." She pulled open the curtains and let the morning light into the room.

"I'm not hungry." She closed her eyes against the light and snuggled deeper under the covers and Sam's dressing gown, still worn over her chemise.

"I imagine not, but a cup of tea would do you good. My mama put a bit of peppermint in it. It will soothe you."

"I don't need soothing. I need Sam," she muttered.

"I'll leave the tea here all the same." She heard Beck grasp the doorknob, but the door didn't open. She opened her eyes a slit to see Beck standing, one hand on the door, looking at her intently. "You said, once Mister Sam left, we'd make plans for my escape."

"It's too soon," she protested. She didn't have the energy to get out of bed, much less help Beck escape. Not today.

"Why?" Beck persisted. "He's gone. There's no point in delaying."

He's gone. She didn't want to think about the fact that he was gone. She could still smell his scent on her. Why did Beck have to remind her he was gone. She stifled a sob. "Please let me get my equilibrium, okay. I'll help. I swear. But let me…I don't know…give me time."

"Fine," Beck said, in a tone of voice that meant it

wasn't fine at all. "What's it to you anyway, if I spend more time as a slave?"

"Please!" She couldn't keep tears from coming back to her eyes. "At least let me get one good night's sleep so I can think straight. Is that so much to ask?"

Beck left the room without further comment. After a few minutes, the scent of the peppermint wafting from the tea was too tempting, and she got out of bed and picked up the cup. She took it over to the window. In the fields the hands worked, hoed, weeded, whatever it was they did at this time in the planting cycle.

In the rose garden Mr. and Mrs. Marshall walked arm in arm, heads close together. How much harder must it be for them to have Sam go off to war. He was their son, their only son. They had known and loved him for over twenty-five years. She had only known him a few weeks. If they could go on with their lives, so could she. It was only fair.

She wished she could forget what that woman at the inn had said. If she hadn't heard he would die in the Civil War, she would be fairly confident he would return. But she *had* heard that woman say that. Of course, she'd been fairly drunk at the time, maybe she had misheard. That was entirely possible. She took a sip of the tea. The peppermint was soothing. Certainly she had misunderstood what the woman had said. She couldn't trust anything she heard while she was drunk.

There had been something else too. A poem. The woman had said Sam was a poet of renown. He wasn't yet. She was pretty sure someone would have mentioned it, like perhaps Sam, himself, if he had a reputation as a poet. She didn't think she could marry someone and not know that about them. Then again, she didn't know very much about him at all. Still, if he was going to be known as a poet, he needed time to write that poetry, and clearly he hadn't yet.

There had been a poem at the inn. She'd read it. What on earth had it been about? Oh! It had to do with *her*. Shivers went up her arms and she clutched the tea cup a little tighter. So, this was meant to be, her coming here and meeting Sam. It had happened before it ever happened. How was that possible?

She shook her head to try to clear it and took another sip of the tea. What did she know for certain? She knew she was from the twenty-first century and now in the nineteenth, so time travel was possible which made pretty much anything else possible. She knew that Sam would be a poet and possibly die in the war. But she knew he wasn't a poet yet, at least she didn't think so, so there was time. Time meant that he might get leave and come to see her, or at least time to write letters to each other. She would not give up yet. And that meant getting dressed and meeting the day, even without Sam here by her side.

She finished her tea and ate the cinnamon bun that Beck had brought up. She needed to start putting in place the plan to free Beck. Today or tomorrow she needed to mention some distant relative in Philadelphia that she would like to visit, perhaps get train tickets or something. That would be good.

She took off Sam's dressing gown and hung it on the hook by the door. She pulled on her bloomers under her chemise and managed to get into the corset by fastening it up the front. The petticoats and hoop she could manage on her own, but the dress with its yards of cloth and buttons up the back, was too much for her.

She made the bed, laid the dress across it, and straightened up the rest of the room, knowing that Beck would be back at some point to help her.

She sat at Sam's desk and opened the drawers hoping to find some writing paper. She would start a letter to him now. She found some paper and pulled it out. The first page had some writing on it.

A sprite from the land of Faerie
Bewitching me with a glance
She touched my hand and stole my heart
Our meeting: more than happenstance

She shivered. She recognized that. It was the beginning of the poem she had seen the night of Dayna's wedding. She was almost certain. If the poem wasn't finished yet, then certainly Sam had to stay alive at least until he could write the rest. There was something reassuring in that. She took out another piece of paper, fussed with the fountain pen until she got it to provide her ink on demand, and began a letter.

Dearest Sam,
You've been gone a few hours now, and I can still feel your touch on my skin. I already miss you so much it is hard to describe, but yet, I know you are going to be okay and come back to me. I can feel it. I know I will see you again. Any other possibility is simply not thinkable.

The door opened, and Beck poked her head in. "You ready to get dressed, miss?"

"I am," she answered.

Beck came into the room. "You're getting better at doing more yourself."

"I try. I don't know how someone can get dressed themselves with all the buttons up the back though." She tucked her started letter into the desk drawer.

"You can't," Beck agreed. "You need some skirts and shirtwaists and maybe a day dress with buttons up the front. Tell Mrs. Marshall you need these things, but don't say it's because I won't be here."

"Okay. I can do that. And don't worry, I won't give anything away." She stood, in preparation for Beck to finish dressing her. "Do you think they'll mind buying me more clothes?"

"You're Mrs. Samuel now, they'll get you whatever you need." Beck picked up the dress and eased it over Emily's head. "Right now, Mr. Marshall wants to go into town to pick up the photographs you and Mister Sam had made. He hopes you'll go with him."

"Of course I will," she answered as she emerged from the yards of material.

"The tea helped?" Beck deftly buttoned up the back of the dress.

"Very much so," she said. "Thank you, and thank your mother for thinking of it."

Before heading downstairs to the family, she took a deep breath. The important thing to remember was that Sam didn't belong solely to her, and she couldn't act as if he did. To wallow in her own misery would make her a chore for these people, and that was not what she wanted.

Mr. Marshall greeted her with a warm smile when she got to the bottom of the stairs. "Emily! How are you this morning? I know it must be difficult to have your husband leave so soon."

Deep breath. Don't let the tears win. Be strong. She smiled back at him, hoping it didn't look forced. "I imagine it is even more difficult for you, you've known him so much longer."

Mr. Marshall took her hand and led her toward the carriage where Mrs. Marshall and Elizabeth were waiting.

"That's sweet of you to say," he responded, "but I don't believe for one minute that it's true. We'll do our best for you, though, until he can be with you again."

She could only hope that day would actually come.

****

She lived through that day and the next. She began planning a trip to Philadelphia with Beck as her companion. She mailed Sam the picture and her letter and got a letter from him telling her not to worry, that the worst they had encountered so far was a rogue coyote, which they dispatched quickly. She did worry though, and the nights were the worst. She couldn't sleep, for wanting him there with her and imaging all the horrible things that might happen to him.

She got up and pulled back the curtains. The moon was full and inviting. Perhaps if she went for a walk she could clear her mind and maybe eventually sleep. She took Sam's dressing gown from the hook by the door and wrapped it around her chemise. She had no slippers to put on, and so went out barefoot, enjoying the coolness of the dirt and the grass in the moonlit evening. She found herself by the fishpond and she marveled at the way the full moon seemed to fill the whole pond. It was almost magical in its way.

She thought of the magic spell, or instructions or whatever they were that had been passed down through the ages: *Lorsque la lune remplit l'étang / Offrez-argent / Et marcher sur les faisceaux de lumière / à un autre moment.*

> *When the moon fills the pond*
> *Offer it silver*
> *And walk on the beams of light*
> *to another time.*

The moon was filling the pond. She could go home. She could go back to her parents and her apartment and her job. Assuming after a month she still had a job or an apartment. She could go back to her friends. Her life. But she'd be leaving Sam. She couldn't leave Sam. Not until she knew there was no chance.

The moonlight reflected off her wedding ring. She brought it up toward her lips and kissed the ring. *Oh, Sam. How much it hurts, not having you here with me.* A mist started to arise around the pond, and she pulled the dressing gown a bit tighter around herself. Then she froze. She remembered this mist. It was what brought her to the past. But she couldn't be trapped in it now. She needed to stay here for Sam. She promised Sam she would be here. She tried to move, but her body didn't respond to her commands, in the meantime the fog rose and encompassed her, wiping out everything around her.

Something scraped against her knee and she reached down and felt the wall around the fish pond. The wall that was not there when Sam's family owned the plantation.

The fog drifted away.

She looked at her finger. The ring was gone.

She was still dressed in Sam's dressing gown.

From the inn, sounds of a party were going on.

She edged closer to the patio, where guests were spilling out of the ballroom. She saw Dayna, in her wedding gown.

Had no time passed? Had it even happened? But she was wearing Sam's dressing gown, it must have happened. She'd slipped back through time without even going in the water. Of course, she'd fallen in the pond when the wall she'd been sitting on disappeared because there was no wall there in the past. All that dunking in the pond, and it wasn't even an essential element to the time travel.

She hurried up to her room. Sam's room. Her room. What was it now? It was her hotel room again. A flick of a switch turned on the lights, and she saw her own modern things strewn around the room. She sat down on the bed and tried to gather her thoughts. She was home. But she didn't want to be. She'd left Sam, but she hadn't meant to. Her heart ached. A physical pain so intense that for a moment she wondered if she were having a heart attack.

Why was the world messing with her, constantly taking her places against her will? It wasn't fair. Tears came to her eyes and she let them fall. It wasn't fair at all. None of it. She had promised Sam and now he would think she'd abandoned him, but what could she do about it? She could go back to the pond. Go back to him.

She looked at her hands. She had no silver. No

wedding band. Why did even that last bit of Sam have to be taken from her? Back home she had more silver jewelry, but nothing with her. She looked out the window toward the pond, the moon was already moving, no longer filling the pond. The opportunity had passed for this month.

She should go downstairs to the party before people started worrying about her. She wanted to curl up on the bed that should be her marital bed, but obviously wasn't, and cry. She wanted to be in Sam's arms. She wanted a drink.

The drink she could maybe manage. She got off the bed and opened the mini bar. She'd always considered these little bottles of alcohol vastly overpriced. Right now, as she opened a tiny bottle of whiskey, she decided they could charge whatever they wanted and it would be worth it.

She drank the whiskey right out of the bottle, which was probably not the way it was supposed to work, but she was wearing a nineteenth-century dressing gown, "how things were supposed to work" was all relative.

A shower to clear her head. That's what she needed. Then maybe she could be with people again. Maybe.

The only person she wanted to be with was Sam and now she'd made it impossible.

She wasn't sure how she would go on from here.

She took a deep breath. One step at a time, that was how she would do it. One step at a time and thinking about Sam every second.

Chapter Thirty-Two

Sam

Sam sat crouched on a campstool in his tent, trying to use his trunk as a desk to write on, while rain pattered on the canvas above him, threatening to come in at the seams. He looked one more time at the picture Emily had sent him in her letter, holding it close to his dwindling candle. It was almost hard to believe she was real. But as she had said in her letter, he too remembered the feel of her skin. He had to stop himself from remembering it sometimes if he wanted to accomplish anything else. But the picture, that made it all real. There she was, in that fabulous dress, the creamy top of her breasts showing, her shoulders alluringly bare. He ached to touch her once more.

Emily may have heard that he died in the war, but he wasn't going to let that happen, not if he had any say over it. He would get home to her. It was the only thing keeping him going through the boredom and the rain and the bad food.

His tent flap lifted, causing his candle to flicker. Sam looked up, prepared to be annoyed, but it was George peeking in at him, and he was nearly always happy to see George.

"Writing to the little woman?" George asked with a nod at the paper.

"Already did that." Sam pointed to a sealed envelope.

"Ah, more poetry?"

It was the only thing keeping him sane in this insane world, putting his experiences into words and putting them on paper.

"Crazy, huh?" He wasn't quite sure what the men in his platoon thought of his poetry writing. He kept it mostly to himself, but he knew word had gotten around about his odd pastime.

"No." George helped himself to a seat on the cot. "In fact the men were saying you should send some to *Harper's Weekly*."

"Really?" Sam thought of the poetry as something for himself. "Do you think other people would be interested in them?"

"I do," George said with a small shrug "They capture the feel of what's going on, without being overly flowery or so full of imagery that you really don't know what's going on. They're real. You should try it."

"Okay, maybe I will." What did he have to lose? "Is that what you came in here to tell me?"

"No." George stood again. "Yuengling says we're moving out tomorrow. He wants all the officers for a strategy meeting in his tent. Now."

"Finally. Maybe something will happen." He'd anticipated being scared of war, not numbed with ennui.

"Didn't your mama ever tell you to be careful what you wish for?" George tapped him on the shoulder.

"Ha Ha. I don't want to die of boredom, I know that much." He put his papers away and blew out the candle and followed George to Yuengling's tent.

The tent was hot and smoky and crowded, and he wished he were pretty much anywhere else.

"We're going to meet up with Braxton's regiment tomorrow up by Allen's Creek. He's expecting a skirmish with some rebels who are gathering over by him. We'll need to leave early and be ready to fight. Have your men leave everything that can't be easily carried with the supply train. They'll catch up with us."

His pulse quickened. They were headed toward a battle. It's what he had signed up for. They had drilled and marched and practiced and now they would get to put all that training to use. He was ready. He knew his men were too. Back in his tent he wrote another letter to Emily. Then he put all his poems together and put them in an envelope addressed to *Harper's Weekly*. Maybe George was right, and other people would like to see them.

He didn't sleep well that night. He dreamed of Emily, wishing she were in his arms, in his bed. He didn't actually want her to be in an army camp, so he supposed what he really wished was that he was back home, with her. When the bugler played reveille, he didn't feel rested at all, but he was eager to get up. Today he would face his first real battle. He was anxious to see what that would be like. He packed up what he would carry, put the rest in his trunk to go with the supply train, ate a bit of biscuit and coffee and took down his tent.

The sun was up by the time everyone was ready to leave. Sam mounted his horse and rode at the front of his platoon, occasionally doubling back to make sure that all was in order. He needn't have bothered; his sergeants were exceptionally well organized.

Around noon a scout approached out of breath, his horse lathered. "The rebels are right ahead. Braxton's regiment is set to take them on. He wants you to stake out this ridge line and cover their right flank."

Sam passed the instructions on to his sergeants and he watched while his platoon got in position. Things were going according to plan. He was ready for this fight. It was time. He rode to the back of the lines and dismounted. Leaving his horse, he grasped his gun and walked the lines, making sure his men were ready and knew what to do.

He wasn't expecting the first bullet.

He thought there'd be more time. He didn't even see the rebels, but clearly they saw him and his men.

"Careful," he called to the men around him. "There's no need to all fire at once. Take your time. See what you are firing at."

He ducked behind a tree and loaded his musket. His heart pounded so loud in his ears he could barely hear himself think. Energy flowed through him. He looked from behind the tree and scanned the area until he saw a rebel coming up the hill. He took aim and fired. His target did not fall though. Perhaps he should have waited for him to get closer. He moved farther along the lines, trusting his men to do their job.

A runner came up to him. "Lieutenant, the captain says advance!"

"Right," Sam yelled back. Personally, he would have preferred to keep the high ground, but he wasn't exactly schooled in the science of battle. He found his sergeants and told them to watch him. On his order they would go down the hill and meet the enemy.

It started out all right, they headed downhill,

stopping every few feet to fire at the advancing rebels. One of his men was hit, and he saw a medic run to him. That was all right then, he'd be taken care of.

Then everything went wrong. Suddenly the rebels were behind them as well as in front. Shots were coming at them from every direction. His men broke formation. Some ran one way, some another, but there was nowhere to go that didn't seem to be in the way of the firing.

He tried to keep his men together, but it was a rout. Okay, fine. If he could not control his men, he could at least control himself. He loaded the musket again and took aim at the rebels advancing on him. One fell. Ha. Take that you nasty cowards, shooting at us. Okay, true, they were shooting back, but it made him feel better to think bad things about the enemy. He advanced to the next tree and fired again. When he went to advance again, a flash of blue cloth caught his eye.

It was a man down, one of his. There were no medics around, he'd need to get this man to help himself. He approached him cautiously, hoping that when he got to him, he would still be alive. He turned the man over and saw the blood pouring from a wound in the chest. But that wasn't what froze him in his tracks.

It was George.

"George. George old boy, can you hear me?" He took his friend in his arms.

"Aye, Sam. But, it hurts, I tell you."

"Right, sure, but I'll get you help."

All the training they'd had in what to do for an injured man went out of his head. This wasn't just a soldier. This was George. Think. He had to think. Get him to a medic. But no medics were close. Stop the bleeding. Yes. Stop the bleeding. He ripped cloth from the hem of his shirt and pressed it against the wound, and then wrapped it with another strip of cloth. Red soaked through almost instantly, but it was the best he could do. Now, he had to get him help.

"Can you stand do you think, with my help?"

"With your help…"

George's voice was faint.

"Come on George, you can do it." He pulled his friend to a standing position. He draped George's arm around his neck and grabbed him around the waist. He took a step, but George's feet dragged on the ground. This would never work.

"I'll carry you." He managed to get George onto his back and staggered to his feet. He would get his friend to help if it was the last thing he did. They had gone through too much together. They were like brothers. He wouldn't let him down now.

"Remember the time we saddled the pig with my mother's corset?" Sam said. "Boy was there hell to pay after that one."

George let out a feeble laugh in reply.

"Or how about the time we ate all the pies that Sally had cooling on the counter. Five pies we ate between the two of us. I was in the outhouse for hours." Sam stumbled under George's weight but steadied himself and continued on.

There was a brief chuckle from George.

"Hang on there, George. I'm going to get you help. Don't you worry about a thing."

He had to stop talking to save his own breath, George was not light, and the terrain was uneven. He'd lost track of their unit, gotten turned around in the smoke of the battle. The sounds of battle were muffled now, he'd gone the wrong way. Or had he? He didn't want to bring a wounded man into the middle of battle. But where were the wagons, the doctors? Where was everyone?

The weight across his back shifted some and he realized that George's breathing had gotten too quiet.

"George?"

No answer.

He laid down his burden. Whatever had animated George, made him who he was, was gone. George was dead. Sam sat beside his best friend, his brother, buried his face in his hands and cried. Perhaps men weren't supposed to cry in battle, but he didn't care. How could he go on without George?

But what now? Did he carry him back to the others? Did he bury him here? He'd been told that generally the men who fell would be buried by the battlefield, the army could not ship bodies home to family except in rare circumstances. If that were the case, what would be the point of carrying him any farther? He could bury him here amid the trees. George would like that.

Sam had no shovel, but he detached his bayonet and started scraping at the earth, keeping up a one-sided conversation as he did so. "I don't know how I'll tell your mother, old boy. She'll be beside herself. And Elizabeth, I think if she ever stopped swooning over Joseph she would have fallen in love with you. Yes, indeed. We could have been brothers for real. And did I ever tell you Emily's secret? She was from the future. The future, can you believe that? She says we'll win. So there's that, old buddy. We're going to win."

He couldn't do this. He had barely scratched the surface of the earth. It would take hours to dig a hole deep enough to properly bury George. He wiped tears from his eyes, took a drink from his canteen, and settled in to dig some more. If he got enough of a depression dug, he could cover the body with leaves and dirt, maybe that would be enough. It didn't seem like enough. George should rest in a pine box in the churchyard. That's where he should be, not covered in leaves in the woods.

"Marshall!"

Sam jerked his head up. Who was here? He had been certain he was alone. But someone who knew him would be a friend, could help him with George. He looked around, but only saw the trees and leaves shifting in the wind. Perhaps he had imagined it. But then he saw him. Daniel Wilkins stood about fifty yards away.

Thank God. Someone to help. Someone who knew George and would understand how important it was to bury him properly.

"Phelps is dead," Sam called out. "Help me dig a grave for him!"

"I don't work for you anymore, Marshall," Wilkins said. He raised his musket to his shoulder and aimed it at Sam.

Sam stood, unable to process what he saw. "Wait!" He held out a hand in supplication. "No, Daniel, what are you doing? We're on the same side! Help me with George!"

Wilkins pulled the trigger.

Sam didn't even hear the blast until the impact of

the bullet in his shoulder had pushed him off the edge of the bluff. He tumbled and fell, saplings doing nothing to break his fall, only adding to his injuries. He came to rest, face down, on the edge of the creek at the bottom of the ravine. As if from far away he heard another shot, and pain ripped through his lower leg.

He only had time to think that Emily was right, he *would* die in the war, before everything went black.

Chapter Thirty-Three

Emily

Emily got out of the shower, feeling cleaner, but no less dazed. Had she really spent a month in the past? Fallen in love? Gotten married? Sent her husband off to war? Of course she had. She knew it was more than a dream. And if she needed more proof than her own memories, there was always the matter of the dressing gown.

In the meantime, downstairs, as impossible as it seemed, Dayna's wedding reception was still going on.

There was a knock at the door and a soft voice called out "Emily?"

For a brief, disconnected second, she thought it might be Beck bringing her a cup of tea.

She hurried to the door and opened it a crack, pulling her towel tight around her. Celia, a college friend of hers and Dayna's, stood there. "There you are!" Celia said. "I was wondering what happened to you? What did happen to you?" she asked, taking in the towel and dripping hair.

She could tell her the truth, that she'd spent a month in the past, but she didn't think that would go over so well.

"I had an accident." She opened the door a little farther. "Come on in while I get dressed."

"Did you spill something on the dress?" Celia asked as she came into the room. Emily closed the door behind her.

"Yes." Though not technically true, it would do as an explanation. "I can't wear it."

"Find something else to wear before Dayna starts wondering where you are."

She grabbed the dress she'd worn to the rehearsal dinner the night before. "I suppose no one will care if I wear this again."

"Since the other option seems to be a towel, that is your best bet."

She brought it into bathroom and slipped it on. Looking at herself in the mirror, she was once again her proper twenty-first century self, but it didn't feel right, she missed the person she had been when she was with Sam, and now she didn't even look like her anymore. She stuck her head out of the bathroom. Celia sat on the bed, her shoes off, rubbing her feet. "You can go back down. You don't have to wait for me. I still have to do my hair and my make up."

"Eh, it's nice and quiet up here. I don't mind a bit of a break. I'll wait."

There'd be no excuse then for simply climbing under the covers and letting herself dream of Sam. Soon enough her hair was styled and mostly dry and her make up was acceptable, and it was time to go downstairs.

"You're not going to lock up?" Celia asked as they left the room.

"My key is in my bag downstairs," she said.

"How'd you get in before?"

"Didn't lock it before." Emily shrugged. It was

undoubtedly careless of her, but it had saved her from traipsing through the ballroom in Sam's dressing gown, so there was that.

At the entrance to the ballroom, she paused. She didn't feel at all like the same person who had originally been at this party.

Celia headed straight to the dance floor, but she wasn't ready for that. She made a beeline for the bar and asked for a whiskey sour. She didn't have a dollar to put in the tip jar, her purse was probably still by the table, she'd have to make up for it later. She took the drink as if it were a lifeline and took a big sip. The world didn't make any more sense, but she could feel herself starting to calm down a bit.

Johnson, resplendent in his tuxedo, spotted her. "Did you change your dress, Emily?"

"Oh, yes," she said, surprised he noticed. But then, he was a detective, trained to notice details. "I spilled something on the other one."

He accepted that as perfectly natural. "Dayna was looking for you before. I guess you were changing."

"Probably," she answered. It was at least an explanation people would believe. "Where is Dayna?"

"She was heading to the bathroom last time I saw her." He turned to the bartender and got himself a beer.

Ah, Dayna wanted her for bathroom duty again. She grinned to herself and thought of Beck helping her with her voluminous gown at her own wedding a few days ago, a few hundred years ago. She took a gulp of her drink.

"Go easy there," Johnson said, eyeing the drink in her hand.

"I'm fine," Emily assured him. And in regards to

alcohol at least, she was. She'd walked back in that door relatively sober, except for the lingering effects of the minibar whiskey. She actually needed to remedy that. Tonight, right now, was not a time she particularly wanted to be sober.

Someone else came up to talk to Johnson, and she used that opportunity to slip away. She headed toward the patio for a bit of air and respite from the noise. It had been a month since she'd heard anything at the volume the band was playing. She had become unaccustomed to it, and she'd thought it was too loud earlier anyway.

She sipped her drink, standing on the patio, the party swirling around her, lost in her own thoughts. Could she go back? Since she had no silver, and the moon's reflection no longer filled the pond, she'd have to wait for the next full moon, but should she do it? Take the chance that he was still alive there, and she could see him again? When exactly did he die? She needed to find out. She needed to learn all she could about him and what had happened to him. Maybe she'd even find out that they'd had six kids, in which case, she would know she had to go back, so that could happen. And if after a month in the past, virtually no time had passed in the present, who was to say that if she waited until the next full moon, she wouldn't go back to exactly the same time she had left. Time travel apparently worked by its own rules.

Draining her glass, she walked back through the ballroom to the entry hall where the portrait hung. There he was, her Sam, looking so much like he had when she'd last seen him. But the portrait didn't really capture him all the way. It didn't show the way his eyes glittered when he laughed or the way his dimples appeared when he was really happy. Looking at the portrait you would never know that he smelled of cinnamon and peppermint and sometimes horses, you wouldn't know that he had gentle hands and soft lips and was an amazing lover. The portrait told you none of that.

"I see you are fascinated by the portrait." The owner was beside her again.

"I am." She couldn't even begin to tell this woman just how fascinated she was by the portrait. "What do you know about him?"

"This was his family's plantation. He died in the Civil War. He was a poet. I showed you the poem already, didn't I?"

"You did, but I'd like to look at it again, if I may." Emily tried to keep her hands from trembling.

"Of course." The woman pulled the laminated copy out of the drawer and handed it to her. "And you said you were Emily, right? This could have been written for you."

Emily's Song
A sprite from the land of Faerie
Bewitching me with a glance
She touched my hand and stole my heart
Our meeting: more than happenstance

Bewitching me with a glance
Her laughter was like bells in the wind
Our meeting: more than happenstance
I knew I had to have her; if only for a while.

Her laughter was like bells in the wind

As we danced the Zingirella for the ball
I knew I had to have her; if only for a while
For when I was with her time stood still

As we danced the Zingirella for the ball
The waterfalls played the only music we needed
For when I was with her time stood still
My sprite would be my bride

The waterfalls played the only music we needed
She touched my hand and stole my heart
My sprite would be my bride
Emily you have my love forever.

This *was* written for her. By her husband. However, she couldn't possibly begin to explain that to this woman, or anyone. She read the words, and Sam was so alive to her that she expected to look up and see him. When she looked up, all she was his portrait and the owner.

The owner. Why did she look so familiar? Emily glanced farther down the wall to another painting that she was so used to seeing in the Marshall home, then back at the older woman in front of her.

"Elsbeth!" She could barely breathe.

The woman's eyes opened wide and then narrowed. "So, you *are* Emily after all."

"I think so." Right now, she wasn't even sure of that.

"Tomorrow, before you check out, you come to my office. I have some things you might be interested in seeing." Her eyes glimmered with hope and happiness and Emily realized that this woman was the key. That if there was a way to get back to Sam, she would know it.

"But how did you get here?" There was so much she needed to know. So much this woman could tell her.

"We'll talk in the morning, dear," Elsbeth said and with a gentle pat on her shoulder moved on, leaving her dazed and confused. She wanted to chase her down and ask her a dozen questions, but she'd have to wait for morning, which suddenly seemed way too far away.

She took one more look at her husband's portrait and headed back into the ballroom. There was no waltzing or dancing the Zingirella, but she thought she could have a good time anyway, for the last hour of the reception, now that she knew she could get answers. She danced with Johnson and his friend Brian and Dayna's brother and with all the bridesmaids and then the band announced the last song, and the reception came to an end. Everyone gathered around Dayna and Johnson to wish them well as they started their life together. She watched from a distance, remembering her wedding dance with Sam in this same room.

Dayna caught her eye and signaled to her to come over. She wanted to tell Dayna everything that had happened, she needed to tell her, but how could she possibly begin? And this wasn't the time or the place. She went to her.

"Em, sweetie," Dayna said. "We want to have the bridal party in our room for one more celebratory glass of champagne, but we can't let it go on too long because our taxi is getting here at five to take us to the airport. Can you gather people, and shoo them out again before it's too late?"

"You know I can," she said, relieved to have

something concrete to concentrate on.

Dayna grabbed her arm as she started to leave. "You okay?"

"We'll talk later." She made sure to smile so Dayna wouldn't worry. She gathered the bridal party, made them swear to leave after one or two drinks and ushered everyone up to the bridal suite. Mr. and Mrs Marshall's bedroom. But of course, she was the only one here who knew that.

Dayna and Johnson simply glowed with happiness, and their joy was infectious. They poured the champagne and everyone made toasts and then they filled glasses again and more toasts and Emily found it impossible not to be happy with them. But two bottles of champagne had been emptied and the bride and groom needed their privacy. Emily herded everyone out the door.

Soon she stood at the door to the suite with Dayna, itching to tell her everything that had happened, but knowing it would have to wait. She gave Dayna a hug.

"Have a great time in Hawaii!"

"We'll talk when I get back," Dayna said and Emily shut the door behind her, leaving the newlyweds alone.

She went down the hall to her room. Sam's room. Her bridal suite.

She undressed and climbed into bed. The bed was different, larger, more comfortable all around, but it was missing Sam and therefore completely unsatisfactory. She got up and wrapped herself in Sam's dressing gown. It had been real, here was the gown to prove, it. She looked out the window at the stars and the moon and wondered where Sam was, and if there were any way at all to ever find him again.

****

Morning came and she lay in bed wondering what was real and what wasn't. It was the morning after Dayna's wedding, yet she had very vivid memories of her time with Sam. Could it all have been a hallucination of some sort? Did she make it all up? But if she did, then how to account for the dressing gown, and the chemise? Both of which did not belong in her twenty-first century wardrobe. She dressed in jeans and a tunic top, relieved at not having to wear a corset or yards of material, but yet oddly missing the elegance those items brought to her look.

She set about packing. Her bridesmaid's dress was gone. Good thing she hadn't really been planning to wear it again. Instead of course she had the nineteenth-century dressing gown. She held it to her nose and sniffed, yes, she could still smell the scent of Sam on it. The cinnamon and tobacco smoke and peppermint. Her heart did a little tumble, but she took a deep breath. There was no reason to panic until she found out what Elsbeth could tell her. Once her bags were packed, she looked around the room one last time, but she couldn't bring herself to leave yet. This was Sam's room. It might not look like his room anymore, but it was still his room. If she left, would she lose any connection she had with him?

No. That was silly. Her connection with Sam went much deeper than a room. She picked up her overnight bag and garment bag and went downstairs. She grabbed a cup of coffee in the breakfast room, or dining room, as she couldn't help thinking of it, and went in search of Elsbeth.

"Ah, you've come," the woman said with a smile. "I imagine you have questions. Let's go into the parlor. It is more comfortable."

She followed her into the parlor, which was now set up like a tearoom for small events. She put her bags by the door and sat in one of the wing back chairs when directed. Elsbeth took the other chair. They were not the same chairs from Sam's time. She wasn't sure if it would have made it easier if they were.

"Thank you so much for seeing me, Ms. Marshall," she said, sitting primly on the edge of her chair, holding her coffee like a life line.

"Winters," Elsbeth corrected. "Mrs. Winters. And you are Mrs. Samuel Marshall, is that correct?"

Emily nearly spilled her coffee.

"How did you know?" she asked.

"The same way you knew who I was, though I must say you look much more like your picture than I look like that portrait in the hall anymore."

"What picture?" She was afraid to hope it could be her wedding picture, taken only days before.

Elsbeth held out a scrap book, and Emily put down her coffee and took it. She opened it to see exactly what she had been hoping to. Her wedding picture. Her and Sam. She reached out and gently touched his face in the photo, while tears pooled in her eyes.

Elsbeth handed her a tissue, and she wiped her eyes.

"I'm sorry."

"What for?" the older woman asked. "For breaking down crying when you see a picture of the husband you will never see again? No, I think that's a perfectly fine reason to cry. Trust me, when I first ended up here, in an abandoned house, my family over a hundred years away and no way to get back, I cried plenty. No shame in it."

"Then you don't think I could go back?" The last hope gone. If her heart wasn't already shattered into pieces, it would have broken.

"It only works in one direction."

"But it doesn't!" She sat up straighter, closing the scrapbook on her lap. Elsbeth might not have the answers she needed after all, but perhaps between the two of them they might figure something out. "I was here, you saw me, at the wedding, and then I went to the pond and it was the full moon and next thing I knew I was in eighteen sixty-one."

Elsbeth stared at her, eyes wide. "You were here first? You came back? To the same day?"

A shiver went down her back and she grabbed her coffee for fortification. "It was like no time had passed."

"And how long were you in eighteen sixty-one?" Elsbeth leaned forward in her seat, intent on her answer.

"A month. From one full moon to the next." Had it only been a month. It seemed like a lifetime.

"Tell me your story," Elsbeth said.

So Emily did, as completely as possible, including figuring out what the magic chant was that the slaves thought was the key to time travel.

"Ah, that's my fault, I'm afraid," Elsbeth said. "When I questioned DayJon and found out what I could about how he got here, he told me the poem, such as it is, in English. I didn't want to be found out, so I translated it into French. He must have taught it to the slaves in French, Or maybe young Moses overheard me, since I repeated it over and over so I wouldn't forget what I had to do.

"So, you left on purpose." She was starting to piece things together.

"I did. I was engaged to a man I could not stand and saw it as a perfect opportunity to get away."

"Will you tell me your story?" She took another sip of her coffee and saw the cup was nearly empty.

Elsbeth saw and took her cup, refilling it by a coffeemaker in the corner. She filled a cup for herself before settling back in her chair.

"My story," Elsbeth said thoughtfully. "You realize I've never told anyone."

"No one? Not even your husband?" She couldn't imagine keeping a secret that big from Sam.

"No. I didn't think anyone would understand. But you would, wouldn't you?"

Yes, she would. She took a sip of her coffee and waited.

"You know about DayJon," Elsbeth began and Emily nodded. She still needed to warn Dayna about that, but there was time, plenty of time for that. "He came and his stories were fascinating, and while the slaves thought he was a conjurer and the overseer thought he was a trouble maker, I understood that he offered hope for a better future for me. I memorized his poem and waited for the next full moon, which, as luck would have it was mere days before my wedding day. It was cutting it close, I know, but I saw no other way out."

"What if it hadn't worked?"

"I'd have been married to a man I did not love and

would have made the best of it, as people do." Elsbeth took a dainty sip of her coffee. "But that is not what I did. I went to the pond, with a silver bracelet my father had given me, and when the moon filled the pond, like in the poem, the mist came and when it had gone, the house was abandoned. In ruins. I wasn't prepared for it to work. I didn't know what to do. I sought shelter in the house until I could get my wits about me."

"What did you do?" Was it worse to be thrust back in time like she had been, or forward. Either way everything was different, and there were no friends or family to help.

"Looked around, got my bearings, figured out how to dress and get around in my new world. Made friends with people who knew things, who helped me get ownership of the plantation, and I started working to make it what you see today. I got married. I lived a rather wonderful life, really."

"What year was it?"

"Nearly fifty years ago now," Elsbeth answered with a far off look in her eye.

"When I saw your family, you'd been gone for nearly sixty years." If they could figure out the vagaries of time travel, it would help a lot.

She shook her head. "There doesn't seem to be a rhyme or reason to it, does there? What did they think happened to me?"

"They thought you were spirited away by fairies. At least that's what Moses thought."

She smiled, wistfully. "Little Moses. He would think that. And the family?"

"They didn't really offer any explanations." Of course she hadn't even heard Elsbeth's story until right

377

before Sam left. There'd hardly been time to process it, much less find out more.

"Does anyone know the portrait in the hall is of you?"

"No." Elsbeth gave her a sad smile. "People don't see what is impossible to them. If you showed all your friends this picture," she pointed to the scrapbook, "not one of them would realize that was you. It's impossible, so it couldn't be."

"Except, we know the impossible is possible."

"Indeed."

Emily clutched the scrapbook, afraid to open it and find what she really wanted to know. "Sam. Did he survive he war?"

Elsbeth shook her head. "No, I'm sorry. I told you already, he did not. Everything I have on Sam is in that book. I'll get a copy of everything made for you."

"Thank you." She braced herself to open the book and look for herself. First of course she had to study the wedding picture some more. "It's impossible to think this picture was taken only a couple of days ago for me, and yet..."

She ran her finger lovingly over the picture of her and Sam and then with a deep breath turned the page. There was a clipping from a newspaper listing those dead at the battle of Allen's Creek, less than a month after she'd last seen Sam. She'd never heard of the battle before, it must not have been an important one in terms of the war, but she saw both Sam and George's names on the list. Her heart ached, but she forced herself to continue. There was the poem that she'd seen before. "Emily's Song."

"And of course, you are Emily." Elsbeth smiled at

her. "It's nice to have some things come together. I'd always wondered why I'd never found anything about the woman in that picture. Now I know. You weren't there to find things about."

"I suppose not. So that does answer one of my questions. You didn't find that Sam and I went on to have six children or something. I don't go back?"

"No point in going back," Elsbeth pointed out. "He died. I know it's harsh to say it like that, but you have to accept the truth."

The words pierced her heart like a sword. She turned another page in the scrapbook and found a part of Sam she'd never known. His poems, all apparently published in *Harper's Weekly*.

And then, two letters, to her, old and brittle, pasted in the scrapbook as artifacts. She read them, his details of mundane camp life, his proclamation of undying devotion. Her eyes overflowed, and she wiped them with the tissue.

"People won't believe you," Elsbeth said. "After all, what we've done is impossible."

She nodded, unable to speak over the lump in her throat.

"But." The woman wrote something on a piece of paper and handed it to her. "Here's my address and phone number. Anytime you want to talk, I'll listen. I'll believe."

She took the paper. "Thank you. I will definitely be in touch. I think I need to process some of this."

"Of course you do, dear."

Emily stood, and so did Elsbeth. "It may be hard to explain to others, the details, but I'll always know you are the wife of my nephew, Sam. Therefore, you are my niece, and to me you will always be Emily Marshall. As for the rest of the world, might be easier if you stuck with your maiden name. Hard to explain a wedding when there is no groom to show for it." Elsbeth tapped the scrapbook, "And I don't think that picture would convince anyone but me."

"Thank you, Aunt Elsbeth," she said and reached out and hugged the older woman. "I'm very glad I met you."

"I must say the same. It's been a long time since anyone knew the real me."

Emily reluctantly said goodbye. It was time to go home and piece her life back together.

****

She looked around her apartment. It was impossible that it looked exactly like it had when she had left it only the other day. She'd lived a lifetime since then. How could the same dirty clothes be in her hamper? How could the milk in the fridge not have gone bad? Even the lettuce hadn't wilted.

Getting back into normal routine was easier than she would have thought. She did laundry, checked email, watched some TV. Had she really spent a month in the 1860s? It must have been a dream. Except she could still feel Sam's touch, and she had his dressing gown. If it weren't for that dressing gown, and the picture Elsbeth had, she would think she had made it all up.

She looked up Sam on line and found reference to the poems, but nothing more. There was nothing on George Phelps. She looked up Elizabeth and discovered she'd married Joseph Fitzsimmons and had six children. So, she'd been right about him after all, Emily smiled at that. At least someone had a happy ending.

Monday morning found her back at her accounting job, dealing with the minutia of debits and credits. Her co-workers asked about the wedding, and it took everything in her not to tell them about the real adventure of the weekend.

Her big regret about her sudden return from the past, other than the obvious, was that she hadn't been able to help Beck. She had promised to help her escape, and although she had started the ball rolling, in the end had done nothing. This was a case where good intentions really were rather useless without results.

Every night she dreamed about Sam. It was like they were together again, and then each morning she woke to the realization he was gone from her for good. She couldn't make that reality stick in her mind.

She invited Aunt Elsbeth over for dinner. She'd had a professional copy of the scrapbook made and gave it to Emily, as well as a framed enlargement of the wedding picture. Emily hugged it to her. What would people say if they saw it on display in her living room? Though, as Elsbeth had pointed out, no one would actually believe it was her.

Over a dinner of chicken cordon bleu, her one guaranteed-to-work company meal, she told Elsbeth about the Marshall family as she had known them and they traded stories about the difference between living in the 1800s and now. There was no one else Emily could possibly have that conversation with. The person she wanted to discuss it all with was Dayna, but Dayna was on her honeymoon, and when she did get home, how would she even begin to tell her what happened?

Life did fall into routine though, and the days

passed, though her longing for Sam didn't diminish. Then, finally Dayna and Johnson were home.

"Come for dinner," Dayna texted her. "We'll bore you with vacation photos."

"Be there at six," Emily texted back. She couldn't wait to see her friend, there was so much she wanted to tell her. She knew the pictures wouldn't be boring. She picked up a bottle of wine on the way over, knowing that would always be appreciated. She hoped her stomach would cooperate, lately a lot of food hadn't been agreeing with her.

Dayna wrapped her in a hug before she was even all the way through the door. "Oh. My. God! I missed you!"

"You shouldn't even have been thinking about me. It was your honeymoon!" She handed the wine to Johnson, who also gave her a big bear hug.

"Trust me, she didn't think about you *all* the time," he said.

"How do you know?" Dayna asked giving him some serious side eye.

He grinned. "Oh, I know. Trust me."

This was quickly going to an awkward place.

"So, show me pictures," Emily said.

"Let me pour the wine first." Johnson took the bottle out to the kitchen.

"How are you?" Dayna took her by the arm and steered her into the living room. "Was everything okay at the reception? You seemed a little out of it."

"I'm fine. I'll tell you all about it, but maybe not quite yet." She hoped her smile was sufficiently reassuring. "I want to see the pictures and hear all about your trip."

Johnson joined them with the wine. He handed a glass to Emily. Dayna plugged her memory card into the TV, and they sat back and watched the pictures. Dayna and Johnson kept up a running dialog about all they had seen and done. Emily let the words flow over her.

Imagine if she and Sam had been able to take a honeymoon. Where would they have gone? Probably nowhere, it was war time. She did have one picture of their honeymoon. She'd brought the scrapbook with her, it was in her bag. She wasn't sure how she was ever going to tell them the story though.

"You need a refill, Em?" Johnson asked.

"No, I'm fine, thanks." She still had more than half of her glass of wine.

They sat down to eat. In the spirit of just coming back from Hawaii, it was a stir fry with pineapple in it. It was delicious, but her stomach was doing funny jumping things and she couldn't eat much. She was too nervous about what she wanted to tell them.

"This is off topic," she said, because most of the conversation had centered around Hawaii, but she needed to find something out. "But Dayna, do you know the story of how your great-great-great grandmother Rebecca escaped from slavery?"

Dayna looked up at her, eyes wide. "I do. Why?"

"I realized I never asked, and lately I've been thinking about family history, and I was curious."

"Actually, I have something kind of remarkable." She stood up from the table and a few minutes later came back with a photocopied paper. "This is a copy of a letter she wrote to someone. I don't know if it was ever mailed. It was stuck in an old family bible. It's a little cryptic, because obviously the person she was writing to knew a lot of the details, but it does give a fascinating glimpse." She handed the paper to her.

The first thing she saw was the heading: "To Mrs. Samuel Marshall." She almost dropped the paper right there. Beck had written this letter to her. It had never been mailed, because the only way for her to get it was to leave it someplace where her great-grandchildren would find it and show it to their friends. It had worked. More than a hundred and fifty years later, she had the letter.

"It all worked out okay," was the next line. Did Beck know she'd feel bad about disappearing on her? "Your sudden departure was the perfect cover for my own. I packed a carpet bag with the new day dress and had Dolly button me into the other. Your hoops and corset were a bit large on me, but I'm making it work. It's too bad the skirt and shirtwaist hadn't come yet, those would have been handy. Buttons up the back are annoying when there is no one to help, as you know." She smiled. Yes, indeed, she did know. "When I realized you weren't coming back, I took off. They'd be looking for a young lady with her slave, not a young lady on her own. I wore a floppy brimmed hat and gloves and had the tickets they had purchased for you. No one gave me a second glance all the way to Philadelphia. So thank you. It worked. I hope my grandchildren are successful, I mean, I gave up a lot for them, they better make it worth it. Love, Rebecca."

"As you can see," Dayna said, "some of it doesn't make a great deal of sense."

"Oh, no," she said. "It makes perfect sense to me. Thank you for sharing. Do you think I could possibly have a copy of this for myself?"

"Sure," Dayna said and ran one off on the printer.

Emily took another sip of her wine. Should she tell them? Tell them that she was Mrs. Samuel Marshall? But as Elsbeth had said, no one would believe her, how could they? She would tell Dayna. Someday. But tonight was not the night. She tucked the letter into her bag beside the scrapbook and ate the ice cream that Dayna brought out and let the conversation return to Hawaii.

On her way home, she stopped at the drug store and bought a pregnancy test.

Chapter Thirty-Four

Sam

Something tickled his ear. He tried to brush whatever it was away from him, but he found he couldn't move his arms. Why couldn't he move? Where was he? The babble of a flowing creek came from somewhere to his right. The coppery scent of blood was mixed with fresh dirt and moss. Ravine. He'd fallen down a ravine. He'd been shot. By Wilkins. Shot and fallen down the ravine. George. George was dead.

He should be dead too, but he didn't seem to be. As awareness flooded back to him, so did pain. The tickling by his ear was forgotten as the throbbing in his leg and shoulder took precedence. He shivered with cold. He opened an eye and saw nothing. Had he gone blind? No. It was dark, and the moon was hidden by clouds and trees. He needed to get to help, and to get warm, and to not be lying in the bottom of the ravine. How long had he been here? Would he bleed to death? He'd done nothing to stop the bleeding when he'd been shot. Had he awakened only to die before sunrise?

Emily. He wanted Emily. He would not die before seeing her again.

First things first. He had to bind his wounds. He could not lose more blood. He tried to move and again was unable. Okay, thing before the first, get to a sitting position so he could assess his wounds and bind them. It took him awhile. He wasn't sure how long. Time had no meaning. It was dark. It stayed dark. Did the moon move across the sky? Possibly. It was too shrouded from view for him to be sure.

The shoulder wound seemed to have stopped bleeding, had the mud he lay in staunched the flow? His leg, although it burned and throbbed did not seem too badly hurt. The bullet did not go into his leg but grazed the side. That didn't seem to be pouring blood. He ripped off a piece of shirt and wrapped it around the wound on his leg. He wasn't quite sure how to bandage the wound on his shoulder. It would have to wait for now. There was no point in trying to climb out of the ravine while it was still dark, but he needed to get warm.

His coat was wool, and the night air did not feel frigid, yet he shivered. Was that a result of his injuries? He had no blanket. Perhaps a fire. Except he could barely move and he couldn't see, he'd never gather enough kindling. Instead he piled leaves and pine needles on top of himself as some sort of cover and waited for morning.

He awoke, dripping in sweat, and his throat dry as dust. He reached for his canteen, but it wasn't on his belt. He opened his eyes to sunlight glittering through the leaves of the trees. He glanced up to the ridge he had fallen from. It was a nearly vertical drop. It didn't seem likely that he'd be able to make the climb in his condition, but that's probably where his canteen was. Yet, there was a creek beside him, that would provide him water. He dragged himself closer to the bank so he could dip his head in. That cooled him off some, and he drank, slaking his thirst.

He couldn't go back up the way he'd come down, that much was obvious, but yet he certainly couldn't stay here. There was a roaring in his head, and over top of that he could hear the burbling of the water and the leaves rustling in the trees and birds chirping. He heard no sign of human activity. Staying here in the hopes that someone found him would almost certainly mean someone finding him dead. He needed to move.

Follow the creek. Wasn't that the conventional wisdom? Water flowing downhill will lead you somewhere: a mill, a town, something. Plus, he would know he wasn't going in circles. He'd have to end up somewhere. And it was a better plan than trying to climb back out of the ravine.

He felt around, and his fingers touched a fallen branch. He pulled it close and used it to help stand. The roaring in his ears grew so great he was afraid he would fall right back over again, but he managed to stay upright, clutching to his stick like a life line. One step and then another. He made it a few dozen yards before his head was spinning too much, and he needed to sit. He fell to the ground and cupped his hands to get more water. There was a large flat rock some distance ahead. If he could make it to that he would take a break there.

A goal. He had a manageable goal to achieve.

The sun was high overhead when he reached the rock, and he collapsed on it as if into a warm bed. Despite the sun and the exertion of exercise, he was shivering with cold again. He curled up like a ball in the rays of sunshine on the rock and let himself drift off to sleep.

He dreamed of Emily. She was here with him,

lying beside him, keeping him warm, loving him. He woke up, sweating again. No Emily. Where was his Emily? She was home waiting for him. He needed to get to her. To get home. Would following the creek get him home? It would get him somewhere. He forced himself to walk again. One step and then another. Each step one step closer to Emily. To his love.

The sides of the ravine lowered, and soon the creek flowed through fields. A farm up ahead promised something more than water for sustenance. He stumbled to the door and fell against it instead of knocking. The woman who opened the door nearly screamed at the sight of him. "Please help," he managed to say before he passed out.

He came to as she cleaned his wounds. She bandaged them and gave him some stew, never quite meeting his eye. Her husband came in and glared at him through narrowed eyes.

"You a deserter?"

"No, sir." It took so much energy to even form words.

"Where's your unit, Lieutenant?"

"I'm not sure. I got separated from them when I was wounded." He told him the unit name and number and commanding officer's name.

The farmer rubbed his chin. "Can't say as I know where they are. Probably south of here, that's where most of them have gone." The farmer cleared his throat. "You can sleep in the barn tonight. Tomorrow you'll have to move on. You can't stay here longer than that."

"Yes, sir," he said. "Thank you for your hospitality." He finished his stew, and the farmer handed him a blanket and led him out to the barn. He collapsed in the hay, barely bothering to cover himself and fell asleep in seconds.

In the morning he shivered with fever. That's what it was, this alternating shivering and sweating. He needed to be safe in bed with someone taking care of him, not wandering the countryside. Standing up to take a piss used up most of his energy and he let himself collapse back into the hay until he thought he could safely move again. He wished the farmer would let him stay here longer. He just wanted to sleep, he'd bother no one. Perhaps there was another farmer, down the way, who would share his barn. If he couldn't stay here, he also knew he wasn't going to look too hard for his unit. He didn't know where they were and didn't particularly care. He wanted to find Emily. Needed Emily. He would go home, step by step, hay loft by hay loft, until he got to her.

Days drifted into other days, melding together until he could not discern what had happened at any given time. Some nights he slept under the stars, others in a barn, either by invitation of the owners, or by his own choice. His leg ached, making every step torture. The pain from his shoulder spread to his whole arm, and he found he couldn't really move it, nor did he try. The fever never left him. Sometimes he shivered as if in the middle of winter; sometimes he burned and sweat. Always he shook. Sometimes he had nothing to eat. When he did have something to eat, he often couldn't stomach it. His pants were getting loose on him, and he had to poke a hole in his belt to keep them from sliding down his hips all the way to his ankles.

Now he didn't only dream about Emily during the night, but during the day. He talked to her as a vision of her walked along side of him. He wasn't sure why he was still searching for Emily, since she was right here, with him, all the time, but yet, he kept, day after day, putting one foot in front of the other and hoping it was bringing him closer to home.

Sometimes George walked with him, and it was nice to see his old friend again. He wasn't sure where George was the rest of the time.

There was a constant roaring in his head these days, whether he was near the creek or not. It made it hard to think. All he could concentrate on was one foot in front of the other until he fell and slept and when he got up he did it all over again.

Then one afternoon things looked familiar. There was an abandoned barn near the creek, and he knew this barn. He and George had many adventures in it when they were small. It shifted and creaked in the wind and sagged dangerously in the middle. Even his fever-addled brain was able to realize that taking shelter there was a poor idea. But he didn't need to take shelter there. If that was the old barn, then his own place was less than a day's walk away, even at the snail's pace he was keeping.

He would get home.

He would see Emily.

He trudged on, step by tired step.

Night fell, but he forced himself to continue. Home was close. Home and a hot meal and a warm bed.

Home and Emily.

Overhead a full moon rose, lighting his way.

There was something important about a full moon, but he couldn't remember it now. He would think about it after he got some sleep. The moon lit his way, guiding him, pulling him home. Step by step. Then he emerged from the woods and saw the house, looming in front of him. Warm light spilling from windows. Home. He was home.

The full moon, which had led him this far, reflected in the fish pond. He stopped and looked, mesmerized at the way the moon filled the whole pond. It was almost as if it was shining from in the pond, not from the sky. A mist came swiftly up from the ground, encompassing him. He collapsed to the ground as the mist turned to an all enveloping fog.

The moon glinted off his silver wedding band, and then the ring started to disappear as the fog immobilized him.

Emily! His mind cried out to her, and he let himself be swallowed by the fog and mist.

Chapter Thirty-Five

Emily

Emily stared through the window of the inn at the full moon.

"It's mesmerizing, isn't it?" Aunt Elsbeth said to her. "I always come to the inn on a full moon. I can't seem to stay away. That's why I invited you to dinner tonight. I thought you might have the same urge."

Her throat was suddenly too tight to speak. Yes, she wanted—no, that wasn't the right word—needed to be here. She needed to see the full moon over the fish pond. She needed to see if a mist always came or only sometimes.

"There's not always a mist," Aunt Elsbeth said as if reading her mind. "Even after all these years, I haven't figured out all the vagaries of the pond."

She took a sip of her water, then set it down.

"Aunt Elsbeth, I need to talk about something with you."

"Something's wrong," Elsbeth said with perception. "It has something to do with the fish pond?" They didn't talk about time travel, not when they might be overheard, but they used fish pond as sort of a shorthand.

"Indirectly," she said. She took a deep breath before blurting out the news. "I'm pregnant."

Elsbeth's face lit up. "Why that's wonderful news. Babies brighten the world."

"By Sam," she finished.

Elsbeth's joy seemed to lessen a bit. "That is a conundrum, isn't it? On the one hand, you'll have a constant reminder of Sam. On the other, how do you possibly begin to explain the child's advent?"

"Exactly." She'd told no one so far, not Dayna, not her mother. She was pregnant by her husband, there was no shame in that, but said husband died in the Civil War, and that part might be a bit hard to explain.

"I suppose telling the truth is out of the question."

"You're the one who told me no one would believe me."

"And they probably won't, it's true," Elsbeth said, holding her fork and knife suspended above her steak, while she contemplated. "Do you have anyone willing to step in and take over as a father figure?"

"No, not really," she said.

"You're not dating anyone?"

"I'm a fairly recent widow." There was a touch more harshness in her voice than she meant to have. "I mean, I know he died over a hundred and fifty years ago, but to me it was only last month."

"Yes, yes, of course," Elsbeth said soothingly. "I'm sorry. I'm trying to figure out an easy way for you to explain the pregnancy."

She sighed, "I'll have to say it was a one night stand, I suppose. I don't see any other alternative." She glanced out the window at the full moon, and the fish pond. And the mist.

She nearly dropped her water as she stood up. "Aunt Elsbeth, there's mist!"

"Wait!" Elsbeth reached out to her and grabbed her hand. "Are you wearing any silver? You don't want to find yourself sometime else. Not now."

She did a quick inventory of her jewelry. Gold chain, gold earrings, no rings. Silver bracelet. She pulled the bracelet off and left it on the table, then she rushed outside. She didn't know what she expected to see or find, but she had to see that mist. Had to be a part of it. Had to see what it meant that it was here again.

She ran toward the fish pond, but before she could get there the fog dissipated and there, sitting against the wall, looking half dead, was Sam.

"Sam!" She fell to her knees by his side and took him in her arms. "Oh, my darling Sam. What happened? You need a doctor. And an ambulance." She glanced up and saw that Aunt Elsbeth had followed her out of the inn. "Call nine one one! It's Sam, and he needs a hospital. He's been hurt."

Elsbeth stood frozen.

"Please!" she cried. "Please call!" She turned her attention to her husband.

"It's okay, Sam. You're here with me. It's all going to be fine. We're together; it's what matters."

His skin was hot with fever. His lips chapped from dehydration. His coat was filthy with dark brown stains. Blood. It was blood. Was it his? What had happened?

"Emily." It came out more as a whisper than anything else. "I knew I'd get home to you, Emily." He closed his eyes.

She could feel the rise and fall of his chest, and as long as he kept breathing until the ambulance got here he'd be fine. She was sure of it.

With a cacophony of sirens and flashing lights the

ambulance arrived. Paramedics pushed her aside to get to Sam.

"What happened to him?" one of them asked her.

"I don't know for sure," she said. "I think he's been shot. He's definitely feverish. He just showed up like this."

Every word was true.

They put an oxygen mask over his face and loaded him on a stretcher.

She tried to climb into the back of the ambulance with Sam. "You can't."

"He's my husband," she said. "Please!"

The medics exchanged a look and relented. They helped her in, and she held Sam's hand during the ride. He was here. He was back. She didn't know how or why or what would happen next, but she had a second chance with him and that was all that mattered.

Once at the hospital, they rushed him inside, and she was left alone in the waiting area. A nurse came up to her. "That's your husband?"

"Yes," she answered feeling numb. Sam was back, but for how long?

"Can you fill out paperwork for me?"

"I can try." She went to sit with the nurse, trying to keep her hands from shaking

"His name?"

"Samuel Allen Marshall."

"Date of birth?"

Emily stared at her for a second. Of course she knew when Sam was born, but saying it was in the 1830s was going to be hard to explain. Instead she gave the month and date and added a birth year that would make him the right age.

"Address?"

She gave her own. Same for phone number.

"Health insurance?"

"No."

"No?" The nurse looked surprised.

"It's a long story. Don't worry, we'll pay. We'll find a way."

"Everyone always thinks they're not going to need insurance," the woman sighed. "Until they do."

"Yes." She tried not to snap. "We've learned our lesson."

"What happened to him?"

"I don't know." She couldn't do this anymore. She needed to be with Sam. Barring that, she needed a drink. Or Dayna. She had to contact Dayna. "I'm sorry. Are there many more questions?"

"No, that's good for now," the nurse said. "And don't you worry, he'll get the best care here."

"Thank you." She moved away from the intake desk to a quiet corner and called Dayna, not trusting her fingers to text a message. "Please come to the hospital. I'm here and I need you."

"What happened? Were you in an accident? I'll be right there."

"I'm fine. I'm here with…someone else. I'll explain it all when you get here. Please come."

Dayna and Johnson were there in fifteen minutes. Dayna rushed in looking frantic, found Emily, and grabbed her in a hug before even asking what going on.

Before she had a chance to say a word the nurse approached her. "Mrs. Marshall, your husband is going in to surgery. You can wait in the third floor waiting room. It might be more comfortable."

"Thank you," she said. "Come on. Maybe it's quieter there."

"Mrs. Marshall?" Dayna asked. "What are you playing at?"

"Not playing. Let's go upstairs. We need to talk."

"I'd think so," Dayna said. The three of them found the third floor waiting room, which was mercifully empty.

Emily took a deep breath. "I'm married."

"And you didn't invite me?" Dayna looked hurt and confused.

"Day," Emily shook her head. "It wasn't possible. Trust me."

"Let her tell her story," Johnson said. "I have a feeling it's a doozy."

He had that right.

"Johnson, go get us some coffee, will you?" Dayna said.

"I don't want to miss anything."

"You won't," Emily promised. With that Johnson headed out in search of coffee. She was glad Dayna had thought of it. Brandy would be really appreciated right now, but lacking that, coffee would do.

"Married?" Dayna asked again.

"I'll tell you when Johnson gets back," she said. Her hands were still shaking. "We promised not to leave him out."

"But for real? Are you married?"

"I'm not sure I have any valid documentation." That was true enough. Even if there was a copy somewhere of the marriage certificate she and Sam had signed, it was from the 1860s, hardly considered proof in today's world. "I suppose it's a bit unconventional. But yes. Married."

Johnson came back and handed each of them a coffee. Emily put hers down on the side table. She needed to tell them before anyone else came in to share this waiting room.

"Remember your wedding?" she asked.

Dayna nodded, looking at her skeptically. "Vaguely," she answered.

"Okay, remember when I changed clothes partway through the reception?"

She nodded again.

Emily took a deep breath and let it out slowly. She could do this. Besides, telling them the story of what happened kept her mind off the fact that Sam was in surgery.

"You're not going to believe what I have to tell you," she said. "But trust me, it's true."

"With a lead up like that, this is going to be good." Johnson came over and sat beside her, putting a comforting arm around her shoulder. She leaned into him, drawing energy from his strength.

How to even start?

"Remember that letter you showed me that Beck wrote?"

"Who?" Dayna looked lost.

"Beck." Wait that wasn't right, she signed it Rebecca. Her free name. "Rebecca. Your great-great-grandmother."

"Oh, right. The one addressed to Mrs. Samuel Marshall," Dayna's voice trailed off and she studied Emily trying to see where this was going.

"Right. That was me. That's my husband Sam in

surgery. He was a soldier in the Civil War and was shot. Beck was his slave. I was going to help her escape, but I ended up coming back to the future instead."

"Back...to the future?" Dayna said slowly. "You were in the past?"

"Yes. I fell in the fish pond at the reception and ended up in the past."

"That's not possible," Johnson said, stating the obvious.

"I know," she answered. "Except it happened."

"Okay, baby." Dayna knelt in front of her, taking her hands. "Tell us everything. From the beginning."

She did and when she was done Dayna stared at her, dumbfounded. "And he's here now. In surgery?"

"He is." The reality of that coming home to her. Was she going to get Sam back just to lose him? "Oh, and one more thing. If in the future I simply say I met him at your wedding, can you guys back me up on that."

"Sure," Johnson said, still looking slightly shell shocked. "We've got your back."

"And also, if I tell you how I think it all works, how I went back in time, and you have a son, don't tell him how it works. There's a scary story about a man who went back in time, named DayJon and bad things happened. Don't let it be your son. Don't name him DayJon, then nothing bad will happen to him."

"Sure, sweetie," Dayna said, "we'll be sure nothing happens."

A surgeon walked into the waiting room. "Mrs. Marshall?" he asked looking at Emily.

"Yes." She stood, flanked by her friends. It felt so

odd to be able to claim that name again. "How's Sam?"

"He's out of surgery. Everything went well, but he's going to need some recovery time." The surgeon, however, still looked concerned. "It appears he was shot with a musket ball some time ago, and the wound festered and got infected. Luckily, he's not going to lose his arm. Do you know what happened to him?"

It seemed fairly clear to her he was shot by someone with a musket, but while that would have raised no questions in 1861, what with there being a war and all, now it was a bit unusual.

"You see," the surgeon spoke over her hesitation. "We need to report any gunshot related wounds to the police."

She looked at Johnson in a panic; she really didn't need the police involved here. That would complicate things far beyond anything she was capable of dealing with.

Johnson approached the doctor, held out his hand and introduced himself, and handed the doctor a business card. "Detective Johnson Brown. I'll take care of everything."

The doctor looked relieved that it was one less thing he had to worry about.

"Can I see him now?" she asked. "Can I see Sam?"

"We'll be moving him to a room in about an hour. It's unlikely he'll wake up before then. I'll let you know when you can go to him." The doctor hurried out again.

She sank down into one of the chairs and picked up her coffee. It was cold by now, but she didn't care.

"Oh, one more thing," she said to Dayna. "I'm pregnant."

****

Emily sat by Sam's bed holding his hand. She'd been sitting by him for an hour, and he hadn't stirred. Dayna and Johnson were still in the waiting room, ready to take her home when visiting hours ended. She was glad she had told them the story. So far, they seemed like they believed it, but maybe they hadn't taken it all in yet.

"Em?" Sam's voice was cracked and soft.

"I'm here, Sam," she said. "Let me give you some water."

She poured some from the pitcher into the glass and put in a straw to make it easier. He took a sip. "Nice," he said. "Where am I?"

"You're in the hospital," she said. "The doctors have already operated. You're going to be fine; you just need to regain your strength."

"But where am I?" he asked again.

"Oh," she said, understanding. "You mean, 'when'?"

"I suppose I do."

"My time," Emily said. "And I'm pretty sure that's why they thought you died in the war. Because you were never seen there again. Because you are here. With me."

"And there is no place I would rather be." He grasped her hand.

She leaned over and kissed him, and her heart overflowed with happiness.

Chapter Thirty-Six

Sam

Sam stood in the front of the church in a rented tuxedo, Johnson Brown by his side. If anyone had ever told him his new best friend would be a black man, he would have laughed at them. It's funny how things worked out. The church was different than what he was used to. Plainer, airier. The altar a free-standing table instead of against the back wall. But the candles, the crucifix, the stations of the cross, those were all identifiers. He was in the right place.

So much was strange to him. The hospital had been odd enough with the variety of blinking machines that all seemed to be operating all the time. The bright lights, the constant sounds. It was unnerving. Then he had gone to Emily's place to continue his recuperation. She'd bought him modern clothes and showed him how to use a computer and a phone. He realized how odd everything must have seemed to Emily when she'd come to his time. Though, he was getting quite used to these futuristic things and feeling more and more comfortable with it all the time.

His Great-Aunt Elsbeth—imagine finding her here—had worked some magic of her own to get him identity papers so he could function in this society without raising endless questions. He smiled at her now, sitting there on the groom's side. She had been so excited to be invited saying she'd never gotten to go to a blood relative's wedding in all these years and was glad she finally had the chance. The reception, later, would be at the Plantation of course. Maybe he'd even get Emily to dance the Zingirella with him again. At the very least she'd promised him several waltzes.

The organist started playing Pachelbel's Canon in D and the bridesmaids came down the aisle. Emily's cousins and friends, and then Dayna as matron of honor. Finally, on the arm of her father, stood his Emily. She was so beautiful. Even more beautiful now, a few months pregnant, than she had been before. She simply glowed. Her dress was white and lacy, and she looked like a princess in it, or perhaps the belle of the ball.

She walked slowly down the aisle to where he waited. Her father kissed her on the cheek and placed her hand in Sam's. Yes, they were already married, but as Emily had explained, in order for them to go forward they would need some modern documentation and besides, her parents had missed their real wedding, she wanted this. And he wanted that for her. So here he stood, marrying his wife, but that was fine with him.

The ceremony started, and Sam marveled at the twists of fate that had brought him to this place. They weren't beginning a new life in his time, no they were in hers. But it didn't matter, because as long as he was with Emily he was home.

The time for the vows came.

"Do you, Samuel Allen, take this woman, Emily Anne to be your lawful wedded wife, to have and to hold, for richer and for poorer, as long as you both shall live?"

He looked into her eyes.

"I do," he said. Their life together was just beginning.

A word about the author...

Christine Marciniak has been writing since she can remember because she loves to tell stories. She lives in New Jersey with her husband and two children.
christinemarciniak.com

Thank you for purchasing
this publication of The Wild Rose Press, Inc.

If you enjoyed the story, we would appreciate your
letting others know by leaving a review.

For other wonderful stories,
please visit our on-line bookstore at
www.thewildrosepress.com.

For questions or more information
contact us at
info@thewildrosepress.com.

The Wild Rose Press, Inc.
www.thewildrosepress.com

Stay current with The Wild Rose Press, Inc.

Like us on Facebook

https://www.facebook.com/TheWildRosePress

And Follow us on Twitter
https://twitter.com/WildRosePress